ANDARTA

THE ASCENDING VEIL, BOOK 1

THE AMIDEI EDITION

Andarta – The Amidei Edition: The Ascending Veil, Book 1

1st Edition

Books may be ordered through popular online retailers and Page Turner Books, Inc.'s online stores, or by contacting the publisher at:

Page Turner Books, Inc.
222 N. Lafayette St., Suite 11
Shelby, NC 28150

www.ptbooksinc.com

(702) 606-1775

ePUB/iBook: 978-1-967289-63-9
Hardcover: 978-1-967289-61-5
Paperback: 978-1-967289-62-2

Also available in Kindle on Amazon!

Audiobook coming March 2026!

exactly what I expected while also being nothing like what I expected...The writing is brilliant and immersive. I was hooked right from the prologue to the last chapter. There was never a drop in the story's pace, even through all of the introduction, backstory, and world-building...This book is a must-read for fantasy and mythology fans!"

~bookishrebel01 for BookInfluencers (South Africa)

"Authors Leanne Staback and S. Kennedy have crafted a compelling narrative that seamlessly weaves together elements of mythology, history, and modern issues...The vivid descriptions brought the world of *Andarta* to life, transporting readers right into the magic and danger...*Andarta: The Ascending Veil* is a thrilling adventure that explores the timeless themes of good versus evil and the power of human resilience. I enjoyed every moment of the story and highly recommend it."

~*Rabia Tanveer for Readers' Favorite*

"Staback and Kennedy excel in creating rich characters in Emilia and Clara...A thoughtful fantasy novel...that spotlights the problem of human trafficking..."

~*Kirkus Reviews*

"What truly makes this book unique is the addition of human trafficking, an unfortunately relevant issue in our society, blended within the fantasy storyline, including epic battles. I loved the main characters, Emilia and Clara, and all the amazing secondary characters woven into this incredibly emotional story. The worldbuilding is also descriptive and immersive, adding another layer to the overall reading experience. I highly recommend this book for fans of Norse mythology, urban fantasy, and dark storylines."

~*Michelle Godard Richer for BookInfluencers (Canada)*

"Their nuanced approach to storytelling creates a rich tapestry that explores themes of justice, sacrifice, and personal transformation within an exciting fantasy...Vivid descriptions of exotic new places like Seraphim City reveal a complex urban landscape that feels both familiar and fantastical, with just the right amount of grit...The authors also masterfully balance intense action sequences with moments of deep introspection, ensuring readers remain deeply connected to the characters' internal journeys...a compelling and thought-provoking read for fantasy fans."

~K. C. Finn for Readers' Favorite ★★★★★

"The magic, the mythology, and the modern-day setting blend so well, and the sibling dynamic? It's so raw and relatable, filled with tension and love! What made the story stand out for me is how it weaves in a very real-world issue: human trafficking. The way it touches on the topic is subtle but so powerful. I love how fantasy was able to make me think about real-world issues in a totally new way. And I love that the authors even set up a hotline (1-567-ANDARTA) connected to the Human Trafficking Hotline. That small detail gave the story so much more purpose. If you love stories that grab your imagination, while leaving you with something to think about, this is an absolute must read!"

~onemorechap on Instagram

"*Andarta* is a fantastic start to this fantasy series. It began with multiple different storylines that seemed very different from each other. However, they all came together in an unconventional way."

~Jill Jemmett for BookInfluencers (Canada) ★★★★★

"Filled with emotions, filled with human connection, two strong girls (twin sisters), and topped up with love and magic, the book will live rent-free in your head for quite some time after having read it."

~This.human.reads on Instagram

"...this was a really amazing story! ...I found myself turning the pages faster and faster to find out what happens. This is just book one in a new series, so I'll definitely be on the lookout for book 2! I also can't wait to check out the graphic novel releasing this summer!"

~Nissa_thebookworm for BookInfluencers (United States)

"It kept me on the edge of my seat, and I couldn't put it down. This book is a must-read if you love mythology, urban fantasy, strong female protagonists, or just a gripping, emotionally charged story!"

~Theratherslowreader on Instagram (South Africa)

Andarta

THE ASCENDING VEIL, BOOK 1

THE AMIDEI EDITION

STABACK, KENNEDY & AMIDEI

SHELBY, NC, USA

DEDICATIONS

To the survivors of human trafficking, the lost, and the resilient,

This book is for you—for those who have endured unimaginable pain and for those still fighting for freedom. May your strength light the way for others, and may you always find allies, hope, and healing on your journey. This story is woven in honor of your courage, and with a commitment to a world where no one else suffers as you have. With endless respect and unwavering solidarity, we dedicate Andarta to you.

With all our hearts,

Leanne Staback, S. Kennedy, & Aria Amidei

Leanne also dedicates this story to her family, especially her mother Lauri, who has been extremely patient with the amount of time she has taken away from being with her to write this important novel. Her brother, Kent, for giving up hours of his life to design our website. Last, but never least, her children. Christopher, who has been the most vocal supporter of this project and provided costume ideas for Magnus' character; Marc and Alex who have helped with marketing; my co-author, S. Kennedy, and Micah, who has been forced to read several drafts since day one. Thank you and I love you all, whether you are mentioned here or not.

S. Kennedy dedicates this book to her friends who provided constant feedback for cover designs, fonts, and plot ideas to the point that it must have driven them insane. To Micah, her husband, who traveled back and forth with her to see her co-author and help with everything book related. To Leanne, who took this story and made it what it is, who put down every plot point and created this vision in its entirety, and without whom this book would not exist.

Aria dedicates this book to all of those who helped her escape from her own human trafficking situation. She is eternally grateful and indebted to you for giving her her life back.

ACKNOWLEDGEMENTS

To everyone to has helped and encouraged us along the way when things got rough, we thank you from the bottom of our hearts. The people listed below have really gone above and beyond in making this book happen and deserve mentioning by name. We are equally grateful to each and every one of them, so we are listing them by surname alphabetically and not by order of importance.

Greg Adams from the Apple Store for helping with data recovery when Leanne's computer completely died and everything seemed lost forever.

Steve Bentley, graphic novel illustrator for the graphic novel version of this book (coming in the summer of 2025), who quickly and fantastically created the prologue in graphic novel format for our special edition prologue promotional graphic novelette, which we handed out to promote this series.

Eduardo and María Corrales for picking up the slack to keep things running smoothly at home when Leanne was deep in the writing process. And a special, heartfelt thank you to María for nursing Leanne back to health after multiple surgeries throughout this project. You will always be *skuldaliò*.

Jason Letts for his amazing editing skills.

Eileen Raye, also *skuldaliò* and a fellow author, who provided much needed encouragement when health issues continued to get in the way of progress on this novel.

Levi Sagi, creative director of Vie Sauvage Couture for designing the Andarta and Eir costumes, **and his team** who created the costumes in time for the book launch book signing at Planet Hollywood in Las Vegas, Nevada, and for providing the inspiration for the Victim Rescue Pods (VRPs) on Andarta's costume.

Table of Contents

MAIN CHARACTERS IN BOOK 1
(in order of appearance, without too many spoilers,
but enough to help you follow along)

BRENNHIR TOROX/JUDGE SKARSGAARD
(Brennhir Torox is pronounced "Brenner Tore-ox")
(Judge Skarsgaard is pronounced "Judge Scars-guard")
- Ancient, notorious Viking leader
- Emilia's employer
- Andarta's main, modern-day trainer
- Member of Andarta's *skuldalið*

MAGNUS VON CATHBAD
(AKA "CATHBAD" AND "MAGNUS")
- Angel
- Ancient Druid Priest
- Modern day spy for the gods
- Member of Andarta's *skuldalið*

EMILIA BENNING
- Human daughter of Cauley and Amalia
- Twin sister of Clara
- Human host to Andarta, the ancient goddess

CLARA BENNING
- Human daughter of Cauley and Amalia
- Twin sister of Emilia
- Human host to Eir, the ancient goddess

GABRIEL CONTRERAS
- Close, childhood friend of Emilia and Clara
- Immigrant from Guatemala
- Human trafficking victim

LEANDRO MAMMON
- Lead human trafficker
- Human host to Mammon, the evil demon

AMALIA BENNING, R.N.
- Human mother of Emilia and Clara
- Wife of Cauley
- Head Nurse by profession

JUDGE CAULEY BENNING
- Descendant of Brennhir Torox
- Human father of Emilia and Clara
- Husband of Amalia Benning
- Superior Court Judge by profession

EIR *(pronounced "Air")*
- Ancient Norse goddess of protection, help and mercy
- Member of Andarta's *skuldalið*

ANDARTA *(pronounced "On-dart-uh")*
- Ancient Gaulish/Norse goddess of strength, courage and divine protection

ETHAN QUADE
- Childhood frenemy of Emilia

KARA
- Norse goddess of communication between gods and men
- Andarta's secondary, modern-day trainer
- Emilia's college roommate
- Member of Andarta's *skuldalið*

SECONDARY CHARACTERS IN BOOK 1

*(in order of appearance, without too many spoilers,
but enough to help you follow along)*

TORREYA PELLE *(pronounced "Tore-ay-uh Pell-ay")*
- Ancient, female Senmarian warrior
- Modern member of Andarta's *skuldalið*

NANA PETROSYAN
- Mother to Amalia Benning
- Maternal grandmother to Emilia and Clara
- Wife to Papí
- Lives in London and owns The Petrosyan Club

PAPÍ PETROSYAN
- Father to Amalia Benning
- Maternal grandfather to Emilia and Clara
- Husband to Nana
- Lives in London and owns The Petrosyan Club

GRANDPA BENNING
- Descendant of Brennhir Torox
- Father to Cauley Benning
- Paternal grandfather to Emilia and Clara
- Husband to Grandma
- Lives in Ottawa, Illinois, USA

GRANDMA BENNING
- Mother to Cauley Benning
- Paternal grandmother to Emilia and Clara
- Wife to Grandpa Benning
- Lives in Ottawa, Illinois, USA

CHASE DOUGHERTY
- Close high school friend of Emilia and Clara

BRANDT *(pronounced "Brant")*
- Tattoo covered, Norse god
- Modern member of Andarta's *skuldalið*

LEILANI *(pronounced "Lay-lawn-ee")*
- Hawaiian goddess
- Modern member of Andarta's *skuldalið*

VAHAGN *(pronounced "Vawn")*
- Armenian god of thunder

HERMES *(pronounced "Her-meez")*
- Greek god of mischief and trickery
- Member of Andarta's *skuldalið*

GUNGNIR *(pronounced "Gung-neer")*
- Norse god of war (originally Odin's spear but gained Odin's powers and took on a human-like form when Odin impaled himself on Gungnir in sword form)

MIHR *(pronounced "Meer")*
- Armenian goddess of water
- Member of Andarta's *skuldalið*

ANAHIT *(pronounced "On-uh-heet-uh")*
- Armenian goddess of fire
- Member of Andarta's *skuldalið*

ÁNGELA
- Mexican human trafficking victim
- Member of Andarta's *skuldalið*

PROLOGUE

SENMARIAN FJORDS, 966 CE

I cy winds howled across the frozen Senmarian fjords, biting at the skin as Brennhir Torox stood tall upon a rugged cliff, withstanding the wrath of nature with a smirk.

His red hair and beard whipped around his body in the fury, ice catching in the strands like ashes in a dying fire. Though the winds blew leaves and snow around him and his legion, Brennhir's piercing blue eyes could clearly see his Viking brethren preparing for battle alongside him, the cold an afterthought to their excitement.

Brennhir's ruthlessness was legendary and came as a trait handed down from his ancient bloodline through generations of Viking men and women.

None in his army dared oppose him, knowing they would meet a gruesome and painful end. They were all too familiar with the bleeding corpses of their unfaithful comrades, left to the elements for the wild animals to feast upon.

With a fiercely determined glint in his eye, Brennhir addressed his warriors.

"Brothers!" His voice boomed across the plains, echoing across the cliff to the near thousand men and women ready to fight at his word. "Today, we carve our names into yet another piece of this forsaken rock we call home. With the fire in our hearts and the edges of our blades, we will conquer these lesser tribes and expand our glorious empire!"

The people shouted in agreement, bumping heads and pushing each other around with anticipation as their leader continued.

"For GLORY!"

"For HONOR!"

"*SKOL!*"

"*SKOL!*" The warriors yelled back, raising their axes and swords in unison, the might of their roars causing the very ground beneath their feet to tremble.

Brennhir basked in the energy of his men, knowing victory was assured. He had never been defeated in his decades of leading this ever-growing horde and didn't even bother to consider such a thing as an afterlife, knowing that when his end came, he would live on through legends told about him. His purpose would keep his spirit alive. He would conquer every last man and woman in Senmar.

Afterward, they would drink from the skulls of the fallen, honoring his foes as their souls were sent to oblivion.

Brennhir's fist tightened around the hilt of his blade, unconcerned about the imminent battle, one in a long line of victories yet to come.

ᛏᚢᚨᛒᛟᛟᚲᛟᚢᛗ

Across the desolate field, hidden between boulders and hills, Senmarian warriors prepared for the assault. Their leader, Kimbel Murphy, stood solemnly as his men surrounded him and awaited orders.

He knew this day would come, having received ravens for many years from other fallen tribes warning of the danger of Torox. The other tribes were ill-prepared and lacking enough warriors to withstand such an assault.

Murphy had sent ravens of his own to leaders who had yet to encounter the bloodthirsty Vikings, begging to unite against their shared foe. The ravens that returned accompanied a small number of tribesmen. It wasn't nearly enough to hope for a victory, and most of the ravens went unanswered, as the tribes were wiped out one by one.

Realizing their numbers were too few in this fight, Kimbel turned to faith. The gods would occasionally make their presence known, especially to fierce believers such as Kimbel and his Druid priest, Cathbad.

The priest hadn't left Kimbel's side in months, whispering the songs of their gods and repeating prayers to him and the tribe members, making every attempt to boost morale and strengthen the warrior's conviction. Through faith and honor, they would not fall.

He stood next to his trusted leader and friend and prepared to address his fellow tribesmen behind the wall of wind that separated them from the Vikings.

Cathbad cleared his throat, lifted his chin, and released his voice in a strong, clear timbre. His dark robes, adorned with sacred golden symbols, whipped about, giving him a seemingly holy aura.

"Brothers and sisters of the Senmarian tribes," he began, "we stand on the cusp of battle, our hearts filled with bravery and uncertainty."

His thick brow wrinkled, and he took a determined step toward the men and women.

"Fear not! We do not go into battle alone!"

Cathbad took in a deep breath and looked to the sky.

"We call upon the aid of Andarta, our mighty goddess of war and victory, to watch over us and strengthen our spirits in this time of need."

To the right, Kimbel raised his sword high and repeated the practiced mantra of prayer in unison with the Druid.

"Andarta, hear our plea! Look down upon your loyal warriors with favor and grant us your protection in the coming conflict. With your guidance, we shall triumph over our enemies and secure our lands for generations to come!"

The confidence of his comrades grew with his declarations of faith.

"Let us join our voices in supplication to the goddess," Cathbad called. "Repeat after me."

He shut his eyes against the wind and fell into something of a melancholy trance.

"Oh, mighty Andarta, we beseech thee, grant us strength and victory."

The group quietly repeated after him, heads bowed and hands clasped.

"Guide our blades. Steady our hearts and hands. In your name, we play our parts."

"In your name, we play our parts."

The wind diminished to a gentle breeze at the conclusion of the prayer. The sky above darkened slightly, and the presence of the goddess herself flowed through every man and woman in Kimbel's army.

Cathbad continued, "Let us make an offering to Andarta, a token of our devotion and gratitude."

In his right hand, he held up a finely crafted sword, adorned with intricate Nordic carvings. Symbols decorated the hilt and danced along the razor-sharp blade. Kimbel reached up and gently received the hilt of the sword from Cathbad's hand.

When he had the sword hilt fully in his grasp, the carvings on the blade began to emit a vibrant, purple glow.

The warriors gasped and cheered quietly in their excitement, knowing they had captured the attention of the goddess, who was now by their side.

Half a mile behind Kimbel's brethren stood an ancient, curving oak tree. Its branches twisted toward the sky, its dark leaves untouched by the cold of winter, and a strange mist surrounding the base. It was a place of worship, where the Senmarian's could feel the energy of their faith and gods. It connected all of the tribesmen in Senmar, a place where weddings, memorials, and births took place in the eyes of the divine.

Kimbel began walking toward the tree, sword still held aloft and glowing, leading the tribe through the mist. The Nordic script pulsated, the heartbeat of the goddess pounding, a gentle drum to lead her believers to victory.

Reaching the tree, Kimbel gazed upon it in reverence as Cathbad set a hand upon the weathered trunk next to a name that had been carved centuries before in the same Nordic script as on the sword, "Helagher Eik".

Cathbad whispered the name aloud, and the petrified wood came to life beneath his touch, recognizing its name on his lips. The lettering softly glowed, matching the color of the sword's aura.

Kimbel thrust the sword into the soil at the tree's roots and spoke, "In honor of Andarta, we offer this blade, forged with skill and purpose. May it symbolize our commitment to the cause, our faith in her protection."

As soon as he removed his hand from the sword hilt, the colors changed to a vibrant green then faded away until it looked like any other sword. The intricate carvings disappeared as well, leaving the blade smooth on all sides. The tree seemed to take in the energy of the sword, absorbing it from the roots and settling at its core.

The warriors bowed their heads as Druid Cathbad began an incantation, invoking the blessings of Andarta upon the army.

The Druid concluded the ritual and said, "Go forth, brave warriors, knowing Andarta watches over you. Let courage be your shield and victory your reward. Today, we fight with the might of the goddess on our side!"

With a resounding cry, the soldiers raised their weapons high, their spirits lifted by the invocation of Andarta's protection. Filled with newfound confidence, the Senmarians turned to face the notorious Vikings.

ᛏᚾ�

The Senmarians marched across the bitterly cold fjord, making their presence known to Brennhir Torox and his Vikings.

Upon clearing the hill, the Senmarian leader peered into the foggy distance and found the menacing shape that was Torox and his thousand-man army.

Kimbel Murphy shouted out with ferocity, spittle flying into the face of his right-hand man.

"Brennhir, your reign of terror ends today! You and all of your men shall meet the devil upon this battlefield, for it will be the last place you'll ever see!"

Brennhir laughed heartily, unsheathing his mighty sword.

Grinning menacingly, he growled, "We shall see, Murphy. First, let our blades meet!"

With a thunderous cry, the two armies charged toward each other, shields raised and weapons at the ready. The clash of metal echoed through the fields as the warriors collided, each side fighting with unbridled ferocity.

Amidst the chaos, Brennhir yelled to his men, "Stand firm, brothers! Victory is within our grasp!"

The battle raged on for what could have been mere minutes or hours. Sprays of crimson stained the ice and snow, fingers, weapons, and tufts of hair along with them.

Kimbel had cut down more Vikings than he thought to count, while constantly searching for the bloodthirsty leader of the group and trudging through the gore. He could still end up a corpse himself...which would be fine so long as he accomplished his mission.

And then Kimbel spotted him.

ᛏᚾᚠᛒᛟᛟᚲᛟᚼᛗ

As the sun began to dip below the horizon, Brennhir realized too late that the masses of men lying wounded or dead on the battlefield were his own. Determined to defeat his enemies, he closed his eyes, raised his face to the sky, and gave a bone chilling, tribal yell in an attempt to shake off the weariness that always came with such battles.

Unbeknownst to him, Kimbel Murphy had been watching, waiting for a break in the constant swings of Brennhir's massive claymore. Murphy knew the opportunity was his to take when the warrior paused and took a deep breath.

As Brennhir Torox raised his sword to the sky, yelling heartily for all his surviving men to hear, Kimbel raised his own weapon from behind the Viking, swiping with all his might at Brennhir's exposed neck.

As he did, the weapon became lighter, faster, and sharper. He felt invisible hands wrap around his own as he swung.

Heads from both sides turned in their direction when Torox's roaring came to an abrupt halt. Blood began shooting out of the stump of his neck, covering Kimbel in scarlet. The hairy head landed with a thump on the ground next to Kimbel, eyes and mouth wide open. He appeared to be looking at Kimbel, but he was dead and on his way to Hel, Kimbel was certain.

Kimbel fell to his knees, exhausted yet triumphant.

The terror that had reigned over the land for decades came to a definite end, silenced by Andarta's wrath. He'd *felt* her there for a moment. He had no idea what to make of it.

Druid Cathbad walked over to Murphy as he knelt, bloodied, over his fallen foe and patted him on the back gently.

"Good work, my son. The fight our people gave was worthy of Andarta's protection, and she is pleased beyond measure."

The Druid had a knowing look in his eye.

Cathbad then bent down and placed his fingertips on Brennhir's forehead, which rolled a bit at his touch, having lost the anchor of its body.

"You may have died valiantly in battle, but you spent most of your life being a scourge. You filled peaceful lives with terror. You uprooted people from their homes and tore women and children away from their husbands and families. From this point forward, you will *serve* Andarta by protecting people who have the misfortune to come across the path of evildoers such as yourself."

The curse was set upon Brennhir as Cathbad removed his fingers from his forehead. He then turned back to Kimbel.

"It is done. Time to honor Andarta for her protection and strength by celebrating with your army."

He smiled for the first time in his life, which gave Kimbel quite a start.

Bolstered by the Druid, Kimbel Murphy turned toward his army, expecting to see only a few remaining. When he saw how many were still standing, he couldn't believe what he was seeing. Kimbel began to take count, filled with more gratitude than he ever imagined as he surveyed the ranks.

"By Andarta, everyone has survived! We have prevailed!" he declared, his voice ringing out triumphantly. "Let us feast tonight and share the good news with our kin! Before we leave these hallowed grounds, let us gather round the magical sword through which Andarta blessed our battle and bow down to her greatness."

ᛏᚨᚹᛒᛟᛟᚲᛟᚾᛖ

Kimbel and his warriors trod over the battlefield, strewn with the mangled bodies of their foes, focused on reaching the ancient oak tree with quiet reverence.

The Vikings who still lived met their end quickly, either too injured or too exhausted to fight back. Killing them after the fall of their leader was a mercy.

"What is to happen to their souls?" asked a young warrior who was seemingly fascinated by the violence.

Cathbad gave an uncharacteristic chuckle.

"They will certainly not be greeted by Eir at the Hall of Souls, if that's what you're asking."

The Druid reached the tree first, standing a few feet from Andarta's sword. As he began the prayer of praise to their goddess, something in the sky shuttered. Any light from the fading sunset was washed away, and dark clouds rolled in faster than the Druid had ever seen.

"What?" Kimbel gasped, searching the heavens.

Before anyone caught sight of anything, the clouds suddenly opened, and the visage of a huge beast dropped to the ground in front of them, its landing producing a wave of pressure that pushed the warriors back several feet and shook the ground beneath them.

It landed on top of the sword and faced the warriors with a calm demeanor, flicking the tip of its fluffy tail up and down gently. Stunned by the vision before them, the group froze in place, hardly daring to breathe lest the massive dragon hear them and attack.

The dragon settled down, closed its eyes, and began making a very loud, deep purring sound as it seemed to fall asleep.

The warriors, still stunned, stepped back carefully and looked to each other in confusion and a healthy amount of fear.

"A dragon!" they gasped.

None of them had ever seen the beast they all thought to be of myth and legend.

One of their commanders approached Kimbel and Cathbad, warily eyeing the dragon.

"How are we to praise our goddess without the sword?" Torreya Pelle whispered.

Torreya was one of the female warriors who was always in high demand when a battle was afoot. Striking in appearance and intelligence, she could be counted on to direct her soldiers effectively for a positive outcome. Her beauty often distracted opposing foes, allowing Torreya's soldiers additional time to fulfill their deadly duties.

Seirri, a mighty warrior who often acted in haste, offered a plan to retrieve the sword so the group could finish their task.

"The beast appears to be sleeping soundly. I'll go around it and see if I can fetch the sword from behind."

"Wait, Seirri!" Torreya commanded in a panic. "He does appear to be sleeping, but none of us have ever come across a dragon before, let alone one so massive. I suggest we leave and come back tomorrow. Surely, he will be done with his nap and gone by then."

Seirri huffed in frustration.

"I'll not be coming back this way tomorrow, Torreya. I want it to be over."

He then began striding purposefully alongside the sleeping beast, watching for any indication that it was awakening, intent on reaching the opposite side of the tree.

Kimbel and his soldiers watched with bated breath as Seirri walked none too softly toward the dragon's right end, where the tail curved back along its body. When he reached the opposite side of the tree, Seirri saw the tip of the sword glinting in the moonlight.

"I see it!" he yelled excitedly.

Jass, Seirri's brother, had also been watching the dragon's eyes for signs of awakening. As soon as Seirri yelled out, the dragon's eyes snapped open and sent a small stream of smoke and fire out of its nostrils toward the soldiers.

"RUN!" screamed Torreya.

"My *brother* is back there!" Jass argued vehemently. "I'll *never* desert him!"

He ran toward the dragon, brandishing his sword while quickly looking for what could be the best place to embed it into the beast's massive body. Any second, he expected to be incinerated by the fire-breathing dragon.

ᛏᚨᚠᛒᛟᛟᚲᛟᛁᛗ

Tyrell, the dragon, was amused at these tiny creatures. He saw the little man running toward him and knew he wanted to hurt him, but he was only there to protect Andarta's sword. They had offered it to her for protection in battle, and she provided that protection. Tyrell knew the sword was now the property of the goddess Andarta, and these mortals seemed to want to take it back.

He could not let that happen.

When Jass got close enough, Tyrell flicked him gently with the tip of his furry tail, which sent the man hurtling through the air sideways at least four meters.

He didn't want to hurt people who Andarta had protected, but he couldn't let them get the sword. He was in charge of protecting it until Andarta needed it once more, however long that may be.

Suddenly, Tyrell felt a sharp sting on the back of his neck and growled in irritation. He turned toward Seirri, who had shot him in the neck with an arrow.

With a look of abject terror on his face, Seirri screamed and started running away toward his countrymen, who were already far ahead of him. Before he could reach them, he felt sharp teeth on both sides of his hips, anticipating the excruciating pain that was surely to come next.

Please make it quick, he prayed silently.

Suddenly, he was lifted high up in the air and flung so far that he landed in front of his fleeing fellows. Both of his legs buckled and broke under the strain of falling from such a height, and he screamed in agony.

Unbeknownst to the group, Tyrell immediately felt remorse at the pain he caused the man. He didn't mean to hurt him, but these creatures were so fragile it was hard not to.

Jass and Torreya quickly bolstered the broken Seirri, one shoulder under each of his armpits, and ran as fast as humanly possible.

Kimbel looked back, expecting to see an angry, advancing dragon on their tails, but he was nowhere in sight.

"Oy!" Kimbel yelled. "Stop! Stop!"

"*Stop!*" yelled Jass, who was further up in the group.

One by one, everyone stopped running and looked at Kimbel, who was pointing back to where the dragon had been.

The fjord was silent, except for the ever-present wind.

In the distance, the warriors could still see the tree where they left the sword at its base. A fluffy tail, much smaller than the one boasted by the dragon, scrambled around the gnarled roots of the tree and up to the branches.

"Did it…fly away?" asked Kimbel, staring in confusion at the tree.

"I believe we would have heard the wingbeats if that were the case. But what was that other creature?" asked Cathbad, who squinted to try to see in the dimming light.

Torreya, also rather puzzled, said, "I think it was a *cat*."

The cat reappeared as it chased a mouse down the tree and across the field, the moonlight glinting off of something around the cat's neck.

Torreya craned her head forward and squinted her eyes in disbelief.

"Did that cat...*sparkle*?" she asked nobody in particular.

Seirri, seeing the same thing but not believing his own eyes, said, "Nooo..."

"Oy!" Torreya exclaimed, brushing it off. "That must be the moonlight playing tricks on our eyes..."

Squaring his shoulders and donning a brave face, Kimbel announced, "Now that the beast is gone, I'm going to go back to the tree to give Andarta our thanks. Torreya, please keep to our mission if I do not return."

"Aye," she replied solemnly, nodding in confirmation.

The group nervously watched their leader as he strode toward the offering tree. He reached the tree after several minutes, put his hands on his hips, then scratched his head. Next, he walked around the tree.

Seirri commented, "Is that some ritual of gratitude he's performing? I admit, I haven't seen it before."

"No," Torreya replied, squinting. "Something is wrong."

The group stood silently as they watched Kimbel return.

When he reached them, he had a blissfully happy smile on his face and announced, "Andarta has accepted our offering! It is nowhere to be found! Praise Andarta!"

"Praise Andarta!" All the warriors responded.

"And now, brethren," Kimbel announced, "we celebrate our victory!"

He thrust his sword, bloodied and dirty from battle, into the air, overjoyed that his unspoken plan had worked.

The warriors followed suit with a thunderous roar, not knowing all that their leader was celebrating. Their spirits were high once again as they celebrated their hard-won victory under the watchful gaze of their indomitable leader.

ᛏᚾᚠᛒᛉᛉᚲᛉᚺᛗ

In the darkness, moonlight glinted across watchful yellow eyes, pupils constricted into fine lines that peered through the leaves.

An ethereal voice echoed in Tyrell's mind. "Not yet."

CHAPTER 1

EMILIA & CLARA

S mall hands held tightly to tough, glass-like scales, the wind playfully pulling at coppery hair as Emilia pretended to soar side-by-side with her twin, Clara. The beat of wings was almost tangible as each movement released a strong pressure of wind at their sides, as they imagined jumping across trees and mountaintops.

"*Faster!*" Emilia yelled against the gale, urging her dragon to pivot precariously around each massive obstacle.

Emilia looked toward the dark clouds looming from the southwest when a large streak of lightning crackled down from the heavens and touched the ground several miles away. A thunderstorm was brewing, which made this the best time to fly.

Her horned helmet, secured around her chin, kept the wind from her face as Emilia pushed forward through the sky.

"Wait for me!" Clara whined, gripping her own beast as tightly as she could with her dainty fingers.

She tried to catch up to Emilia, but the girl was *too* fast! Clara's coordination was thrown off, and within seconds she found herself sprawling on the ground covered in thistles and stone.

"Come on!" Emilia yelled over her shoulder, laughing gleefully.

"I can't," Clara whimpered.

Emilia looked over her shoulder and saw Clara on the ground grabbing her knee and crying. Her plastic Viking helmet and broomstick were forgotten in the dirt next to her. Her strawberry blonde braids were askew, random hairs sticking out in every direction from the electricity in the air.

Immediately brought back to reality, Emilia dropped her own broom and ran to her twin's side.

"What happened? Are you okay?" she asked with concern.

Clara shook her head and sniffled as tears ran down her face and dripped off the end of her chin and nose.

"Come on," Emilia urged. "Let's show Mama so she can fix you up."

She helped Clara stand up and supported her on the way back home. Before they could reach the house, another lightning flash and frightful growl of thunder came simultaneously, causing Clara to let out a short scream.

"It's okay. We're almost there," Emilia assured her sister, urging her along as quickly as possible.

Clara's eyes were red from sobbing when they reached Amalia, the girls 'mother.

When she saw Clara, she exclaimed, "What happened, my little fawn? Did the dragon get you?"

Clara shook her head sadly.

"No...the broom was broken, and it made me fall and hurt my knee."

"Oh, what a nasty broom that is, but thankfully it's only a little scratch. I'll patch you up, and it'll be better in no time. I bet you'll be back on that dragon tomorrow morning," her mother said with a quick kiss on Clara's forehead.

Clara smiled up at her mother and then watched as she cleaned the scrape, added some antibiotic ointment and put on a bandage.

Amalia said cheerfully, "There now...all better!"

"Thanks, Mama!" Clara hugged her mom and mumbled, "I hate thunder. It's so scary."

"I—" Amalia was cut short by the loudest clap of thunder they heard yet.

All three of them jumped and yelled when the windows in the house shook violently. The rain then began pouring down so heavily that they couldn't see the other side of their backyard outside the window.

"Did something hit the house?" Amalia asked in a panic.

The girls followed her as she ran through each room in the house looking for damage, but they didn't see anything out of place, other than items the girls left on their bedroom floor.

"Let's go watch the telly while we wait out the storm," Mama suggested. "Something funny!"

"Okay!" the girls yelled with enthusiasm, not recognizing the concern in their mother's eyes.

They spent the rest of the afternoon watching comedy shows, some of which relaxed them enough to be able to laugh at the funny parts.

Right when Mama said it was time to make dinner, the power went out.

"Good Lord," she mumbled. "What next? I'm going to call Daddy and see if we can go out to dinner tonight."

"Yay!" Emilia yelled.

ᛏᚾᛒᛟᚱᚱᚲᚱᛁᛗ

The next afternoon, the girls came in from the backyard to have lunch with their mother. Clara's face was flushed from the heat that developed after yesterday's storm. The humidity hanging in the air made the heat even worse.

"Clara, hurry up!" Emilia scolded before taking a bite of apple.

"I am," Clara shot back.

"No, you're not! You eat like a slowpoke!" Emilia complained. "I want to go back outside. Let's go!"

"Okay," Clara mumbled slowly and then finished the water in her glass before standing up.

She could never match her sister's never-ending supply of energy and excitement.

Amalia could easily see Clara's discomfort and suggested, "It's getting rather warm outside, girls. Why don't you go change into something cooler and take it easy for the rest of the day?"

Clara smiled at her mother with relief, and Amalia winked at her. She knew this meant they could stay inside the house where the air conditioning kept them comfortable and safe.

"There's nothing to do, Mama!" Emilia whined. "I'm so bored!"

"We could do a puzzle," Clara offered.

"An excellent idea, my little fawn!" Amalia replied. "You got that beautiful fairy puzzle a few months ago at your birthday party. I've never seen you girls even open the box. Why don't you do that one?"

"I hate puzzles!" Emilia complained. "I want to do something fun!"

Emilia was still pouting because her best friend, Gabriel, couldn't come play with them. He had to work on his parent's farm.

She told him to tell his parents they were his best friends and surely they would understand, but they didn't. Having never met his parents, she assumed they must be really mean!

"Come on, Emi," Clara pleaded, using her nickname for Emilia, hoping it would soften the impending explosion.

Clara hated confrontation and was trying to avoid having her mother and Emilia start yelling at each other.

The girls were seven years old, and as long as Clara could remember, Emilia and her mother were always butting heads. Although the girls were twins, they were as polar opposite as two people could be. Emilia was the taller of the two, the stronger of the two, and the more outgoing of the two.

She was also loud…*really* loud.

If she couldn't be found in a crowd by her bright red hair, no one ever had to work hard to find Emilia—all they had to do was follow the noise. She was also fearless and never had trouble making new friends with people and animals alike.

Clara wished she could be like Emilia, but she was painfully shy, very quiet, and didn't have any friends of her own because of these qualities. Emilia's friends were her friends, mostly because they put up with her to be around Emilia. They didn't dislike her, because she was very sweet, but she did tend to put a kink in their plans because she was afraid of doing things that might be dangerous.

Every now and then, when Emilia's friends complained about Clara tagging along, Emilia told them they weren't her friends anymore.

She'd always say, "Where I go, Clara goes."

Most of her friends stayed around, especially Gabriel and Ethan.

Gabriel was good friends with both of them, at least at school. He never had time after school. He had a great imagination and played Vikings with them whenever they could at recess. Every once in a while, they wanted him to be a mean Viking. He didn't play that role very well, but he did his best to appease the twins. Gabriel was very softhearted and always gave up the fight way too easily for Emilia's satisfaction. Secretly, he had a crush on Clara and didn't want to scare her or make her think he was a bad person.

Emilia was born first, by twelve minutes, and was therefore the oldest. Due to this, she felt it was her duty to protect Clara. Since she was also stronger and more confident, this helped when she needed to protect her sister…which seemed to happen a lot. Too many times, Clara was helpless and at a loss as to how to handle what seemed to Emilia to be simple problems.

One time, when her parents brought her a brand new beach ball when they came back from a trip to Le Meadows, Clara took it out to the front yard to play. Within minutes, she lost control of the colorful ball. It bounced across the street and went into the neighbor's yard, getting caught in some rose bushes.

Clara panicked.

She didn't know the neighbors, and they had a dog that she was sure would attack her if she went across the street to get her ball. She spent the next several minutes pacing back and forth on the front lawn before running inside to tell Emilia what happened.

"So go get it!" Emilia snapped.

She was busy coloring a picture of a cat. Emilia loved cats and wanted one more than anything, but her father was allergic to them.

Clara's face paled at the very idea.

"I can't do that! Their dog will kill me," she said seriously, her eyes wide with fear.

Emilia sighed.

"Clara, you have to get over your fear of dogs. Besides, their dog is in their backyard. Your ball is in their front yard. There's no way their dog is going to get you."

Clara began crying.

"Emi, please, I can't do it! Can you please get it for me?" she pleaded, small and nervous hands tightly grasped together.

Seeing how much distress Clara was in, her heart softened, and she replied, "Okay."

She went over to Clara and gave her a hug before heading out the door to get the ball.

When Emilia returned with the ball, it was flat. It had popped against the rose bushes' thorns. Clara was crushed. She never had such a beautiful ball before, and now the one she had was ruined in less than five minutes.

Emilia felt bad for her sister. She gave the ball to Clara, who appreciated the gesture but was now worried about how she was going to tell her parents what happened. She always worried about how other people were going to react to her, so she went out of her way to do what she could to make them happy…even if it made her unhappy.

One of the things that made Clara unhappy was Ethan. He was one of Emilia's friends who simply put up with Clara. Always walking around with an air of superiority, Ethan was unfortunately very smart and made sure everyone knew it. The only person in their grade who could match wits with him was Emilia. That was what their friendship was based on – competition. At times it seemed like they were fighting, but they were really arguing some point to prove which one of them knew more about a topic. Over time, they seemed to be equally knowledgeable, often about the same topics. This resulted in the two of them rolling with laughter on several occasions, while Clara would be left feeling completely out of the loop.

"I don't like, Ethan," Clara whined one day after he had left their house.

"Why not?" Emilia asked.

"He's mean!" Clara pouted.

"Ethan is not mean!"

"He is too. He's always walking around like, 'Look at me! Look how smart I am!'" she mimicked, doing her best imitation.

Emilia collapsed on the bed in laughter.

"Oh Clara, that is so funny and so true!"

The sisters laughed together, which cheered Clara up immensely.

ᛏᚢᚱᛒᛟᚷᚷᚲᛟᛁᛗ

The next day at lunch, Emilia and Clara were eating with Gabriel and Lisa, discussing plans for the week.

"Hey, Gabriel, want to come over after school? Lisa and Chase are coming over," Emilia asked, her eyes sparkling with excitement.

Gabriel hesitated, his gaze dropping to his food tray.

"I can't. I have to work," he mumbled.

Clara frowned, her brow furrowing in confusion.

"Again? But you always have to work. Don't you ever get a break?"

She really liked Gabriel a lot and wanted someone she considered to be her friend at their house too.

Gabriel forced a smile, shrugging nonchalantly.

"It's how things are in my family. We all have to pitch in."

"We do too, but not every day!" Emilia pointed out. "Don't your parents want you to have friends?"

Gabriel shrugged again without responding.

"I'm sorry, Gabriel," Clara said solemnly. "We'll miss you."

Gabriel's heart warmed, and he smiled at her with a slight blush in his cheeks. She gave him a small smile back then noticed Emilia give her a knowing look, so she quickly looked away. The girls accepted his explanation and changed subjects.

There was the occasional chill in the air and the leaves were starting to change colors. They knew his family lived on a farm and the fall harvest was in full swing. What could they do but wait until winter when farming came to a standstill?

As the weeks passed, they noticed Gabriel appearing more exhausted and he became withdrawn – even from them. Emilia and Clara grew increasingly concerned about him so one day at recess, when they were out of earshot of other students and staff, Clara broached the subject with gentle concern.

"Gabriel, are you okay?" she asked. "You seem really tired lately. Have you been sick?"

Gabriel hemmed and hawed for a moment, his gaze distant as he struggled to respond.

"I…I'm fine," he replied weakly.

Clara could see that something was terribly wrong, but if Gabriel wouldn't tell her what was going on, how could she possibly help him?

That night, while the girls were in bed waiting to fall asleep, Emilia asked, "Clara, have you noticed that Gabriel always says he can't hang out with us after school or on the weekends?"

"Yes, I have! I think it's sad he has to work so much. He's a kid! He should be able to play with his friends after school every now and then. Don't you think?"

Emilia was taken aback by the passion with which Clara spoke about Gabriel's situation.

Oh, she thought, *this was more than puppy love!*

"Of course! I don't know what I would do if Mama and Daddy wouldn't let us do stuff with our friends. I'd probably go bonkers!" Emilia said and made a funny face.

Clara giggled, "You already *are* bonkers, Emi! That's what makes you so fun."

Emilia's smile quickly turned to a frown as she lamented, "I feel like there's something else going on with Gabriel. Something not good."

Clara sat up in bed and looked at her sister with alarm.

"Like what?"

Emilia shrugged.

"I don't know. Maybe we should talk to Mama and Daddy about it."

Before she even finished speaking, Clara was out of bed and shoving an arm through a sleeve of her robe.

"Let's go," she stated.

Emilia quickly followed suit, and the girls ran downstairs to find their parents in the family room watching a game show.

"What are you two doing down here? I thought you were already in bed!" Amalia exclaimed.

"Mama, Daddy, can we talk to you about something?" Emilia asked.

"Of course, girls," their father, Cauley replied, pressing the mute button on the television. "What's on your mind?"

Clara explained, "It's about our friend Gabriel. He always says he can't hang out with us because he has to work."

"That's interesting." Amalia said. "I know different families have different responsibilities, depending on what they do for a living. Maybe Gabriel's family needs his help with something important."

"That's what I thought too, Mama," Emilia said, "but it seems like he is *always* working! It doesn't seem normal for someone our age."

Daddy said, "They probably have a lot of chores to do around the farm or something. It's not uncommon for families to rely on each other for help."

Clara's shoulders relaxed a bit, since her father's explanation seemed to go along with what Gabriel had been telling them.

She nodded slowly.

"I guess that makes sense, but I still feel bad that we never get to see him outside of school."

"Clara has a crush on him," Emilia teased.

"*I do not!*" Clara shouted.

"Yes, you do," Emilia laughed.

"*Take that back!*" Clara cried and tried to slap Emilia, but she was too fast.

As Clara chased after her, Emilia sang, "Clara and Gabriel, sittin' in a tree, K-I-S-S-I-N-G! First comes love, then…"

"Alright, stop it you two!" Cauley yelled.

Both girls stopped running, and Clara sat on the floor and continued to cry while hugging her knees.

Amalia sat down next to her and wrapped her arms around her.

"It's okay to like boys, Clara. There's nothing wrong with it, as long as you stay friends until you're old enough to date."

"When will that be?" she sniffled.

"Um…" Amalia looked up at Cauley with a questioning look.

"Not until you're at least fifteen years old," he replied, looking sternly at both girls then at Amalia with a questioning look.

Amalia added, "I was going to say sixteen, but I guess fifteen would be okay. In the meantime, maybe you girls could help out more around the house. You have plenty of chores that need to be done too."

"But Mama…" Emilia whined.

"No buts, Emilia. It's important to help out your family and take care of your responsibilities."

Clara could tell Emilia was regretting coming down here and bringing up Gabriel's work.

"Okay, Mama!" Clara said cheerfully. "As soon as we get home tomorrow, we'll do our homework and then clean our room right away."

"Great!" Amalia replied. "And no shoving things under your bed either. I want everything to be put where it belongs."

"Okay," the girls replied. "Good night again!"

Once back in their room, Emilia sighed.

"That didn't go like I planned. Instead of figuring out a way to help Gabriel we ended up getting more work for ourselves!"

Clara nodded.

"Yeah, that was a bust. I wish we could do something to help him, but our parents are right. We do have our own stuff to do."

"I know, but it still doesn't feel right. You know how Mama always says to listen to your gut instinct? My gut instinct is telling me that something is really wrong in Gabriel's family. I don't know what it is, but something is definitely not right," Emilia announced with conviction.

"Maybe we can find a way to help him when we're older," Clara mumbled.

Suddenly, a loud burst of thunder shook the house as incredibly bright blue light filled the room briefly.

"I thought the storm was over!" Clara cried, pulling the covers up over her head in fear.

"Maybe it's starting again," Emilia shrugged.

A faint sound mingled with the clatter of the storm.

"Meow."

"Clara!" Emilia shouted. "There's a cat outside!"

"So?" Clara sneered, convinced her sister was trying to take her mind off the thunder. "We see cats all the time."

She pushed the covers back down and looked at Emilia quizzically.

"No...*look*!" Emilia pointed at their bedroom window.

Both girls looked at the window and could clearly see a huge gray cat sitting on the windowsill looking in at them with its amber eyes.

"How did it..." Clara started to ask.

"I have no idea!" Emilia stated.

"We're two stories up!"

"Maybe it climbed up the side of the house."

"Cats can't climb up the side of a house," Clara retorted.

"We should let it in before it gets wet from the rain," Emilia said and walked toward the window.

"What if it bites?" said Clara, worried.

"Ugh!" Emilia rolled her eyes as she opened the window to let the cat in.

Once the window was open, the cat simply sat there looking at her.

"Come on, kitty-kitty!" Emilia called.

The cat gracefully jumped down onto the floor, walked over to Emilia's bed, and jumped up, settling itself in a ball next to her pillow.

"Look! It knows that's my bed!"

"How could a cat know which bed is yours?" Clara argued.

"Maybe he likes me best!" she replied, sticking her tongue out at her sister.

"Whatever," Clara mumbled. "You know you can't keep it. Daddy's allergic."

Emilia's mouth twisted to the side as she considered her sister's warning.

"Yeah, you're right."

She walked over to the cat curled up on her bed with its eyes closed, apparently sleeping.

She petted the long, soft fur on top of its head between its sharply pointed ears and said sadly, "Sorry, kitty, you have to go."

"Meow."

The cat licked Emilia's hand with its rough tongue, jumped down off the bed and walked over to the window.

"Okay," Emilia sighed as she got up to open the window for the cat.

She was surprised to see it was not raining. Not only that, but the ground outside was bone dry. She stuck her head out the window to look up at the night sky. Emilia couldn't figure it out. That bright flash and loud boom surely had been a storm…evidently a very quick one.

And why didn't their parents come up to make sure they weren't scared with a noise that loud?

For the first time in her life, Emilia found herself with unsettling thoughts. As much as she and Ethan liked to think they could explain away any mystery, she was definitely stumped.

Not wanting to frighten Clara any further, Emilia kept her thoughts to herself and mulled them over throughout the night.

CHAPTER 2

THE SYNDICATE

Diego Contreras watched the cool mist blanketing the Santa Susana Mountains begin to burn off as the sun made its way above the horizon. He loved this time of day when it was humid but still cool enough to enjoy. In a few hours, the temperature would climb into the mid-nineties and the humidity would lessen, but Diego was still glad he was not one of the crop pickers.

Being outside in the direct sunlight, working in the dirt and dust, was miserable. Diego had seen plenty of farmworkers collapse in the sweltering heat of the strawberry fields because they didn't drink enough water to keep them hydrated.

Of course, the bosses didn't provide water for the workers. They had to bring it themselves. Since many of them didn't have a pot to piss in, let alone a thermos, they went without anything to drink during the long, hot hours in the fields. It was an effort for them to ensure they didn't pass out from exhaustion.

Diego had been a farmworker when he was a child. His grandfather, whom he called *abuelo*, constantly told him how fortunate he was to have a job in the United States.

Diego remembered crying a lot when they first arrived at the border in Southern California. He recalled watching in horror as his parents and baby brother, Gabriel, were forced into the back of a truck and driven away from his grandfather and him.

"Mama! Mama!" he cried and reached out for his mother as she was taken further away from him.

His mother cried out in anguish as the vision of her little son and father got smaller and smaller. Too soon, they were out of sight, and their hearts were broken.

Diego was only six years old when his family was torn apart. It all started before they even reached the border. His grandmother and older sister, Flora, died in the truck before reaching the States, due to the heat and lack of fresh air. Diego's mother was too weak to cry aloud in the pain and sorrow of losing both her mother and daughter in the same day, but he remembered her holding tightly to both of them, weeping silently and letting out an occasional moan of grief for an extremely long time.

She didn't let go even when the truck stopped, and the driver opened the back to let the cargo out to relieve themselves. When the driver saw the dead in her grasp, he cursed and called his partner to come out.

"Shit! Billy, help me get rid of these," the driver yelled as he climbed into the cargo hold.

Billy waited on the ground, hand on the butt of his gun should any of the cargo get out of hand – or try to escape.

The driver forcefully dragged Diego's mother away from her daughter and mother's stiff bodies. He watched as his mother screamed in agony, and he started crying too. Seeing his mother like that scared him and made his chest hurt. The bodies of his sister and *abuela* were dragged out by their feet far enough for the driver's partner to take them by the ankles.

The driver picked them up by their heads and walked them to the edge of the cargo hold. As soon as the bodies were clear of the truck bed, both men dropped the bodies with a muffled thump onto the dirt road. The driver jumped down off the truck and dragged the bodies separately into a ditch near the road.

It was the worst day of his life…until the rest of his family was taken away from him.

This was definitely not the wonderful picture his parents painted for them before leaving Guatemala. He had been looking forward to growing up with his baby brother in America, teaching him the things Diego knew, playing with him at the beach, having family picnics.

Now, that was never to be.

His baby brother was taken with his parents to a different place than Diego and his *abuelo*. Nobody ever told them where they were taking his family, so they were lost to him forever. His *abuelo* was never the same after that and died of a heart attack three years later.

At least, the doctor told him it was a heart attack, but Diego knew his grandfather really died of a broken heart.

After all the trauma he and his family had been through, Diego learned a long time ago that emotions were for the weak and only led to heartbreak. It was then that he began building a mental wall around himself. No way was he going to let anybody close enough to hurt him again. No way!

One thing he did agree with his *abuelo* on was that he was lucky to have a job in America, and he actually did get paid.

His payment was the opportunity to sleep on a blanket on the floor of the bunkhouse and eat a bowl of oatmeal every morning. He also got a cup of water every day. Plus, during the winter, he would get a small cup of fresh orange juice when the oranges were in season.

When Diego was fourteen years old, Leandro—the big boss—offered him a job that paid actual American money. He was the first person in his family to get a paycheck in the United States, and he was very proud of the one dollar and thirty-five cents an hour he made. Diego was more than happy to be taken on as Leandro's right-hand man, once he had proven himself to work quickly and follow orders. The other workers enjoyed Diego's way of managing things and that he made a good referee between the workers and Leandro's fiery temper.

Leandro was a mean son of a bitch.

Anybody with good sense would steer clear of him, but since Diego worked directly for the man, he had to be constantly on guard and do exactly as requested and *pronto*.

Diego sipped his still hot coffee and flicked the ash off the end of his cigarillo as he saw Leandro, heading his way.

"Hola," Diego greeted the man warily.

Leandro was known to be the meanest man around, and nobody knew what to expect from one minute to the next. It was best to always be cautious around him, lest he lose his temper.

Leandro ignored the greeting, walked over to Diego and Magnus – one of the new farm foremen – and said, "What do we have lined up for today?"

Diego was quick to report, "We've got a shipment coming in. Should be here very soon."

Thankfully, Leandro looked pleased with a brief twitch of the corners of his mouth in what seemed to be a smile.

"*Bueno,*" he replied, nodding. "We must meet our quota for the month, and with the season coming to its peak, the more help we can get, the better off we'll be."

Diego saw the cargo truck rambling along the dirt road next to the strawberry fields and announced, "Here they come!"

He put his arms up and began waving so the driver would know where to go.

"Who's they?" Magnus asked.

"The workers, you idiot!" Leandro snapped, looking at Magnus with disdain.

Diego snorted with laughter.

"Where did you find this *imbécil?*" Leandro demanded of Diego.

Diego shrugged.

"The owner said he was here to run the workers. Make sure they don't slack off."

Leandro looked Magnus up and down, still unsure of this newcomer.

He was a gringo. Leandro hated gringos, but they were an unfortunate part of life in this country. He turned his head and spat at Magnus's feet then walked away toward the bunkhouse.

"That was wonderful," Magnus commented sarcastically.

"*Ay Dios mío!*" Diego blurted in shock. "Do you know who that man is?"

Magnus shrugged," No."

"*Mi amigo*…that man could kill you with the flick of his little finger. You need to show him some respect!" Diego warned.

"I'll show him some respect when he gives me a reason to," Magnus replied nonchalantly.

Diego looked horrified.

"You have got some mighty *grande bolas, mi amigo!*"

16

He then made the sign of the cross on his chest, kissed his fingertips, and walked quickly away from Magnus toward the truck that had come to a stop.

Magnus shrugged and followed Diego to the truck.

"There's only two people in the truck," Magnus commented. "How are they going to pick that many strawberries in a month?"

Diego shook his head as he walked toward the back of the truck.

The driver and passenger from the truck cab met them at the back of the truck and unlocked the sliding door at the bottom. Diego shoved the door upward, allowing the back to be fully open.

Inside were at least fifty men, women and children, all sweating from the heat inside the truck in which they had been trapped for who knew how long.

Magnus couldn't believe what he was seeing. These people were brought here like this? They must be miserable! Most of them appeared to be Hispanic, but he noticed one little girl who looked Asian.

"Where did they come from?" he asked Diego.

"Oh, here and there," Diego said with a smile.

He then gave a sharp, quick whistle and began directing the people in the back of the truck to get out.

Slowly, one by one, every person climbed down out of the truck. Able-bodied adults helped the smaller children who were too little to get down on their own and the elderly who moved slowly due to the arthritic pain that inevitably came with age.

When the truck was empty of its human cargo, the driver jumped up onto the platform and pulled the rolling door back down and locked it in place.

"Where's Leandro?" the driver barked at Diego.

"I'm coming," Leandro called, appearing around the opposite side of the truck, a thick envelope in his left hand with a rubber band around it.

Diego and Magnus stood silently as Leandro handed the envelope to the driver, and then the two of them shook hands.

"What time will you be here with the next delivery?" Leandro demanded.

The driver shrugged while counting out the hundred dollar bills contained inside the envelope.

"No later than noon on Tuesday. Possibly sooner if we don't have any problems with Immigration Patrol."

Leandro gave a quick nod of his head then turned to the people who had exited the truck.

He gave them instructions in Spanish, pointing to the bunkhouse and the strawberry fields. He indicated a stack of open topped boxes in which the workers were to place the picked strawberries, clapped his hands, and said to Diego, "They're all yours now. Get to work."

He started back toward the office building next to the bunkhouse.

"*Señor!*" one of the older women in the group said loudly. "*Agua por favor?*"

Leandro stopped in his tracks.

He turned slowly toward the woman with an evil glint in his eyes.

Walking up to the woman, he gently said, *"Que?"*

"*A..Agua...por favor?*" The woman asked again, hesitantly.

"No," Leandro smiled. "No *agua.*"

He chuckled, turned, and started walking away from the woman again.

"*Señor...por favor!*" the woman pleaded, tears forming in her eyes.

"Dolores, no!" a man standing next to her admonished.

Leandro stopped walking again, turned slowly, walked back toward the woman, pulled his Desert Eagle out of its holster, and shot her right between the eyes.

"Agh!" Magnus yelled, covering his ears from the loud pop.

In mere seconds after Leandro pulled the trigger on his Desert Eagle, Magnus and Diego watched as Dolores's corpse crumpled to the dusty ground in a heap as the gunshot's echo ricocheted off the surrounding hills.

Several people gasped in shock. The children began screaming and crying, while the adults in the group looked on in horror, trying to calm both the children and themselves.

"Anybody else want...*agua?*" Leandro asked menacingly.

Nobody did.

Leandro slowly turned back toward the buildings and began walking nonchalantly away.

Magnus could feel his blood boiling.

18

"HEY!" he shouted at Leandro.

Leandro stopped once again.

Diego quickly grabbed Magnus's arm as he saw the man was headed toward Leandro and slapped his hand over his mouth.

"Callate idiota!" Diego said angrily. "Shut up, man! Do you want him to kill you next?"

Magnus stopped in his tracks, knowing he had bigger things to deal with and had to somehow hold his temper until the time was right. These people made him sick!

Diego could still feel the tension in his arm and he dared not let go yet. He didn't know Magnus and could not imagine what might happen if he removed his grip.

"I need your help here," Diego pleaded with Magnus. "You need to watch yourself around Leandro. He will not hesitate to kill any one of us."

When Leandro turned back around, Diego looked toward the people who had exited the truck and yelled, "Hey! You heard the man… Get her over to the dumpster! *Inmediatamente!"*

Diego mumbled to Magnus, "Act like you were telling them to get rid of her body. If he thinks you were yelling at him, you'll be thrown in on top of her."

"I'm not touching a dead body!" Magnus recoiled in horror.

"Aye, estúpido hombre blanco," Diego mumbled under his breath. "If he doesn't see you touching a dead body, you'll become a dead body. Get it?"

"Fine," Magnus grumbled as he walked over to the corpse.

In a fit of rage over having to deal with this, Magnus snapped angrily at those closest to him, "Help me!"

He immediately regretted it, seeing the fear in the workers 'eyes. He wasn't here to frighten them.

Afraid of what this gringo might do, several men in the group helped hoist the woman's body and carry it over to the closest dumpster, trembling all the while. Dolores landed on the bottom with a loud, metal thud since it had been emptied early that morning.

Magnus followed Diego's lead as they got the workers onto the field and quickly trained them how to be strawberry pickers.

So this is what the gods meant by, "you will have to blend in with the most evil among them". Magnus hoped it didn't last too much longer.

CHAPTER 3

OVERSEAS

The girls celebrated their tenth birthday that summer and were becoming more aware of how people viewed them… especially Emilia. She couldn't pass a mirror without looking at herself.

Already packed for the trip to see their grandparents in England, Emilia began pulling her hair out of her face while looking in the mirror on her parent's closet door.

"Mama? How come I have red hair, and you have brown hair?" Emilia asked.

"That's the way God made us," Amalia responded with a shrug.

"Brown hair is prettier than red. I want brown hair," Emilia pouted.

Amalia laughed.

"Oh, darling, many people would beg to differ. Some of the most beautiful people in the world have red hair! You should consider yourself lucky."

Emilia made a face of disgust behind her mother's back but stopped talking about her hair for the moment. No matter what she complained about regarding her appearance, Amalia always brushed it off and said she should feel lucky.

The girls were the only people in their entire school with red hair. Clara was always getting teased about being a ginger, which brought her to tears every time. Nobody said any such thing to Emilia because she would stand up to anyone who crossed her. They usually didn't tease Clara in front of Emilia because of this, so Emilia didn't hear about it until later when Clara was already upset and in need of consoling.

"Girls, let's go!" Cauley called up the stairs. "The shuttle is here!"

Emilia and Clara quickly grabbed their suitcases and coats and ran down the stairs to the front door. Clara was out of breath and panting, her breath leaving huge plumes of mist behind her as they walked down the front steps toward the airport shuttle.

Emilia was her usual, joyful, loud self.

"I can't believe we're going to London!" she yelled. "This is so exciting! We finally get to see Grandma and Grandpa's restaurant and Buckingham Palace! I wonder if we'll see the queen!"

Clara was too out of breath to respond and smiled at her sister's excitement.

"Come on. Get in, you two," their father laughed, helping the driver with the luggage.

The girls climbed into the back seats. Their parents followed by settling into the middle seats of the shuttle van. Once the driver got into the driver's seat and started the engine, they drove away from their house.

The girls looked at the house one last time, knowing it would be at least ten days before they saw it again. It was a strange feeling. They had never been away from home longer than a weekend before.

"I wonder if the house will be lonely without us," Clara said.

"I don't know…maybe," Emilia agreed.

Their mother turned around in her seat.

"The house will be fine. Mrs. Ameday is going to put our mail in the kitchen for us every day and make sure everything is fine while we're gone."

Both girls gave a sigh of relief and stopped worrying about the house. They then started talking about London and all the things they wanted to do and what they hoped to see there.

On the drive to the airport, it began snowing so heavily that they could barely see the road outside the windows of the shuttle. Traffic slowed to a crawl, and the girls heard their father worry about whether they would make it in time for their flight. The driver assured him they would make it in plenty of time.

As they approached the airport, both of the girls were in awe at the size of the buildings that made up the airport property. They had never been to the city and had never seen anything that huge before! There were so many buildings—how could they possibly know where to go?

Planes were everywhere, and they were huge too! They looked so tiny in the sky, so to see them up close was quite a shock.

Too soon, the driver pulled up to the drop-off area and opened the doors. As the Bennings climbed out of the van, the driver unloaded the luggage. Everyone was in charge of their own suitcase, carryon bag, and coat. This of course, was a struggle for Clara, so their father helped with her suitcase.

"Here, let's make this easy and do curbside check-in," Amalia suggested.

"Good idea," Cauley agreed.

They rolled their bags over to the curbside check-in desk, and Amalia was immediately deflated when she saw the sign on top, "Closed due to weather."

"Oh well," she sighed.

Defeated, the family trudged into the building to stand in the check-in line, which seemed a mile long. Luckily, it moved fairly quickly, and they were able to move on to the security checkpoint in less than forty minutes – almost unheard of for the holiday season.

"Gate C11," Cauley read off of the flight information display board. "That's our gate. Let's head over there first before doing anything else to see how much time we have before we need to board."

The family began the long walk to Gate C11, taking in their surroundings of people, restaurants, and shops along the way.

"Look!" Emilia shouted. "That store has a stuffed animal cat! Can I get it? I brought my allowance money!"

"Not now, Emilia," Amalia replied sternly. "We need to get to the gate first. If we have time before we have to board, maybe we can come back and get it."

Emilia grumbled but kept moving while Clara looked at her sister with sympathy.

When they arrived at the gate twenty minutes later, the passengers were already boarding.

Emilia's grumbling turned into a loud moan, and her father snapped, "Stop it right now, young lady! I'm sure there will be stores in London that sell stuffed animals. Be patient."

Patience was not one of Emilia's strong suits. She crossed her arms and pouted.

"You're going to have to pout with one arm if you want your luggage to come with you," her mother said sternly with a glare at Emilia.

Slowly, Emilia put her arms down and took ahold of her carryon, pulling it along behind her forlornly down the walkway to the airplane.

Clara reached over and held onto Emilia's free hand as they walked. When they got to the plane, she let it go, since they could only enter the plane one at a time. They found their seats and settled in for the eight hour flight.

Emilia and Clara couldn't help but touch everything within their reach, curious about the new things they were seeing on the airplane.

"Look! A magazine!" Emilia shouted with enthusiasm.

She had started to enjoy magazines for young teenage girls and was thrilled to find one on the plane.

"Okay," Amalia said quietly, trying to shush Emilia. "It's a magazine. You see those every day."

Emilia quieted down and began looking through the magazine, quickly getting bored with the endless ads and articles about travel that could only appeal to adults.

Clara noticed there were television screens on the back of the seats in front of them and curiously poked at hers until it lit up, displaying dozens of film and television selections.

"Wow! Emi, they have so many movies!"

She smiled and continued touching the screen, looking through the catalogue.

"How much longer till we get there?" Emilia demanded, ignoring her sister's excitement.

Cauley leaned forward and looked at Emilia.

"Once the plane takes off, it will take about eight hours to get to London."

"Eight *hours?*" she moaned. "What are we supposed to do for eight hours?"

"Sleep," Amalia responded firmly. "It's an overnight flight, so sleeping is the best thing to do to pass the time."

Emilia turned away from her parents, looked at Clara, and rolled her eyes.

Clara giggled with her hand over her mouth in a sad attempt to keep quiet.

"Here, Emi, you pick the movie," Clara offered.

The plane continued to fill with passengers until there were no seats left. The girls were fully ensconced in their movie when the loudspeakers burst to life.

"Ladies and gentlemen, on behalf of British Airways, we welcome you to flight BA 1541 with service from Chicago to London."

The announcement began going over safety regulations, which Clara listened to carefully. Glancing over at Emilia, she realized her sister was not paying attention in the slightest and gave her a nudge. When Emilia glanced up, Clara nodded toward the stewardess who was giving the safety presentation.

ᛏᚾᚦᛖᚱᚱᚲᚱᛉᛗ

When the plane landed at Heathrow Airport eight hours later, the girls were surprised there was no snow on the ground. It always snowed this time of year where they lived in the suburbs of Chicago.

"Aren't we going to have snow for Christmas?" Clara wondered.

Amalia smiled and shook her head slightly.

"No, it doesn't snow much in London."

"Why not?" Emilia asked. "Aren't they higher on the globe than we are?"

Cauley looked surprised and with a smile said, "Why yes, it is! How did you know that?"

"Our teacher was talking about latitude and longitude in class the other day, and she said it got really hot at the equator and really cold at the poles. I figured London was much closer to the North Pole than Chicago…and we always have snow for Christmas in Chicago," Emilia replied vacantly while looking out the tiny airplane window at the workers waving their lighted batons around as they directed the plane to the gate.

"How close are we to the North Pole?" Clara asked excitedly. "Will we get to see Santa Claus?" She clasped her hands together.

Amalia and Cauley looked at each other in surprise. They always knew the girls were smart, but it was something else to hear them make such connections at their age.

"You never know…you just might!" Cauley said with a twinkle in his eye.

"Gabriel said there's no such thing as Santa Claus," Emilia retorted. "He said the three kings come to visit his family on January sixth…not even on Christmas."

"Who are the three kings?" Clara asked.

"You remember," Emilia started. "He told us about the three kings who went to visit baby Jesus when he was born. They're the same kings who bring presents to Gabriel and his family."

"Santa doesn't visit everyone, love," Amalia began. "He only visits those who truly believe in him. Plus, other cultures celebrate the holidays differently, and maybe they have their own version of Santa Claus."

This explanation put an end to questions about Christmas gift givers and gave the girls something to think about. Never had it occurred to them that people celebrated the holidays any differently than they did.

Suddenly, they heard a loud mechanical whooshing sound as the door to the airplane opened, and the captain announced they could unbuckle their seatbelts and get their carryon luggage. He ended his announcement by saying, "Welcome to London! We hope you have a very happy Christmas and New Year."

"*Happy* Christmas?" Clara asked in confusion. "Isn't it supposed to be *Merry* Christmas?"

"Different cultures, my dear!" Amalia sang and winked at Clara.

Clara leaned over to Emilia's ear and whispered, "This is weird. These people speak English and look like us, but they don't even know how to say Merry Christmas."

"Different cultures, my dear!" Emilia imitated Mama, and the girls fell into a fit of giggles as they started walking down the narrow aisle of the plane toward the exit.

"I heard that, young lady," Amalia admonished Emilia.

Emilia gave a sheepish smile to her mother, which made Amalia smile as well. They were all so excited to be in London that it was hard to get too upset with each other.

When they finally retrieved their luggage from baggage claim, the Bennings went to find a ride to their hotel. As soon as they exited the airport doors, they saw a long line of taxi cabs. Cauley hailed one of them, and the driver pulled up to the curb within seconds and got out to help them load their luggage in the vehicle.

"Where can I take you?" the cabbie said in a very strong British accent.

The girls giggled again at hearing his accent.

"To the Kensington Arms, please," Amalia responded with a slight British accent.

Never having heard their mother speak with any kind of accent, the girls looked at each other in shock.

"Mama?" Clara asked. "Why does your voice sound like that?"

"Like what?" Amalia looked confused.

"You sound like them!" Emilia pointed out.

"Oh!" Amalia laughed. "I grew up here, darlings. When I visit, I tend to pick up a bit of my old accent. You'll do the same if you ever leave the Midwest. When you come back to visit, you'll pick up your accent as well."

The girls looked at each other in confusion. *They* didn't have an accent!

"You grew up here?" Emilia asked in shock.

"Of course!" Amalia began. "That's why my parents live here. I was born and raised in London. Your father and I met at The Petrosyan Club when he was here on holiday with some friends."

"On holiday? What does that mean?"

"That's what the Brits say for vacation. Instead of going on vacation, they 'go on holiday,'" Amalia explained.

"This place keeps getting weirder," Clara mumbled so only Emilia could hear.

Emilia nodded, looking at her mother in a whole new light.

In a matter of hours, Amalia had become a completely different person to her…a more sophisticated person. So bizarre.

"I remember that like it was yesterday," Cauley smiled as he looked over at his wife. "Your mother is still as beautiful today as she was then. Maybe even more so."

"Aw, you're so sweet, bubby," Amalia replied with a blush in her cheeks as she reached up to give her husband a quick kiss on the lips.

"Okay, you guys are creeping me out," Emilia grumbled.

Cauley and Amalia laughed at Emilia's discomfort, knowing she would be in a romantic relationship at some point and would understand.

As they drove to the hotel, Emilia and Clara did their best to take in the sights. Everything looked so old but so very cool! They couldn't wait to get out and explore London.

When they arrived at the Kensington Arms, a bellhop was waiting outside before the cab even stopped. As soon as it did, he opened the passenger doors to help Amalia and the girls out with a proffered hand. Amalia and Clara were grateful for the assist, but Emilia waved his hand away and climbed out on her own. She was no damsel in distress and did not want to be treated that way. She was a ten year old, able-bodied girl who could take care of herself.

The cabbie chuckled at her attitude then went to help the bellhop with the Bennings 'luggage.

"How much do I owe you?" Cauley asked the cabbie.

"One hundred pounds thirty," the cabbie replied.

Cauley counted out the total from the British pounds he had gotten at the bank before they left Illinois.

"My apologies, but how much should I give you for a tip?"

"Oh, give us a fiver," the cabbie responded with a smile.

Cauley counted out an additional five pounds sterling and handed the money to the cabbie.

"Happy Christmas!" the cabbie said with a wave as he got back into his cab.

"Happy Christmas!" they all replied.

Again, the girls began giggling uncontrollably.

"I know you're having fun, but some might consider your giggling rude, since it's at someone else's expense," Cauley admonished.

The girls fell silent while they went to the hotel's registration desk and then up to their room.

"Wow!" Emilia exclaimed upon entering the hotel room. "This is so cool!"

"It's huge!" Clara proclaimed. "Do you think it's haunted? Gabriel told me some hotels are haunted, especially the old ones."

"I'm sure it's fine," Amalia calmly replied in an attempt to keep unnecessary fears out of Clara's head during the trip.

"When do we get to see Nana and Papí?" Clara asked.

"In about an hour. We need to unpack and get cleaned up, then we'll head down to the restaurant."

"Do they have spaghetti?" Emilia asked.

"Spaghetti?" Amalia asked, confused.

"Yes, I don't want anything weird or gross. I want spaghetti. That way I know it'll be fine."

"I don't think they have spaghetti, but they do have many other things you'll probably like," her mother replied.

"Like what?"

Amalia sighed in frustration.

"You'll have to wait until we get there and see what they have. You have to remember, I haven't been here since before you girls were born. I'm sure some things have changed since then."

Emilia crossed her arms, sat on the bed she was to share with Clara, and pouted until it was time to leave.

CHAPTER 4

GABRIEL

Gabriel's earliest memories were entwined with the earth – its feel beneath his bare feet, its scent after the rain, and the relentless rhythm of work that began before dawn until school started and started again after school until the stars came out.

He didn't know it yet, but he was a slave, bound to toil on the vast farms that stretched across Illinois, his life a cycle of seasons and servitude. His parents worked alongside him in the corn and soybean fields, but they worked all day long, from dawn until nighttime.

He was told the people they worked for were his grandparents, but he began to doubt this as he got older since they didn't sound like either of his parents. They didn't look like them either. When he began asking his parents about this, they told him to stop asking questions and do as he was told.

During the winter break from school, when Gabriel turned ten, his life took an unexpected turn.

His father told him that he was going to the sun-drenched fields of California, where the land bore the sweetest strawberries ever found on Earth. He was to go there to work in those fields with an uncle of his he had never heard of named Quinto.

"When are we leaving?" he asked his father.

"*We* are not leaving. *You* are leaving…without us," his father said gruffly, quickly tearing his gaze away from Gabriel's uncomprehending expression.

Gabriel felt a heaviness in his chest and a lump in his throat at the thought of going so far away from home without his family.

"Will I come back at the end of strawberry season?" he asked hopefully.

"We don't know, *Papito*," his mother replied sadly.

"When will I see you again?" Gabriel cried.

"We don't know," his father whispered and began crying silently.

"I won't go!" Gabriel announced, vehemently.

"You have no choice," his father replied sadly.

"I'll run away!" Gabriel announced stubbornly.

"*Ay Dios mio!*"

His mother panicked, placing her hands over her face.

"If you run away, we'll all get killed!"

She looked terrified.

Gabriel gave his mother a suspicious look.

"Why would we get *killed?*" he asked in horror.

He had never felt unsafe before, so this revelation led to a multitude of thoughts and emotions he couldn't quite understand at his young age.

His parents told Gabriel the truth about how they came to the United States from Guatemala. They were illegal immigrants and were forced into slavery by the people who sent them to Illinois to work on the farms. This was because they didn't have any papers that made it legal for them to get regular jobs in America, so they had no choice, but they didn't think it would last this long. He learned about the people he called his grandparents and how they worked for the slave owners. They told him about his older brother Diego and his real grandfather who were taken somewhere else, and his real grandmother and sister who died on the truck on their way to this country.

In order to protect his parents and himself, Gabriel went to California on the truck the very next day without incident. He didn't even get a chance to say goodbye to his friends since everyone was on winter break from school, and school was the only place he ever got to see his friends.

He was going to miss Clara the most.

As soon as he arrived in California, he was put to work on a strawberry field so large it reminded him of the soybean fields he worked on in Illinois. There were no strawberries because it wasn't the season for them, but he was put to work preparing the soil for spring planting.

Knowing what he knew now about his circumstances, he found himself constantly depressed and angry. His days were long, starting before the first light crept over the mountains and ending only when darkness enveloped the land. He began to wonder if there was any hope of him getting out of his situation and living a normal life.

Despite the physical exhaustion, his Tío Quinto tried to get Gabriel to embrace the simplicity in this life, measured by the changing of the seasons and the growth cycles of the crops he tended.

One night, after work, Quinto took Gabriel outside of their sleeping quarters, put a fatherly arm around Gabriel's shoulders, and said, "Look over at the hills, Gabriel."

Gabriel followed where Quinto was pointing and saw big, beautiful, and probably comfortable, houses dotting the hillside. Their security and landscape lights added a warm glow to the vision.

"Yeah, what about them?" Gabriel mumbled.

He honestly didn't care about the hills, so he didn't understand why Quinto was pointing them out.

"Do you see those houses on the hills?" Quinto asked.

"Yeah."

"People who live in houses like that have a lot of responsibility that doesn't go away when the sun goes down," Quinto began. "They might have beautiful houses, but how much money do you think it costs them to live there?"

Gabriel shrugged.

"*A lot!*" Quinto exclaimed. "Those are the people you see who are always on their phones or on their computers...because they *never* get to rest. They are *always* working!"

"So?" Gabriel grumbled. "*We're* always working."

Quinto hugged Gabriel to him and chuckled, saying, "At least we get to rest at the end of the day, *mi amigo*. Some of those people keep working even at night. Keep that in mind."

Gabriel appreciated that Quinto was trying to cheer him up, but for him this move wasn't only a change in geography. He had *lived* in a decent house in Illinois...the only home he had ever known until now.

This new life represented a cold, dark, deep plunge into the harsh realities of his captivity.

California's strawberry fields promised the allure of something new but delivered only more of the same: relentless work under a blazing sun, hands stained red with juice as if to mark him with the evidence of his labor.

As he grew older and stronger, the work he was given intensified, and the weight of his situation bore down on him unrepentantly.

The change also brought with it a sense of isolation and displacement.

Removed from the familiar surroundings of Illinois, Gabriel found himself navigating new waters. The fields of California, with their vibrant hues and sweet scents, could not mask the bitterness of his situation. Quinto tried to get Gabriel to accept his life for what it was, but Gabriel felt he was meant for something better than this.

Amidst the struggle and strife, Gabriel's dream of freedom began to crystalize. The very extremity of his circumstances, the change from one form of servitude to another, spurred within him a deeper yearning for liberation.

During late spring and early summer, work in the strawberry fields was backbreaking. Gabriel spent long hours bent over rows of strawberries, picking fruit under the blazing sun. He was young and turning into a man more each day, but the physical toll brought sore muscles, blisters, and the exhaustion that came from repetitive motion and constant bending. Gabriel had to contend with extreme weather, ranging from scorching heat to sudden rain, which made the fields muddy and even more challenging to navigate. There was little to no protection from the elements, and breaks were few and far between. The pay was meager, and the wages were often not commensurate with the amount of work and hours put in.

The economic exploitation was a bitter reality for Gabriel, who depended on the income from these fields to survive. Working every possible moment for his captors meant he had no way of seeking additional employment to better his lot in life. Moving to a new place every few months meant adapting to a different community and often facing language barriers and cultural differences.

Gabriel felt isolated from the migrant worker community, struggling to find a sense of belonging. Having gone to school in Illinois and being raised there since infancy, he spoke perfect English with hardly any accent, but he looked like any of the other immigrants from Mexico or other places south of the border. They talked about things that went on "back home," things he could not relate to because he was taken away from it when he was a baby. Even Quinto was no help there since he too was born and raised in Chihuahua, Mexico. He had more in common with their fellow workers than Gabriel could ever hope for.

The work in the fields offered little room for advancement. Gabriel faced a future with no opportunities for education or alternative employment, trapping him in a cycle of poverty and hard labor. His new bosses did not allow for any education for the workers.

He had been looking forward to continuing school but learned very quickly that was not to be. Still grappling with feelings of hopelessness, fear for the future, and the stress of supporting himself under such dire circumstances, Gabriel's physical and emotional well-being were greatly affected.

His parents had explained how they were undocumented, and he was too, so now he had the added fear of deportation and limited access to legal employment opportunities. As a result, he knew he could not seek help from the authorities.

One thing that was very different in California was that he moved from job to job with the other migrant workers. He found he had no social life whatsoever now, which made it difficult to build any lasting relationships or become involved in a community. As a result, Gabriel felt very lonely and disconnected.

He missed his family very much and wished he could see them one more time or even hear their voices on the phone. Tío Quinto was family, but to Gabriel he was virtually a stranger. Any closeness he might have developed with Quinto was a lost cause since they were so different in age and background.

At each job, Gabriel and the other workers lived in overcrowded and substandard housing. Oftentimes, they were only given a blanket to use and slept on the floors. He saw many workers get sick from their poor living conditions and worried about how long he could manage to live like this.

CHAPTER 5

THE PETROSYAN CLUB

When everyone was ready to go, Cauley locked their hotel room, and they headed downstairs to the street.

Across from their hotel was the famous Hyde Park, and it was extravagantly decorated for Christmas. The girls instantly wanted to go over and look at everything but knew they had to meet their grandparents, so they kept quiet for the time being.

The Petrosyan Club was two blocks away from the hotel, so the walk was short. Clara was grateful since she still hadn't recovered her breath from when they left Illinois. The cold really bothered her breathing, but she dared not say anything and ruin the trip for her family.

Upon entering the restaurant, Amalia's mother and father came rushing out of the back, arms outstretched, smiling widely as they welcomed their family into the restaurant for the first time.

Amalia's mother hugged her first, tears of joy streaming down her face.

"Oh, my beautiful daughter! I'm so glad you're here! And Cauley…you're still as handsome a devil as ever!" she exclaimed as she reached over to hug her son-in-law.

"And who do we have here? The most beautiful twins God ever created," their grandfather said with a wink at the girls.

He reached over and hugged them both in a group hug so tight that Clara thought her head would pop off. Thankfully, it didn't last long so she was able to catch her breath before her grandmother gave them welcoming hugs.

"Come, have a seat! You must be starving after that long trip."

Nana handed everyone a menu.

"Pick whatever you want. It's our treat!"

Nana then sat down at the table and continued to exclaim how thrilled she was to see them again.

The girls looked over the menu, attempting to find something…anything, that looked familiar.

"What's *tabouleh* and *lavash?*" Emilia asked with a confused look, left eyebrow cocked as it always was when something didn't make sense to her.

"*Tabouleh* is a salad, and *lavash* is a type of bread," Papí explained. "The salad has parsley, tomatoes, mint, onion, bulgur, olive oil, lemon juice, salt and sweet pepper. Sometimes we add lettuce to it too."

"You put mint in *salad?*" Emilia questioned, eyebrow still cocked. She had never heard of such a thing.

"Yes," Nana confirmed, "it's absolutely delicious! If you like salads, you should try it. That's one of the neat things about traveling to a foreign country. You get to experience things you would never have at home…and it broadens your horizons."

"What does 'broaden your horizons' mean?" Clara asked, imagining the flat, never-ending horizon she sees at home every day.

Why on Earth would she care to have them broadened? To her, it seemed like she would be seeing more flat land filled with corn and soybean fields. That didn't sound very exciting.

"It means your mind will begin to change from thinking about the world as you experience it every day to learning about things you haven't seen before," Amalia began. "It helps you understand how people in different parts of the world live, and one thing to keep in mind, girls, is that England was here *long* before the United States, and they're still one of the major influential countries on this planet."

Neither Emilia nor Clara knew how to respond to this, but Emilia was curious about one thing in particular.

"Nana, if you live here, how come you don't sound British?"

"I was born in Turkey, dear," Nana replied, "but my accent is Armenian, since that's what my parents and those around us spoke."

In all the times the girls had been visited by their grandparents in the United States, it had never occurred to them that their accent was something different than the other people who they lived among. Never had they been exposed to a British accent until they arrived in London, so they assumed their grandparents 'accent was a British one. They definitely preferred the British accents they'd been hearing since they arrived. It sounded so elegant and refined.

"Where's Turkey?" Clara asked. "Is it around here?"

Papí chuckled, "No, Clara, Turkey is in the Middle East."

The girls looked at each other in surprise then turned back to their grandfather, urging him to continue.

"How did you end up in London?" Emilia asked.

Their grandparents reached out to each other and held hands. The solemnity that took over their grandparents told them this was not a happy story.

Nana began, "Have you ever heard of the Armenian genocide in school?"

Both Emilia and Clara shook their heads.

"Have you ever heard of the Holocaust?" Papí asked, knowing full well the answer was yes.

The girls nodded.

"The Armenian genocide was a lot like that, only it happened much earlier. As a result, many Armenians who survived left Turkey and settled in other countries. Our parents were some of those Armenians who left Turkey," Papí explained.

Emilia and Clara were shocked. They had never visualized their grandparents as anything but happy British people who loved to visit them in America. Like most children, they thought of their grandparents as always having a perfect life, spending their time focusing on how to make their grandchildren happy. Now, their grandparents were humans with a painful past.

"How sad," Clara whispered, her eyes round as saucers.

"You have no idea how sad," Papí replied softly. "When we get together with our Armenian friends here in London, we often talk about those we lost – even those we never met."

Nana spoke up, "Before we get too far into the weeds on this, let me get some food and drinks. They've come a long way, Papí."

The girls 'grandfather nodded and smiled before turning to Cauley and Amalia to make small talk.

"Girls, would you like to help?" Nana offered.

They both smiled and followed her into the massive, restaurant kitchen, watching as Nana bustled around, quickly gathering appetizers for them to share.

She handed Clara a basket of bread and said, "Please take this to the table and ask your Papí and father what they want to drink."

Clara skipped gleefully out of the kitchen and into the seating area of the restaurant with a warm breadbasket full of *lavash*.

"I brought bread!" she announced proudly to the men. "Nana wants to know what you want to drink."

"Ah, that's a good little pumpkin!" Papí exclaimed with a huge smile on his face.

He took the basket from Clara and placed it in the center of the table.

"Tell Nana that your dad and I would like the pomegranate wine and that you and Emilia should each have a glass of *tan*."

"Tan?" Clara asked skeptically.

The only "tan" she'd ever heard of was when someone's skin changed color in the sun. She never tanned, but Emilia did sometimes.

"You'll love it!" Papí touted. "Tell her to bring out some of the cheese *börek* too."

Cheese? Clara *loved* cheese!

"Okay!" she said with a smile and skipped back to the kitchen with their requests.

When she returned to the kitchen, she announced, "They want to drink pomegranate wine, and Papí said Emilia and I should have *tan*. Oh! And he said to bring out some cheese…cheese…," she couldn't remember the last word.

"Börek?" Nana asked.

"Yes! *Börek!*" Clara said enthusiastically while clapping her hands.

"Okay, give me a few minutes to warm the *börek*," Nana said.

She headed to the drink counter to prepare the beverages. When they were done, she put them on a brown tray and asked the girls to take them out.

"Um…maybe let me get that," Amalia said, having followed Clara into the kitchen. "I don't want them dropping it and breaking your dishes."

"They're almost old enough to start working, Amalia! They can handle this," Nana said pointedly.

"Okay…" their mother said with furrowing brows.

"We can do it, Mama," Emilia said.

After hearing her grandfather's story, she felt like she was capable of anything with the Armenian blood running through her veins.

Emilia took the tray from Nana and asked Clara to open the door to the dining room for her.

Clara ran toward the door. As she began to push on the heavy door, she slipped and fell face first into the door, causing her nose to bleed.

"I *told* you!" Amalia grumbled to her mother, who looked defeated.

Amalia quickly arrived at Clara's side and began wiping the blood away from her nostrils. Clara was crying, which made things even worse. She wanted to blow her nose, but it hurt too much to touch. As Amalia gently tried to wipe some blood from the bottom of one nostril, the tip of Clara's nose bent to the side and flattened against her right cheek.

"*OW!*" Clara cried, pushing her mother's hand away.

"Oh dear," Nana lamented. "I'm afraid it's broken. We need to get her to hospital right away."

To hospital? Emilia thought. Shouldn't it be "to *the* hospital?" Having learned all the new things she did today, she dared not question her grandmother at a time like this.

Amalia sighed and nodded then headed out into the dining room to explain to the men what happened.

Immediately, they were both on their feet and running into the kitchen to check on Clara.

"We'll take her to the hospital. You stay here and visit," Cauley said.

The women watched as the men carried Clara out the back door and placed her gently into Pap'ís car. They quickly climbed in the front and left for the hospital.

As they drove away, Nana patted Mama on the back and said, "She's in good hands. Don't worry. Come, let's finish preparing the food so we can eat. I can warm their food for them when they get back."

The three worried ladies locked the front door and headed back into the kitchen.

CHAPTER 6

THE LEGEND OF ANDARTA AND EIR

When Cauley and Papí returned with Clara, she had a nasty looking bandage over her nose and bruises under both eyes. Nana, Mama and Emilia were awaiting their arrival with a warm dinner.

"Oh, my poor baby!" Nana crooned over Clara. "Here, have some *tan*. It will make you feel better."

She handed Clara a short glass with a thick, yogurt-looking substance inside.

"Thanks, Nana," Clara replied pitifully with a very stuffy sounding nose.

She took a sip of the drink and smiled.

"It's good!"

"I knew you'd like it!" Nana replied, clapping her hands gleefully. "Everybody sit. Let's eat. I have a special surprise for dessert."

The girls watched as Nana bustled around the table making sure every plate was full of steaming hot food. The aromas were making their mouths water. As Nana sat down, everybody began eating. For quite some time, all you could hear was the clinking of flatware on porcelain and the sounds of people eating.

Suddenly, loud bells chimed as the front door swung open.

"*Whew*, it's cold out there!" a familiar voice announced.

Emilia yelled, "Grandpa!"

She jumped up from her seat, ran over to the man by the door and gave him a big hug.

"What happened to your face?" Grandma shrieked, hands covering her face in horror at Clara's appearance.

"Oh my goodness!" Amalia cried and also ran over to the door to hug her mother-in-law.

Papí and Nana were clapping and grinning.

"Surprise!" they both yelled.

"Dessert came early!" Nana laughed.

"What are you two doing here?" Cauley laughed as he gave his parents a warm hug.

"It's a surprise these two cooked up," Grandpa winked, indicating the grandmothers.

"Come sit!" Nana instructed happily. "Have something to eat."

Cauley and Papí took the newcomers' luggage upstairs to the apartment where Nana and Papí lived, while Grandma and Grandpa got settled at the table.

ᛏᚨᚹᛒᛟᛟᚲᛟᚾᛖ

"If you want to hear a *really* cool story, you should hear about your Viking ancestors!" Papí laughed.

"Oh, we know all about them," Emilia replied. "Grandpa talks about them all the time."

"Does he now?" Nana asked. "And what has he told you?"

"He told us about how they were warriors and explorers," Clara said as best she could.

"And how they flew around on dragons!" Emilia shouted, laughing.

"Did he mention Andarta or Eir?" Papí asked.

"No?" Clara gave Emilia a quizzical look.

Emilia shrugged.

"That doesn't sound familiar. Are those places in Turkey too?"

"They're not places," Nana said, leaning forward conspiratorially. "They're ancient goddesses."

"Goddesses?" Emilia said with excitement.

Emilia and Clara were eager to hear another story. This was turning out to be the best visit with their grandparents they could ever remember.

"I don't think they're quite ready to hear all of this yet, Dad. They're only ten years old," Cauley warned.

"They don't have to hear everything, but they should know some things by this time. None of us knows when they're going to need it," Grandpa argued.

"Need what?" Emilia asked skeptically.

"The…history…for when you might have to…" Amalia said nervously while looking at the other adults.

"Write a report about them at school," Cauley finished.

Emilia got the feeling the adults were trying to keep a secret from her and Clara.

"Let's have some dessert while I tell them the story," Grandpa suggested.

"Yay, dessert!" the girls yelled.

Nana laughed, "Okay, give me a few minutes. Does anybody want coffee?"

All of the adults wanted coffee.

"Can I help?" Emilia offered.

"That would be lovely," Nana smiled.

Several minutes later, Nana and Emilia returned from the kitchen with trays full of Turkish coffee, cream, sugar, more *tan* for the girls, honey cake, and Armenian Delight.

Once everyone had taken their share, they settled in for what promised to be another of Grandpa's exciting Viking stories.

"I call this 'The Legend of Andarta and Eir'," he began. "In the ancient days of the Viking age, among the clash of swords and the roar of the sea, twin sister goddesses stood side by side, their destinies entwined by the threads of fate. One of them was the revered goddess of war, Andarta. Warriors prayed for her protection and guidance in

44

battle, mostly against the notorious Vikings, who were ruthless in their ways. The other goddess, Eir, was the goddess of healing. She tended to the fallen warriors, guiding them to the Hall of Souls where she would oversee the healing of their broken souls before sending them off to Valhalla."

"What's Valhalla?" Emilia inquired.

"Valhalla is like heaven for warriors," Grandpa explained. "Although they didn't look like twins, both had red hair and blue eyes…like you two."

Emilia and Clara smiled at each other proudly. As much as Grandpa talked about their Viking ancestors, he had never mentioned twins, let alone twin girls with red hair and blue eyes. This was getting better already! They looked back at Grandpa with rapt attention as he continued the story.

"They were Vikings by blood but were left orphaned as babies when their parents were killed in battle. The Senmarian warriors with whom their parents were at war were determined to rid their land of the Viking savages and went from tent to tent murdering any Vikings that remained.

"When they came across the babes, kept warm only by the large cat that traveled with their family, they could not continue the bloodbath.

"'Kill them!' one of the men outside the tent yelled at those standing inside.

"'They're mere babes,' someone pleaded.

"'Babes who will grow up to be murderous savages and bring Hel back to Earth! If none of you cowards will do it, I'll finish this.'"

"Girls, I tell you, before that man even made it to the tent…which was a few feet away…a huge *dragon* came charging out of that tent, snatched that man in its jaws, and flew away with him!"

Grandpa's eyes were as big as saucers.

"What did he do to the man?" Emilia whispered, looking like she'd seen a ghost.

Grandpa spread his arms wide.

"I don't know, sweet pea. That man was never seen again."

Clara, realizing that the babies were in the tent where the dragon came out of, shrieked, "Did it eat the babies?"

"No," Grandpa chuckled. "The babies were fine."

Emilia yelled, "Oh no, did it eat the cat?"

All the adults in the room burst out in uproarious laughter at Emilia's expression when she thought the cat had been eaten.

Grandpa, seeing how upset she was by the adults laughing, shrugged and said, "I don't think so, but nobody ever saw the cat again."

"Oh no," Emilia replied softly.

She loved cats and always wanted one. The thought of a cat keeping the twin babies warm as its last good deed on Earth was so sweet that it made her cry.

"Do you want to hear the rest?" Grandpa asked.

"Maybe you should stop for now," Mama suggested.

"No!" the girls shouted in unison.

They loved hearing Grandpa's stories, which were always so exciting and the basis of most of the girls 'imaginary play sessions.

The adults laughed at the girls 'reaction.

"Okay," Mama relented.

Grandpa cleared his throat and took a sip of his Turkish coffee before continuing.

"The people of Senmar were very superstitious and took it as a sign that these babies were to be protected…not killed. The warriors discussed their fate. Their leader, a man named Kimbel Murphy and his wife, were childless and decided to take them home and raise them as their own."

Both Emilia and Clara breathed an audible sigh of relief.

"Since they didn't know the babies 'names, or even if they had names yet, they named them Andarta and Eir after goddesses in their culture. Little did their adoptive parents know, but they had saved the lives of two actual goddesses. This didn't become known until the girls became of age – ten in that day and time."

"Hey! *We're* ten!" Clara shouted, and Emilia smiled gleefully.

"You are?" Papí looked astounded.

Both girls nodded vigorously, still smiling widely. This story was already so much more exciting than any they'd heard before. They didn't notice how somber the other adults had become or that they were looking at each other with concern.

"Go on, Grandpa!" Emilia shouted, eager to hear more.

After a long pause, he took a deep breath, looked over at the girls ' parents, then continued in a more serious vein.

"The girls themselves didn't know they were goddesses until they were in the midst of their first battle against the dreaded Vikings. Up until then, they were raised in a fairly peaceful time and lived as normal girls. They did their lessons, did housework, took care of the animals, practiced archery and other battle strategies…the same stuff other children did in that time and place.

"Right before the battle began, their Druid priest gathered the warriors together and invoked the goddess Andarta's name for protection – as they had always done since the beginning of their civilization. The last time it had been done was when the twin goddesses were newborns, and many of the people there felt it was good luck having a warrior named after the goddess in their midst.

"The priest went through his usual routine and prayers, but when he said, 'We call upon the aid of Andarta, the mighty goddess of war and victory, to watch over us in this time of need,' the ten-year-old Andarta was filled with an overwhelming feeling of strength and power. She ran toward the enemy in silence and killed all of them in a matter of seconds.

"Her sister, Eir, followed after her but tended to the mortally wounded to ensure a quick escape from their pain and suffering, so they could enter the hallowed halls of Valhalla.

"When they returned to their stunned comrades, neither girl had one scratch on them…not one hair out of place. Andarta and Eir had returned to their mortal selves and had no idea what they had done.

"They stood there looking at the rest of the warriors, waiting for instructions about what they were to do in the upcoming battle. The girls didn't realize they *were* the battle and that it was over. Neither had any memory of what happened."

Emilia, never missing a thing, interrupted, "I thought you said the twins were Vikings. Why would Vikings protect other warriors against Vikings?"

Grandpa was impressed.

"Good question! First of all, the girls didn't know they were Vikings. The Senmarians who raised them from infancy never told the girls the story of how they were rescued. They let them believe they were born from their own race. The other people in their caravan kept their secret because they worried if the girls knew the truth that they might turn on them and kill them all in their sleep.

"Vikings were vicious barbarians whose sole purpose in life was to conquer other people and take their land. They would even murder or abandon their own people if they were sick or injured – babies, the elderly…it didn't matter to them. If they couldn't help the Viking cause, they were discarded. Being raised by people who were not Vikings gave the goddesses a different perspective than the people they were born from."

"That's awful," Clara said, deeply affected by the images swirling around in her mind.

Everyone nodded solemnly.

"I don't want to be a Viking anymore," Emilia stated and crossed her arms in a pout.

"Me neither," Clara mumbled.

Grandpa chuckled.

"Don't be so hard on yourselves. Many people have a little Viking in them whether they want it or not. The Vikings made it a habit of having babies with the people they conquered, so their bloodline runs far and wide. It doesn't mean that everyone with Viking blood in them is a bad person. Look at the twins, Andarta and Eir. They were Vikings. Do you think they were bad?"

The girls looked at each other and shook their heads.

"No!" Nana agreed passionately. "They were *good* people!"

"Where are they now?" Clara asked. "Valhalla?"

There was an unbearably long silence.

"It's hard to say," Grandpa began slowly. "We know that since the advent of Christianity, many people have stopped worshipping other gods and goddesses…even helpers like Eir and Andarta. When they stopped being called upon, they seemed to go into a hibernation of sorts. Do you know what hibernation is?"

"It's when animals go to sleep for the winter and get skinny," Clara explained.

Grandpa smiled.

"Yes, sort of like that."

"So, they can still be brought back?" Emilia asked.

Another very long pause permeated the room.

"Yes," Grandpa said carefully, then pressed his lips together firmly.

"How?" Clara asked. "I want to meet Eir!"

Grandpa let out a big breath and looked over at the girls 'parents.

"I can't tell you that. What I can tell you is that the twins have been walking the Earth disguised as mortals ever since. They take over the bodies of twin girls in their bloodline until such time as those girls ' human bodies pass away. Girls with red hair and Viking blood. Waiting for the day when they will be needed again…and called upon to help those being forced into horrible circumstances. People who cannot get out of their situation without powerful forces behind them.

"Bound by blood and purpose, Eir and Andarta made a solemn pact to fight against the darkness that plagues the realms of gods and mortals alike. Andarta's invincible spirit and Eir's healing touch allowed them to forge a bond stronger than steel, a beacon of hope in a world gripped by chaos. Disguised as humans, they swore to protect the innocent and bring justice to evildoers. Over time, as men began to battle in the name of Christianity, the damaged souls were no longer completing the journey to Valhalla, because Eir was no longer known to humankind. The Hall of Souls was bursting at the seams with wounded warriors stuck in limbo. It's still like that today, as we speak."

"So, who's going to help them?" Clara asked, worry lines etching her forehead.

Grandpa quickly pulled his gaze away from Clara and mumbled, "Eir will help them…when it's time."

"When will it be time?" Emilia demanded.

"When Eir's human body…is no longer available to her," Grandpa's voice cracked.

The girls looked at each other.

"What does that mean?" Clara whispered.

"It means the twins have to separate. Eir has to go to beyond the veil to the Hall of Souls. Andarta has to stay here on Earth," Mama explained gently.

The thought of being apart from her sister forever was incomprehensible. Clara instinctively reached over and grasped Emilia's hand, as she was reaching out for hers.

When their hands touched, they both sensed a strong, warm vibration start in their palms, move up their arms, pass across their shoulders, and then permeate their entire beings. The air was being forced out of their lungs and felt as though they were momentarily weightless while everything turned blindingly white.

Before they were alert and could make sense of what was happening, the girls felt a light tapping on their cheeks and something solid against their backside.

"Wake up," Cauley said. "Clara! Clara!"

Emilia felt something cool on her forehead and slowly opened her eyes.

"She's awake!" Nana said.

"Thank God!" Mama cried, quickly appearing in Emilia's line of vision.

Emilia heard a loud, masculine sob and looked over at her father's back. He was bent over Clara's still body.

"Clara…" He began sobbing wholeheartedly.

Clara's eyes suddenly opened.

Everyone watched as she reached up and placed her hand on her father's cheek and spoke very clearly in what sounded like an ethereal woman's voice, "Don't worry, Cauley. It's not time yet."

Her eyes closed again.

Everyone was left speechless at this turn of events.

"Cl... Clara?" Amalia said timidly, afraid to touch her body.

Papí brought another cool washcloth over and placed it on Clara's forehead.

"She'll be okay," Papí said to console his daughter. "She said it herself. Give her some time to come around."

"They're only ten years old, Hayrig!" Amalia began crying. "They're too young!"

Nana went over to Mama and put her arms around her shoulders.

"Yes, they are too young, Amalia. Eir told us it's not time yet. Don't worry, love," she told her daughter.

"Grandma," Emilia corrected. "That was Clara…not Eir."

"Ah, yes," Grandma said, ducking her head away. "My mistake."

Clara opened her eyes and tried to sit up.

"What happened?" she said groggily.

"Oh nothing!" Nana said cheerfully. "You slipped and hit your head. You'll be fine. I think it's time you get back to your hotel so you can get some sleep. It's very late, and you all must be very tired from the trip and the time change."

Cauley and Amalia agreed and hurried the girls along to gather their things. Everyone gave their goodbye hugs as the Bennings headed for the door. Once outside, the air was crisp, and they could see their breath in the air. The walk back to the hotel was quiet.

CHAPTER 7

THE ENCHANTED SWORD

Although the girls were tucked into bed and kissed goodnight, as soon as their parents left the room, they started talking about the story Grandpa told.

"Clara, do you remember anything when you were asleep on the floor?" Emilia asked.

"No," she mused. "The last thing I remember was Mama telling me that I have go to the Hall of Souls, and you have to stay here," Clara recounted.

Emilia shot up in her bed and stared at Clara in a panic.

"*What?* She didn't say that, Clara! She was talking about Eir…the Viking goddess…not *you!*"

She was quite frightened now.

First, Clara talked like a woman and called their dad by his first name, and now *this?* Emilia wanted to cry but was afraid it would scare Clara, who obviously thought this was all normal.

What is going on? She thought frantically.

"I'm sorry, Emi. I know you're not ready, but it's going to happen. I don't know when, but we have to be prepared," Clara explained calmly.

"No! Clara! Stop! It's a story!" Emilia argued and began crying.

Clara got out of her bed and climbed into Emilia's, wrapping her arms around her sister, who was sobbing hysterically.

"It'll be okay, Emi. This is why we're here."

"Why?" Emilia sobbed.

"It's been centuries! The world needs us. We can't back down. It's in our blood. You know this," Clara said firmly.

"I don't want to be Andarta!" Emilia cried.

"You already *are* Andarta," Clara said forcefully. "You always have been. You've never been afraid before. Why would you be now?"

Emilia shook her head. She'd never seen her twin this passionate about anything.

"Were you listening to Grandpa?" Clara continued. "You took out an entire Viking army in a matter of seconds when you were ten years old. That was *centuries* ago…way before the advanced weapons we have today. Imagine what you can do *now!*"

"Maybe when it's time, I'll be able to understand this…but right now, it's really scary," Emilia moaned.

"I know," Clara said.

"How certain are you about this?" Emilia asked.

"As certain as you and I are talking right now."

This was a side of Clara that had never appeared before, and her maturity and absolute conviction about their fate was difficult for Emilia to grasp. It was usually Emilia comforting Clara, and she didn't know how to accept this change in her sister.

For the first time in her life, Clara did not seem to be afraid of what was happening, and Emilia felt that now, if ever, was the exact time for Clara to be afraid.

"If I'm Andarta, then you're Eir. That means you have to go to the Hall of Souls. How will you get there?"

"The same way everyone goes to the Hall of Souls," Clara replied with a shrug.

The girls settled down again in Emilia's bed and stayed there for the rest of the night, holding hands and contemplating their futures as Andarta and Eir.

"I hope it doesn't happen for a very long time," Emilia said.

Clara gave Emilia's hand a comforting squeeze but said nothing.

ᛏᚾᛒᛉᛉᚲᛉᚺᛗ

The next morning, the Bennings went back to The Petrosyan Club to meet with the rest of their family.

"What should we do today?" Cauley asked cheerfully over breakfast.

Several ideas arose – the Tower of London tour, a ride on the London Eye, and a trip down the Thames River.

"I want to hear more of Grandpa's story about Eir and Andarta," Emilia said seriously.

"You're in a new country, darling! It's time to get out and experience new things," Nana encouraged.

"Can't I hear a little more before we go out?" she asked.

Everyone looked at Grandpa, who nodded.

"Okay, what would you like to hear?"

"When the sisters get separated, do they ever see each other again?" Emilia asked.

"Oh, yes!" He smiled. "They're goddesses who can go between realms whenever they want. You can almost think of where they live as where they work. When your parents go to work, they come back home and see each other. With the gods and goddesses, it's similar. Where they live is where they work, so in order to see each other, they have to go visit each other at work. Also, Andarta and Eir work *together*, but in different realms, so they *have* to keep in touch."

He hoped that was a simple enough explanation for them to understand.

This did provide some comfort to the girls. Neither one knew whether or not the adults in their family knew who they really were, so they had to be skillful in the way they posed their questions. Emilia in particular wanted to know about Andarta's battle skills and weapons.

"How did Andarta kill all those guys in the Viking army so fast? Did she have some kind of big weapon?" she asked.

Grandpa rubbed his chin and looked aside thoughtfully before answering.

"You know, I'm not sure. I do remember hearing about an enchanted sword she had – something with old Norse words carved into the blade, but it was never mentioned in the story about that battle when it was told to me."

"Tell me more about the sword," she encouraged, leaning forward so as not to miss a single word.

"Oh, I don't know much about it, except that it was gifted to her by a Senmarian tribe before a battle. Do you remember me mentioning a Senmarian tribe leader named Kimbel Murphy?" he asked.

The girls both nodded.

"He was the one who adopted the Viking babies who were in the tent with the cat," Emilia answered.

"Very good! Kimbel's mother was a Viking who died giving birth to him. His father was from Senmar but was killed in a viciously bloody battle against the dreaded Vikings at the very time his wife was passing into the Hall of Souls. He was quickly adopted by others in his Senmarian tribe and felt it was his duty to do the same for the babies in the tent.

"Kimbel Murphy found the sword at the edge of a cooled lava flood from the *Elkgjá* eruption, which happened many years before. He was out hunting for food when he saw something glinting brightly in the sunlight under the lava rock. Out of curiosity, he went to explore and found the blade of the sword partly buried under the rock. Using an axe, he spent days breaking apart the rocks and pulling on the sword until it finally came free. As soon as he picked it up, the words etched in the blade began glowing different colors. The blue and purple jewels around the hilt, emblazoned with gold filigree, were unlike anything he had ever seen. He was truly mesmerized by its beauty and couldn't wait to take it home and show his wife."

"What did the words say?" Emilia whispered, completely engrossed in Grandpa's story.

"I don't know if these are the exact words. It was written so long ago that I'm sure some things have been changed in the telling throughout the years, but it's something like this…Andarta, the goddess of war, is the sole owner of this sword. Hammered by the gods before the existence of humanity, it shall only be wielded by the goddess. It shall never be used by another but remain protected until

Andarta has need of it. When she touches this sword, the powers bestowed upon it will come to life. Hidden by her human bloodline until such time as her earthly guardian takes possession of it and bestows it on the goddess to keep until the end of time. This sword, if taken into any other's possession, will instantly cause the bearer's death, and the weapon will be returned to its current protector."

"*How* did you memorize all that?" Amalia asked her father in amazement.

Grandpa offered a small smile and said, "I've been reciting the story in my mind all my life."

"Cool!" the girls exclaimed.

All the adults laughed at the girls 'excitement.

"When Kimbel showed the sword to his wife, she asked him what the markings on the blade were, but he didn't know. It was a language he had never seen before and didn't look like any letters he'd ever seen. He assumed they were scratches from being buried under the lava, and as the lava cooled and turned to stone, it left the marks on the blade," Grandpa explained.

"His wife, being taken in by the sword's beauty, wanted to touch it, so Kimbel placed it on a table so she could look at it closer. As soon as he put that sword down…do you know what happened?"

Emilia and Clara shook their head, eyes wide with anticipation.

"The colors *disappeared!* The *words* disappeared!" He whispered mysteriously. "Except for the jewels and gold on the hilt, it looked like any other sword they would see every day."

"Wicked!" Emilia whispered.

Grandpa laughed and continued, "His wife ran her finger along the blade, touching the smoothness of it, and then the worst thing happened. She picked it up by the hilt and immediately dropped dead. Kimbel was horrified and heartbroken at the same time. He looked over at his girls playing in a corner of the tent and was overcome with fear for them, realizing he would have to raise them himself.

"Of course, when word got out about what happened to his wife, several women in his tribe helped raise the girls, easing his burden. That was a benefit of being their leader.

"Kimbel did his best to rid himself of the sword, lest anyone else succumb to the same fate as his beloved wife. He worried about his daughters finding it and touching it. He took it back to the lava flood where he first found it and placed it atop the lava rocks before heading back to his camp. When he re-entered his tent, the sword was lying on the table again in plain sight of anyone who should happen to enter."

"How is that possible?" Emilia demanded.

Grandpa shrugged, "Nobody knows."

"So, what happened?" Clara prodded.

He grinned, "Next, he took it far away to the edge of the land, climbed into his boat with the sword and sailed far out into the Denmark Strait. When he had gone so far that he couldn't see land in any direction, he knew he had reached his destination. He lifted the heavy sword and dropped it over the side of the boat into the frigid water below. When he could no longer see it in the murky depths, he sailed back to land and made the long trek back to his people.

"Weary from his trip, Kimbel Murphy approached his tent with relief. Before he was able to enter, he heard a loud crashing noise from within. Concerned, he rushed into the tent to find one of his tribeswomen lying on the ground with the sword mere inches from her hand. The woman was already turning an ugly shade of bluish gray, having touched the sword.

"Kimbel was in a panic and very distraught about the sword and what it was doing to those he cared about. It was obvious that no matter what he did, he could not rid himself of the sword. He was stuck with it forever and did his best to keep it hidden from prying eyes, but one of his comrades happened to come across him in the forest one day, holding it in his hands while trying to make sense of the glyphs on the blade. Since everyone, except him, who touched it died instantly, he began to think the glyphs were words of some kind and that the sword was cursed. But why not for him?

"When his friend reached out to touch it, Kimbel pulled it away sharply and shouted, 'No! Don't touch it. People who touch it have died immediately. I don't know if it's because of the sword, and I don't want to lose any more people.'

"'But, my friend, you are touching the sword, and you are as alive as me!' the man replied, perplexed by Kimbel's behavior.

"'It doesn't affect me the same way,' Kimbel argued.

"Since the words were written in old Norse, which was not a language any of them could read, none of them even knew the markings were words. His friend suggested he take it to one of the Druids to see if they could find out if the sword was cursed.

"The following day, Kimbel took the sword to the tent of Cathbad, the most powerful Druid he knew. He told Cathbad the story of the markings glowing and fading away and his wife and tribeswomen's untimely deaths upon touching it.

"'I feel this weapon is cursed,' Kimbel told Cathbad.

"The Druid looked over the sword very carefully, while Kimbel held it.

"'These are not mere scratches from lava rock,' Cathbad cautioned. 'These are words…ancient Norse words.'

"Kimbel watched as Cathbad transcribed the words on the sword on a piece of parchment. When he had copied everything, he translated them out loud.

"'This is a very powerful sword, Kimbel,' Cathbad proclaimed. 'Do not let it fall into the wrong hands. It must stay in the Viking bloodline to which it has been given until it is bestowed upon the goddess Andarta. When she is no longer in need of it, it will be returned to the same bloodline and must be kept safely for her future needs.'

"'But I was adopted. I don't know what my bloodline is,' Kimbel said.

"'Your parents were Vikings, were they not?'"

"Kimbel hated to be reminded of that fact but nodded in confirmation.

"'Your children are of Viking blood,' Cathbad added.

"At this, Kimbel looked at Cathbad in horror.

"'My wife and I didn't have any children before she passed away. Only the two girls we adopted, but they are not of our bloodline.'

"'They are of *your* bloodline,' Cathbad replied knowingly.

"'That's not possible! I have never sired a child!'

"'*You* may not have sired them, but your daughters are from your Viking bloodline. That is why they were given to you to rear,' Cathbad explained. 'They are next in line…the next chosen to protect the sword. You are the first.'

"When Kimbel left Cathbad's tent, he was very upset at what he had been told. Thinking of his children becoming guardians of a mystical sword that had immense powers truly frightened him.

"And then he remembered what his daughters had done during their first and last battle against the Vikings...without instruction or provocation. They had single-handedly wiped out the entire legion waiting to battle against Kimbel's army. He still couldn't figure out how they had done it and assumed it must be something in their Viking blood. Seeing what they were capable of terrified him. He had never seen his warriors do anything like that...ever. All the more reason to get rid of the sword.

"Kimbel spent many months trying to figure out what to do with the sword. He hardly slept out of worry that someone would find it and die, or worse, steal it. He decided that at the beginning of the next battle he would keep his daughters out of the fray and leave the sword as a gift for Andarta. If the gods permitted, she would take it and relieve him of this burden. If not, it would end up back in his possession again.

"The next battle came much sooner than expected, but he was ready. He told Cathbad of his plan. After invoking the protection of Andarta, Kimbel put the sword at the base of an old oak tree as an offering, the colors and carvings on the blade disappearing as always."

Grandpa leaned forward conspiratorially and said, "Legend has it that when Andarta holds it in her hand, the sword comes to life. The carvings reappear, and the words glow again. Supposedly, when the goddess wields the sword in battle, it never misses its mark."

"*Whoa!*" Clara shouted.

"*Sweet!*" Emilia said, nodding and smiling. "So where do I...I mean, where does she keep the sword?"

She noticed Mama look at her quizzically.

"Nobody knows," Grandpa said. "We don't even know if she *has* the sword. The last time it was seen was at the base of that tree. When the warriors went back to the tree to thank Andarta for her protection in that battle – which they won, of course – a gigantic dragon was sitting on top of the sword."

The girls eyes bulged at this revelation.

"Anyone who tried to go near it to collect the sword was tossed away by the dragon. The warriors weren't stupid, so they got out of there quick! As they were running, they heard their leader yelling for them to stop. When they looked back at the tree, both the dragon and the sword were gone! All they could see was the tree and a big, fluffy cat running around chasing something on the ground."

Grandpa sat back and put his fingers on his chin, deep in thought.

"I remember hearing something else that was rather interesting. The strangest thing about that cat was that it looked like it had something silver around its neck – like a collar, but pets didn't have collars back then. This was during the first century, in the 900s!"

The girls 'eyes bulged even more as they stared at each other in astonishment.

They've been on Earth *that long?*

"Okay, that's enough of the Valkyries for now," Grandma said and stood up.

"The Valkyries?" Clara asked.

"Valkyries are beautiful and powerful warriors and are also known to escort chosen warriors to Valhalla," Cauley explained.

"Wow, there is so much to this stuff. How am I ever going to learn it all?" Emilia wondered.

"Why do you have to learn it all?" Mama asked with a smile.

"I don't *have* to. I think it's really interesting, so I want to learn as much as I can about it," she explained.

"Well, one thing you *can* learn about while you're here is how the German's celebrate Christmas!" Papí exclaimed.

"Um…aren't we in *England*?" Emilia asked.

"Yes! The perfect place to attend a *Christkindlmarkt*. That's German for Christmas Market. They have one over at Hyde Park every year called Winter Wonderland. It's spectacular!"

"Oh, is that the thing we saw last night with all the lights and the rides?" Clara asked gleefully.

"The very same!" Papí confirmed.

"Can we go?" Emilia begged her parents.

"Yes, we can do that tonight," Mama replied. "Today, we're going to do something else though."

"Why don't we go to the Tower of London?" Dad suggested.

"What's that?" Emilia asked.

"It's a castle where the kings and queens used to live a very long time ago," he replied.

Excited at the prospect of seeing a real castle, the girls were anxious to get going. Luckily, there was a bus stop on the corner where they got onto a red double-decker bus. The girls immediately ran up the stairs to the top deck so they could see everything as they drove to their destination.

Shortly after the tour began, the guide was telling their group about the Tower crows.

"It's been said that if the crows leave London, England will fall," he announced.

A black raven came swooping down and landed in front of Emilia, bent forward as if bowing, then looked up at her and cawed before flying away.

Everyone in the group laughed at the funny occurrence before continuing on to the Tower itself.

Once inside, the girls soon lost interest. It was too dark inside, and there were so many steps to climb that they got worn out pretty quickly.

The only part that Emilia was interested in were the swords. There were swords of different lengths and widths, too many to count. She wondered if any of them were the fabled Andarta sword; but since she wouldn't know unless she touched it – and she wasn't allowed to touch them – there was no way for her to find out.

By the time the tour was over, it was late afternoon, and they were getting hungry. Since restaurants in London didn't open for supper until eight o'clock, they went back to their grandparents restaurant to eat.

When everyone had their fill and the dishes were cleaned and put away, the girls were begging to go to Winter Wonderland across the street.

CHAPTER 8

CHRISTMAS IN LONDON

The Benning family had been eagerly anticipating their trip to London for months. Finding out about the Winter Wonderland event in Hyde Park only heightened their excitement.

As evening approached, they bundled up in their warmest coats, scarves, and hats, brimming with excitement as they went to Hyde Park. The air was filled with the scent of roasted chestnuts, mulled wine, and the sound of joyful laughter.

Stepping through the gates, they were greeted by a spectacle of twinkling lights, towering Christmas trees, and festive decorations adorning every corner of the park. The girls' eyes widened with wonder as they took in the sights and sounds of Winter Wonderland.

As they walked along the pathways through the park, they were fascinated by everything they saw. Their first stop was the ice skating rink, where the entire family laced up rented skates and glided across the glistening ice. Laughter filled the air as they twirled and spun.

Next, they visited the *Christkindlmarkt*, where rows of temporary wooden chalets offered an array of festive treats and handcrafted gifts. Papí couldn't resist sampling a warm mince pie, while Cauley indulged in a steaming cup of mulled wine.

Emilia and Clara found a vendor stand filled with toys, and Emilia asked, "May we please go look at the toys?"

"Sure," Dad replied, "I'll go with you. There are a lot of people here, and I don't want you to get lost."

"Cauley, they have an archery range here!" Mama announced gleefully. "We're going over there, so when you're done with the toys, come meet us."

"Okay," he said chuckling.

He knew how much Amalia loved archery. She had been the star of her high school archery team and practiced back home whenever she had some free time.

As they got closer to the toy vendor, Emilia shouted, "They have stuffed animals! I'm going to see if they have a cat!"

She took off running toward the vendor stand.

"Hey, slow down!" Cauley called, but it was too late, and there was too much noise and loud music for Emilia to hear him.

"I think she's going to grow up to be a crazy cat lady," Clara laughed.

"I think you're right!" Dad said, as they entered the vendor's tent.

When they found Emilia, she was sitting down on the ground with a huge gray cat sitting on her lap, gently lifting its tail up and down. Emilia was in a world of her own, scratching the cat behind the ears and running her hand along it's fluffy back.

"I thought you meant a *stuffed* animal cat?" Dad gasped with a frown.

"I did. When I was looking at the stuffed animals, this cat came up to me and kept rubbing up against my legs and purring. He wouldn't leave me alone, so I sat down to pet him, and he climbed into my lap. I think he likes me!"

"What's his name?" Clara asked.

Emilia looked perplexed.

"I don't know! He doesn't have a collar or anything," she shrugged.

"How can you tell with all that fur?" Dad laughed.

Both the girls giggled.

"True," Emilia said and began feeling around the cat's neck for a collar.

Bingo!

She found a solid, silver collar hidden beneath the cat's extremely thick fur. The cat sat there contentedly while she twisted the collar around looking for a tag with the cat's name on it. Not only was there no tag, but there also didn't seem to be an end to the collar itself. It was almost like a solid bracelet around the cat's neck.

Disappointed, Emilia sighed, "Well, I found a collar, but there's no tag, so I *still* don't know what his name is."

One of the workers came over to see what the commotion was about.

"Hello, is everything alright?" he asked in a strong British accent.

"We're trying to find out this cat's name," Emilia responded.

"I've never seen him before. Does he have a collar?" the worker asked.

"Yes, but no name tag," Emilia replied.

"That's a bit funny, isn't it?" the man commented.

Emilia nodded.

"My name is Tyrell, but you can call me Ty. Let me know if you'd like to look at anything in the shop. I'll be right over there," Tyrell said with a wink, pointing toward the cash register.

"Thank you, Ty," Emilia said.

She took an immediate liking to him. She loved the way he talked, and he was so friendly. Emilia thought she might even be developing a little crush on Ty. She giggled at the idea.

Clara and Emilia spent the next fifteen minutes looking at all the toys Tyrell's shop had to offer. Clara found a play stethoscope, a nurse's hat, and a toy medical case that she wanted.

Emilia scoured through all the stuffed animals until she found a cat that looked like the one she had been playing with, only a *lot* smaller. Regardless, it was still a stuffed animal cat, and much nicer than the one she saw at the airport in Chicago. Secretly, she was glad her mother told her to wait until they got to London.

With the girls' purchases in hand, Cauley led Emilia and Clara from the toy store and through bustling crowds of holiday revelers, searching for their mother. After some time of poking at candy stalls that offered sugary samples, clothing booths with faux fur coats and knit scarves, and even a pop-up tavern offering spiced mead, which Cauley had to explain was not for little girls, he finally stumbled across a decorated sign that pointed in a direction they hadn't gone yet. He was absolutely sure he'd find his wife there.

ᛏᚨᚠᛒᚷᚷᚲᚷᚻᛗ

Thunk. Thunk.

Emilia watched with wide eyes as she witnessed her mother shooting arrows at a faraway target. Each arrow whizzed past her and landed with precision, getting closer and closer to the bullseye every time.

Thunk.

"GO, MAMA!" she yelled, clapping hard when the arrow struck dead center on the circular target.

Amalia turned in surprise and saw them all standing there, shopping bags in hand, clapping at her achievement.

"Thank you!" she bowed with a huge smile.

"Can I try?" Emilia asked gleefully.

"Sure!" Amalia replied, handing her bow to Emilia.

"Are you sure that's such a good idea, honey?" Cauley asked with apprehension.

"It's fine," she assured him. "I learned archery when I was six years old. She's ten."

She patted her husband on the chest.

When Amalia turned toward Emilia to offer her some quick lessons, she was stunned to find Emilia already in the range, nocking an arrow onto her bow. There were five targets on the paper. One large one in the middle and four small ones in each corner.

Her family watched in disbelief as she shot one after another in rapid succession, each arrow narrowly missing the bullseye.

"Oy!" The archery range keeper shouted at Emilia. "What do you think you're doing there, missy?"

"Archery?" Emilia responded quizzically.

"This range is for adults only. You need to leave."

Emilia slowly bent down to place her bow and the remaining arrows on the ground when someone from the crowd behind her shouted, "Let her be, Ian! She shoots better than *you!*"

The crowd jeered and chittered.

"She's a little *girl!* How *dare* you say she's better than me! I won the gold medal in the eighty-four Olympics, didn't I?" he shouted back at the person in the crowd.

"I'll wager ten quid she can beat you," the man argued.

"Ten?" Ian spluttered. "Make it twenty, you sodding idiot!"

Once the laughter died down, another man called out, "Make it fifty."

At this latest bet, the crowd grew quiet.

"I think we'd better go," Amalia whispered to Cauley.

"And have this crowd turn on us too? No way!" he chuckled quietly. "She obviously has her mother's gift!"

Amalia smiled and wrapped her arms around her husband and placed her cheek on his chest, watching to see what would happen next.

"How about we stay at ten for now," Ian said hesitantly, which brought uproarious laughter from the crowd.

"That's fine with me," the first man replied.

"Okay, ten paces from the target," Ian said to Emilia.

She nodded.

They both walked to the target and then took ten paces toward the crowd. Since the man's legs were much longer than Emilia's, she ended up much closer to the target than Ian.

"That's not ten paces!" Ian argued.

"It is for me," Emilia argued, "but if it makes you more comfortable, I'll move back to where you are. It makes no difference."

This brought more laughter from the crowd and caused Ian's face to turn purple with embarrassment.

Emilia skipped back toward the crowd with a smile on her face, receiving an encouraging smile from her family in the process.

Once she had reached the same distance from the target as Ian, she stopped, turned, nocked her arrow, released it, and hit mere centimeters from the bullseye, eliciting cheers and applause from the crowd behind her.

"Oy!" Ian shouted. "I didn't say go!"

"Oh, sorry," Emilia shrugged.

She quickly walked to the target, pulled the arrow out, and walked back to her spot.

Preparing again, as soon as she heard Ian give the signal, she released her arrow, this time hitting the bullseye dead center.

"Damn it!" Ian moaned.

She looked over at his target and saw that he had hit outside the bullseye.

"Again!" Ian shouted.

Emilia nocked another arrow, shot it, and watched as it sank into the target alongside her other arrow, as close to the center of the bullseye as it could get with another arrow already embedded there.

"AGAIN!" Ian screamed in frustration.

Emilia was worried she wouldn't be able to make another bullseye because there were already two arrows in its place. She nocked another arrow, pulled back further on the bow string, made a little prayer to Andarta for guidance, and immediately felt a strange tingling all over her body. She felt as though she were suspended, and all sound disappeared into the void.

Emilia knew it should have frightened her, but all she sensed was complete peace as she felt another hand take control of hers, pull the arrow back even more, and release. The tingling rapidly disappeared through the tips of her fingers, and the sound from the crowd reappeared. She was surprised to hear a loud cracking sound instead of the usual thump she heard the previous times she shot the arrows.

The crowd behind her went wild, and Ian threw his bow on the ground and stomped his feet in fury. He was shouting several curse words and using the word "bloody" a lot.

Emilia didn't quite understand what happened until she looked closer at her target. There she saw what looked like four arrows sticking out of the center of the bullseye. Confused because she knew she had only shot three during her competition with Ian, she walked up to the target for further inspection.

She was stunned to find that the last arrow had not only hit the bullseye dead center but had shot *through* the first arrow she shot, splitting it in half.

"Great job, honey!" Mama shouted as she ran up to Emilia, hugging her tightly and lifting her up in celebration.

"How did you do that?" Clara asked in admiration.

"That was spectacular!" Dad announced with a huge smile on his face. "I am very proud of you, Emilia!"

Emilia was dumbfounded at what had happened but didn't want to scare her parents, so didn't tell them about it. Plus, she was still amazed at that last shot.

Several people in the crowd came up to her to tell her how amazing she was, shaking her hand and wanting to take their picture with her. She felt like she was famous for a brief moment. It was so exciting.

Emilia felt something brush against her leg and looked down to see the cat she had played with in Tyrell's Toy Shoppe.

"Hello, Ty!" she crooned.

"Ty?" Dad asked.

"Yes," Emilia smiled. "I'm going to name him Tyrell, Ty for short, since he doesn't have a name yet."

"Isn't that the name of the man at the toy shoppe?" Dad asked teasingly.

Emilia blushed slightly and nodded.

They all laughed, still overjoyed at Emilia's success in the archery range.

As the night drew to a close, they gathered around the towering Christmas tree in the center of Winter Wonderland for the grand finale—a dazzling light show set to classic holiday tunes. They oohed and aahed as the tree sparkled and shimmered in a mesmerizing display of color and light.

As they returned to the hotel, cheeks flushed and hearts full of joy, the girls reflected on their magical day at Winter Wonderland. They knew that they would cherish these memories for years to come.

Quietly, they could hear a group of carolers outside and crept over to their window. Dad opened it enough to hear, but not enough to let too much cold in.

They sang a carol none of them had heard before, but it was very ethereal and quite beautiful.

"What are you doing?" Mama whispered to Clara.

"I'm writing it down, so I can remember it and sing it to the children," she whispered back.

"What children?" Nana asked quizzically.

"The ones who need peace," Clara replied calmly.

Mama smiled and turned back toward the window.

When the carolers had moved on, they closed the window and gathered around Clara to read the lyrics she had written.

Softly falls the winter night,
Blankets pure in silver light,
From a star so high and bright,
Guiding hearts in gentle flight.

Angels hum a lullaby,
Through the dark and silent sky,
Bringing hope, a love so wide,
For all to find, for all to bide.

Star of peace, shine clear and true,
Light the path for me, for you.
May we walk in love's embrace,
Underneath your gentle grace.

In the stillness, voices rise,
Soft as snow, yet bold as skies.
Every soul, in silent praise,
Joined as one, our hearts ablaze.

Let no fear or sorrow stay,
Bid them softly drift away.
In this light, all burdens cease—
Wrapped in quiet, endless peace.

Star of peace, shine clear and true,
Light the path for me, for you.
May we walk in love's embrace,
Underneath your gentle grace.

From mountain high to valley low,
Wherever weary travelers go,

A whispered prayer, a healing song,
To guide the lost, to make us strong.

So let this light within us glow,
Brighter than the stars we know.
Hand in hand, through frost and flame,
Kindness calls us each by name.
Star of peace, shine clear and true,
Light the path for me, for you.
May we walk in love's embrace,
Underneath your gentle grace.

As the dawn brings morning's hue,
Hope is born, and hearts renew.
Star of peace, forever stay,
Guide us on our sacred way.

"Oh, that's lovely!" Nana exclaimed, clasping her hands together joyously.

"What's the name of it?" Emilia asked.

Clara looked surprised. "I don't know."

"How about 'Star of Peace?'" Papí suggested.

"Yes! 'Star of Peace,'" Clara happily agreed and quickly wrote it at the top of the paper.

ᛏᚾᚦᛐᚱᚱᚲᚱᚼᛗ

The next morning, everyone gathered their gifts and met at the grandparent's apartment and placed the presents under the Christmas tree. Emilia and Clara were surprised to see Christmas stockings, filled to the brim, hanging on the fireplace mantle for them.

"Oh, how pretty!" Clara exclaimed.

"Can we open them now?" Emilia shouted.

Nana laughed and said, "Of course!"

The girls quickly ran over to the fireplace and took down their stockings, taking them over to the carpet where they began removing little treats and gifts.

Shiny red wrappers hid delicious fudge-filled chocolate balls. Pretty paper bags held lacy ribbons for their hair, and they each had a homemade doll with red braided hair and blue paisley dresses.

"These are so cool!" Emilia cried with laughter. "Thank you, Nana, and Papí!"

Both girls gave their grandparents very tight hugs of appreciation.

"Thank you! I love my presents." Clara smiled.

Mama helped Nana serve breakfast with delicious Christmas beverages before the family began opening the rest of the gifts.

When Grandpa announced he had something special for his granddaughters, they could hardly contain their excitement.

"Clara…your mother tells me you like to take care of things. Perhaps you will be in the medical field someday. I saw this and thought it might help you make a decision one way or the other," he announced.

He handed Clara a large, gift-wrapped box with a big bow on top. She tried to open it carefully without tearing any of the paper.

Emilia got impatient waiting to see what was inside and urged, "Rip it open!"

"I can't," Clara replied. "It's too pretty!"

"Ugh!"

"Emilia!" her mother snapped. "When it's your turn, you can rip it all you want, but it's Clara's turn now and you have to be patient."

Emilia crossed her arms and pouted in protest.

Finally, Clara got all the paper and ribbon off the box, in one solid piece. Underneath the wrapping was a plain brown box. She slowly removed the thick piece of tape holding the flaps down, eliciting another moan from her sister.

Once the box was finally opened, Clara had to stand up to see what was inside. Emilia came running over to see as well. It looked like a box of medical supplies and books. The girls looked at each other quizzically.

"What is all this stuff?" Emilia asked Grandpa.

"It's all the stuff someone might need to perform first aid!" he said with a big smile.

"What's first aid?" Clara asked.

"First aid is the treatment people get when they first get injured somewhere," Mama explained. "Like, when you get a cut at home, and I patch you up, *that's* first aid."

"Or when someone gets into a car accident, an ambulance comes and the paramedics bandage up those who are injured to stop the bleeding before they can get to the hospital," Grandma added. "That's also first aid. It's the aid injured people get first."

"When soldiers are injured on the battlefield, there's a special kind of soldier called a medic who gets to them and treats the worst wounds first. That's also first aid," Papí contributed.

"Wow…there's first aid *everywhere,*" Emilia said.

"Indeed, there is," Dad responded, nodding.

While everyone was explaining the different first aid situations, Clara was pulling each item out of the box and examining it. As she looked closely at each item, she set it to either her left or right.

Once she was done, she gave Grandpa a hug and said, "Thank you so much! I already know how to use these," she said proudly, pointing to the pile on her right, which contained a box of bandages, a scalpel, antibiotic ointment, cleanser, a bottle of water, rolls of gauze, a tourniquet, tongue depressors, cold compresses, tweezers, scissors, vinyl gloves, and cardboard that she had ripped off the box flaps.

"But I'll have to learn how to use those."

She indicated the pile on the left, which included hydrocortisone cream, trauma pads, a CPR valve, an emergency blanket, a sling, a thermometer, and a first aid guide.

She looked down and put her fingers to her chin.

"I'll have to get a few things that are missing though."

Grandpa looked confused.

"There's something missing? I thought this had everything."

"Yes, I'll need matches or a lighter, some washcloths and towels, some small wood planks, and healing herbs like chamomile, nettles, horehound, yarrow, and mug wort. I'll also need some leeches, plantains, onions, garlic, and quartz."

The adults in the room looked at each other questioningly, then noticed the faraway look in Clara's eyes.

"How do you know how to use *those*?" Mama asked, pointing to the pile on Clara's right.

"I've seen you and our doctors use a lot of that stuff," she said with a shrug.

"You've never seen them use these!" Mama argued, pointing at the scalpel and tourniquet. "And what do you need cardboard for?"

"The knife is to cauterize open wounds. That's why I need the matches or lighter – to get it hot enough. The tourniquet is to control heavy bleeding, and the cardboard is to brace broken bones once I put them back in place. Wood would be better though," Clara explained with way more knowledge than she should have had at ten years old.

"It's not a knife. It's called a scalpel, and you're too young to have something that sharp," Amalia said, glaring at her father.

"I'll be careful, Mama," she assured.

"Tell me about the other things you said you need," Grandpa said, kneeling next to Clara.

He was fascinated to see Eir's true nature speaking through his young granddaughter.

"Huh?" Clara looked confused.

"You mentioned some herbs and other things you wanted."

"I did?"

Noticing the moment had passed, Dad said, "Okay, let's clean up this mess and get ready for church!"

"Wait!" Grandpa said loudly. "I have something for Emilia too."

Emilia's eyes twinkled in excitement, waiting for her gift, but she grew disappointed when Grandpa handed her an envelope.

"Thanks," she mumbled as she opened it.

Inside was a piece of very old parchment with strange markings on it.

ᛏᚺᛖ ᛟᚹᚾᛖᚱ ᛟᚠ ᛏᚺᛁᛊ ᛊᚹᛟᚱᛑ ᛁᛊ ᛏᚺᛖ ᚷᚱᛟᛏᚲ ᚷᛟᛑᛑᛖᛊᛊ ᛟᚠ
ᚹᚪᚱ ᚹᚢᚱᛊᛖ ᚺᛖᚱᛖ ᛗᛏ ᚲᚱᛖᛗᛏᛁᛟᚾ ᚹᚪᛊ ᚪᚾᛑᚪᚱᛏᚪ. ᚺᛟᚹᛖᚹᛖᚱᛑ

ᛒᛊ ᛏᚺᛖ ᚷᛟᛑᛊ ᛒᛖᚠᛟᚱᛖ ᛏᚺᛖ ᛗᛒᛁᛊᛏᛗᛁᚲᛖ ᛟᚠ ᚾᚢᛗᚪᚾᛁᛏᛊ,

ᛏᚺᛁᛊ ᚠᛗᚱᚲᚪᚾ ᛊᚹᚪᚱᛏ ᚪᚹᚱᛊ ᛒᛖ ᚹᛁᛖᛏᛑᛖᛑ ᛒᛊ ᛏᚺᛖ
ᚷᛟᛑᛑᛖᛊᛊ ᚪᚾᛑ ᚹᛁᛏ…

She grimaced and said, "What is *this*?"

Grandpa smiled, bent down close to Emilia's ear and whispered, "Focus…Andarta."

Emilia instantly felt that strange tingling again and looked at the parchment, eyes glazing over with a bluish fog. She watched in amazement as the markings turned into words she could easily read, and she read them out loud for everyone to hear, but even Emilia didn't recognize the voice that came out of her mouth.

> "The owner of this sword is the Gaulic goddess of war whose name at Creation was Andarta. Hammered by the gods before the existence of humanity, this weapon shall only be wielded by the goddess and will remain hidden until Andarta reclaims it once again. Upon her touch, the powers bestowed upon it will come to fruition. Hidden by her human bloodline until such time as her earthly guardian takes possession of it and bestows it on the goddess, this sword, if taken into any other's possession, will instantly cause the bearer to perish and spend all of eternity in Hel… and the weapon will be returned to its present guardian."

As soon as she finished reading, the tingling disappeared, and the words returned to their former markings.

Grandpa clapped and shouted, "Yes! I knew it!"

He reached over and give Emilia a huge bear hug.

Everyone else came over to look at the paper and were confused by the markings on it. They looked from the paper to Emilia to Grandpa and back to the paper.

"What happened?" Nana asked with a confused look.

"Andarta is *here* with us!" Grandpa said gleefully. "She's back!"

"How do you know?" Papí whispered.

"Because Emilia was able to read the Old Norse writing on that parchment, and she read it correctly, including the parts I left out and messed up when I told the story about the sword," Grandpa laughed, tears of happiness streaming out of his eyes.

"Where did you get that?" Amalia asked her father-in-law.

"It's been in my family for generations! I don't even *know* how long. My grandmother gave it to me and told me to keep it until I either found Andarta or passed away. If I died before meeting Andarta, I was to leave it to Cauley, and the same rules applied to him. If he died without meeting her, he was to leave it to the girls for safekeeping, and so on," he explained.

Emilia felt a glowing warmth from head to toe, knowing she was already feeling some of the powers she would hopefully have control over someday.

"Thank you," she said to her grandfather in an otherworldly voice, eyes still swirling in a mysterious blue haze. "I've been waiting for far too long."

"The thanks is all mine, Andarta," he replied seriously.

"Do you have my sword?" she inquired.

He shook his head slowly.

"Do you know who does?" she asked, getting impatient.

He shook his head again.

"No, I'm so sorry. I have never seen the sword. I don't know who has been protecting it. The last I ever heard of the sword was when it was left by Kimbel Murphy at the old oak tree on that battlefield."

She sighed and nodded.

"It is safe then," she confirmed. "I'll find it when I need it."

Not knowing how to react to this news, everyone else was quiet as they gathered up the gift wrapping, ribbons, and tags and tidied up the room before changing out of their pajamas.

This was their last day together before the Bennings had to return to Chicago, so they had to make the best of it.

ᛏᚾᚦᛉᚱᚱᚲᚱᚻᛗ

Tyrell closed up his toy shoppe after waiting out the last-minute shoppers and children wanting to play in the store. As he counted the money from the registers and cleaned up fallen plush animals, he noticed one shoved under a shelf haphazardly.

"What're you doing down there?" he grunted as he leaned down to grab the stuffed tail.

The tail immediately whipped away and disappeared even further under the shelf, its owner now emitting a low growl that sounded much deeper and more guttural than an animal should.

"That damn cat," Tyrell muttered, looking for a broom to poke at the animal and get it out from beneath the shelf.

He grabbed one from behind the register and got to his knees by the shelf to search for the animal.

The area was empty, and his eyes began to water as a remnant of smoke wafted out from under the shelf.

The cat was gone.

CHAPTER 9

THE UNDOCUMENTED

Manolo was brimming with excitement, now that the day to leave Mexico and start his new life had finally arrived. Before he left Sinaloa, he was promised transportation to the United States...that magical land of opportunity so many of his family and friends vied to become a part of. In preparation, he carefully filled his old canvas bag with essential items like clothing, a toothbrush and toothpaste, a hairbrush, his travel visa, and some money, which would ensure a quick entry into his new country.

His mind was swirling with the unknown adventures to come, while he waited in line behind the others as they boarded the bus one by one.

When it was his turn to board, the man at the door asked, "Visa?"

Manolo gladly handed over the only documentation he had of his existence on this Earth.

Instead of giving the visa back, the man simply waved Manolo aboard and said, "Find a seat. It's time to go."

Climbing the steep steps of the old bus, Manolo felt like a child climbing up the steps to a slide in a playground. His heart was so light and exuberant.

Until he turned toward the aisle of the bus and noticed the dejected faces of his fellow passengers.

"Why does everyone look so sad?" he asked with a smile. "We're going to *America.* You should all be celebrating!"

Manolo quickly stopped trying to cheer them up when they looked at him glumly. He moved further into the dusty bus, his heart pounding in his chest. He clutched his worn-out bag tightly, eyes darting nervously around at the faces of the other passengers. Everyone wore a look of resignation, their spirits crushed under the weight of their circumstances. Manolo heard the engine start and bus doors squeal as they were shut.

"Sit down," the burly driver barked, his voice echoing through the cramped interior of the bus.

Manolo hurried to find a space to sit, squeezing into a space next to a middle-aged woman with haunted eyes.

"What's wrong? Why does everyone look so sad?" Manolo whispered, his voice trembling with fear.

The woman glanced at him with a weary expression and then turned her head back toward the window before mumbling, "Because we're being trafficked."

Manolo's stomach churned at the thought. She had to be wrong.

"Uh...excuse me," he said loudly. "How long will it take for us to get to the border?"

A man with an AK-47 came walking over to Manolo and said, "We'll get there when we get there. Now, shut up!"

He heard stories of what awaited those who fell into the clutches of these kinds of people. A life of slavery, abuse, and exploitation awaited them, but he never imagined he would become one of the victims.

"Oh," Manolo panicked. "Uh...I need to get off the bus. I need to get back home. My mother is sick."

The man and the bus driver burst out laughing, and the man returned to his seat but kept an eye on Manolo.

He could tell that one was going to be trouble.

As the bus lurched forward, Manolo couldn't shake the feeling of dread that settled over him like a suffocating blanket. He stole a glance out the window, watching as the familiar streets of Sinaloa faded into the distance. As each mile passed, he felt himself being pulled further away from everything he had ever known...and loved.

Hours stretched into eternity as the bus rumbled on through the night, the silence broken only by the occasional whimper of despair from the passengers.

Manolo's mind raced with thoughts of escape, but he knew it was futile. They were outnumbered, outmatched, and at the mercy of their captors.

How did this happen to me? He wondered in despair.

Manolo always thought of himself as very cautious but also a very faithful child of God. He knew God was with him…with all of them…whether they acknowledged that or not. Manolo knew this was not how his story would end.

It couldn't be. God wouldn't let that happen.

When the bus finally came to a stop, they were in a desolate warehouse on the outskirts of a sprawling city. The doors creaked open, and Manolo felt a chill run down his spine as he was herded out onto the cold concrete floor along with the others.

"Welcome to your new home," a gruff voice announced, sending shivers down Manolo's spine.

They were met by a group of menacing figures, their faces obscured by shadows. Manolo could feel their eyes boring into him, stripping him of any semblance of dignity or hope.

Being one of the few men in the group, and having a strong faith that God would protect him from evil, Manolo stood up and demanded, "What do you want from us?"

One of the figures stepped forward, a cruel smile twisting his lips.

"Everything," he said and then laughed.

Manolo knew his life would never be the same again. He was another pawn in their twisted game, trapped in a world where the only way to survive was to lose a piece of himself with each passing day.

Days turned into weeks, and weeks turned into months as Manolo toiled away in the darkness, his spirit slowly eroded by the cruelty of his captors. He watched helplessly as his fellow victims were bought and sold like cattle, their humanity stripped away until they were nothing more than shells of their former selves.

Despite the despair that threatened to consume him, Manolo refused to give up hope. Deep down, he knew that somewhere out there, someone was searching for him. Someone who refused to let him become another statistic in the grim underworld of human trafficking.

After several months, those who remained were taken in a shipping truck to a farm somewhere in California to do agricultural work.

He did his best to give hope to his fellow victims by telling them God was with them as often as he could. He could tell the older ones didn't have his faith, but the young children still had hope in their eyes.

Although he was still a slave and under the control of these despicable people, his new living quarters were better than the last.

They were now located on a fruit farm near the coast of the Pacific Ocean and appreciated the temperate weather and the constant sea breeze. The landscape surrounding them was quite beautiful and made for a peaceful workday…provided the bosses left them alone.

When the sun went down and they were done working for the day, the workers were allowed to leave – supervised, of course - for an hour to get food and any other necessities they needed. Unfortunately, their pay was subpar, so they could not afford much. Many of them lived on beans and refilled used water bottles to satiate their thirst. If they saved up enough, they would occasionally treat themselves to a small Mexican meal from the taco shop down the street.

In his makeshift bed at night, he stared up at the cold, unforgiving ceiling. Manolo whispered a silent prayer for salvation, knowing that even in the darkest of times, there was still a flicker of light waiting to be found.

One such night, he overheard two of the bosses talking about them. He knew one of them was Leandro, the one everyone was afraid of. The other one might be that gringo, Magnus.

Something about Magnus told Manolo that he was inherently good but was putting on a show for the other bosses so they wouldn't kill him. He had seen Magnus appear angry with some of the victims, but his heart didn't seem to be in it, like with the other bosses. When the other bosses yelled at you, you did what they said right away. When Magnus yelled at you, you still did what he said but weren't driven by the same fear of retaliation if you worked a bit more slowly.

The walls were slightly thicker than paper, so Manolo was able to hear their conversation fairly well.

"Yeah, but I hate how we have to resort to this. These people have families and dreams," Magnus lamented.

"Dreams?" Leandro laughed. "Give me a break. They're bodies to fill our pockets. You need to stop thinking of them as people, *amigo*. You'll end up losing sleep for nothing."

"But they *are* people," Magnus argued. "They don't deserve to be exploited!"

Manolo could only imagine the expression on Leandro's face. He'd never heard anybody challenge Leandro before, not even the other bosses. It wouldn't surprise him if Magnus suddenly "disappeared," as sometimes happened when people crossed Leandro.

Suddenly he heard Diego's voice. He liked Diego. Not only did they both come from south of the border, but hey had a lot in common.

"Desperate or not, man, they're the perfect workforce for us. Cheap, disposable, and easily replaceable," Diego said, backing up Leandro's take on things.

Manolo felt an overwhelming weight crush down on him in an instant and wanted to vomit. *How could Diego think of his people like that?*

He heard a loud sigh and then Magnus's voice again.

"I can't shake the feeling that what we're doing is wrong. We're ruining lives and destroying families. It's not right!"

"Look," Leandro said sharply, "we didn't create their circumstances. We're taking advantage of the situation and making our own jobs easier. It's survival of the fittest out here."

"That doesn't make it right," Magnus continued to argue. "These people deserve better than to be treated like property."

"Stop being so sensitive, man," Diego said. "This is the real world. If we don't exploit them, someone else will. At least with us, they have a chance to earn a living of sorts."

Magnus sighed again, "I guess."

Manolo heard shuffling and footsteps as the men walked away from the bunkhouse.

He was surprised to hear Magnus's voice again.

"Andarta, where *are* you? How much worse do things have to get until you come back? These people need you...*now!*"

Magnus was mumbling to himself, but Manolo heard him quite clearly.

Andarta? Manolo thought. *Who is Andarta?*

He had never heard the name before, but the way Magnus was talking about this person gave Manolo more hope than he had in a very long time.

CHAPTER 10

CARING FOR MAMA

When Emilia and Clara returned to school after the winter break, they were excited to tell their friends all about their trip to London.

At school on Monday, they had fun recounting all the different sights and food they experienced. They told everyone but Gabriel, who was nowhere to be found. Nobody seemed to know where he was either. It wasn't like Gabriel to miss school. He *loved* school. Emilia figured he must be sick. The flu was going around after all. When the following Monday arrived and he *still* wasn't at school, she asked their teacher if she knew anything.

Her teacher said sadly, "Yes, Gabriel moved over the break."

"He *moved?*" Emilia seemed astonished and left her mouth hanging open.

How could he move without telling her? She thought they were best friends.

Sorely disappointed, she told Clara what the teacher had said, and Clara began to cry.

"Why wouldn't he tell us?" she sobbed.

"I don't know. It seems really weird, doesn't it?"

Clara nodded her head and kept sobbing.

Just then, Ethan came sauntering up.

STABACK, KENNEDY & AMIDEI

"Hey, did you hear about Gabriel?"

"Yeah," Emilia replied.

"Bummer, huh?" Ethan said with a smile.

Emilia looked at him inquisitively.

"Why are you *smiling*?"

"Because it turns out he wasn't a normal kid after all. He worked like an adult. No wonder he never did anything with us outside of school. I mean, what a weirdo, huh?" Ethan chuckled.

"How does that make him a *weirdo*?" Emilia said defensively, curling her hands into fists at her side.

"It's not normal. *That's* what makes him a weird," Ethan argued.

"Maybe his family is poor and needs the extra help!" Emilia yelled. "Something *you* wouldn't understand, you self-righteous creep!"

Ethan held his hands up in surrender and chuckled again, "Okay, you win. I still think it's weird though."

Emilia sighed and shook her head in disgust at Ethan.

"Come on, Clara."

The girls went to the library for some peace and quiet before the lunch break was over. Ethan really could get on Emilia's nerves sometimes.

ᛏᚢᚠᛒᛟᛟᚲᛟᛏᛗ

"Mama, Gabriel's gone!" Clara cried to Amalia as soon as they walked in the door.

Amalia had been watching the news when the girls arrived.

"What do you mean he's gone?" Amalia asked in alarm.

"He's *gone!* The teacher said he moved during the break, and he didn't even say goodbye to me!" Clara wailed.

Amalia quickly walked over to Clara and put her arms around her to calm her down.

"Shhh…it's OK. I know he was your friend, and it's always sad when a friend leaves, but your paths might cross again someday. It happens, especially now with the internet. People are always finding their old friends online."

84

"Do you really think I'll see him again?" Clara whimpered.

"Perhaps!" Mama said cheerfully. "Maybe not for a long time, but I do think you will at some point."

"I hope so," Clara whispered.

"Me too," Emilia added.

Cauley returned home from work.

"Dad," Clara began, "Gabriel moved, and he didn't say goodbye to me."

She stuck her lower lip out in a sad pout.

"Oh, I'm sorry, pumpkin. That happens sometimes," he said calmly.

"I miss him," she said quietly.

"I know you do," he said sympathetically. "You'll make new friends."

Clara tried to give her dad a smile. She knew he meant well, but he didn't know how difficult it was for her to make friends. Gabriel was the only friend she ever had who was friends with her outside of their friendship with Emilia. He was friends with Emilia too, but he would play with both of them – together *and* separately.

Nobody else did that. He made her feel like she mattered.

ᛏᚾᚠᛒᚱᚱᚲᚱᚺᛗ

The school year passed with both girls missing Gabriel, but as time went on, their memories of him faded into the recesses of their minds. Not having had the opportunity to see him outside of school helped.

Emilia and Ethan spent more time together, much to Clara's chagrin. The more he was around, the more she disliked him.

That summer, when school was starting back up, the girls were beginning middle school as sixth graders. They were going to be attending a new school and would have to change classrooms for each subject. Emilia was extremely excited about this, but Clara was worried she was going to get lost, miss some of her classes, and get in trouble. She hated getting in trouble. It truly traumatized her whenever she thought someone was angry with her.

Luckily, each student was given a map, and Clara carefully highlighted the rooms she was to go to and numbered them in the order of attendance to help guide her.

She and Emilia only had homeroom together because they had the same last name. After that, they were on their own.

Well, Clara was on her own. Emilia always had a gaggle of friends surrounding her everywhere she went. If they happened to pass by each other in the hall, Emilia would wave to her or give her a hug, depending on how close they were, but Clara definitely felt like an outsider.

"Mama, I'm so sad," Clara cried to Amalia one day after school. "I don't have any friends, and Emilia has tons!"

"Oh, I'm sure you have friends, my little fawn!" Amalia said, trying to cheer up her suffering daughter. "You're so sweet and kind! Who wouldn't want to be friends with you?"

"Everybody," Clara mumbled sullenly.

Amalia's heart broke at seeing Clara so despondent. She was definitely aware of the difference in her daughters 'personalities and knew this had always been an issue as they were growing up. Clara had always been so sensitive and a people pleaser that she ended up only hurting herself in the long run – never really getting close to anybody except family.

"Do they have any clubs or teams you might be interested in?" Amalia suggested.

Clara shrugged," I don't know."

"When you go to school tomorrow, talk to someone in the office and see if they can tell you. Maybe something will perk your interest!" Amalia said cheerfully.

She certainly hoped something would interest Clara, for her daughter's sake.

"Okay," Clara said without conviction.

The next day, Clara came running into the kitchen with a piece of paper.

"Mama! The have a bunch of really fun stuff to do at school! *Look!*"

She shoved the paper in front of Amalia's face.

Amalia laughed, "Wonderful! Let's see."

She took the paper and sat down at the kitchen table with Clara to go over the offerings. She noticed Clara had already circled several activities and clubs on the paper, some with stars scribbled next to them.

"Look! They have dance and *cooking*!" Clara pointed to the items on the paper she had written stars next to. "Can I do those, Mama? Please?"

She had her hands folded tightly and a puppy dog look in her eyes.

"Yes, I don't see why not," Amalia replied with a smile. "What do you need to do to get started?"

"I need to have you, or Dad, fill out these forms and get the dance uniform, and there's a fee for the cooking class," Clara jabbered breathlessly.

"I'll take care of the forms and the cooking class fee right now. You can turn them in tomorrow," she replied while getting up to grab a pen and her checkbook. "We can go after school tomorrow to get the dance uniform."

"Yay!" Clara shouted, jumping up and down.

"What's all the excitement about?" Cauley said as he walked in from the garage to see Clara jumping.

"Dad, I'm going to be taking dance classes and learn how to cook!" Clara said gleefully.

"How fun!" Cauley laughed at her exuberance.

It was good to see Clara happy for once.

Over the next month, she attended every dance and cooking class and practiced at home every day after she completed her homework. Everyone in her family noticed that she became more graceful and much less of a klutz. Clara insisted on cooking every Wednesday night, which Amalia deeply appreciated. Her cooking, while basic, improved with each meal until her family looked forward to her Wednesday night meals.

One such night, Clara skipped into the kitchen to begin her dinner preparations, her small frame brimming with energy. She found her mother sitting at the table, her face drawn in pain.

"What's wrong, Mama?" Clara asked, concerned.

Amalia winced as she attempted to stand, clutching her side.

"Oh, Clara," she mumbled and waved is if to indicate it was nothing, "I think I pulled a muscle while gardening. It hurts to move."

Instantly, Clara's playful demeanor shifted to one of determination.

"Don't worry, Mama. I'll take care of you."

Amalia said, "Thank you, my little fawn."

A sharp pain stabbed her in the side again, and she doubled over in pain.

"I think I need to see a doctor."

Clara ran over to the phone and called her father at work. His secretary told her he was in court and would call her back.

Clara panicked and cried, "But…it's an emergency! Mama is hurt!"

"Hold on," the secretary said with a sigh.

After several long minutes, her father picked up the phone.

"Hello? Clara?" he asked anxiously. "What's going on?"

"Mama hurt herself gardening, and she's laying on the kitchen floor. She's in a lot of pain and needs to see the doctor," Clara explained.

"Can she talk?" Cauley asked.

"Yes."

"Please give her the phone," he said with urgency.

Clara handed the phone to her mother and waited while she and her father talked. She heard Amalia tell Cauley the same thing she told her, and then she hung up the phone and handed it back to Clara to put on the charging cradle.

"Your dad's coming home," Amalia gasped. "He's going to take me to the emergency room."

"Can I come?" she asked a bit too excitedly.

Amalia nodded.

"Yay! When will Dad be here?"

"As soon as he can," Amalia struggled to reply before beginning to fade in and out of consciousness.

"Mama?" Clara asked timidly.

No response.

Clara made sure her mother was breathing, then went into her parent's bedroom and grabbed a pillow and blanket. She brought them to the kitchen, placed the pillow under her mother's head very gently, and then covered her with the blanket.

Twenty minutes later, her father arrived still dressed in his judge's robe. Her mother had woken up several minutes before but wasn't talking much. Clara told her dad what happened since they hung up the phone. Cauley picked up Amalia and carried her to his car. Clara opened the car door for him, and he slowly placed her in the front passenger seat and buckled her seatbelt. Clara climbed into the back seat, Cauley took the driver's seat, and they quickly drove to the Ottawa Hospital Emergency Room.

Although they were in the emergency room for almost eight hours, the time flew by for Clara. She was so thrilled to be inside of an actual hospital and watch all the comings and goings of hospital staff. She couldn't wait until she was old enough to become a candy striper! Three and a half more years and she would be old enough to volunteer.

Lab technicians came and went from Amalia's room, some to take her blood, some to take her away for scans, and others to look at the readings they printed out from machines that had been attached to her body with various tubes.

Clara asked as many questions as she could of the staff and explained to each one that she was going to be a nurse when she grew up, eliciting smiles from everyone and brief explanations of what they were doing to her mother.

Once the results came back, Dr. Moul came into the room and told Amalia that she had acute appendicitis and needed to have surgery to remove her appendix. He gave Cauley a prescription for medications that Amalia would need after surgery and then sent the nurse in to schedule her surgery for the following day.

Cauley and Clara wished Amalia a good night and promised to see her bright and early the next morning before her surgery. Emilia was due back from an after-school function within the hour, and they needed to get back home.

ᛏᚾᚠᛒᛉᛉᚲᛉ�

When school got out the next day, Cauley was waiting in front of the school so they could go together to pick Amalia up from the hospital and bring her home.

Once home, he helped Amalia walk to their bedroom, which went painfully slow since she needed a walker and was still groggy from the anesthetic.

Clara and Emilia fussed over their mother, making sure she was perfectly comfortable before starting their homework. Luckily, it was a Friday, and she would end up sleeping most of the day, according to the discharge nurse. Although they had the weekend to work on their homework, Clara was anxious to get it done while her mother was sleeping so she would be able to help her mother all weekend.

She already dreaded going back to school on Monday. What if Mama needed something while she was at school?

For the next week, Clara became her mother's devoted nurse. She fetched ice packs, prepared meals, and gently helped Amalia move around the house. As the days passed, Clara's tender care brought a glimmer of relief to her mother's pain.

"You're such a good little nurse, Clara," Amalia said with gratitude.

That echoed in Clara's mind, igniting a spark within her young heart. She found satisfaction in caring for her mother, a sense of fulfillment she had never known before. She always knew she wanted to be a nurse, but this experience gave that idea solid ground and a much deeper sense of purpose.

ᛏᚨᚹᛒᛟᛟᚲᛟᚾᛖ

One afternoon, while her mother was sleeping, Clara began thinking about Gabriel. Even though she had begun to make some friends of her own, Gabriel's absence still bothered her. He was her first friend outside of her family, and she still felt very frustrated at not knowing where he went and why.

Thank God she still had Emilia. She desperately wished she had the social skills of her sister. She was so strong and not afraid of anything. Clara was afraid of her own shadow and spent most of her free time writing poems or reading books.

The gloomy weather outside, matched her mood. She felt as if the Earth itself could feel her sadness at losing Gabriel and was crying with her. Melancholy took ahold of her, and she began writing down the lyrics to a song that she knew would never actually become a song.

Amalia woke up and saw Clara furiously writing in a chair next to her bed.

"Hey, what've you got there?" Mama asked Clara.

"I'm writing a song for Emilia," she said, holding up the paper to show her mother.

"Oh, how nice," Amalia said sweetly. "I didn't know you knew how to write songs."

Clara considered what her mother said, and replied, "It's like writing a poem but different because you have the big parts and music."

"The big parts?" Mama asked.

"I don't know what they're called, but they're parts that a song has that repeats a certain part. They're usually the best parts of a song."

All of a sudden, it dawned on Amalia what Clara was referring to.

"I think the big parts you're talking about is called a chorus."

"Yes, that's it. The chorus!" Clara smiled and giggled.

She picked up her pen and crossed out "BIG PART" and wrote "CHORUS" next to it.

"And you've written a chorus into your song for Emilia?" she asked, glancing down at the paper Clara handed her.

Clara smiled and nodded.

"But I've only written poems before...never songs, so I'm not sure if I did it right. Can you please read it and help me fix the bad parts? Please?"

"Oof," Amalia said, shaking her head slightly. "I don't know anything about writing songs, but I'll try."

Clara smiled nervously as she watched her mother read her song for Emilia. Pretty soon, her mother began crying quietly.

"What's wrong?" Clara panicked. "Is it that bad?"

Amalia shook her head, wiped the tears from her eyes, and said, "No, little fawn. It's beautiful. It's absolutely amazing. I hope Emilia appreciates this. It's so precious!"

Amalia grabbed Clara up in a bear hug and gently rocked her sensitive daughter.

"You're wonderful, Clara! I wish more people had your heart," Mama said.

Clara was relieved and happy at her mother's reaction to her song.

"When are you going to show Emi?" Mama asked.

Clara shrugged," I don't know. Maybe when she gets home from the mall, but not if she brings her friends with her. I want her to read it, but not if they're going to laugh at me."

"Maybe wait until you girls go to bed tonight," Mama suggested.

"Yes, that would be better," Clara agreed.

Then they heard the front door open and slam shut. Clara and Mama looked at each other and laughed.

"She's home!" they said in unison.

"Hi!" Emilia said as she came barreling into the room, out of breath.

They both greeted her, and then Clara asked, "Did you bring anybody with you?"

"Nah, they all had to get home," Emilia explained.

"Yay!" Clara exclaimed. "I wrote a song for you!"

Emilia's expression changed immediately.

"You wrote a *song*?"

Clara nodded vigorously, grabbed the paper off the table, and took it to Emilia.

"It's only the words..."

"Lyrics," Mama corrected her. "The words to a song are called lyrics."

Clara giggled and said to Emilia, "I wrote the lyrics to a song I wrote for you."

Emilia still looked stunned. Writing songs or even poetry was not something she was ever interested in or thought about.

"Read it out loud!" Clara said, clasping her hands together.

Emilia looked over at her mother, not quite sure how to handle this situation. Amalia smiled and nodded to her.

Emilia took a deep breath, took a seat and read Clara's lyrics.

Lullaby for Emilia

Always happy,
Voice like a chime,
Nobody can resist her.
She's got my back,
And I've got hers.
For she's my
Loving sister.

(BIG PART) CHORUS

I'm so thrilled to do life with you,
In this world we will explore.
I can't wait to see what we'll do,
With our lives beyond that door.

Your acceptance of everyone
Has brought you a lot of friends.
I'll do my best to measure up
And do what the group intends.

(BIG PART) CHORUS

I'm so thrilled to do life with you,
In this world we will explore.
I can't wait to see what we'll do,
With our lives beyond that door.

You're strong and loud and beautiful,
Someone I wish I could be.
But I'm quiet, shy and struggle
To find the magic in me.

(BIG PART) CHORUS

I'm so thrilled to do life with you,
In this world we will explore.

I can't wait to see what we'll do,
With our lives beyond that door.

I know you'll do amazing things.
The world is blessed to have you.
You want the best for all you see,
And work hard to make it true.

~~(BIG PART)~~ CHORUS

I'm so thrilled to do life with you,
In this world we will explore.
I can't wait to see what we'll do,
With our lives beyond that door.

With our lives beyond that door.

With our lives beyond that door.

When Emilia finished reading, she grabbed Clara and hugged her tightly.

"I love you, Clara. You're so sweet, and the song is perfect."

Clara, hugging Emilia back, had the biggest smile on her face. Emilia's approval meant everything to her.

As the days went by, Clara watched with pride as her mother's strength slowly returned. Bedridden at first, Amalia began to move with ease, and her laughter was filling their home once again. She didn't realize until now how much she enjoyed gardening.

During the days she took care of her mother, it was the time of her life when Clara could pinpoint her decision to become a really good nurse. She didn't want to be an average nurse. She wanted to be the best nurse in the world.

An added bonus was getting to spend so much one-on-one time with her mother. During their intimate conversations, she learned things about her mother she never knew before. Her mother told her that she had been a pilot in the Royal Air Force and became a nurse upon her retirement from the Air Force. Clara thought her mother had *always* been a nurse!

CHAPTER 11

BAD NEWS

It was a dreary winter day, and a slushy snow had been falling nonstop. The ground was too slippery to go outside and play after school. When the girls arrived home, they went into the family room where Amalia was watching the news. The girls began their homework on the floor in front of the cozy fireplace, where it was warmest.

An hour later, Amalia went into the kitchen to begin preparing supper so it would be ready and hot when Cauley got home.

Emilia finished her homework first and waited for Clara to finish hers. While she was waiting, her attention was drawn to the news lady announcing the next topic after the commercial.

"Authorities uncover a human trafficking ring in a major city…after these messages," the news lady said in a grave tone.

Human trafficking? What the heck is that? Emilia wondered.

It must have something to do with traffic, she decided. Her parents were always complaining about it. The lady had also said "ring" after it though. Emilia remembered hearing that term in regard to criminal organizations mentioned on the news and from her father talking about work stuff. Maybe it had to do with stealing cars, since they had to do with traffic? She decided she'd have to ask her dad about this, because the answers she was coming up with really didn't make sense.

The same news lady came back on the screen and began talking about it.

"Dozens were rescued from horrific conditions, and several human traffickers were apprehended this morning in Seraphim City.

"In a shocking revelation, authorities have uncovered a large-scale human trafficking ring operating within the heart of Seraphim City. The investigation, which spanned several months, culminated in a series of raids on multiple locations believed to be connected to the illicit operation. According to sources close to the investigation, dozens of victims, including men, women, and children were rescued from deplorable conditions in various clandestine establishments. Many of the victims were found in cramped quarters, deprived of basic necessities and subjected to physical and psychological abuse.

"'We were horrified by what we discovered,' stated Detective Danielle Rodriguez, who led the operation. 'These individuals were living in unimaginable conditions, stripped of their dignity and forced into a life of servitude.'

"Among those rescued were individuals from diverse backgrounds, highlighting the global reach of human trafficking. Some had been lured with false promises of employment and a better life, only to find themselves trapped in a nightmare of exploitation and coercion.

"'This is a stark reminder that human trafficking knows no boundaries,' remarked Terry Bronson, a spokesperson for a local advocacy group. 'It's happening right here in our own communities, hiding in plain sight.'

"In a coordinated effort, several law enforcement agencies apprehended numerous suspects believed to be responsible for orchestrating the trafficking operation. The individuals, whose identities have not been disclosed pending further investigation, are facing a litany of charges, including human trafficking, kidnapping, and conspiracy.

"'We are committed to bringing those responsible to justice and ensuring that victims receive the support and resources they need to rebuild their lives,' stated Chief Darryl White of the city's police department.

"In the wake of the raids, authorities are urging members of the public to remain vigilant and report any suspicious activity that may be linked to human trafficking. They are also urging lawmakers to

enact stronger measures to combat this pervasive crime and protect the most vulnerable members of society. As the investigation continues to unfold, the rescued victims are being provided with medical care, counseling, and assistance in reintegrating into society. Their stories serve as a sobering reminder of the harsh reality faced by millions of individuals around the world who fall victim to the insidious crime of human trafficking.

"Next up, Dakota is going to interview author Eileen Raye on her new release Alaine of Hawthorn*! Stay tuned!"*

"Mmm…something smells delicious!" Cauley called from the front door.

"Hi, honey!" Amalia called back. "Dinner's almost ready!"

"Hi, Dad!" the twins yelled in unison from the family room.

"Hi, girls, how was your day at school?"

"Good!" they yelled and came running over to give him a hug.

"Dinner's ready!" Amalia announced. "Wash your hands and come to the table."

As they ate, Emilia blurted out, "What's human trafficking?"

Amalia dropped her fork, and Cauley's fork stopped halfway to his mouth.

"Where did you hear that?" he asked suspiciously.

"On the news."

"It can be a lot of different things, but it boils down to slavery," he answered succinctly.

"*Slavery?*" Emilia gasped.

"I thought slavery ended with the Emancipation Proclamation?" Clara argued.

"Legal slavery ended then. Human trafficking is *illegal* slavery, and it's still happening," he explained in a very serious tone.

"Slavery was legal?" Emilia was shocked.

"Yes and no. It was legal in some of the states in America for quite some time, but the other states disagreed and made it illegal. That's what caused the Civil War. Have you heard about that in school yet?" Cauley asked.

"Yes, we learned about that before winter break," Clara said.

"That same kind of slavery is still going on today, but not necessarily on southern cotton plantations," he explained.

"Oh," Emilia said. "Then why don't they call it slavery? Why do they call it human trafficking?"

"There's a lot that goes into it, but one of the easy ways to tell the difference is back when it was called slavery, the slaves usually stayed in one place, on the plantations where their owners lived. Nowadays, the slaves are moved from place to place based on where they are needed. Sometimes only for a few weeks or months, and then they're moved again."

This explanation gave the girls some serious food for thought. They were certainly glad they were not in such a situation.

CHAPTER 12

CANÐY STRIPER

As they grew older, Emilia and Clara began leading separate lives, but the ties of sisterhood that bound them together were as strong as ever. Despite their shared DNA, they couldn't have been more different.

Emilia, with her vibrant personality and infectious laughter, was the darling of their middle school. Her charm drew people to her like moths to a flame, and she effortlessly navigated social circles with ease. She was the epitome of popularity with a wide circle of friends and a magnetic presence.

Clara, on the other hand, was the quiet counterpart to her vivacious sister. Shy and introverted, she often found solace in the pages of her books, content to observe the world from the sidelines. While Emilia thrived in the spotlight, Clara preferred the comfort of solitude, her gentle spirit a stark contrast to her sister's exuberance.

Middle school was a challenging landscape for Clara. While Emilia effortlessly made friends wherever she went, Clara struggled to find a place among her peers. She was often overlooked, her timid nature overshadowed by Emilia's larger-than-life presence. The few friends she had were merely extensions of her sister's social circle, their loyalty more to Emilia than to Clara herself.

Emilia was acutely aware of the divide between her and her sister when it came to friendships. She watched with a heavy heart as Clara struggled to find acceptance among her peers, her fragile confidence eroded by the indifference of those around her.

One day, as Emilia sat with her friends during lunch, she overheard them whispering disparaging remarks about Clara.

"I don't know why Emilia insists on bringing her sister everywhere. She's such a drag," one of them muttered.

Emilia's heart saddened at their callousness, but she remained silent, contemplating her next move. When the conversation turned to Clara once again, Emilia knew she couldn't stay silent any longer.

"Hey, if you have a problem with Clara, then you have a problem with me," Emilia declared, and her friends looked taken aback. "Wherever I go, Clara goes. If you don't like it, find another friend."

To her surprise, most of her friends nodded in understanding, their respect for Emilia outweighing any misgivings they had about Clara.

In that moment, Emilia realized the true meaning of friendship — standing by those you love, no matter the cost.

From that day forward, Emilia's friends accepted Clara as part of their circle, embracing her quiet strength and unwavering loyalty. As they navigated the tumultuous waters of middle school together, Emilia and Clara stood side by side, their bond stronger than ever before.

As the school year came to a close, the twins celebrated their fourteenth birthday, and Clara happily announced she was old enough to volunteer at Valley Veteran's Hospital as a candy striper. It was the same hospital where Amalia worked, and she agreed to take Clara to work with her on Monday to get her signed up and introduce her to the volunteer supervisor.

Clara could hardly sleep until Monday came!

ᛏᚪᚠᛒᛟᛟᚱᚳᛟᚢᛗ

Finally, the day she had been waiting for so long was here at last. Clara happily woke up at six o'clock in the morning to join her mother for the forty-minute drive to the hospital. They discussed where and when to meet for lunch before they got out of the car. As they walked through the lobby doors, Clara was once again hit with the heady scent of sanitizer and the thrill of seeing all the medical personnel running here and there. Everyone seemed to be in a hurry. She couldn't wait to be in a hurry alongside them.

"Good morning, Sheila! I would like to introduce you to my daughter, Clara. She turned fourteen and wants to be a candy striper," Amalia said to a woman wearing a pink lab coat.

"Hello, Clara! It's so nice to finally meet you," Sheila said with a welcoming smile and a proffered hand.

Clara gently shook Sheila's hand, and said, "Thank you. It's so nice to finally be here."

Sheila and Amalia laughed, and Clara smiled at them both with a huge grin. She couldn't believe how alive she already felt, and she hadn't even done any volunteering yet!

"Okay, I'll leave you to it," Mama said, giving Clara a quick kiss on the cheek. "I'll see you in the cafeteria at twelve."

"Okay," Clara smiled. "I'll see you then."

"What days can you work?" Sheila asked.

"As many days as I can," Clara laughed. "My mom works here, so I can come every day that she's here…so Monday through Friday."

"Wonderful!" Sheila exclaimed. "Although, we can't have you every day because we can only let you work twenty hours a week during the summer and ten hours a week during the school year."

Clara felt instantly deflated.

"How come?"

"It's the law, dear," Sheila explained.

"But my friend Gabriel worked all the time…after school and on the weekends," Clara argued.

"How old was your friend, Gabriel?" Sheila asked.

"Well, he was ten the last time I saw him."

Sheila looked appalled and said, "He worked that many hours when he was *ten*?"

Clara nodded.

"That doesn't sound right. Are you sure?"

"That's what he told me," Clara said with a shrug.

"Mmm…if it's true, it sound illegal to me," Sheila mumbled. "Let's go to my office so you can fill out the paperwork. Once that's done, then I can show you around and get you started."

"Okay," Clara responded, thoughts of Gabriel quickly flying out of her head at the prospect of being an official candy striper.

Once in Sheila's office, Clara completed her paperwork neatly and quickly. Sheila perused it for errors and found none. She then took Clara to the uniform closet and found a new pink-striped candy striper apron for Clara to put on. Clara was so excited to have her very own uniform.

Next, they began a tour of the hospital so Clara could learn the layout. Sheila introduced Clara to different people in the various offices. They always seemed to light up when she told them that Clara was Amalia Benning's daughter, which made Clara quite proud to be her mother's daughter. She was going to have to remember to tell Emilia about this.

They visited the second floor maternity ward. Clara fell in love with the babies she saw in the Neonatal Intensive Care Unit window.

"Oh, they're so cute!" she crooned. "Can we hold them?"

"No, dear. Those babies are in bad shape. They need a lot of care, so only the nurses who specialize in neonatal intensive care can touch them," Sheila explained.

Clara immediately felt sorry for the babies.

"Oh, how sad," she lamented.

By the time they had completed the tour and Sheila had shown Clara where to find all the things she would need to fetch for people in the hospital, it was noon and time to meet her mother for lunch. Sheila told her to return at twelve-thirty, and then she would be able to start doing some things on her own.

Over lunch, Clara regaled her mother with stories of her adventures with Sheila, the people she had met who knew Amalia, and the things she was going to be doing as a candy striper. She complained about not being able to work every day but said she couldn't because Sheila said it was the law. It was decided that she would come in Monday, Wednesday, and Friday with Amalia.

The rest of the day was spent with calls coming into the volunteer office from patients, nurses, and doctors with requests for the volunteers.

When it was something that Clara could do, Sheila sent her to complete the task. At five o'clock, Amalia went to the volunteer office to collect Clara on her way out, but Clara was off running an errand for a patient who wanted a magazine.

When Clara returned to the office, her mother and Sheila were laughing.

"Hi, Clara!" her mother said with a big smile. "Sheila was telling me what a wonderful job you've been doing."

Clara's smile matched her mother's.

"She did?"

Sheila nodded.

"So, I'll see you back here on Wednesday?" Sheila asked.

"Yes, ma'am!" Clara said happily.

Amalia and Sheila laughed again and bid each other farewell as mother and daughter headed out for the day.

"That was the best day *ever!*" Clara yelled as soon as the lobby doors closed behind them.

Amalia laughed and said, "I'm so glad you liked it."

"I *loved* it," Clara stated.

ᛏᚹᛖᚾᛏᚤᛏᚹᛟ

On Wednesday morning, when they arrived at the hospital, Clara went to the volunteer office by herself, her uniform clean and freshly pressed and hair pulled back in a ponytail. She greeted the receptionist with a warm smile and checked in for duty.

"Good morning, Clara," Sheila said in greeting. "Can you please go to the pediatric unit and pop into each patient's room and see if they need anything?"

"Sure!" Clara said and headed up to the fourth floor.

Why did it have to be the pediatric ward? Out of all the places in the hospital she could have been sent to, she got sent to the one that made her the most uncomfortable. Not wanting to miss out on any experience that could get her closer to becoming a nurse, she would agree to anything…even this, but it still gave her the heebie-jeebies.

Once on the fourth floor, she slowly headed toward the first patient room. There she found a little girl named Aimee with blonde curly hair and big blue eyes. She looked to be about four years old.

"Hi," Clara said softly with a big smile. "I'm Clara. I'm a candy striper. Can I get you anything?"

This seemed like an odd question to ask someone so young, considering she probably didn't know what to ask for, but Sheila hadn't shown her anything to offer patients this little.

Aimee nodded and pointed to the floor.

"Fifi."

Clara looked down and saw a gray plush mouse about twelve inches tall. She bent down and picked it up.

Showing it to Aimee she asked, "Fifi?"

Aimee smiled and reached out for the mouse, which Clara immediately handed to her. She watched with satisfaction as Aimee hugged Fifi to her chest, settled back down on her bed, began sucking her thumb, and closed her eyes to go back to sleep. Clara reached over and pulled the covers back up to Aimee's shoulders and quietly left the room to head into the next patient's room.

As soon as the coast was clear, she let out a sigh of relief. Well, that went better than expected! Clara felt more confident now. Going into the next room, she saw two boys about her age. Both were fast asleep, so she quietly closed their door and went to the next room.

"Hi, are you a candy striper?" the occupant said as soon as she walked through the door.

"Yes, I'm Clara," she responded to a heavyset teenage girl with a shiny head and no eyebrows. "How are you today?"

"I'm great. My name's Emily," the girl responded. "How old are you?"

"Fourteen," Clara replied.

"Hey, I'm fourteen!" Emily said.

Clara was certain she was much older, sixteen at least.

"Cool!" Clara said. "Can I get you anything?"

"Like what?"

"We have a library. I can get you a book or some magazines," Clara offered.

"Do any of them have cute guys in them?" Emily giggled.

Clara blushed and said, "I don't know. Maybe."

"Well, check them out. If they do, bring me some, okay?"

"Okay. I have to check on the other patients and then I'll be back with something."

"Cool beans," Emily said.

Clara left Emily's room and headed into the next room. Before she opened the door, she could hear rock music playing quietly. She knocked and then slowly opened the door. Sitting up in bed, playing on his phone was Chase Dougherty, one of the football players from her school and one of Emilia's friends.

"Chase?" Clara asked in surprise. "What are you doing here?"

He looked up briefly then glanced back at his phone. When it registered who had walked into his room, he put his phone down and gasped.

"Clara? What are you doing here?"

"I work here," she responded with a slight smile.

"You *work* here?" he spluttered.

"Yes, I'm a candy striper," she replied sheepishly.

"That's hot," he grinned.

Clara blushed crimson from her chin up to her hairline.

Ignoring his comment to the best of her ability, she said, "I've come to see if I can get you anything to read."

"To read?" He looked confused and then chuckled. "No thanks, I'm good."

He held up his phone as if to indicate he was already well taken care of in the entertainment department.

"Okay, if you change your mind, call the volunteer office and let them know," she replied and then backed out of the room.

"You can bet on it," Chase replied with a wink before turning back to his phone.

When Clara stepped back out into the hallway, she had to take a moment to get her emotions under control.

A guy called her "hot." That had definitely never happened before. She simply didn't know what to make of it. Was he teasing her? It didn't seem like it. Plus, he was being nice to her without Emilia being around, which was a first for him. Usually, he ignored her. All of a sudden, she was seeing Chase differently.

After checking in with the remaining patients in the pediatric ward and making a list of what each one wanted, she collected the various items and placed them on the serving cart kept in the volunteer office storage closet. Clara headed back to the fourth floor, delivered the requested items and spent a minute or two making pleasant conversation with the patients who had deliveries. Several patients told her how cool she was and how they were glad to have someone their own age to talk to. Clara decided the pediatric ward wasn't so depressing after all.

When nine o'clock arrived, Clara was given the job of escorting family members to their loved ones 'rooms. As she walked with them, Clara offered a sympathetic ear and words of encouragement to those who were anxious or overwhelmed. It was during this time she learned that many people were deathly afraid of hospitals, even when they were simply visiting someone who was in the hospital. This seemed like such a foreign concept to her, since she had been coming to the hospital off and on her whole life with her mother. It felt like a home away from home to her.

At noon each day, Clara and her mother continued to enjoy their lunch breaks together and talk about their workdays. Both of them had come to really look forward to these times together. It was like being in a place that was theirs to share.

After lunch one day, Clara joined a group of volunteers in the hospital's recreation room, where they organized arts and crafts activities for patients of all ages. She helped children create colorful drawings and handmade cards to brighten up their hospital rooms. She also joined the hospital's pet therapy program, where she assisted with caring for therapy animals and accompanied them on visits to patients 'rooms. She loved seeing the joy and comfort these furry companions brought to patients.

As her shifts ended, Clara reflected on her day and the impact she had on the lives of patients and their families. She felt extremely grateful for the opportunity to serve others and looked forward to returning to the hospital to continue her volunteer work in the days ahead.

CHAPTER 13

HIGH SCHOOL

As the humid, hot days of summer began to change into the crispy, fresh air of autumn, Clara's volunteer work at the hospital ended. She missed it terribly, but the girls were starting high school in the autumn, and their parents were worried they would fall behind in their studies if they worked in addition to attending school and being involved in school activities.

"When can I work at the hospital again?" Clara asked her mom.

"Let's see how you do in school, and if things go well then you can be a nurse's aide when you're sixteen," Amalia explained.

"What's a nurse's aide?" Clara's interest was piqued.

"It's someone who helps the nurses with their daily duties. The nurse's aides change bed linens, give patients bed baths, change diapers, clean the bedpans, bring meals, among other things," Amalia explained.

"Oh, that sounds so exciting!" Clara said breathlessly. "I can't wait to be sixteen!"

"Yes, you can," Amalia retorted. "Don't be in such a rush to grow up, Clara. Enjoy the time you have now because you won't get it back."

No, thought Eir, speaking into Clara's mind, *I'll be around until the end of time, but at least I'll be able to help people in the Hall of Souls.*

"I already know what I want to do with my life, Mama," Clara replied calmly. "I'm anxious to get started."

"I know how you feel," Amalia agreed. "I felt the same way once I decided to become a nurse. It was all I could focus on until I actually became one. It was a very satisfying feeling. But it is a shame the nurses don't look like nurses anymore."

Clara looked confused, "What do you mean?"

"They look like everyone else now. There was a time when a nurse was a highly respected position, and everyone knew you were a nurse because of your white cap."

Clara chuckled and said, "I don't care what I look like as long as I get to help people feel better, but why don't they wear their caps anymore?"

Amalia sighed and shrugged, "I don't know, my little fawn. The world has changed so much since I was your age. Professional and public standards have dropped drastically, and it seems like nobody cares about making a good impression anymore."

"Will I get a white cap when I get my nursing license?" Clara asked.

Mama looked at Clara, deeply in thought.

"I don't know if they even do that anymore."

Huh, she thought. When *did* she last see a nurse wearing a white hat who wasn't a child in a costume for Halloween?

"I promise to always be as professional as I'm allowed to be when I become a nurse. I want people to look up to me like they look up to you."

This brought a huge smile to Amalia's face. She had no doubt that Clara would be an amazing nurse. She was such an empathetic person and could quickly tell when something was bothering someone. Clara always went out of her way to do what she could to make someone feel better.

"Hey, what are you guys talking about?" Emilia asked as she entered the living room.

"Nursing," Clara replied lightly.

"Oh," Emilia's interest immediately dissipated.

"How are you doing, Emi?" Clara asked.

"I'm bored!" she grumbled. "I can't wait for school to start. There is *nothing* to do around here!"

"Only one more week!" Mama promised.

"It can't come soon enough," Emilia stated.

"Have you girls thought about any sports or clubs you might want to join at school this year?" Amalia asked.

"I want to join the debate team, the archery team and take Krav Maga," Emilia announced.

"That's an awful lot to take on in your first year of high school," Amalia warned. "Maybe choose one for now. Your homework is going to be a lot more that it has been in the past, and your homework comes first before anything else."

"I can take debate team as a class and get credit for it. I can join the archery team in place of P.E., and I want to take the Krav Maga class at the training center down the street on Saturdays," Emilia stated, showing that she had it all figured out.

Amalia smirked.

"The first two make sense, but why do you want to learn Krav Maga? It's so violent!"

"I need to be able to fight, Mama," Emilia replied quietly.

"Why on *Earth* do you need to be able to fight?!" Amalia asked in alarm. "Who is threatening you?"

"Nobody," Emilia said straight-faced, "but I still need to know how to fight in case I need to defend myself…or someone else."

She glanced at Clara briefly.

"I don't like this, Emilia. Let's discuss it with your dad when he gets home," Mama replied.

Emilia crossed her arms in a pout and said, "Fine."

ᛏᚾᚦᛒᛜᛜᚲᛟᛁᛗ

Cauley arrived home late that evening due to a court case that extended beyond the normal hours.

"Emilia wants to take Krav Maga lessons," Amalia stated unhappily as soon as he walked in the door.

"She needs to," he replied.

Emilia shouted, "Yes! Thanks, Dad!"

"*Why*?" Amalia was astonished.

Cauley stated, "She…needs to. Like Clara needs to learn nursing, Emilia *needs* to learn how to fight…and how to fight dirty. In case you didn't notice, those things did not carry over completely. They still have to learn the modern ways of doing things."

Cauley's firm stance on the issue left no room for discussion, and Amalia's eyes welled up with tears as she left the room.

The following week, Emilia and Clara entered Ottawa High School for registration. The school was gigantic. Emilia loved it immediately, but Clara was apprehensive as usual.

The one thing she *was* happy about was being able to choose a few of her classes. Clara again signed up for cooking and discussed her nursing plans with the school counselor. Mrs. Rayburn became very animated and told her about a program called Health Occupations Students of America. She called it HOSA for short.

"How serious are you about becoming a nurse?" Mrs. Rayburn asked.

"It's all I've ever wanted to be," Clara replied with a laugh.

"Then we need to get you into this program. It will not only show others in the medical profession how dedicated you are to becoming a nurse, but it also opens many doors for you to become involved while you're still in high school. Have you done any training yet?"

"Training?" Clara questioned.

"Yes," Mrs. Rayburn began, "First aid certification, CPR training, nurse shadowing…anything like that?"

"I was a candy striper over the summer," Clara offered.

The counselor smiled.

"That's a good start. Would you be interested in taking any of the courses I mentioned?"

Clara thought about the seven courses she already had on her schedule.

"I'm not sure. Would it be classes I can take toward my high school diploma, or are they additional?"

"The first aid certification and CPR training can be taken as a course, but nurse shadowing would be outside of school hours. Have you considered becoming a CNA?" Mrs. Rayburn inquired.

Clara remembered hearing that term at the hospital but couldn't remember what it stood for.

"What's a CNA?"

"It stands for certified nursing assistant," Mrs. Rayburn began. "It's a good way to get your foot in the door to becoming a nurse, and you get lots of hands on experience working in doctor's offices, hospitals, home health agencies, and other places."

Clara's interest was definitely piqued!

"I would *love* that! What do I have to do?"

She and Mrs. Rayburn spent a good part of the next hour creating a plan for Clara's high school career, which would ultimately lead to her dream job of becoming a registered nurse. Clara was on cloud nine.

ᛏᚾ�ᚱᚱᚲᛟᛁᛗ

When she and the counselor were finished, Clara ran off to find Emilia and tell her the exciting news Mrs. Rayburn shared with her.

There were hundreds of students either milling about or standing in lines in the wide hallway, so it was difficult to find any one particular person.

Then she heard her sister yelling from somewhere behind her. Clara spun around and followed the shouts until she found Emilia and Ethan in a heated argument about some girl.

"No way!" Emilia shouted, her face turning almost as red as her hair.

"It's not up to you, Emilia!" Ethan shouted back. "If I want to ask her out, it's nobody's business but mine and hers!"

"She'll never go out with you anyway," Emilia said more calmly with an evil smirk.

"Why not? I'm good-looking, and she's known me for years!" Ethan blustered.

"Because…she *hates* you," Emilia smirked again, much closer to Ethan's face.

Clara rolled her eyes at what was apparently an incredibly petty argument. She could tell that Emilia was more hurt than angry at Ethan, probably because she wanted Ethan to ask her out, not some other girl.

Clara decided to interrupt and break up this disaster.

"Hi, guys!" she said cheerfully. "Emi, guess what? My counselor told me about this cool program I can get into that will help me get into nursing faster."

Emilia kept glaring at Ethan but replied to Clara, "Nice, let's go."

Emilia threaded her arm through Clara's and pulled her down the hall away from Ethan. The girls heard a loud, metallic bang behind them.

Ethan griped, "Gah! Damn it!"

Clara tried to turn around to see if he needed help, but Emilia kept pulling her along and mumbled, "Forget it. He's stupid."

"What happened?" Clara demanded. "I thought you two were best friends?"

"Not anymore," Emilia declared.

"Why?" Clara asked. "Emi, stop!"

She stopped walking and refused to be pulled along any further until she got to the bottom of this. Noticing that Clara was no longer willing to go along, Emilia stopped and said that Ethan wanted to ask out one of her friends who hated him. She tried to dissuade him, but he became belligerent, and they began arguing. Emilia claimed that Ethan had become too full of himself and wouldn't listen to reason, therefore she was done with him.

"That doesn't seem like a reason to stop being friends with someone," Clara replied softly.

"It would if you knew who he was talking about," Emilia carelessly snapped.

"Who was he talking about?"

Emilia stopped and looked at Clara for a long while, moving her jaw around as she sometimes did when clenching her teeth.

"Nobody," she finally replied. "Drop it."

Emilia began walking toward the exit, since the girls had completed their school tasks for the day. Clara was utterly perplexed but knew better than to keep pushing Emilia when she was in this kind of mood.

CHAPTER 14

CHASE

Hey, what's with your sister?" Chase asked Clara when the bell rang releasing the students from fourth period.

"What do you mean?" she asked innocently.

"Ethan told her that he wanted to ask you out, but she went completely nuts on him!" Chase exclaimed with a chuckle.

Clara looked at him to see if he was serious. He certainly seemed to be.

"Ethan wanted to ask *me* out?" she squeaked.

"Yeah!" Chase nodded with a smirk.

"Since when did he even start to notice I existed?"

Chase laughed and said, "Clara…we *all* notice you exist. Emilia's fun and all, but she's more like one of the guys. *You* on the other hand are more...girlfriend material."

"Me?"

This was complete news to her. She always felt like she lived in Emilia's shadow.

Chase nodded with a look of confirmation.

"How so?" she asked with a baffled look on her face.

Chase thought.

"You're more feminine. You're *much* quieter."

They both giggled in agreement.

Chase blushed and gave a half smile.

"And since you popped your cute little head into my hospital room, I haven't been able to get you out of *my* head, so it only seems logical that Ethan would be attracted to you too. After all, he spends way more time with you two than I do," he said, supplying her with a full dazzling smile this time.

"Oh my…" Clara covered her mouth with her hands. "You think about me?"

"Who wouldn't?" he whispered, looking into her eyes with a soulful look.

Clara felt the breath leave her lungs, and her knees almost buckled. Chase reached out to grab her and keep her from falling.

"Whoa, you okay there?"

"Uh-huh," she breathed, looking deeply into his eyes and feeling that effusive connection.

She had always been a romantic at heart, believing in love at first sight. Although she and Chase had known each other for quite some time, she always felt he was mean and didn't give her a second thought. She thought he put up with her because she was Emilia's sister, like most of Emilia's friends did. But now, when she looked into Chase's turquoise eyes, she could feel her heart melt, and her feelings for him change dramatically.

"So, since Emilia has such an issue with you going out with Ethan, what do you think about going out with me instead?" Chase asked.

Clara giggled, and her cheeks burned. Here was Chase, now the quarterback on the junior varsity team at their high school, one of the most sought-after guys, and he was asking her out...Clara Benning, the invisible twin. She didn't know what to make of this strange new twist but knew she liked it.

"Okay…" she said hesitantly.

"You don't seem too sure there, Clara," he teased.

"I've never been asked out before. I also never thought I *would* be asked out, so it's kind of weird."

"My dad always says there's a first time for everything," Chase said. "So, there you go. This is your first time being asked out, and I hope you'll say more than 'okay, 'because I really like you."

Clara smiled and looked at his handsome face again and responded more positively this time.

"Yes, Chase, I would love to go out with you."

"Sweet!" he yelled and thrust a fist up in the air, and Clara laughed.

"Can I call you tonight?"

Clara nodded, "Yes."

Chase's smile widened.

"Alright, I'll call you after practice…around seven-thirty?" he asked.

"That's perfect," she confirmed.

"Great, I'll talk to you tonight," he smiled.

Clara watched as he walked back to his friends, who were waiting on the other side of the lunchroom. Her heart skipped a few beats while the butterflies fluttered around in her stomach. She felt like she was floating for the rest of the day and couldn't pay attention to anything her teachers or other students said to her. All she could think about was Chase. He was so handsome and charismatic and had a smile that could light up the darkest room.

CHAPTER 15

SHATTERED DREAMS

Clara found herself drawn to Chase, her heart beating faster every time he flashed her that charming grin.

As they spent more time together, Clara fell deeply in love with him. She believed with all her heart they were meant to be together, destined to build a future filled with love and happiness. She imagined walking down the aisle toward Chase, then facing him while saying "I do" in front of all their friends and family.

Finding it impossible to think about anything else, Clara's grades began to slide. The poor besotted girl didn't even care. All she wanted was to spend time with Chase. Whenever he had football practice or anything else she could attend, she was always there to support him. When he saw her, his face lit up, bringing a warmth to her from head to toe.

Clara especially loved the times when they were alone, when she could have him all to herself for a brief moment. When he put his arms around her, she felt things she never thought were possible. Love and protection were things she had only felt from her family until this point in her life. Chase made her feel special in a way that her family never could.

Even though Clara loved Chase, she was still hesitant to do anything beyond hugging and kissing...even though she definitely thought about doing more. She assumed they would wait until they were married to do anything else, but she didn't know if she was willing to wait that long. Chase stirred feelings in Clara that were hard to resist.

"I have something for you," Chase said as he smiled at her from across the table and reached out a hand for hers to hold.

Clara couldn't control the huge smile that lit up her face! Oh, he was so sweet! She reached over and lightly wrapped her fingers around his large, warm hand.

"What is it?" she asked, trying to keep her excitement under control.

With a big grin, Chase pushed a small jewelry box across the table toward her and said, "Open it."

Oh my goodness, Clara thought. *Is this a ring? Is he proposing?*

Her thoughts ran wild as she reached out for the tiny box.

Slowly she opened the lid and saw a gold pin in the shape of a football.

She was so disappointed but couldn't let Chase know how she felt. He was obviously so proud of his gesture. She smiled at him with a questioning look.

"It's my first varsity pin! I know most guys put them on their varsity jackets, but I wanted my girl to wear mine." He winked.

Clara did her best to keep the impending tears at bay, but they came anyway.

He took her hand and said, "That's right, baby. Everyone will know we're exclusive now, so maybe the other guys will stop flirting with you finally."

"Nobody flirts with me," Clara replied, looking confused.

"Oh, please," Chase began. "I'll bet you probably have at least twenty guys hitting on you before you even get to your first class in the morning."

They both laughed, but it definitely made Clara feel better to hear such a compliment.

ᛏᚾᚦᛟᛜᚲᛟᚻᛗ

Things were going so well. Before they knew it, their six-month anniversary was approaching. Clara planned to cook a nice dinner for Chase, but he had other plans in mind.

"Happy six month-iversary!" Chase shouted across the bustling hall at school that morning, waving vigorously at Clara so she could find him in the crowd.

Chase wasn't hard to miss. He was taller than most of the other students and almost always had a smile on his face to greet anyone who crossed his path.

She didn't even attempt to yell back to him over the hubbub but quickly made her way over to her boyfriend. Chase quickly snatched her up and gave her the sweetest kiss they had shared in a while. Clara hadn't noticed a change in how he kissed her until then but quickly disregarded any negativity, since he certainly seemed to be crazy about her right in this moment.

When he finally released her, Clara smiled and said, "Happy six month-iversary, baby!"

"I love you so much," Chase said.

"I love you so much, too," Clara said as she gave his large, calloused hand a squeeze.

"I have something special planned for tonight," he said. "Dress nice."

"What are we doing?" she squealed.

The only time she had been told to dress nice before was on holidays when her relatives were getting together. Clara was so excited.

"It's a surprise."

"Eeee!"

Chase laughed. "You're so cute, baby!"

ᛏᚾᚦ᛭᛭ᚳᛉᛏᛗ

"Clara, get OUT!" Emilia banged on the bathroom door. "I need to use the bathroom!"

She banged again several times for emphasis.

"Hold on!" Clara yelled back.

She was carefully twisting strands of hair around the hot curling iron, getting ready for her big date that night with Chase.

"Mom!" Emilia's voice faded as she went to find their mother.

Good...now she could at least have a few moments of peace and quiet before her mother and sister came back to the bathroom. Clara was so focused on Chase and the surprise he promised her that night that she didn't care if Emilia was upset. After all the years of Clara being invisible because of her sister's popularity, she felt it was finally her turn to be the focus of attention. Emilia would have to deal with it.

Clara faintly heard the doorbell ring and panicked when she heard Chase's voice in the house. She wasn't ready yet, and curling hair was not something that could be rushed. Her watch alarm sounded, reminding her it was time to leave.

"Ugh!" she groaned as she quickly broke up the tight curls for a softer look.

She heard another knock on the door, and her father say, "Clara, Chase is here."

"Okay, tell him I'll be there in two minutes, please," she begged.

She heard her dad chuckle and say, "Men don't like to be kept waiting, Clara."

"I'm hurrying!"

Her dad laughed again and said, "Okay, I'll let him know."

With a last spurt of perfume on her wrists, Clara checked her reflection in the mirror. Satisfied, she grabbed her purse from the bedroom and headed downstairs to greet Chase.

He gave an appreciative whistle when he saw her.

"Wow! Look at you! Baby, you're gorgeous!" Chase enthused.

Clara blushed deeply and said quietly, "Thank you."

He laughed and said to Cauley, "She's so modest. I love that about her."

Cauley smiled proudly and replied, "Yes, she's a very special girl, and we love that about her too. You two be careful tonight and have fun."

"Thanks, we will!" Clara smiled as she took Chase's hand, and they walked out the door.

Amalia and Cauley watched them through the window as they walked to Chase's car. They saw Chase open the passenger door for Clara and make sure she was inside safely before closing her door. They were comforted by his gentlemanly ways toward their daughter.

"I think I'm beginning to like that kid," Cauley commented.

Amalia laughed and gave him a playful slap on his arm.

"The girls have been friends with him for years! You're just now beginning to like him?"

Satisfied that Clara's life finally seemed to be on a happier path, they both laughed and grasped each other's hands as they headed toward the family room for a relaxing night at home.

ᛏᚢᚠᛒᛟᛟᚱᚲᚱᚢᛗ

When they pulled up to the restaurant, Clara was a bit intimidated to see it was the fanciest place in town. She felt very insecure about her rather plain outfit. She was wearing the dress she usually wore to church, with its tiny floral print, a lavender cardigan sweater and white sandals. Everyone else in the restaurant was dressed much fancier than she, and Clara was suddenly embarrassed by her childish outfit.

Moon River Resort & Trattoria was a place she had heard about on social media but had never seen before. Chase gave his car keys to the valet and took Clara's hand as they walked toward the old-fashioned riverboat turned restaurant.

"It's an actual boat?" Clara exclaimed.

"Yes, ma'am," Chase smiled.

"This is so cool!"

"I was hoping you'd like it."

As they were seated at a window-side table, their server appeared in a tuxedo and took their drink order.

Another server came over and placed some artisan bread and butter on the table. Clara was already impressed and hadn't even looked at the menu yet.

"Chase, this place is amazing," she said quietly, giving him an appreciative smile.

He said, "So are you, baby."

Clara blushed as their server came over with their menus and recited the specials of the day. Most of it was dishes Clara had never heard of before, and she didn't want to ask what they were, so she kept quiet.

Although the food took a while to arrive, it was the best thing Clara could remember ever eating. She thanked Chase for bringing her here and suggested they go to a movie afterward. They still had a few hours before her ten o'clock curfew.

"Actually, I had something else in mind," Chase said and held her hand again.

"Like what?" she asked with a smile.

"You'll see."

They strolled along the cobblestone pathway, bordered by lush green ferns and other tropical plants, enjoying the coolness of the evening. Arriving at the door to the Moon River Resort portion of the property, Chase held the door open for Clara.

"What are we doing here?" Clara asked.

"I got us a room." Chase grinned.

Clara began to panic instantly. *A room? What does he think we're going to do in a hotel room?*

She was so stunned and disappointed that she didn't know how to react. Clara watched her boyfriend check in at the front desk and felt like she was in a dream...or a nightmare. This was *not* what she wanted, but she loved Chase so much.

While struggling with her dilemma, Chase came over and happily showed her the card key to their room. He took her hand again and lead her down the hall to the elevator and pressed the button. When the elevator arrived at their floor, she dutifully went along to the hotel room Chase booked for the night. Opening the door gave Clara another jolt when she could see the large bed waiting for them. It seemed ominous.

Chase took her purse off her arm and set it on the table, then pulled Clara close to him. He began kissing her like he always did, but then he began running kisses down the side of her face to her neck.

She simply couldn't say no to Chase and gave in to his desire, telling herself it would just be this one time.

ᛏᚾᚦᛒᛉᛉᚲᛉᚺᛗ

"They're back!" Amalia exclaimed when she heard the front door open and close.

She went to see Clara and hear all about her magical anniversary dinner, but her daughter didn't want to talk. She feigned tiredness and went straight to bed.

Amalia was alarmed. This was not like Clara, who always wanted to talk about good things that happened.

"What on Earth?" Amalia murmured to herself as she walked back to the family room and Cauley.

"Well?" Cauley asked. "Did she have a good time?"

Amalia shrugged, "I don't know. She didn't want to talk."

"What?" Cauley asked, also worried now. "That's not like her. What do you think happened?"

Amalia shrugged again.

"I don't know," she replied, clearly dismayed. "Hopefully, she'll tell me tomorrow after she's gotten a good night's sleep."

"You don't think he hurt her, do you?" Cauley asked angrily.

"No." Amalia shook her head. "She looked fine."

The parents were once again deeply concerned about their youngest child.

Alone in her room after their anniversary date, Clara went over the night's events in her mind. It had started out so beautifully, but almost as soon as they left the hotel room, she noticed a change in Chase. He became distant and aloof. She tried to ignore the sinking feeling in her heart, but deep down she knew that something was wrong.

ᛏᚾ�ᚱᚱᚳᚱᛁᛗ

The next morning, Clara sat on the edge of her bed, her heart heavy with sorrow. Tears streamed down her cheeks, and she sobbed as quietly as possible while reading and re-reading the message Chase sent to her phone late last night when he got home. The message shattered her world.

"Hi Clara," she read through blurry vision, "Sorry to do this over text but, I need some space. I'm not ready for a serious relationship right now, and I want to see other people. I hope you can forgive me. <3"

Emilia walked into the room to grab her backpack and found her sister in misery. Her eyes widened with concern as she took in Clara's distraught expression.

"Clara, what's *wrong?* Why are you crying?" she asked gently, putting an arm around Clara's shoulders.

Her voice trembling with emotion, Clara replied, "He broke up with me, Emilia! I thought we were going to be together forever."

She burst into tears again, leaning on her sister for comfort.

Emilia frowned and said, "Why would he break up with you? I thought everything was fine between you two?"

Clara nodded, her voice choked with emotion.

"I did too. I guess I was wrong. How could I be so stupid?"

"You're not stupid, Clara," Emilia snapped. "Don't ever say that about yourself. You're smart and beautiful, and any guy would be lucky to be your boyfriend. Chase is a freaking idiot!"

"Maybe," Clara sobbed, "but he was *my* idiot!"

Emilia nodded in understanding.

"It hurts so much," Clara keened, curling into a ball and pushing her fists against her mouth to try to keep quiet. "I don't know how I'm going to get through this, Emi. I want to die!"

"You'll get through it, Clara," she soothed.

"When?" she demanded.

Emilia sighed and said soothingly, "I don't know, but it did *just* happen. You need to give it some time. Look at people who are married and get divorced. They get through it...somehow. You and Chase only dated for six months. You'll feel better soon."

Clara suddenly panicked and said frantically, "I can't go back to school!"

"What?" Emilia looked shocked. "You have to go to school. Mom and Dad would kill you if you dropped out, especially for something as stupid as a boy!"

"I can do homeschool," Clara argued, fists rubbing furiously at her red-rimmed eyes.

"You're not going to be homeschooled. You'll never see any of your friends again. And what about me? How do you think I'm going to feel without you there?"

"You have a ton of friends," Clara pointed out. "You'll be fine."

"Not without you, I won't. You're my twin sister. If you're gone, every day will be awful. I don't care about anyone else right now. I only care about you. Now, come on, let's get you ready for school."

"I can't," Clara whimpered.

"I know you're hurting," Emilia said softly, trying not to cry herself. "You're a strong girl, and you'll get through this. I promise. And I'll be there for you whenever and wherever you need me."

"Thank you, Emi," she said, leaning against Emilia's shoulder for comfort.

"Of course," Emilia replied gently.

"I miss Gabriel," Clara sobbed. "He would never do this to me."

Emilia nodded in agreement.

"I know. Gabriel was such a nice guy. I miss him too."

"I wish we knew where he moved to," Clara sniffed. "I would try to find him."

"Hmm..." Emilia said with a smirk. "It sounds to me like you're already moving on."

For the first time that day, Clara braved a small smile at her sister.

"That's it. Keep that smile on your face as much as possible when you're at school. Try to hold off on breaking down until we get home and can be alone. Also, may I remind you, dear sister...*you* are a freaking *goddess*, Clara! The goddess Eir was created to help all of mankind make it to the next plane. Don't you dare let some silly human boy take you down. You've got way more important things to deal with than this!"

Eir...

At hearing her goddess name, Clara felt a surge of confidence and peace flow through her. She immediately stood up and began getting ready for school. There would be no more tears over the lost Chase.

Clara nodded to herself while thinking, *If Eir can live through centuries and still be willing to help people, then I can deal with something as inconsequential as losing a boyfriend I only had for half a year*.

As time slowly passed, she began to heal, her shattered dreams replaced by the promise of a brighter tomorrow. With Emilia by her side, she knew that no matter *what* life threw her way, she would always have someone to lean on and a shoulder to cry on.

Sisters really were handy at times.

CHAPTER 16

GOLD COAST

The California sun beat down mercilessly on the barren strawberry fields as Gabriel trudged along, dragging his weary feet through the dirt. At fifteen years old, the weight of the world rested heavy on his shoulders. For months, he had been trapped in a nightmare of forced labor. When he first started, he hoped that if he worked hard enough, he would be recognized by the bosses and be given a regular job, one that he could afford to live on. Those hopes had long faded to the dark recesses of Gabriel's young mind.

"Hey, Gabe," his friend Angel greeted him.

"Hi, Angel," he mumbled.

"Did you hear they're moving us today?" Angel asked, squinting against the harsh sun.

Gabriel looked at Angel.

"Where?"

Angel shrugged and tossed a clump of dirt across the field. Both boys watched the dirt clump smash apart as it hit the ground.

"Does it really matter anymore?" Angel replied.

"Nothing matters anymore," Gabriel said bitterly, wishing he could hear that he was being sent back to Ottawa…back to Clara and Emilia.

God, how he missed them! Especially Clara.

Angel gave a wry chuckle and said, "I feel ya, bro."

Gabriel had finally found a friend in Angel…another teenager who was brought to California from a farm in Iowa. Angel was also raised from infancy in the United States, so his English and way of life was very similar to Gabriel's. Both having felt like outsiders when they first arrived, they hit it off immediately and developed their own "family," which helped immensely in getting through the day-to-day awful situation in which they found themselves.

ᛏᚾᚠᛒᛟᛟᚲᛟ�

A piercing whistle flew through the air. Both boys turned and looked toward the sound and saw a man waving to them, while standing next to a moving truck.

Angel sighed and said, "Here we go again. You ready, bro?"

"Do I have a choice?" Gabriel replied.

"No, none of us do, at least not when it comes to where they take us, but we're still *familia*, Gabriel, and we'll help each other through it," Angel said.

"That's true. At least we have each other."

He attempted a smile as he wondered if Angel had ever had any close friends like he had in his past life in the Midwest.

"And we'll have each other forever. *Familia*?" Angel asked.

Gabriel reached out his fist, which Angel bumped gently.

"*Familia*. If we can't have our real families, we'll make our own family. Brothers for life, man."

As they climbed into the back of the truck, several other captives were already seated. The suffocating heat was overwhelming, making the inside of the truck even more oppressive than usual. This time, they were each given a brand new, eight-ounce bottle of water to drink on the drive to their next job site.

Finally, after what felt like an eternity, the truck stopped, and the captive laborers were unloaded next to a cherry orchard. The air was heavy with the scent of ripe fruit, but there was no sweetness to be found in their surroundings. They didn't even know where they were, and nothing looked familiar to Gabriel or Angel.

As usual, they were set to work immediately. Since they knew this would happen, both boys saved their water bottles, not knowing if they would get any more during their stay.

ᛏᚾᚠᛒᚱᚱᚲᚱᛁᛗ

Picking cherries was much easier than picking strawberries. They didn't have to bend over as often, and there was a slight ocean breeze that came through the orchard, giving some reprieve from the heat every now and then. They worked alongside the other captives until it was too dark to see anything, and the new boss rang a metal bell telling everyone it was time to come in for the night.

When the boys saw their new living quarters, they groaned in misery. Their living conditions were deplorable. Crammed into dilapidated shacks with leaky roofs and dirt floors, they saw that the only "beds" available were straw mattresses that lined the floor. While they had been working, the harsh California sun beat down on the shacks relentlessly, turning their makeshift homes into ovens.

Despite their dire circumstances, Gabriel found comfort in his free time with Angel and some of the other laborers. There was Jacinta, a skinny teenage girl with a mischievous grin and a knack for making the best of a bad situation. She had been brought to the farm from Chihuahua, Mexico, her dreams of a better life destroyed by the harsh reality of forced labor. She never let it change her outlook on life though. All of her real family members were killed trying to cross the border. She was the only one left and very happy to still be alive. Gabriel and Angel definitely needed her around to lift their spirits.

"What should we do tonight?" she asked with enthusiasm as they opened the doors to their sleeping quarters to let it air out and cool down before going inside for the night.

Gabriel chuckled at her energy. Despite being exhausted from the long day of arduous labor, her vivacity was contagious. He reminded her so much of Emilia from Illinois.

Remembering Emilia immediately brought back warm and loving thoughts of her sweet twin, Clara. They had shared a very special bond. Gabriel felt an ache in his heart at the thought of them and dared to hope that he might see them again one day.

Xerxes, a young man with a fiery spirit and a heart of gold, replied sarcastically, "Hey, how about we go to the opera?"

He had been trafficked from Honduras. He had dreams of becoming a doctor, but his dreams of a brighter future were quickly crushed by the merciless hands of his captors.

The group laughed, knowing the likelihood of any of them every having such an opportunity – or desire – was highly unlikely.

"Opera sucks, man," Angel commented. "I'd rather hear some good old Mexican music."

Jacinta giggled with a gleam in her eyes.

"Look what I found!" she whispered with glee as she held up a small portable music player with the headphones still attached.

Gabriel looked around to make sure none of the bosses had seen her treasure.

"*Aye*, 'Cinta!" he whispered her nickname. "You need to be careful with that. If they catch you, there's going to be trouble."

"They won't do anything to me," she replied glibly. "They like me!"

"*Eres una idiota*, Jacinta," Xerxes retorted with a roll of his eyes. "They don't like any of us."

"They may not like *you*, Xerxes, but they *do* like me!" she insisted.

Angel chuckled, "What makes you so special, *mija*?"

She smiled slyly at him and then began to dance seductively, coming close to each of the guys who could feel their loins stirring at the vision of her gyrations. When she got close to Xerxes, she turned her back to him and rubbed her backside against him until she heard him moan and then shove her away.

"Stop that!" he demanded angrily, embarrassed at his reaction to her.

She giggled and said, "*That's* what makes me so special."

Gabriel was extremely uncomfortable with Jacinta's sensual display. He really hoped in his heart that Clara and Emilia weren't like that, although it really didn't matter anymore since he would probably never see them again.

"I think I'm going to turn in," he yawned. "I'm beat."

As he turned to enter the shack that made up their sleeping quarters, he could hear his friends chattering and Jacinta giggling behind him.

As he settled down, he wondered why he had been thinking about Emilia and Clara so much lately. He hadn't seen them in over five years.

Wow...five *years?* Has it been that long? The more he thought about it, the more his heart began to break. He began weeping silently at the life, friends, and innocence he had lost in Illinois. Gabriel fell asleep feeling very sorry for himself. Even though he and his new friends attempted to create their own family unit, it simply wasn't the same. *Tío* Quinto was still being used at the strawberry farm, so his only real family was lost to him once again.

Luckily, a fellow cherry-picker, Mateo, quickly filled his uncle's role. Mateo was a quiet older man, very gentle, but had a haunted look in his eyes. He had been working on this farm for many years, and his spirit was long since broken by the endless cycle of exploitation. Gabriel and Angel both felt that Mateo was too old to continue working like this but didn't say anything. After all, what could Mateo do? Nobody *retired* from slavery.

The friends who made up his makeshift family now, bound together by shared suffering and the faint glimmer of hope that burned within each and every one of them, were something at least. They worked tirelessly under the scorching sun during the day, but at night they entertained each other with jokes, stories of the past, and shared their pre-slavery dreams.

Despite their resilience, Gabriel knew that escape was a distant dream, a fading flicker of light in the darkness that their lives had become.

ᛏᚾᚠᛒᚱᚱᚲᚱᚺᛗ

The following morning, Gabriel surveyed the endless orchard stretching before him and vowed to never give up his hope of finding Clara again, to keep fighting for something better even while faced with overwhelming odds.

The bond his little family had formed gave all of them the strength to endure, survive, and to never give up their hopes of breaking free from the chains of their oppression and reclaim their stolen freedom.

The hard part was keeping their new family together when they all knew they could be torn apart by their oppressors whenever they decided to send them to separate locations. It was a constant struggle to hold onto people who mattered in one's life when one was a victim of human trafficking.

Hope was the only thing they had left.

CHAPTER 17

SHAPING THE FUTURE

As soon as school ended, the Benning family moved to Forest Hills, a suburb of Seraphim City. The girls were very excited at the prospect of living in Southern California. It seemed like such a glamorous place, and it had an actual beach. Other than having gone to Lake Michigan in Chicago a few times, the girls had never been to a beach and definitely not one on the shores of an ocean. They moved during the last week of July, so there was still plenty of hot days to spend at the beach.

Their first trip to the beach was quite memorable. The scenery during the drive through Malibu Canyon was spectacular. Emilia and Clara had never seen mountains before, and these were ginormous. Cauley and Amalia laughed every time the girls crowed about the scenery, although they enjoyed it as much as the girls. As soon as the car parked along the curb on Pacific Coast Highway, Emilia jumped out and ran toward the ocean. She couldn't wait to swim and cool off.

"*Aaaagh*!" Emilia screamed as she put her feet into the frigid water.

"What's wrong?" Clara yelled.

"It's *freezing*!" Emilia yelled back.

Clara trudged through the thick sand to Emilia's side.

"Oh!" Clara yelped when the wake ran over her feet. "You're right! It *is* freezing! I thought oceans were warm."

"Me too," Emilia replied. "But it's still an ocean, and I love it. Can you believe we're actually living in Southern California, little sister?"

"It really is beautiful, Emi," Clara agreed with a sigh of contentment as she took in the new scenery.

"I want to come here every day," Emilia stated.

Clara smiled at her sister's enthusiasm.

The Bennings stayed at the beach until sunset so they could watch the sun dip below the ocean's horizon. It was stunningly beautiful to see it in person.

On their way home, Emilia said, "I love this place, and I know you've kind of explained already, but...why did we move to California?"

"Your dad got a promotion at work, and they moved him out here because they figured he could do more good here than in a little town like Ottawa," Amalia replied with a smile, facing the girls as she twisted herself around in the front passenger seat.

"You got a promotion?" Emilia asked her dad.

"Yes, it was quite unexpected, but I wasn't going to pass up a chance for us to live in Southern California!" He chuckled.

"That's awesome, Dad!" Clara exclaimed.

"Yeah!" Emilia chimed in.

"Thank you, girls!" Cauley basked in his family's pride.

Judge Cauley Benning was promoted to the federal courthouse downtown. He was to be a federal judge now.

Although he wasn't allowed to talk about the cases he worked on, every now and then he would say things like, "There are some truly bad people in this world. I don't understand it."

"There are also some truly *good* people in this world, Dad," Emilia pointed out.

Cauley looked over at his oldest daughter, surprised at her comment. He thought about how grown up she seemed lately and considered beginning talking to his daughters in a way that was more appropriate for their age. Up until now, he still treated them like little girls...but Emilia at least was definitely no longer a child. Clara, too, for that matter with her becoming a nurse's aide and plodding along with her career goals.

"You're right, Emilia," he eventually replied. "There are good people in this world. Perhaps my job has made me jaded, since it seems like all I ever see are criminals. The worst part is when they get away and end up causing more harm. That really is the worst."

Both Emilia and Clara, being mostly around their mother, shared her viewpoint that there was good in everyone, so hearing comments like that from their father confused them. They chalked it up to being a man's point of view and did what they could to cheer him up on days when he seemed down from whatever happened at work that day.

Being sixteen years old, the girls were well aware that people did bad things from time to time but truly felt that people were genuinely good overall.

CHAPTER 18

FOREST HILLS HOSPITAL

Clara was still determined to become a nurse, but her focus had changed to wanting to help children. She found the whimsy of children enchanting and any injury or illness heartbreaking. She was empathetic to their discomfort and would do everything she could to bring a smile back to their cherub faces.

When she turned sixteen, she was able to become a nurse's aide at Forest Hills Hospital. Clara was beyond excited to work, *really* work, in a hospital environment. It's everything she ever dreamed of for her future.

The extremely nervous Clara went to the hospital by herself to apply for the position. It seemed like forever while she waited for the interviewer to call her name, and she almost left.

Then she remembered what Emilia said when Chase broke up with her, "You are a *goddess*, Clara!"

That's right! she thought. *I am a goddess! I can do this! Thank you, Emi,* she prayed silently.

"Are you Clara Benning?" an older nurse asked.

Clara looked over at the woman, smiled, stood up, and walked over to the woman with her hand out.

"Yes," Clara replied, shaking the woman's hand.

"I'm Agnes McBroom. You can call me Agnes," she replied, while shaking Clara's hand.

"Hi, Agnes. It's very nice to meet you!" Clara said.

"And you as well! So you want to be a nurse's aide?"

"More than anything," Clara replied.

"Do you have any hospital experience?"

"I was a candy striper for the summer when I was fourteen, and my mom is a nurse."

"Is there anything that could cause you to call out for a shift?" Agnes asked seriously.

"Absolutely not. I'm dedicated. Trust me."

Agnes was very impressed with Clara's maturity and apparent love for the field of nursing. She hired Clara on the spot and told her to report on Saturday morning at six-thirty.

"I'll be here. You can count on me," Clara assured Agnes, followed by another firm handshake before she left the interview.

Agnes and her coworker, Lauri, watched Clara exit the room, her back straight and confidence filling her aura.

"She is certainly a breath of fresh air!" Lauri commented after Clara left the room.

"Isn't she?" Agnes smiled. "She reminds me of myself at that age."

"Me too," Lauri agreed. "I don't know what is wrong with the younger generation these days, but it certainly seems to have bypassed *that* young lady."

"Amen to that!" Agnes laughed.

ᛏᚢᚠᛒᚱᚱᚲᚱᚼᛗ

On Saturday morning, Clara's alarm went off at 5:30, giving her plenty of time to shower, have breakfast, and still make it to the hospital by 6:30. Luckily, her father agreed to be up and drive her to the hospital on the weekends she worked.

"Are you excited about your first day?" Cauley asked.

"I am so excited. I hope I can calm down enough to focus on what I'm supposed to do," Clara admitted.

Cauley chuckled, "You'll do fine, Clara."

"Do you really think so?"

"I *know* so."

Her father's confidence in her seemed much stronger than her own, but it did help calm her fears.

When her dad pulled the car up to the hospital entrance, Clara gave him a kiss on the cheek and said, "Thanks, Dad. I'll see you at 12:30."

"Have a good day!"

He smiled and waved as she gathered her things from the floor of the car.

The first thing she did was check in with the nursing supervisor, who went over her assignments for the day. He also introduced Clara's mentor nurse, Desha Duncan, and explained that Desha would be training Clara and was there if she had any questions.

Desha and Clara joined the nursing team on the medical-surgical unit where Desha taught her how to take vital signs, assist patients with bathing and dressing, and change bed linens. Together, they ensured their patients were well cared for and comfortable.

Next, Clara went with Desha on her rounds, visiting each patient's room to assess their condition and address any concerns. Desha showed her how to update patient charts and communicate important information to the nursing staff using the hospital's computer system.

Clara was thrilled to be able to transport patients to and from medical procedures and the radiology department for various body scans. She managed to control her excitement when one of the patients she was transporting for discharge was a moderately famous actor she had seen in a few movies.

"Watch my foot!" he grumbled to her as they went around a corner.

His left foot had a large bandage from the toes up to the middle of his calf, and Clara imagined it must be incredibly sore, so she slowed down and was more cautious.

When they arrived at the car parked at the curb, his friend got out and came around to help him get in the car.

"Would you like some help?" Clara offered.

The man looked her up and down and replied, "No thanks, babe. I got it."

Clara's left eyebrow went up, and she was tempted to say something snarky but didn't. It was her first day, and she certainly didn't want any complaints about her getting to the hospital staff. She quickly changed her expression to one of neutrality and patiently waited until the man was comfortably seated in the car before grabbing the wheelchair handles and heading back to the nursing department.

"It's lunchtime!" Desha announced, standing in front of a large cart loaded with steaming food trays.

"Already?" Clara asked, looking at her watch. "It's only eleven."

"We have a lot of patients to feed. If we wait until a time that we consider lunchtime, some patients won't eat until two," she explained.

Clara hadn't thought of that, and she felt like she should have known. How could she though? She had never done this before.

Stop being so hard on yourself, Clara! she thought. *Pay attention and learn everything you can.*

Feeding patients literally meant "feeding patients" in some cases. Desha showed her how to feed and clean a person who needed to be spoon-fed. It saddened Clara to see people in such a weak condition that they couldn't even hold a utensil to feed themselves. When they were done delivering the lunch trays and feeding those who needed assistance, Desha announced that Clara had done an amazing job.

"Since your shift is over, you get to go home and spend the rest of the day relaxing," Desha said pleasantly. "I'll see you tomorrow bright and early!"

"What?" Clara asked in surprise.

She looked down at her watch and was stunned to see that it read twelve-forty.

"Wow! That went fast!"

Desha laughed and nodded.

"Yes, hospital work is very involved, and the time does pass quickly."

"Thank you, Desha," Clara replied with a grateful smile on her face. "I'll see you tomorrow."

When Clara exited the hospital, she saw her mother sitting in her idling car a few feet beyond the patient drop-off area. She ran over to the car and opened the passenger door, giggling as she got inside.

"I take it things went well?" Amalia asked.

"Mama, that was so amazing. I can't believe you get to do this every day."

Amalia laughed.

"Well, it isn't *all* good. There will be stressful days too, Clara."

"Oh, I know," Clara agreed, "but for my first day, it was the best!"

They spent the drive home with Clara talking nonstop about everything she learned and did that day. Amalia couldn't have gotten a word in edgewise, even if she tried. Her heart was overjoyed with Clara's enthusiasm about nursing.

CHAPTER 19

LIKE FATHER, LIKE DAUGHTER

It was during her career development class at Sweet Water High School that Emilia became interested in possibly becoming a lawyer so she could follow in her father's footsteps. She wanted to do it to prove that good people sometimes do bad things and find ways to keep them from doing bad things again. She wanted to rehabilitate people to prevent them from repeating bad behavior. She just didn't know anything about how to do that, yet.

She had an appointment with Mr. Wilder, her guidance counselor, on Wednesday and planned to talk to him about her courses. Emilia wanted to make sure she took the classes necessary to get into law school.

When she walked into his office, she announced, "Hi, Mr. Wilder. I want to be a lawyer when I grow up. Can you help me plan for that?"

Mr. Wilder smiled at Emilia. She was one of his favorite students. Brilliantly intelligent, she would go far if she applied herself properly.

"Good morning, Emilia. So, you want to be a lawyer? What brought you to this sudden decision?" Mr. Wilder inquired.

"My dad is a federal judge, so I've been hearing about the legal system as long as I can remember," she explained. "I feel called to protect the rights of the accused and ensure that justice isn't only about punishment but also understanding and rehabilitation. I've heard about cases where it seems like some people have a disadvantage when trying to navigate the legal system. I want to provide support to those people. I feel that with my debate club experience and the proper education, I'll be able to create arguments to uncover the truth and persuade juries. I've read about some cases where attorneys have made a difference, helping their clients avoid unjust outcomes and find second chances."

Mr. Wilder's eyebrows raised.

"Wow, it sounds like you've given this a lot of thought."

Emilia nodded emphatically and said, "I have, Mr. Wilder. This is what I want to do. It's what I *need* to do."

"Let me research the requirements for law school, and then we can create a plan to get you there."

"Sweet!" Emilia smiled.

ᛏᚾᚠᛒᚱᚱᚲᚱᚺᛗ

Emilia's debate team coach was so impressed with her knack for making cohesive arguments that he put her in the first debate of the year against Calabaza High School's debate team. For the first time in her life, Emilia was actually nervous. She had never done an official debate before, and she heard tales of most of the high schools around that debated and lost against Calabaza High's team.

What makes their team so unbeatable? Emilia thought irritably.

Knowing confidence was a huge part in winning a debate, Emilia did not let anyone know of her fears. She had never lost any competition in her life and couldn't let her anxiety get in the way of winning this debate.

As they entered the auditorium of Calabaza High School, Mr. Bartles, the Sweet Valley debate coach, handed Emilia a pair of nerdy looking glasses.

"Here, put these on," he instructed.

"What? I don't wear glasses," she replied in confusion.

"I know you don't, but glasses are a good intimidation tactic in debates."

Emilia chuckled and said, "You're kidding."

He shook his head and pushed the glasses closer to her. Emilia sighed and put the glasses on. They had glass for lenses, so it wouldn't affect her vision when reading her notes.

"One more thing," Mr. Bartles said as the team was walking to their seats, "if you win this thing, you'll be the new debate captain."

Emilia's head snapped around as she looked at him incredulously. "I'm only sixteen! I'm a sophomore!"

"That's right," he nodded. "You could be the school's youngest debate captain in history."

Oh, wow. Emilia suddenly found it hard to breathe. As confident as she felt when they got to the school, knowing she had spent weeks meticulously planning strategies for her portion of the debate, she now felt the weight of the world on her shoulders. Apparently, Mr. Bartles was depending on *her* to win this thing. She knew she couldn't let him down. She sat quietly watching other teams have their debates. She learned how the scoring system worked and studied the presenters in an attempt to understand why some won their debates while others didn't. Emilia even made a little wager against herself each time a team debated, trying to determine who would win and why.

When it was her team's turn to debate, Emilia was called up onto the platform. She waited anxiously to see who she would be debating against...not that she knew anybody from Calabaza High School.

To her shock and delight, she saw her old friend from Ottawa walk over to the other platform.

"Ethan!" She smiled and gave a little wave.

"Emilia," he replied tersely.

She was taken aback by his coldness. What happened to Ethan since she saw him last to make him treat her this way? She didn't know, but she did know she couldn't let it get to her. Not now anyway. She could brood about it at home later.

He was still his arrogant self. That part obviously hadn't changed. Knowing Ethan as she did, she understood his team's reputation for playing dirty and winning at any cost. *That* was Ethan, hands down. His silver tongue and ruthless tactics struck fear into the hearts of his opponents. Emilia grew up with him though. She knew him like these other teens never would. She decided she would look at this like any one of their usual arguments and relaxed.

They faced off in a heated battle of words. Emilia stepped up to the podium, her confidence radiating as she laid out her arguments with precision and eloquence. But Ethan would not be outdone, not by Emilia and certainly not in front of all these people. He managed to sway the judges in his favor by his smooth demeanor and underhanded tactics.

The Sweet Valley High Team was stunned at the loss. Even Mr. Bartles seemed shocked at the outcome.

"I was *sure* you had it in the bag," he said to Emilia. "You gave the best debate I've ever witnessed. How the hell did that guy beat us?"

"He's a snake, Mr. Bartles," she said with confidence. "I grew up with him, and he's always been like that. Don't worry though. I know what we're up against now, and I can win the next one."

"I don't know, Emilia," he replied with defeat. "Nobody has beat Calabaza in two years. Not even close."

Two years, huh? Emilia thought. *So that must mean Ethan moved here a year before we did. I wondered why I hadn't seen him around campus. Now I know — he was here slicing down team after team with his razor-sharp tongue, but not for long.*

She quietly laughed an evil laugh and mumbled to herself, "You have no idea what's coming your way, my friend."

Emilia refused to let her team lose hope. They gathered together and made plans to redouble their efforts to win against Calabaza. Mr. Bartles managed to get his hands on some of the Calabaza debate team's performance recordings, and the whole team watched them *ad nauseam*, picking apart their arguments and separating them out into categories of valid and just nasty. Unfortunately, in the end, it seemed like it was the use of nasty arguments that made Calabaza win so much.

Knowing she was planning to become a lawyer, Emilia wondered if courtroom arguments were just as dirty. She made a mental note to talk to her father about it.

The next several debates did not involve Calabaza High, so Emilia's team got some reprieve, allowing them to grow stronger and more resilient, learning from their mistakes and adapting their strategies accordingly. Thanks to Emilia, the team managed to win ten out of the next twelve debates. After the last win, Mr. Bartles told Emilia he wanted to make her debate team captain.

"Thank you, Mr. Bartles, but I'm not going to accept that position until we beat Calabaza."

Mr. Bartles looked shocked. He had never had a student turn down such a high honor.

"Emilia, our current captain is leaving at the end of the semester. We need a new captain in place, and you're the obvious choice."

"I'm sorry, but I'm not going to become captain until I've earned it," Emilia stated firmly.

"You *have* earned it!" exclaimed Scott, a fellow team member.

"Yeah!" Tamara agreed. "You argue circles around the rest of us, Emilia."

Many others in the team murmured their agreement.

"Ethan, the Calabaza team captain, I've known him most of my life. He's been my best friend and my worst enemy at times. We have always been very competitive. If I can't beat him, I won't feel like I've earned that title."

When she saw how dejected everyone looked, she continued, "Don't get me wrong. I *can* beat him! I've done it before, though not with these stakes. Let me prove it to myself, to you, and to Ethan, and then you can call me your captain."

"Emi! Emi! Emi!"

They all began clapping a beat and saying her nickname over and over again. Their support bolstered her courage to beat Ethan, and she felt ebullient. She knew she would win the next debate against him. She could feel it in her bones.

As the semester progressed, Sweet Water High and Calabaza High found themselves tied in the standings. It all came down to the final debate, in which Emilia would finally face off against Ethan in their second battle of wit and willpower as debate team contestants. This time, Emilia was over-prepared. She spent months studying Ethan's tactics and devised plans to counter them.

The final debate of the season took place in one of the local courthouse meeting rooms. It was a special treat for the students, since most of them had law school aspirations.

The topic was "How the benefits of social media outweigh the harm." Emilia, as the would-be captain of Sweet Water High's debate team, took the lead.

"Good afternoon, esteemed judges and fellow debaters. Today, my team and I argue that the benefits of social media outweigh the harm. The world becomes more connected every day. Social media serves as a powerful tool for communication, education, and social activism."

She continued her opening statement by outlining the main points her team would be addressing. She presented statistical evidence and real-life examples to support her arguments, emphasizing the importance of social media in today's world.

"Thank you, Emilia, for that interesting speech. However, the reality is that social media poses significant risks to society. Cyberbullying and privacy concerns cause harm that far outweigh any benefits. We cannot ignore the negative impact that social media has on mental health and interpersonal relationships," Ethan replied in an uncharacteristically caring tone.

Ethan countered Emilia's arguments with his usual confidence and charisma. He acknowledged some benefits of social media but focused more on the negative aspects. He used emotional appeals and anecdotal evidence to sway the judges and undermine Sweet Water High's case.

In the cross-examination portion of the debate, both teams engaged in a back-and-forth exchange, questioning each other's arguments and challenging their evidence. Emilia remained composed and logical, shredding Ethan's claims and exposing inconsistencies in his reasoning. Ethan began using aggressive tactics in an attempt to throw Emilia off balance with rapid-fire questions and personal attacks.

Oh, you want to make this personal, do you? she thought as she could feel the ire building up inside.

Emilia turned toward Mr. Bartles and the rest of her team and mouthed, "Watch this."

When it was Emilia's turn again, she directed her focus solely on him, boring into his eyes when he dared to look at her.

"Ethan, you mentioned that cyberbullying is a major harm of social media. Can you provide concrete evidence to support your claim?"

"Absolutely, Emilia. According to a recent study by the Pew Research Center, over forty percent of teenagers have experienced cyberbullying on social media platforms."

"Thank you for that statistic, Ethan. However, I would argue that social media also provides opportunities for victims of cyberbullying to seek support and connect with others who have had similar experiences. Would you agree?"

"While it's true that social media can be a source of support for some individuals, the overall impact of cyberbullying cannot be ignored. The psychological toll it takes on young people is undeniable, leading to increased rates of anxiety, depression, and even suicide."

She noticed Ethan beginning to show signs of unease. This only bolstered Emilia's courage for the final kill in her closing statement.

"I appreciate your concern for the well-being of young people, Ethan. However, it's important to recognize that social media can also be a force for positive change. From raising awareness about social issues to organizing grassroots movements, social media empowers individuals to make a difference in their communities."

Emilia then turned toward the audience.

"In conclusion, my team and I firmly believe that the benefits of social media far outweigh the harm. While it's true that social media presents challenges, we must not overlook its immense potential to connect people, share knowledge, and inspire change. As we move forward in this debate, I urge you to consider the broader implications of your decision. Thank you."

Emilia was so certain her team won that she could not sit still as they waited for the judges to end their deliberations and announce the winner. Everyone held their breath and crossed their fingers as they watched the judge who would announce the winner walk up to the podium.

"Despite Calabaza High's formidable performance, we ultimately award the victory to Sweet Water High's debate team," he formally announced.

A roar of applause and whistles rose up from those in attendance for Sweet Water High School. Emilia was elated and experienced a moment of surrealism. She had done it. She had officially beaten Ethan in a high school debate. She was ecstatic.

"Would the captain of the Sweet Water High School debate team please come to the stage?" the judge requested.

Emilia looked around at her teammates who were all smiling at her.

Marina shooed her forward and whispered, "Get up there, Captain!"

She stood up and walked gracefully to the stage, doing her best to hide her exuberance and avoid sticking her tongue out at Ethan.

CHAPTER 20

HARVEST SEASON

The scorching sun beat down mercilessly on the fields of the farm as Gabriel and his friends toiled under the watchful eyes of their captors. Prisoners of forced labor, they were trapped in a nightmare from which there seemed to be no escape. Ángela, a young woman with a gift for seeing things others couldn't, kept a vigilant watch for the arrival of the bosses. She had a sixth sense that warned her of impending danger, and she used her powers to protect her fellow victims whenever she could.

"Ángela, do you see anything?" Coleta whispered, nervous.

Ángela closed her eyes, focusing her mind as she reached out with her senses.

"Not yet, but we must be prepared. They could come at any moment."

Coleta nodded, her grip tightening on the hoe she held. She was a tough, no-nonsense woman with a fierce determination to survive, despite the odds stacked against her.

They were constantly on edge, their senses heightened as they awaited the inevitable arrival of their oppressors.

Suddenly, Ángela's eyes snapped open, her senses tingling with warning.

"They're coming," she whispered urgently. "Hide!"

The group scattered, diving for cover among the tall stalks of corn as the bosses 'trucks rolled into view. Ángela watched from her hiding spot, her heart pounding in her chest as she prayed they would go unnoticed. Unfortunately, luck was not on their side that day.

One of the bosses spotted Esmeralda hiding among the rows of corn and dragged her out into the open, his fists raining down on her with brutal force.

"Please, no!" Esmeralda cried, her voice choked with tears.

But the boss showed no mercy, his rage consuming him as he unleashed his fury upon the defenseless girl. Ángela closed her eyes, unable to bear witness to the brutality unfolding before her.

When the bosses finally left, the survivors emerged from their hiding places, their faces pale with shock and horror. Esmerelda was motionless on the ground, her body battered and broken. Gabriel knelt beside her, his hands trembling as he checked for signs of life.

"She's gone," he murmured.

Coleta's eyes filled with tears as she knelt beside him.

"She didn't deserve this."

Ángela clenched her fists, her eyes burning with anger.

"We can't let her death be in vain," she exclaimed. "We have to find a way to escape from this hell."

Before they could make even one plan of escape, the sound of approaching footsteps sent a shiver down their spines. The bosses had returned, their faces twisted with rage as they descended upon the group in a fury.

Manolo stepped forward, his voice trembling but resolute.

"God is with us," he declared defiantly.

However, his faith could not protect him from the wrath of the bosses. In a flash of violence, they descended upon him, their blows raining down until he was still and silent on the ground.

ᛏᚪᚠᛒᛉᛉᚲᛟᚺᛗ

For weeks, the survivors of the farm continued to toil under the harsh sun, their spirits battered but unbroken. They found solace in each other's company, drawing strength from their shared determination to survive.

Kahlo, a talented artist with a keen eye for detail, missed the paints, brushes, and canvases he had back home in San Salvador, but his mentor had taught him well. Silvio had shown Kahlo how the cavemen used to make paint out of the earth's elements, and this was exactly what Kahlo did during his enslavement. Painting was the only thing that brought his mind any distraction or peace during this awful time in his life. He used his skills to create portraits of the bosses, capturing their likeness with uncanny accuracy from several different angles. His paintings served as a form of resistance, a silent protest against the injustice they faced. Kahlo painted them on the floor of the warehouse in which they all slept with quick-drying paint before going to sleep at night, and then he made a mud plaster to smooth over them in the morning when the paint was dry. This way, even if the bosses came into their sleeping quarters, there was nothing to be seen but bare floors.

ᛏᚨᚠᛒᛟᛟᚲᛟᚾᛗ

Xiao, a quiet girl from China who had been used as a personal slave by one of the bosses, stepped forward, her eyes filled with steely resolve.

"We can't let them win," she declared, her voice soft but determined. "We have to keep fighting."

And fight they did, their spirits undaunted by the horrors they faced. As time passed, the survivors of the farm grew bolder in their resistance, their determination to escape growing stronger with each passing day. They knew their chances of survival were slim, but they refused to give up hope. Ángela, Coleta, Gabriel, Kahlo, Manolo, and Xiao joined forces, their spirits united in their quest for freedom. They knew the odds were against them, but they refused to let fear dictate their actions.

"We have to make a run for it," Coleta declared, her eyes blazing with determination. "We can't stay here any longer, or we'll all end up dead."

Under the cover of darkness when the harvest was near completion, they made their escape, slipping past their captors and disappearing into the night. They ran until their lungs burned and their legs threatened to give out, their hearts pounding with the exhilaration of freedom. They found shelter in an abandoned house about two miles away from the farm and its depressing warehouse. Everyone was so exhausted by the time they arrived that they all soon fell asleep on the carpeted floors. It was the softest thing any of them had slept on in years, and it felt like heaven.

ᛏᚾᛒᛦᛦᚲᛦᚻᛘ

Gabriel felt someone shaking him and groggily opened one eye to see Ángela standing over him.

"Huh?" he grumbled.

"They're coming!" she announced fearfully as she looked toward the front door of the house.

BANG! BANG! BANG! The insanely loud, rapid, knocking on the door woke them all up in a panic. Judging by the light coming into the house, it was around dawn. The group sat up and looked at each other with dread.

"What do we do?" Coleta whispered.

Kahlo stood up and silently pointed toward the sliding door at the back of the house. Everyone got up and followed him out to the backyard, hoping for an easy escape.

Kahlo quietly surveyed the backyard for an escape route. All he could see from the patio were tall brick walls all around the yard. Far too tall for any of them to climb over. He stealthily walked along the back of the house, seeking alternative escape routes, while the others waited silently for him to return with good news. He finally found the only escape route on the property, a gate that lead to the front of the house where whomever was banging on the door was waiting for them.

"What do we have here?" a voice called from behind them, coming from the opposite direction where they were looking for Kahlo to return.

They jumped at the sound of the voice, sounds of panic uncontrollably escaping their lips.

"Did you all lose the way back to your sleeping quarters?" Leandro asked sarcastically.

This was the worst possible scenario for the escaped victims. Of all the bosses who could have come looking for them, Leandro was the most feared...and for good reason.

Xiao decided to take a stand and said in a clear voice, "We are human beings, free to do as we please and go where we want to go. You don't own us!"

Leandro turned to her, smiled, and said, "Oh, but I do."

"No, you—" Xiao began to argue but was cut off by the bullet that tore part of her cheek off.

The rest of the group began to tremble uncontrollably with fear, knowing they were surely next.

"Get in the truck," he spat to the rest and waved them forward with his gun as he followed them out the gate to the driveway where a big truck was waiting to take them back to the farm.

Distraught, and still in shock over Xiao's death, the group forlornly went into the back of the truck, which had been backed up to the gate with the door up and ready for them. After the last of them had climbed inside, Leandro threw Xiao's body in onto the floor of the truck, pulled the door down, and locked them inside for the trip back to the farm.

CHAPTER 21

LEAVING HOME

The morning of departure dawned bright and clear, the sunlight filtering through the curtains of the twins 'shared bedroom. Emilia and Clara were already awake, their excitement palpable as they prepared for the journey ahead. Emilia stood before the mirror, her reflection a picture of determination and ambition. She smoothed down her crisp, navy-blue blazer and adjusted her crimson tie, the colors of Hereford Law School serving as a symbol of her future aspirations. Clara sat on the edge of her bed, her hands trembling slightly as she doublechecked her suitcase. She always dreamed of becoming a nurse, of helping others in their time of need, and now that dream was finally within her reach. As they went downstairs, their parents greeted them with smiles that barely concealed the sadness in their eyes.

"You sure you're ready for this?" Amalia asked, her voice soft with emotion.

Emilia nodded, her eyes shining with excitement.

"I've been waiting for this moment my whole life, Mom. I'm ready."

Clara took a deep breath, her heart fluttering with nerves.

"I'll be okay, Mom. UCSC has one of the best nursing programs in the country."

Cauley wrapped his arms around his daughters, his voice thick with emotion.

"We are so proud of you both. Remember, no matter where life takes you, you'll always have a home here."

With tearful goodbyes and promises to keep in touch, Emilia and Clara set off on their respective journeys. Emilia's path led her to the hallowed halls of Hereford Law School, where she would immerse herself in the study of law and prepare to make her mark on the world.

Clara, on the other hand, found herself on the bustling campus of UCSC, surrounded by eager students and the promise of a bright future in nursing.

The days turned into weeks and the weeks into months as Emilia and Clara settled into their new lives thousands of miles apart. They kept in touch through late-night phone calls and hurried text messages, their bond as strong as ever despite the distance between them.

As they navigated the challenges of college life, they found themselves growing and changing in ways they never could have imagined. Emilia discovered a passion for advocacy and social justice, while Clara thrived in the fast-paced environment at the hospital, her compassionate nature earning her the respect of her peers.

ᛏᚾᚠᛒᚩᚷᚷᚲᚩᛁᛖ

In the heart of Cambridge, Massachusetts, nestled among the ivy-covered buildings of Hereford Law School, there lived a stray Norwegian forest cat. He had a thick coat of fur that shimmered like moonlight and amber eyes that glinted with intelligence. He roamed the campus with an air of confidence and mystery.

The students and faculty often caught glimpses of him darting between the shadows, his graceful movements betraying his wild nature. Some whispered that he was a ghostly apparition, a guardian spirit watching over the prestigious halls of Hereford Law.

But to Emilia, a bright and ambitious student with dreams of becoming a lawyer, the cat was simply a source of fascination and intrigue. She had always been drawn to animals, their innocence and purity a welcome respite from the complexities of human interaction. Humans were the worst sort of animals. Cats were some of the most peaceful. How could she not love them?

One day, as Emilia sat on a bench outside the library, buried in her books and lost in thought, she felt a soft brush against her leg. Looking down, she saw the familiar stray staring up at her with curiosity, his amber eyes sparkling in the sunlight.

"Well, hello there, handsome," Emilia murmured, reaching out to gently stroke his fur. "What are you doing here all by yourself?"

The cat purred contentedly, his tail flicking back and forth in silent approval. Emilia noticed the shiny, silver collar around his neck, devoid of any name tag or identification.

"You know what?" she said to the cat as she was running her fingers through the thick fur on top of the cat's head. "I saw another cat that looked like you at a toy stand in London when I was ten years old. I named him Tyrell after the man who ran the shop. He was a very nice man. Since you look like that cat, and I don't know if I'm ever going back to London again, I'm going to call *you* Tyrell too!"

From that day on, Emilia and Tyrell became inseparable companions. She would sneak him bits of leftover food from the cafeteria, and he would curl up in her lap as she studied late into the night. Despite his wild nature, Tyrell seemed to sense that Emilia meant him no harm. He would follow her around campus, and Emilia couldn't shake the feeling of sadness that lingered when she realized Tyrell belonged to no one, that he was a stray with no home to call his own. Determined to give him the loving care he deserved, Emilia made a decision. She would take Tyrell in, give him a home, and show him that he was loved.

One crisp autumn day, Emilia gathered Tyrell in her arms and carried him back to the dorm room she shared with her roommate Kara, where he would become a permanent fixture in her life, a constant source of joy and companionship.

CHAPTER 22

CLARA BENNING, R.N.

Clara found college to be much more fun than high school. Perhaps it was because she was taking courses that were going to help her reach her ultimate goal. Since the other students were also no longer in high school, everyone seemed to treat each other better. The entire environment was adult centered, and that provided much comfort to Clara.

In her first semester, she had to take prerequisite courses that were the foundational knowledge needed for nursing school. She found anatomy, physiology, biology, and psychology very enjoyable and passed all of them with the highest grades.

When it came to chemistry though, she really struggled and had to hire a tutor. Her tutor's name was Jessica, a very spunky and friendly fellow student. They became fast friends since Jessica was also going into the nursing program. Clara did her best but ended up with a B in chemistry. She wasn't happy about it but at least passed the class with a high enough grade to get into the nursing program.

The following semester, both Jessica and Clara entered the school's official nursing program. They both intended to get their registered nursing license, and a bachelor of science degree in nursing, and knew they would be together for a while. They were delighted to find they were going to be roommates during nursing school. When Jessica saw their plain dorm room, she suggested they go shopping to decorate the room to their liking.

Clara was so excited to finally have made a good friend on her own. She knew Emilia would be happy for her and hoped that her sister was having as good of a time in law school.

Nursing school courses turned out to be much more rigorous than either of the girls expected. In their first semester, they took courses in pharmacology, pathophysiology, nursing theory, patient assessment, and medical-surgical nursing. Since they were progressing beyond the basic nursing license, they also practiced lab work and clinical skills.

During their lab training, they did their best not to laugh when they had to give injections to oranges. They did, however, pay very close attention to how to do it properly, because they knew they would be doing it to each other next.

The following semester, they began to participate in clinical rotations at the local hospital. This gave them the hands-on experience needed to provide patient care under the supervision of licensed nurses and clinical instructors.

The girls spent the summer working as nurse's aides at UCSC Medical Center and spent all of their free time studying for the upcoming exam required to become a registered nurse.

When the big test came, they felt confident in their ability to pass it. They both took their time and made sure to answer every question thoroughly. When they were finished, they went out to dinner that night to celebrate and relax from the hard months of studying and working. After six long weeks of waiting, they finally received their test results in the mail. Both of them got scores at the highest levels in all subject areas. They danced around in their dorm room in the excitement. Now they only had one more year to go to get their bachelor's degrees.

ᛏᚨᚠᛒᛟᛟᚷᚲᛟᛁᛗ

The sun cast a warm glow over the courtyard of UCSC's nursing school as graduates, their families, and faculty members gathered to celebrate the culmination of years of hard work and dedication. The rows of white chairs were arranged facing a stage adorned with flowers and banners congratulating the graduates. As the ceremony began, the dean of the school of nursing took to the stage, her voice filled with pride as she welcomed the graduates and their loved ones. She spoke of the challenges they had overcome, the sacrifices they had made, and to the bright future that awaited them as registered nurses.

Clara looked around for her family and saw them sitting to the left of the stage with smiles on their faces. She gave them a little wave to let them know she saw them.

One by one, the graduates were called to the stage to receive their diplomas. They walked across the stage with heads held high, smiles lighting up their faces as they enjoyed the culmination of their years of hard work.

After all the diplomas had been awarded, it was time for the traditional pinning ceremony. Each graduate was presented with a nursing pin, a symbol of their entry into the nursing profession. Family members and faculty members pinned their graduates, offering words of encouragement and support as they embarked on their nursing careers. The ceremony concluded with a heartfelt speech from a distinguished guest speaker, a seasoned nurse who shared words of wisdom and inspiration with the new graduates. She spoke of the importance of compassion, resilience, and lifelong learning in the nursing profession, urging the graduates to embrace the challenges and opportunities ahead. As the sun began to set on the horizon, the graduates stood together, their nursing caps and pins shining in the fading light.

ᛏᚾᚦᛒᚱᚱᚲᚱᛁᛗ

In just a few short weeks after graduating, Clara was offered a job as a registered nurse at St. Mary's Hospital, a renowned medical facility known for its commitment to excellence in patient care. More than ready to take on anything her new job threw her way, she approached her new role with confidence and determination, eager to make a difference in the lives of her patients.

CHAPTER 23

EMILIA'S STRUGGLE

Emilia found college to be much more difficult than high school. She knew becoming a lawyer required a rigorous educational journey and the completion of several steps. Her undergraduate studies would provide her with a bachelor's degree in pre-law. She knew the competition was fierce and that it was important to maintain high grades and participate in extracurricular activities that demonstrate leadership, critical thinking, and communication skills.

When she finished these courses, she prepared for the Law School Admission Test. Emilia studied harder for this than any other test she had taken before, putting all social activity on hold until she had finished the test. She even put social media activity on hold until the test was done since the scores she received on this test were crucial to her being admitted into law school. Until she passed, nothing else mattered.

On the day of the test, Emilia was extremely nervous. She knew she had studied as much as possible but was concerned about how much of that she was going to retain in the moment of truth. She had to pass this test and get accepted into law school. She needed to know as much as possible about the law if she was going to be able to help people.

ᛏᚢᚨᛒᛟᛟᚲᛟᛉᛗ

After three unbearably long weeks, Emilia received her test results in the mail. She received passing scores on everything...barely. She curled up into a ball on her bed and cried all night long. There was no way she was going to get into law school now. Only students with the highest test results were likely to get in.

What was she going to do? She did not want to admit to her low test scores to anyone, but she definitely needed her father's advice. She picked up the phone and called her dad.

"Hi, pumpkin!" Her dad sounded so excited to hear from her.

Emilia swallowed the growing lump in her throat and said quietly, "Hi, Dad."

Immediately alarmed by Emilia's tone, Cauley asked with worry, "Emi, what's wrong?"

At hearing his concern, she burst into tears.

"Emilia, talk to me!" her father begged. "Did something happen to you? Are you hurt?"

"No," she moaned.

"Then what is it?" he asked. "Why are you crying?"

Emilia took a deep breath and sniffled before answering.

"I got my LSATs back."

"And?" Cauley urged. "Oh...you didn't pass?"

"I did, but barely."

"Then what's the problem? You passed, Emi!"

"My professors said that only students with the highest LSAT scores will be allowed into law school." She began crying again. "What am I going to do, Dad? I've never wanted to be anything else!"

She heard her father sigh on the other end of the phone.

"How bad were they?"

"*Really* bad! I got a 153."

"Oh, that's not terrible, Emi. You could still be accepted with that score."

"Not at Hereford, I can't!"

"Why don't you wait and see what they say before you do anything drastic?" Cauley advised his distraught daughter.

"I know I'm not going to get into the Hereford program."

"Then apply to other schools. Hereford isn't the only good law school in the country, you know."

Emilia hadn't even considered any other law schools, so she really didn't know what other colleges provided good law programs. She began to calm down, knowing her father – a federal judge – would know a thing or two about this.

"Where would you suggest?" she asked.

"What about UCSC? You could be near your sister, see your family – hint, hint – and still get a great law school degree."

Emilia brightened up at this idea! Yes, she *could* go to a different school, and what better school than the one Clara was attending?

"Maybe…" she replied, thinking rapidly about what she would need to do to be enrolled at UCSC.

"Plus, since you would live closer, I can introduce you to some of the better lawyers, and you'll most likely be able to get an internship through them. It's something you'll have to do anyway, so why not do it here?"

Boy, was she glad she called her dad! He was throwing out positive options she had never considered.

"Dad, you're the best! Don't say anything to Mom or Clara yet. I want to tell them myself when I get accepted somewhere," Emilia urged.

He chuckled, "I appreciate you saying that, but the hard work will all be on you, so don't thank me yet. I won't say anything."

As soon as they hung up, Emilia grabbed her laptop and a fresh coffee and began researching UCSC's law school requirements.

She spent the next week gathering records and other materials the UCSC School of Law required for admission. She reached out to Mr. Bartles, her high school debate team coach for a letter of reference, which he was happy to provide.

Uploading everything to a file on her laptop, she quickly filled out the online application, submitted the requested documents, and pressed the apply button.

Now, she had to wait to hear back.

ᛏᚾᚠᛒᚱᚱᚲᚱᚺᛗ

The following week, Emilia received an acceptance letter and a large packet of material informing her of the UCSC School of Law's course requirements, student housing options, and a calendar of school events. She was elated!

Emilia picked up Ty and danced around her dorm room with him. She put him down on the bed and picked up her phone to call her father. As she waited for her dad to pick up his phone, she scratched the cat's neck, brushing a finger against his collar, which immediately turned a shimmering blue, purple and gold.

What the heck? she thought and began to look closer at the collar, which was still changing colors and getting brighter the longer she touched it.

When her dad answered the phone, she was distracted from the strange colors of Ty's collar and stood up to pace the room while sharing the excitement of her acceptance letter with her dad.

"Well?" Cauley asked as soon as he answered Emilia's call.

"I got in!" she crowed.

"Wow, that's great, Emi! See? I told you it could be done," he laughed.

"You were right! Oh, I'm so glad I talked to you about this. I was really freaking out."

"That's what us fathers do," he said. "It's so nice to hear you happy again. So, when's the big move?"

"Oh, gosh!" she exclaimed. "I don't know!"

Emilia began laughing.

"Once you figure it out, let me know, and I'll come get you," he promised. "If you have some time before you have to be at UCSC, why don't you come home and stay with us for a while? Your mom would love that!"

"Oh, thank you! Maybe I will. Let me figure out my schedule first."

"Okay. Your room is still the same as it was when you girls left. Should I see if Clara can come and visit when you get back here?"

"Yes, that would be awesome," she agreed wholeheartedly.

"Okay, keep me in the loop, and I'll keep your secret until you're home and can tell everyone yourself," he promised.

"Thanks, Dad," Emilia said as she sat down beside Tyrell on the bed and absentmindedly ran her hand down his tail.

Oh no...*Tyrell!* What was she going to do with him? Her father was highly allergic to cats. There was no way she could bring him home.

"Um...I might not be able to stay with you and mom after all," she said sadly.

"Why not?" he demanded curiously.

"I sort of have a cat now," she explained.

"You have a cat?" he exclaimed. "When did you get a cat?"

"He was a stray that lived around the campus here. We took a liking to each other, so I adopted him," she said.

"Oh..." Cauley started, "That could be a problem. Do you know anybody the cat can stay with while you're here?"

"I can't leave him with someone else, Dad. He's my pet. He depends on me."

She heard her father sigh on the other end of the phone.

"I guess we'll have to figure something else out then."

He sounded so disappointed that Emilia felt terrible, but she couldn't abandon Ty. That would be cruel, and who knew how long he had been fending for himself as a stray?

When they hung up, Emilia took a closer look at Tyrell's collar. It looked like the plain, old silver collar he always had. She touched it to see if she could find anything with color or to determine if it was her imagination.

Again, as soon as she touched it, the glowing, sparkling blue, purple, and gold colors reappeared. She moved it around his neck to see if the colors would allow her to find the opening to the collar. The longer she touched it, the brighter the colors got, but still no opening was found.

Tyrell was there and purred while Emilia toyed with his collar.

"What is this, Ty?" she murmured. "Why does your collar glow when I touch it? And why can't I take it off?"

ᛏᚾᚠᛒᛪᛪᚲᛪᛏᛘ

When her roommate, Kara, returned from work, they discussed plans for the weekend. They both finally had two days off in a row and wanted to do something fun and relaxing. It had been ages since they had that kind of free time!

"We should go to Montauk," Kara suggested.

"Montauk?" Emilia mulled the idea over in her head.

She had never been there but had seen photos and heard stories from others about how beautiful Montauk could be in the spring.

"Okay, let's do it!" she agreed.

"Sweet!" Kara exclaimed.

"What do we do with Ty?" Emilia asked.

"Bring him along!" Kara replied.

"Will the hotel let us bring a cat?"

"If we go to a pet-friendly hotel, then yes," Kara pointed out.

"Oh, cool!" she exclaimed. "Ty, want to go on a girls 'trip with us?"

Ty looked up at her, gave his tail a gentle flick up and down, joined by a sweet meow.

Both girls laughed and began packing for the weekend.

As they packed, Emilia told Kara about her acceptance to UCSC and her concerns about what to do with Tyrell in the meantime.

"I can keep him for you until you get settled, if you'd like," Kara offered.

Emilia was surprised at Kara's offer.

"You would do that for me?"

"Of course! What are friends for if we can't help each other out every now and then," Kara laughed.

"Oh, my goodness, you are the best!" Emilia gushed.

"It's nothing, really."

"It is to my family," Emilia began. "My dad is severely allergic to cats, so I can't bring him home. I'm going to have to wait until I have my own place, and who knows how long that will be."

"I've got all the time in the world to keep Ty for you. Literally...all the time in the world. Let me know when you're ready to have him back."

Emilia walked over to Kara and gave her a gentle hug.

"I don't know how I would do this without you," she murmured with grateful tears in her eyes.

"You *can't* do it without me," Kara winked, and they both laughed.

"I promise I will get my own place as soon as possible, so you're not so tied down. Seraphim City is a huge place. I should be able to find something fairly quickly."

Kara's face brightened up and she replied, "I'm going to be moving there myself next week! Do you want to get a place together?"

Emilia's jaw dropped.

"You're moving to California, too? When did this come about?"

"My dad's firm is out there, and they offered me a paralegal position," she said happily.

"What?" Emilia smiled. "Why didn't you tell me?"

"I was *going* to tell you this weekend, but then the issue of Ty came up, and it felt like the right time," Kara explained.

Oh, this was so crazy.

"Yes, let's do it!" Emilia agreed.

This felt like the right decision. All the pieces started easily falling into place...almost too easily.

CHAPTER 24

BACK HOME

Moving all of their belongings from Massachusetts to California was fairly simple. The girls had no furniture to move, since the furniture they were supplied with at Hereford belonged to the school. They had everything packed and in their cars the night before they were to leave.

The next morning after breakfast, Emilia bought a crate to put Tyrell in on the drive. She heard that cats were a nightmare to drive with if left loose.

"Okay, Ty! Time to go home!" she said cheerfully. "Let's get you in this thing."

Anticipating resistance from Tyrell, she was shocked to see him walk right into the crate and settle himself on the blanket she put inside for him.

"Okay then!" she laughed. "I guess we're all ready to go."

"Meow," said Ty.

She and Kara carried Ty's crate to Emilia's car. He was a heavy cat, and the crate added weight. Placing his crate on the front passenger seat, Emilia threaded the seatbelt through the handle on top of the crate to keep it from sliding around too much.

"Ready?" she asked Kara.

"Ready!" Kara confirmed with a nod.

The young women got into their respective cars and drove away from Hereford for the last time.

ᛏᚾᚠᛒᛉᛉᚲᛟᚻᛗ

"I'm home!" Emilia announced as she walked into her parents ' house.

"Emilia!" her mother cried happily. "What are you doing here?"
Cauley winked at his daughter.

"I'm moving back here to go to UCSC School of Law!" she announced happily.

"Oh heavens, how exciting!" Amalia exclaimed. "Does Clara know?"

"Not yet. I want to surprise her," Emilia stated.

"Oh, she will definitely be surprised!"

"What did you do with the cat?" Dad asked.

"My roommate, Kara, is going to keep him for me until we find a place."

"We?" Amalia looked confused.

"Yes, Kara got a paralegal job at her dad's firm downtown, so she's going to keep Ty for me while we go apartment hunting."

"Ty?" Amalia looked even more confused now. "Who's Ty?"

"Wait…like the cat in London?" Cauley said to his daughter.

"The cat?" Amalia wracked her brain to make sense of this. "You mean the one at Winter Wonderland?"

"Yes. Apparently, our daughter got so attached that when she found a stray wandering around the Hereford campus, she adopted him and called *him* Ty too!"

They all laughed at the irony.

"Let me guess," Amalia said. "This cat *also* has a collar that doesn't come off?"

She laughed, knowing how ridiculous that would actually be.

Emilia paused before answering her mother. Ty's collar *didn't* come off. What were the odds of two cats in two different countries having the same issue?

"Uh…actually his collar doesn't come off either," she replied, her face a mask of bewilderment.

Both of her parents snapped their heads around to Emilia, and exclaimed, *What?!"*

"It's true," Emilia insisted. "Not only that, but I was touching it the other night and it turned all these different colors that kept getting brighter and brighter. As soon as I stopped touching it, it went back to its boring silver color."

"Where did you say you found this cat?" Cauley asked.

"He was just a stray cat that hung around campus," Emilia mumbled.

She noticed her parents 'worried look that passed between them and wondered if she too should be worried.

ᛏᚹᛔᛉᛉᚲᛉᛁᛘ

Looking forward to her first day at UCSC School of Law, Emilia began the three-year journey to earn her juris doctorate degree. She dove headfirst into her studies, learning everything she could about the different types of lawyers and the legal system. She took courses in contract law, torts, criminal law, civil procedure, constitutional law, and legal writing...which she disliked the most. The elective courses offered were not as exciting, especially since Emilia decided to pursue criminal law. She figured that was the best way she would be able to find clients who could benefit from rehabilitation into society, instead of spending months, years, or even the rest of their lives in prison.

Emilia faced a number of challenges as she navigated the intricacies of law school and the legal profession. From late-night study sessions to grueling exams, Emilia's journey was filled with obstacles and hurdles. She got to a point where she was despondent over the overwhelming amount of papers she needed to write and studying she had to do.

"Ty, baby," she said while stroking his fluffy fur one day when she was in a funk, "I think I need to drop out of law school. It's more than I expected, and I can't handle it."

Ty looked up at her, blinked, and growled a deep meow of disapproval.

Great, now my cat's mad at me, she thought as she followed him over to the sliding door to open it for him. She watched as he ran across the small yard and jumped over the back fence.

"Okay, don't mind me," Emilia mumbled and walked back to her desk, leaving the door open for Ty to get back in when he returned.

Kara came skipping into the den and announced, "I got invited to a swanky party in Bel Air. Want to come?"

"*Swanky?* When is it?" Emilia asked.

"Tonight!" Kara said with a huge smile.

Emilia sighed and stared at the mountain of books and paper on her desk.

"I guess. I need a break from all this schoolwork."

"Awesome! Be ready to leave by seven," Kara ordered.

"Okay."

"Where's the kitty?" Kara asked.

Emilia waved toward the sliding door and said, "He needed to go out."

"Okay, I'm going to get ready."

"I'll get ready as soon as I finish this paper," Emilia said.

When the women were ready to leave, Tyrell still hadn't come back.

"What do we do about Ty?" Emilia asked. "He's not back yet, and if we close the door, he won't be able to get back in."

"He's a cat, Emi," Kara said. "He'll be fine outside for a few hours.

"Hmm...okay," Emily said, but she still worried.

CHAPTER 25

THE PARTY

The party was in a luxury home built into the side of a mountain. It was really wild to find that what looked like a single story house was actually a three story house, with the two lower levels built into the mountainside.

The view from the deck out back was spectacular. In one direction, they could see the lights of the San Fernando Valley, and the other direction gave them a very distant view of the Pacific Ocean, shimmering in the light of the setting sun.

"Having fun?" Kara asked, joining Emilia on the deck.

"I don't know about fun, but I definitely needed the break. This house is insane. Who lives here, a rock star?"

The girls laughed, and Kara said, "Come on! I want to introduce you to some people."

Emilia followed Kara up two flights of stairs to the main floor, where most of the party was taking place. The partygoers were quite a diverse group. One thing Emilia found amusing was that the people who dressed the fanciest had regular jobs and the people who dressed casually were the ones with the high-paying, power jobs. Then there were the outsiders, as Emilia thought of them. The way they dressed was rather odd, almost like they were attending a costume party.

"Who are those people?" Emilia whispered to Kara, pointing in the direction of the outsiders.

"Oh, they're family," she explained. "I'll introduce you to them later."

"Okay," Emilia said, glancing back at the group once more before following Kara to the library.

They actually had a library in their house, and it was gorgeous. Emilia could imagine spending days studying in this room and never getting tired of it.

"Wow, this is incredible," Emilia murmured.

Kara giggled and said, "Yeah, this is my favorite room in the whole house."

Emilia looked at her quizzically.

"You've seen the whole house?"

"Oh yeah," Kara nodded vigorously.

"How many times have you been here?" Emilia inquired.

"Tons," Kara said, rolling her eyes. "Oh, hey, there's Magnus! Come on."

Emilia followed Kara over to a young man in a long, dark trench coat with soulful, teal-colored eyes.

"Magnus!" Kara shouted over the din and reached up to give him a warm hug.

"Kara!" he said with a huge smile and hugged her back.

"I want to introduce you to On... I mean, Emilia," Kara said. "Emilia, this is my cousin, Magnus Cathbad."

Emilia looked at Kara with suspicion. It sounded like she was going to call her Andarta. She had never told Kara anything about Andarta or Eir. Maybe she was reading into it too much.

She held out a hand toward Magnus and said, "It's nice to meet you, Magnus."

"It's a blessing to meet you...Emilia, is it?" he asked as he gently shook her hand.

"Yes, Emilia," she confirmed.

Before she could ask any questions, a short, muscular man with long unkempt hair approached their little group. He looked like something straight out of the Viking age, and Emilia wondered how he got into this shindig.

172

"Hi, Brennhir!" Kara smiled and gave the man a hug.

Brennhir grunted and hugged her back, all the while keeping his eyes on Emilia.

"This is her?" Brennhir asked gruffly, indicating Emilia.

"Yes," Kara said cheerfully. "This is my *roommate*, Emilia Benning."

Brennhir grunted and mumbled, "Nice to meet ye. Excuse me, but I have to meet someone."

As she watched him walk away and disappear into the crowd, she wondered, *Ye? Who says ye these days?* Brennhir did seem to have some kind of accent, but she was unable to place it. It sounded like German, but not quite.

"Daddy!" Kara shouted, breaking Emilia's thoughts about Brennhir.

"Hi, small fry," replied a very tall, professional-looking man.

"Daddy, this is my roommate Emilia Benning. She's a student at UCSC School of Law. I brought her to drag her away from her studies. She's always got her nose in a book," Kara laughed. "Emilia, this is my father, Judge Skarsgaard."

The man offered his hand, and Emilia shook it.

"It's nice to meet you," she said politely.

"Likewise," he began. "Any friend of my small fry here is family. She really knows how to pick out the best from the rest."

Emilia blushed at the compliment.

"Have you started your internship yet?" he inquired.

"Oh, no, sir. I won't graduate for another year," she admitted.

"When you're ready, let Kara know, and we'll get you into the firm for a paid internship."

Emilia was speechless. Was it really that easy?

"Emi, let's go see who's downstairs," Kara suggested.

"Uh...okay," Emilia replied faintly and then followed Kara to the next level down.

Some people were in the middle of a billiards game, while others were sitting around on comfortable couches, chitchatting and listening to the music being piped throughout the house.

Emilia noticed a young man, about her age, leaning against a wall, flicking a lighter on and off while staring at the flames. He was covered in tattoos from the top of his smooth head, down his neck, and what she could see of his arms. He definitely did not look like he belonged with this group.

"Hi, Brandt," Kara said.

"Hey," Brandt said with a side glance at Emilia.

"I thought you were supposed to be in Europe," Kara continued.

"I am," Brandt replied calmly.

"Oh!" Kara replied. "I see. This is my roommate Emilia Benning."

All of a sudden, Brandt's whole persona changed. His eyes widened, and he looked at Emilia with something akin to awe.

"Oh my gods, it is so nice to meet you," Brandt said with emphasis.

Emilia shook his proffered hand and replied, "It's a pleasure."

Brandt kept staring, which made her uncomfortable.

Kara, picking up on her roommate's uneasiness, announced that they needed to help in the kitchen and dragged Emilia away from Brandt.

"Did he say he was *in* Europe?" Emilia asked.

"Yeah, he's like that," Kara replied nonchalantly and then began talking to the kitchen staff to see if they could do anything to help them.

"No, Missy Kara," Sylvia, the head chef replied. "We all good here."

"Okay, thank you, Sylvia!" Kara replied and then turned to go back to the party.

"How did she know your name?" Emilia demanded.

"I grew up here. She's known me all this life," Kara replied.

"You grew *up* here?" Emilia was flabbergasted.

She had never thought of Kara as being anymore better or worse off than herself...and she grew up in a mansion?

Kara laughed at Emilia's astonishment.

"Yeah, I missed having a backyard."

"Oh, poor little rich girl," Emilia said with mock sympathy.

They both laughed hysterically. Then it hit her...Kara's previous comment of "this life."

"What did you mean when you said, 'She's known me all *this* life?'" Emilia asked.

"Oh, did I say that?" Kara giggled. "I meant all *my* life."

Emilia didn't reply. Strange things and people seemed to be surrounding them, and it made her uncomfortable.

Sylvia came out of the kitchen and announced that dinner was ready, so everyone gathered in the enormous dining room. Emilia's eyes bulged when she saw a dining room table that could easily seat thirty people. There were also eight other round tables placed strategically around the room.

"Let's find our names so we know where to sit," Kara said as she headed to the table seating chart on an easel inside the entrance to the dining room.

"We're at table seven," Emilia said, pointing to their names on the list.

"Hey, how about that?" Kara said happily. "We'll be in seventh heaven!"

She laughed heartily at her own joke. Emilia smiled, and they walked over to their table. By the time they arrived, the other guests at their table were already seated. She was a bit disappointed that they seemed to be sitting at the table of outsiders.

Is that what they think of me? She thought with a bit of worry. She didn't want Kara's father, who offered her a paid internship, to think of her the same way she viewed these people.

Once they were seated, Kara began introducing Emilia to the other people at the table.

"Let's see..." Kara began, "You've already met Magnus, Brandt, and Brennhir. This is Torreya and her daughter, Ko'qleye."

Emilia nodded and said, "Nice to meet you."

Both of the women nodded in return with gentle smiles on their faces.

"And finally, this is Brenda, Thorin, and Leilani," she said. "Everyone, this is my roommate, Emilia Benning."

Emilia heard a few gasps and wondered if something was wrong with her appearance.

"Why are they acting like that?" she asked Kara.

"Like what?" Kara asked, confused.

"I don't know," Emilia replied. "They all seem shocked to meet me."

"Oh, they're just dramatic," Kara replied, brushing off Emilia's concerns. "They're all very nice though and would quite literally kill to protect those they love."

"Do they think I'm going to hurt you or something?"

"No, they haven't been introduced to my friends before, so it's a little unusual for them. Try not to worry about it and enjoy yourself. After all, that's why we came here, isn't it…to let go of your stress for a little while?"

"I guess," Emilia agreed.

Over the seven courses of the meal, everyone seemed to relax and began talking to Emilia in a way that seemed so familiar. It was strange, but it seemed like she *really* knew these people. These outsiders, as she thought of them. She was making light talk with Brennhir when Magnus interrupted their conversation.

"How's Ty?" Magnus asked with a smile.

Emilia whipped her head around toward Magnus so fast that she felt a sharp pain in her neck.

"What did you say?"

"I said, how's—" Magnus was cut off by the host of the party tapping a spoon against his wine glass for attention.

Emilia turned back around and noticed that Brennhir was nowhere to be found.

Once the room had quieted down, Kara's father greeted his guests warmly and thanked everyone for coming to such a monumental event.

"Monumental?" Emilia asked Kara.

She didn't see anything monumental about this party at all. It seemed like a regular party. Kara shrugged and feigned ignorance.

"My daughter, Kara, has finally found a friend worthy of introducing to us!"

The crowd chittered and clapped politely. Emilia wanted to crawl under the table. As much as she enjoyed being the center of attention, it was only within her own family and friend groups...not when she was surrounded by a room full of strangers.

"Emilia," he continued, addressing her directly, "as I told you when I met you, a friend of Kara's is family. So, take a good look around, my child." He spread his arms wide to indicate everyone in the room. "This is *your* family too. Next time we do this, you need to bring Clara along. There are many here who are anxious to meet your twin." He smiled.

"Did you tell your dad about Clara?" Emilia asked Kara.

"Huh?" Kara looked confused.

Emilia said, "He said, 'Next time we do this, you need to bring Clara along.' I haven't mentioned her once since we've been here."

"Oh yeah!" Kara replied, waving in a gesture of forgetfulness. "I've told him about you and your family. Being a lawyer, he's always *en guard* when it comes to the people I spend my time with."

That made enough sense, so Emilia let it go.

ᛏᚾᛒᚱᚱᚲᚱᚼᛗ

When they returned to their condo, Ty was nowhere to be found.

"What do we do?" Emilia asked Kara in a panic. "Maybe he got hit by a car! Maybe someone stole him! Maybe…"

Kara cut her off and said, "Ty is fine, Emilia."

"How do you know?" she asked fearfully.

"Because I know. He's a Norwegian Forest Cat. They are very quick, strong and smart. He'll come back when he's ready. Don't worry. He was a stray for who knows how long, and he managed to survive."

Emilia let out a sigh. "You're right. He'll be fine."

She nodded as if confirming Ty's safety.

CHAPTER 26

TYRELL

A week later, Ty still hadn't returned to the apartment. Kara and Emilia spent hours scouring the streets, parks, and anywhere they thought he might have gone. They created lost-cat signs and put them up everywhere they were allowed. Not one phone call came in, and no new cats had been picked up by animal control, they were told every day they called.

Emilia felt her world falling apart. Ty was everything to her, and she had been so careless to let him leave. She was certain he must have come back while they were at the party, found the door closed, and eventually left.

ᛏᚾᚠᛒᚱᚱᚲᚱᚼᛗ

The soft glow of twilight spilled across the vast expanse of the celestial realm. The gods, seated in a circle, awaited the arrival of their trusted emissary. The air shimmered as a large, gray, Norwegian Forest cat appeared, tail high, eyes glinting with an ancient wisdom that belied his feline form.

"Tyr," boomed Mimir, the god of wisdom, his voice resonating like thunder through the ethereal plane. "You know why you have been summoned."

The cat's form rippled, stretching and twisting until it stood upright. In moments, a mighty dragon with scales that glimmered like deep tanzanite emerged, wings folded neatly against his back. His golden eyes met Mimir with quiet determination.

"I am ready," Tyr rumbled, his voice deep and resonant.

A serene figure, Frigg, leaned forward, her silver hair cascading like waterfalls.

"Andarta's sword must not fall into mortal hands. It is the keystone to her dominion and the balance of realms. Forces conspire against us, seeking to exploit its power."

"I suspected as much," Tyr said, his tone even. "But why now? For centuries, I have guarded the sword without interference."

"A breach," growled Brandt, the god of valor. His fiery mane flickered with intensity. "Mammon has unlocked forbidden knowledge. He approaches the hidden sanctuary even as we speak."

"Then I must act swiftly," Tyr replied.

His wings unfurled slightly, casting shadows that danced across the radiant floor. Mimir's wise gaze lingered on Tyr.

"This is no ordinary mission," Mimir advised. "You will not merely stop him. You must also ensure he does not return with others. The sword's location must remain secret."

"How far am I permitted to go?" Tyr asked.

Frigg's voice softened, "You must not take a mortal life unless absolutely necessary. Redirect, deceive, or incapacitate, but do not sully Andarta's legacy with needless bloodshed."

Brandt snorted, "Soft words. The realm of mortals is not so kind, Frigg."

Tyr interrupted before they could quarrel, "I understand the terms. I will protect the sword's sanctity."

As he turned to leave, a new voice filled the space. It was Nótt, goddess of shadows, her figure materializing from a swirling mist.

"Beware, Guardian. Mammon is not alone. He carries a shard of the Void—a fragment that bends reality itself."

Tyr's golden eyes narrowed.

"A shard of the Void?"

"Yes," Nótt confirmed, her tone as cold as frost. "It will weaken you if you linger near it too long. Act swiftly and decisively."

"Then I must rely on more than strength," Tyr said. He shifted back into his feline form, his fluffy gray fur shimmering under the celestial light. "Trust that I will succeed."

With a final nod from Mimir, Tyr leapt from the celestial plane, descending through layers of reality. His dragon form emerged mid-flight, cutting through the fabric of the mortal world as he raced toward the hidden sanctuary.

ᛏᚾᚠᛒᛣᛣᚲᛟᚼᛗ

That evening while having dinner with her family, Emilia complained to her father, "Dad, I don't think I'm going to be able to finish my program. It's so hard. I don't know if it's worth it anymore."

Cauley looked Emilia in the eyes, and said, "Emilia Benning, you *will* finish law school. This is what you've always talked about, and you will do it. Something worth having does not come easy. You're not in high school anymore. You're in college to prepare for the adult world in a very demanding profession. You have never backed down from a challenge before. Don't let this be the one that takes you down. You're smart, Emi. You're charismatic...everything people want in a lawyer."

Clara leaned over and whispered to Emilia, "He's right you know. And think about it...would *Andarta* give up?"

Emilia sighed. They were right. She had to finish this if she was going to be able to help people the way she wanted. She wasn't happy about it, but knowing her family was right, and knowing that *she* was the one who made such a goal in the first place, she agreed and said she would see it through.

"That's my girl," Cauley said as he patted her on the shoulder. "I'm here if you need help with your studies. I did go through the same program, after all."

"I know," Emilia agreed. "Thanks, Dad."

"Anytime, kiddo," he winked.

ᛏᚾᚠᛣᛣᚲᛟᚼᛗ

When Emilia returned to her condo that evening, Ty was sitting on the doorstep, flicking his tail back and forth, awaiting her arrival.

"Ty!" she shouted and ran toward her cat. "Where have you been? I've been so worried about you!"

"Meow," Ty replied.

Then he let out a big sneeze, and Emilia could swear she saw a little bit of smoke come out of his nose. She looked more closely. Sure enough, there was a fine trail of smoke still wafting out of Ty's nose.

"What the heck?" she said. "Are you okay, Ty?"

"Meow," Ty said again then stood up and began rubbing himself sideways against her legs to show her some love.

"I'm glad you're back too," she said as she petted Ty. "Now, mister, I've got some studying to do. Care to join me?" she asked as she opened the door.

Ty meowed once more and followed his mistress into the condo.

"Kara!" she yelled, hoping her roommate was home.

"Yes?" Kara came out of her bedroom and asked how dinner with the family went.

"Great! And look who's back!" Emilia exclaimed pointing to Ty who had curled himself onto the couch.

"Hey, Ty," Kara said calmly.

"Meow," replied Ty.

"You don't seem surprised." Emilia felt a bit disappointed.

"I'm not," Kara responded carelessly as she was flipping through a magazine. "I told you he was fine. I asked him if he wanted to come inside when he got back, but he said he wanted to wait outside for you."

"Oh, he talks now, does he?" Emilia teased.

Kara laughed it off.

ᛏᚾᚠᛒᛦᛦᚲᛦᛉᛗ

The next week was full of preparations for the upcoming semester, and Emilia had zero time to herself. She was amazed at how efficient she was, considering that a few days ago she was talking about dropping out.

Perhaps the party she attended with Kara was what she needed to clear her head. It was certainly interesting, to say the least.

Finally prepared for the semester to come, Emilia had a couple of days to relax. Classes began on Monday, and she knew it was going to take up all of her time until the semester ended. She was ready to take on the challenge.

CHAPTER 27

UNEXPECTED OPPORTUNITIES

Monday morning, Emilia gathered her school books, writing pads, her laptop, pens, sticky notes, and some highlighters. Surely that would cover any possible need in the classroom.

Over breakfast, she and Kara discussed their week ahead. Emilia was envious of Kara, having already finished law school and working at her father's firm.

"Focus on one day at a time, and before you know it, we'll be working side by side," Kara said, trying to provide some light at the end of Emilia's tunnel.

"I'll try," she replied glumly.

"There is no try, Emilia. Just do it," Kara demanded firmly.

Emilia was taken aback at Kara's demeanor. This was a side of her she'd never witnessed. She wasn't sure how to respond, so she didn't say anything, just took a sip of her coffee and nodded.

ᛏᚾᚠᛒᚱᚱᚲᚷᚼᛗ

Emilia's first course Monday morning involved an overview of the bar exam required of every law student who wished to become an attorney. She wasn't concerned about the multiple-choice questions or the essay questions. Her writing skills were above par, and she felt confident in her ability to meet the demands of the rigorous exam. Emilia was worried about the performance tests portion though. This was where students had to complete a sample work assignment performed by a law firm associate.

"How am I going to be able to answer these parts of the exam if I haven't even worked for one minute in a law firm?" she asked Kara that evening.

"How much time do you have available?" Kara inquired.

"The professor said there could be up to two performance tests, each taking ninety minutes each. It sounds like a *lot* of work and is probably counted as the biggest portion of the bar exam," she signed. "I'm worried about that part."

Kara looked at her and nodded.

"I meant, how much time do you have available outside of school… like during the week?" Kara clarified.

Emilia looked at Kara like she was crazy.

"I *have* no time available outside of school!" Emilia snapped.

"Yes, you do," Kara replied calmly.

Emilia rolled her eyes and sighed with exasperation. Her roommate obviously wasn't hearing a word she said.

"Why are you doing this to me?" Emilia demanded.

Kara gently smiled and said, "If it makes you feel better to have some office experience behind you, I can make that happen."

"That's great, Kara," Emilia grumbled. "Once you figure out a way to add additional time to the minimal twenty-four hours in a day, then I'll take you up on it."

Kara smiled and sipped her coffee.

ᛏᚢᚾᛒᛟᛟᚷᚲᛟᛉᛗ

The first semester flew by for Emilia. Her schedule consisted of sleep, food, school, and studying. She rushed through her personal hygiene routine every morning with barely enough time to grab a cup of coffee and a protein bar on her way out the door. This was final's week, and she was studying anytime she could. She turned down several invitations from her friends and family, citing the need to prepare for finals. Thankfully, nobody gave her any grief about it.

When her last final was finished on Thursday, Emilia breathed a much needed sigh of relief. She was exhausted physically and mentally.

"Finals all done?" Kara asked Thursday evening.

"Yes, finally," Emilia rolled her eyes and sighed.

"How long until the next semester begins?"

"Two weeks," Emilia replied.

Kara nodded.

"Would you like to get away for a mini vacation until you have to be at your folks 'for the holidays?"

"Oh, jeez," Emilia moaned. "I totally forgot about the holidays. I haven't even shopped for one Christmas present yet."

"Why don't we do that then?" Kara suggested.

"Do what?" Emilia's brain was so fried by this time that she could hardly follow Kara's line of thinking.

"Go Christmas shopping!" Kara laughed. "Instead of going away for a few days, we can stay here and spend the days shopping for presents for your family."

"What about *your* family?" Emilia asked.

"Oh, they don't need anything," Kara waived it off. "We're not big on exchanging gifts. We appreciate being together, since it's a rare occurrence."

"Oh!" Emilia replied, feeling empathy for her friend who didn't seem to feel the holiday spirit that she felt herself. "Do you get together with them on holidays?"

Kara shrugged," When they're in town we do, but otherwise no."

Emilia mulled this over.

"I've got an idea! Why don't you come to my parents 'for Christmas?" she offered with a huge smile on her face.

Kara smiled and said, "Wouldn't that interfere with your family time?"

"Not at all," Emilia pressed. "My mom is one of these people who thinks the more people there are, the merrier the celebration."

"I would like that then," Kara replied. "Thank you, Emilia."

"Of course!" Emilia practically shouted. "Oh, this will be so fun!"

She immediately texted her mom to make sure it was okay.

Amalia immediately replied, "Yes, of course! We would love to meet your roommate. But leave the cat at home, please."

Emilia replied with, "You got it, Mom! I love you!"

To Kara she said, "I let my mom know, and she's excited to meet you."

ᛏᚾᛒᛉᛉᚲᛉᚻᛗ

Friday morning, Emilia and Kara headed to the local mall for Christmas shopping. It was a blast. As smart as Emilia knew Kara to be, there were so many things that Kara was unaware of, and Emilia had a great time showing her how things worked.

"Fascinating!" Kara replied many times with a look of wonder on her face.

One of the things Kara enjoyed most was a fidget spinner. She kept playing with it and couldn't put it down. In fact, she was so entranced with the tiny toy that she walked right out of the store with it, without paying.

Emilia didn't realize that Kara still had the spinner until they were about to walk into the next store.

"Did you pay for that?" Emilia questioned Kara.

"Pay?" Kara looked confused.

"Yeah, you know...did you give the cashier your credit card or any...you know...*money* for that?" Emilia pointed to the fidget spinner.

"Oh!" Kara laughed in her embarrassment. "I don't think I did!"

"Come on," Emilia said, looping her arm through Kara's and steering her back to the store they had exited.

Reentering the store, Emilia and Kara went up to the cashier counter, explained the situation, and Emilia paid for the toy.

Kara looked genuinely touched when she asked, "Did you buy this for me?"

"Yes," Emilia laughed. "I didn't want you to get arrested! I need you!"

"Thank you," Kara breathed.

"Merry early Christmas!" Emilia smiled.

They spent the rest of the day purchasing gifts for Emilia's family and had enough time left to have a nice dinner at a The Shakespeare Café – a cute, little European bistro on the outskirts of the mall property.

While they were eating, Kara asked Emilia how well she felt she handled the first semester.

"It was hard work, but I definitely learned a lot," Emilia replied thoughtfully.

"I think you should start your internship now instead of at the end of next semester," Kara announced.

Emilia was stunned. She didn't know any students at her level who were already interning.

"I would love to, Kara, but I will be as busy next semester as I was this semester. I won't have any time for an internship. I appreciate the offer though."

"I can help you," Kara offered. "I really think you should give it a try, Emilia."

Not wanting to let her friend down, she agreed to try it.

"Okay, but if it starts interfering with my study time, I'll have to quit."

Kara smiled knowingly and replied, "Okay, I'll let my father know and we can go in Monday morning to get you set up."

Emilia was still unsure about the internship, which was actually called a clerkship at this level, but decided it was worth a shot. After all, how could she know what she was capable of if she didn't at least *try*? She wasn't going to tell her family about this yet though. First, she needed to know if it was even possible with her school schedule.

"Before we leave the mall, let's go get you a suit," Kara insisted.

"A suit?" Emilia questioned.

"If you're going to work at my dad's firm, you have to wear a suit and look professional. The more professional you look, the more seriously people will take you."

Emilia laughed, "Really?"

She always thought her intelligence and charisma would get her as far as she wanted to go in life.

"What do you think of our current governor?" Kara asked with an amused look on her face.

Emilia burst out laughing.

"He's a freaking joke!" Emilia continued laughing.

"And yet millions of people voted for him and insist he's a great governor," Kara pointed out.

"And your point is?" Emilia prodded.

"He's taken seriously in part because of how he dresses," Kara claimed. "The rest is people saying things through a tiny microphone in his ear so he knows what to say and how to say it to appease the people."

Emilia had never considered this before. Perhaps Kara was onto something with the idea of getting Emilia a suit to wear at the law office.

After dinner, the ladies headed to the women's section of the department store on the property. They had a nice selection of women's suits in different colors and styles. Emilia chose a navy blue, knee-length skirt and a matching blazer.

As she began heading toward the cashier, Kara reminded her, "Blouses, Emilia! And is that the only suit you're getting?"

"Oh, right. And yeah, I think so," Emilia laughed.

She was giddy at the idea of working in a law firm for the first time, and her mind was all over the place.

"Grab at least one more outfit. And nylons and shoes," Kara advised.

"Got it! Thanks, Kara!"

After purchasing several blouses that went with her new suits, some low-heeled pumps, nylons, and professional-looking earrings, she was finally set to check out.

"This is so exciting!" Emilia giggled as they walked toward Kara's car.

Kara smiled and gave Emilia a side-hug.

CHAPTER 28

EMILIA'S INTERNSHIP

The weekend had flown by as Emilia's anxiety came to a head on Monday morning. After multiple outfit changes and hairstyles, finally landing on one of her new fashionable gray pantsuits and slick pony, she now frantically grabbed copies of her resume and tried placing them in her backpack in such a way that they wouldn't wrinkle.

Kara watched the whirlwind that was Emilia and sighed, chuckling to herself.

"Here," Kara said as she pulled a rectangular package out of her own bag and handed it to Emilia, "try this."

Emilia's eyes lit up as she took Kara's gift, realizing that it was a new periwinkle laptop bag. She examined it with excitement, opening the various large pockets and golden zippers. Plenty of room for everything she needed to bring with her.

"It's beautiful! How did you know periwinkle is my favorite color?"

"It seemed to suit you. I'm glad you like it!"

Emilia stood up and immediately embraced Kara in a tight hug. With her confidence boosted, she packed everything up and was ready to take on this new adventure.

ᛏᚾᛒᛖᚱᚱᚲᛟᛗ

When they pulled up to the multi-story office building in which Kara and her father worked, Emilia was rather intimidated. It looked so professional.

"You *are* a professional, Emilia," Kara stated.

Emilia looked at Kara in shock.

"How did you know what I was thinking?"

Kara looked confused. "What do you mean?"

"I was thinking that the building looked really professional, and it was making me nervous, but I didn't say anything," Emilia pointed out. "And then *you* said, 'You *are* a professional. 'It's like you were reading my thoughts."

"Oh," Kara waived it off. "I said that to help calm your nerves and bolster your confidence before we go in."

Emilia bought Kara's excuse and let it go.

ᛏᚾᛒᛖᚱᚱᚲᛟᛗ

As they entered the lobby, Emilia was even more intimidated than before. It seemed as though every surface was covered in marble or gold trim.

Emilia followed Kara as she walked past the front desk security checkpoint toward the bank of elevators with gold doors. One elevator's doors were open awaiting the next group of passengers. The ladies entered the elevator, and Emilia watched Kara press the button for the fifty-fourth floor.

"Wow, that's really high up." Emilia said.

"It's the top floor," Kara said. "My dad likes to be in high places." She giggled.

Emilia laughed along with her friend, grateful for the momentary reprieve from her anxiety.

When they entered the lobby of the law office, a clerk stood up and said, "Good morning!"

"Hi, Sandy," Kara greeted the receptionist with a smile. "Is my dad here yet?"

Sandy said, "I don't think he ever leaves."

All three women laughed at her comment as Kara led Emilia through the double doors of the law firm. They walked to another desk in front of two huge double doors.

"Go on in!" The secretary waved toward the door.

"Thanks, Tisha!" Kara said with a smile.

Emilia and Kara walked into the enormous and tastefully decorated office. Everything in the room was white except for some small decorative items and book spines on the bookshelves.

"There's my girl!" Kara's father said with a smile as he stood up from his desk and came around to give his daughter a hug.

"Hi, Dad. I brought Emilia to set her up for her internship."

He looked surprised.

Turning to Emilia, he asked, "I thought you still had another semester of law school left."

Emilia blushed, but before she could respond, Kara replied for her.

"She does, but she needs to get going on her internship now," Kara stated, looking at her father knowingly.

"Already?" he asked in alarm.

"Yes," Kara confirmed.

"I don't have to start my internship now," Emilia began. "Kara thought I might be able to get in while I'm still in school."

The judge said gently, "If Kara says you're ready, then you're ready. When can you start?"

Taken off guard, Emilia replied, "Um...I don't know."

She looked at Kara for some direction, who responded, "She needs to start as soon as possible."

"Can you start today?" the judge asked, scrutinizing Emilia.

Remembering what her father told her about presenting herself as confident, Emilia replied, "Yes, sir!"

"Great!" he replied then turned to Kara. "Take her down to HR and have them get her set up."

"Will do," Kara said and nodded.

The judge directed his attention back to Emilia.

"You'll be working directly with me. Anything that anyone else wants you to do here goes through me."

"Yes, sir." Emilia replied.

ᛏᚾᛒᛟᛉᚲᛟᚼᛗ

The ladies left the judge's office and went downstairs to human resources.

"Hi, Tom," Kara greeted the man sitting behind the desk. "I've brought Emilia Benning to get her into the system. She'll be working directly with the judge."

"Hi, Emilia," Tom said, standing up to shake her hand. "Please take a seat."

"I'll leave you to it. Let me know when you're done, and I'll come back to give her the tour," Kara advised.

"OK," Tom agreed.

When Kara left the office, Tom turned to Emilia and said, "Welcome to The Law Offices of Skarsgaard and Skarsgaard. We are pleased to have you join us."

"Thank you," she murmured politely.

"Do you know what your duties will be?" Tom inquired.

"Not yet," she admitted. "I know I'll be working with the judge."

He blinked for a moment, then said, "Uh...okay. Do you have your ID and resumé with you?"

She nodded and reached down to pick up her laptop case, unzipped it, and pulled her resume folder out. Then she pulled her wallet out of her purse and produced her driver's license for Tom.

"Thank you," he said. "I need to make a copy of your ID. I'll be right back."

"Okay," Emilia said and looked around the rather plain office while waiting for him to return. After several minutes went by, Tom returned with her ID, which she swiftly placed back in her wallet.

"Here are the employee handbook and forms you will need to complete before we can call you official," he said as he handed her a stack of papers and a small book. "There's a desk over by the water cooler you can use."

"Thanks," she replied.

It took her over an hour to fill out all the necessary paperwork, and she had to stop a few times and ask Tom about the benefits package. There were several options to choose from, and she didn't know which one to select.

When she was finished, Tom called Kara to let her know Emilia was free to go on the tour.

Kara arrived in seconds, thanked Tom for his time, and took Emilia on a tour of the legal practice's offices, departments and other areas.

"And now, the coup de grace," Kara smiled as she opened a set of double doors marked "Attorneys Only."

In front of them was a first-class gym with a sauna, a steam room, equipment and weights for any kind of workout, and a snack bar.

Emilia kept saying "wow" as they walked through the gym to the women's locker room, which contained all the accoutrements of a modern, full-sized gym.

They headed back toward the front of the gym, but instead of leaving, Kara said, "Here's where we usually work through our lunches."

She opened a door to the left of the gym entrance. Inside was a large dining room with elegant tables and chairs, soothing décor, a coffee station, and a fully staffed kitchen.

"Oh my goodness," Emilia squealed. "I can't wait to be an attorney and be able to use this area."

"You work for the judge, Andarta. You're already allowed to use this area," Kara chuckled at Emilia's enthusiasm.

"What did you call me?" Emilia felt an electrical shock flow through her, like she was in a dream and hearing someone else say the words that came out of Kara's mouth.

"Hm?" Kara asked, looking curiously at Emilia.

"You called me Andarta," Emilia pointed out.

Kara didn't respond but looked at Emilia as if she got caught doing something she shouldn't.

"I did?" Kara mumbled.

"Don't try to blow me off, Kara," Emilia demanded. "Tell me what you know. Is this why you wanted me to start my internship before I'm supposed to?"

"Come with me," Kara replied and began walking back toward the gym exit.

"Hey!" Emilia shouted at her roommate.

Kara stopped and turned around, looking at Emilia in shock. She'd never seen this side of her charge before.

"What is going on here?" Emilia demanded and stood rooted to the spot, refusing to budge until Kara talked to her.

"Let's go see my father. He can explain everything," Kara replied calmly.

Emilia continued to glare at Kara for several moments before deciding to follow her to the judge's office.

ᛏᚾ�ᛁᛗ

"Hi, ladies!" The judge welcomed them back. "How did everything go? All set, Emilia?"

Emilia stared at him without responding. She wanted to scream at both of them, frustrated with the current situation, but she knew she wouldn't have a job for long if she did so.

Noticing the tension between the ladies, he offered them a drink from the bar behind sliding doors near the seating area in his office.

"Fireball on the rocks," Emilia requested firmly.

The judge raised his eyebrows at her. It was unusual for a woman, especially one so young, to order such a strong drink.

"I'll have my usual," Kara said.

While the judge put the drink orders together, he asked, "So what seems to be the issue between you two?"

"Andarta," Emilia stated.

The judge stood up straight and turned with the ladies 'drinks in his hands. He walked over to the high-backed, leather chair where he already had his half-empty drink.

"I see," he commented quietly as he set the drinks on the coffee table.

"Please have a seat, ladies," he commanded gently.

Emilia picked up her drink and gulped down a good portion before taking a seat. Once seated, she immediately crossed her arms and began swinging her leg back and forth. It was something she did when her emotions were heightened in some way, good or bad.

"How did this come about?"

Kara opened her mouth to reply, but Emilia spoke up, "She called me Andarta. That's how this came about."

The judge looked at Kara none too happily.

"Does she know?" he asked Kara.

Kara shrugged and said, "I don't know, but considering the case that came across your desk, I would say she needs to be brought up to speed...and fast."

"What case?" demanded Emilia, her emotions changing from anger and frustration to complete confusion.

The judge let out a big sigh, gulped down the rest of his drink, set his glass down, and scrutinized Emilia for the second time that day.

"Why are you here, Emilia?" he probed.

Emilia's expression revealed nothing but confusion.

"I'm here to learn how to be a lawyer and get my feet wet in this field," she stated.

Kara looked back toward her father, noting his acceptance of the plain answer before turning back to Emilia, looking her dead in the eye and asking, "Why are *you* here, Andarta?"

"KARA!" the judge exclaimed, now panic stricken at the woman's boldness.

Kara said nothing as she held up a hand, holding eye contact with Emilia. Except...something had shifted. Emilia's eyes had hardened into a stern expression, her skin emitting a soft glow, and Kara began to smile.

"Andar—"

As Kara spoke her name, the air chilled, and the lights of the office flickered violently with a thundering shake. Kara and the judge shielded their eyes from the sudden strobing light, until they had burnt out entirely and left them in the dark, the only source of light filtering through the tall window behind the judge's desk. They opened their eyes, Kara now nervous and shaken.

Before them stood an enraged goddess wrapped in Emilia's pantsuit, eyes burning with a divine fury and exuding more power than Kara had felt in a long, long time. They were both stunned, not having interacted with Andarta in human form before.

Andarta started, "How many more people were you willing to let this happen to before I showed up?"

Both the judge and Kara were shocked at her outburst. They had known Andarta since the beginning of time and had never seen her this angry.

"Andarta," Kara said softly, "we had to wait until the human race developed enough for your efforts to be successful."

"What the hell does that mean?" she demanded. "You have both seen me rip apart entire armies with my bare hands! You seriously think I'm incapable of bringing down this...this...*sewage?*"

"It's not that," the judge implored. "We need to be able to help the victims who survive and help them acclimate back into society in a healthy way. That's now starting to become a possibility. Before now, and even still now in some cases, once victims are rescued, they don't have anywhere to go. No direction in life. Most of them have been slaves since childhood and need guidance to help them get back to the lives that birth itself promises to all humankind."

Andarta took his response in and mulled it over.

"How is Emilia being an intern going to help?"

"We will explain it to her, but we need you to bring her back now," Kara replied.

Instantly, Emilia's fists unclenched, and her stance relaxed. The judge and Kara breathed a sigh of relief, now that the confrontation with Andarta was over. As the lights flickered back on, Emilia looked around in confusion.

"What happened? Why am I standing up?"

"Have a seat, Emilia. This is going to take a while," the judge said as he downed the rest of his drink.

CHAPTER 29
A Sister's Support

Despite their busy schedules, Clara and Emilia remained as close as ever, spending their free time together and sharing stories about their respective journeys. Clara would tell Emilia about her nursing experiences, and Emilia would eagerly recount her adventures at law school and her internship.

"I've been promoted to head nurse at the hospital!" Clara exclaimed one evening as they sat together in Emilia's apartment, sipping on cups of steaming tea. "Can you believe it, Emi?"

Emilia's eyes widened in surprise and delight.

"That's incredible, Clara. I always knew you had what it takes to succeed. Congratulations!"

Clara beamed with pride at Emilia's support.

Emilia was relieved to know that Clara had finally found her place in this world. Her tender and caring nature had found the perfect home in the medical field. Knowing her sister as she did, Emilia knew Clara had the potential to literally be the best nurse in the world. She had such a tender heart and easily overlooked any negativity from people who were suffering from illness or injury, which allowed her to focus on the job at hand until the patient was as comfortable as possible. Emilia was almost envious of Clara's patients because she knew the kind of tender loving care they received from her sister.

Despite the demanding nature of her job, Clara thrived in her role, drawing upon her newfound leadership abilities and unwavering dedication to her patients. She approached each day with optimism, determined to make a positive impact in the lives of those under her care.

As Clara's career as a nurse flourished and Emilia's aspirations as a lawyer took shape, the sisters found themselves united by a shared vision of making a difference in the world. They shared a deep-seated belief in the power of compassion, justice, and healing, and they were determined to use their talents and skills to create a positive change.

Together, they embarked on a journey to advocate for the rights of patients and the marginalized, fighting tirelessly for justice and equality in their respective fields. They worked side by side, using their unique strengths and perspectives to effect meaningful change in the world around them.

As they stood together on the precipice of their futures, Clara and Emilia knew that no matter where life took them, they would always have each other's backs. For they were not just sisters. They were kindred spirits, bound by a love that transcended time and distance and a shared commitment to making the world a better place.

CHAPTER 30

EMILIA BENNING, ESQ.

With graduation and the bar exam finally behind her, Emilia could actually call herself a real attorney at last.

As the summer sun beat down on the bustling streets of the city, Emilia went to the office. When she entered the building, the entire staff was standing in the lobby with balloons, flowers, and a buffet with a large cake that read, "Congratulations, Emilia Benning, Esq."

Everyone cheered as they came over to pat her on the back.

"Good job, kiddo!" Judge Skarsgaard said as he gave her a bear hug that almost squeezed the very breath out of her.

"Thanks!" she managed to squeak out.

"Now hurry up and thank everyone for this ridiculous feast," he said. "We've got work to do."

She was more than eager to get started on their next project and felt like this party was a waste of time, but she couldn't let her kindhearted coworkers know how she felt. They were all amazing in their own right, and she would do anything for them.

Emilia and the judge held out for a decent forty minutes before Kara came over and acted as if there was an emergency that needed their attention immediately in order to politely get them out of the gathering.

Once the three entered the elevator for the ride to the top floor, Emilia let out a sigh of relief and said, "Thank God. That was nice of everyone, but I want to get to work."

The judge and Kara laughed, and she said, "I know. I could tell the way you kept crossing your arms and tapping your foot."

"Yeah, you don't hide it very well," the judge joked.

Instead of going to the judge's office, they went into another office.

The judge announced to Emilia, "I would like to introduce you to Mrs. Rodriguez. She is a seasoned attorney who works on cases involving human rights violations. I am assigning you to work on a case with her involving human trafficking and forced labor."

Hearing that, Emilia whipped her head toward the judge and questioned, "Human trafficking?"

"Yes, it's a form of modern-day slavery," he explained.

"I know what human trafficking is," she explained. "I've just never been exposed to any cases involving it."

The judge sighed, "Get used to it, Emilia. As long as there are people on Earth, human trafficking will exist."

"I don't understand why or how it still exists," Emilia said with frustration.

"Because powerful people don't want to do the dirty work, so they use forced labor to get their jobs done for free...or very cheaply."

"That's disgusting," Emilia grimaced.

"What's even more disgusting is that they gaslight their victims to believe they are fortunate to be in that position," the judge chuckled wryly.

"How could anyone possibly believe that?" Emilia demanded.

"Because they're desperate," Mrs. Rodriguez replied quietly.

The four stood quietly for a moment, mulling over Mrs. Rodriguez's comment and trying to imagine themselves in such a situation.

"How can we help them?" Emilia asked.

"I'll leave you ladies to it," the judge said. "I'm due in court in thirty minutes."

They said their goodbyes, and Emilia followed Mrs. Rodriguez to her office.

Upon arriving in the cozy yet expansive office, Emilia was surprised to see thousands of folders stacked on most of the furniture surfaces, and all along three walls...some reaching waist high.

"Are these all human trafficking cases?" Emilia asked in astonishment, her mouth open in shock.

"Yes," Mrs. Rodriguez replied gently with a tone of sorrow in her voice. "These are the cases that are still open."

Emilia thought her eyes were going to pop out of her skull. How could there be *that many?* Hard as she tried, Emilia could not wrap her mind around that many people being victims of human trafficking. And this was for *one* law firm. How many others were out there? Emilia was sickened and angry at the idea of so many human beings having been victims of such powerful scum. It wasn't right. Her mother always told her that life wasn't fair, but this went beyond anything having to do with fairness. The more she thought about it, the angrier she became.

Mrs. Rodriguez's voice jarred Emilia out of her consternation.

"I have an important assignment for you today. We have a client who is a victim of forced labor, and I need you to assist with her case."

Emilia's eyes widened with interest.

"Of course. I'm ready to help in any way I can," she replied eagerly.

Mrs. Rodriguez led Emilia to a small conference room where they met with their client, Yazmin, a young woman with haunted eyes and a trembling voice. Yazmin recounted her harrowing ordeal of being trafficked from her home country and forced to work in a sweatshop under appalling conditions.

"I wanted a better life for my family," Yazmin sobbed, her hands shaking as she clutched a crumpled tissue. "But instead, I was treated like a slave, forced to work long hours for little pay and no freedom."

Emilia listened intently, her heart breaking at Yazmin's story. She felt a surge of determination to fight for justice on behalf of Yazmin and others like her who had been victims of human trafficking and forced labor.

"Yazmin, thank you for sharing your story with us," Emilia said gently, her voice filled with empathy. "We are here to help you seek justice and hold those responsible accountable for their actions."

Over the following weeks, Emilia worked tirelessly on Yazmin's case, conducting research, drafting legal documents, and preparing for court hearings. She was determined to use her legal skills to make a difference in Yazmin's life and bring her traffickers to justice.

Finally, the day of the court hearing arrived, and Emilia accompanied Yazmin to the courthouse where they faced Yazmin's traffickers in a tense legal battle. With Mrs. Rodriguez by her side, Emilia presented evidence, cross-examined witnesses, and argued passionately on behalf of Yazmin.

In the end, justice prevailed, and Yazmin's traffickers were convicted and sentenced to prison for their crimes. Emilia felt a profound sense of satisfaction knowing that she had helped secure justice for Yazmin and played a role in the fight against human trafficking and forced labor.

As they left the courthouse, Yazmin took Emilia's hand and squeezed it tightly, her eyes shining with gratitude.

"Thank you, Emilia," she said softly. "You have given me hope for a better future."

Emilia smiled, her heart full, knowing she had made a difference in Yazmin's life and that her passion for justice would continue to guide her on her journey as a lawyer.

CHAPTER 31

HOPE

Gabriel's day began before the sun even rose, the cool predawn air carrying the promise of another grueling day in the strawberry fields of Southern California. As he rose from his makeshift bed in the cramped, dimly lit shack he shared with his fellow laborers, Gabriel's heart felt heavy with the weight of his circumstances. With a weary sigh, Gabriel pulled on his tattered work clothes and made his way to the fields where rows upon rows of strawberry plants stretched out before him in a sea of green and red. The sun beat down mercilessly, its scorching rays turning the air thick and stifling as Gabriel toiled under its oppressive gaze.

For hours on end, Gabriel bent over the strawberry plants, his fingers raw and blistered from the back-breaking labor. The work was relentless, the heat unbearable, and yet Gabriel pressed on, driven by a fierce determination to survive and one day escape the clutches of his captors. But it was not the physical hardships that weighed heavily on Gabriel's spirit. The way he was treated by his bosses, the ruthless overseers who cracked their whips and barked orders with impunity, filled him with a sense of indignation and despair.

One fateful day, as Gabriel toiled in the fields under the scorching sun, he caught sight of a familiar face in the distance at the stand where the strawberries were sold directly to customers. It was Emilia, his childhood friend from Illinois.

What was she doing here in California? With a surge of hope in his heart, Gabriel took a chance that he wouldn't be seen by the bosses and quickly approached Emilia.

"Emilia?" he began tentatively. "It's me…Gabriel…from Ottawa."

"Gabriel?" Emilia's jaw dropped when she saw her old friend.

The huge smile that lit up her face was unavoidable as she reached out and gave him a hard, long hug. At first, his body was stiff with tension but quickly relaxed in her embrace, and he began crying uncontrollably.

"Gabriel, what's wrong?" she asked in alarm.

"I wish I could tell you, but I have to get back to work," he sobbed.

It was then that she noticed his worn and dirty clothing, the sweat and grime on his face and hands, and the overall disheveled look of her old friend.

"What time do you get off work?" she asked.

Emilia knew she needed to get him alone. It was very apparent that something was not right with Gabriel.

He shrugged and said, "It changes every day, but we're always done by dark because we can't see the fields after that point."

"It's usually dark by eight these days," Emilia pointed out.

"True," Gabriel hesitated.

"Can I pick you up at eight?" she asked.

Gabriel looked panic stricken and blurted out, "No, don't do that!"

"Why not?" Emilia was baffled by his response.

And then it dawned on her that her dear old friend might actually be a victim of human trafficking, still…after all this time. She needed to get to the bottom of this, for Gabriel's sake.

"Are you allowed to leave, Gabriel?" she asked gently.

Eventually, Gabriel nodded.

"I can leave for a short time to get food, but not for long."

"Where is the closest place we can meet without being seen?" Emilia pressed.

"There's a taco shop up the street on Rose Avenue," Gabriel said. "I can meet you there at nine."

"Okay, that—" Emilia began, but was cut off by a piercing whistle.

"Oh, shit!" Gabriel exclaimed. "I gotta go. See you at nine!" he said fervently as he rushed back to his post.

Emilia watched him run away from her back to the strawberry fields, worried about how fearful he looked when he heard that whistle.

What are they doing to him? she wondered. She looked at her watch. About four more hours until she was able to meet Gabriel. Emilia pulled out her phone and called Clara.

"Hey, Emi!" Clara said happily. "What's up?"

"Clara, you're not going to believe who I ran into," Emilia said.

"Who?"

"Gabriel."

"*From Ottawa?*" Clara exclaimed in shock.

"Yes," Emilia replied gravely.

"Why do you sound so serious?" Clara laughed.

"I think he's being held captive," Emilia replied.

There was silence on the other end of the phone.

Impatient for a response from her sister, Emilia continued, "I went to the farm to buy some strawberries. While I was waiting to check out, he came up to me looking very grimy and nervous. We made plans to meet at a taco shop tonight at nine o'clock. Can you come? I know he would love to see you, and then we can find out what's really going on with him...and maybe help him."

There was a long pause before Clara answered.

"Yes," she said quietly. "I can come. Can you pick me up?"

"Of course," Emilia promised. "I'll come get you at eight. That should give us enough time to deal with traffic and find the place."

"Thank you," Clara said before hanging up.

ᛏᚾᚦᛉᛉᚲᛇᛏᛗ

The ladies arrived twenty minutes early to the taco shop and were surprised to see that Gabriel was already there. Emilia was relieved to see him clean and wearing fresh clothes. She was sure Clara would have broken down in tears if she had seen how he looked when Emilia saw him earlier.

As soon as they came in the door, Gabriel walked quickly over to Clara and gave her a warm embrace that lasted for several moments. When they parted, both had tears in their eyes.

"Hi," Gabriel whispered to Clara.

"Hi," Clara whispered back.

"I missed you," Gabriel whispered as he leaned forward and rested his forehead against Clara's.

"I missed you too," Clara whispered and then burst into tears. "Why didn't you say goodbye?"

"I didn't have a choice," he explained. "I didn't know I was leaving when you left for London, and when I found out, I only had one day's notice."

Gabriel let out a heart-wrenching sob, and Clara wrapped her arms around him. She held him tightly until his crying had subsided.

Emilia, knowing his time with them was likely limited, interrupted them.

"I hate to break up this little love scene, but we need to talk, guys," she said with authority.

Slowly, Gabriel and Clara untangled themselves from each other but continued holding hands as the three walked to an empty table away from the other restaurant patrons.

Once seated across from them, Emilia began the much needed conversation.

"Gabriel, tell me about your situation at the strawberry farm. I got the impression you don't have a normal job."

He paused, uncertain about how much he could tell them without fear of repercussion.

"Look," Emilia said sternly, "when Clara and I were little, we thought you were a victim of human trafficking because you were always working and never allowed to do things outside of school. And now it *definitely* looks like you're in that situation. Correct me if I'm wrong."

Gabriel glanced at Emilia and then quickly looked down at the table, humiliated that his depressing life was so obvious to the two women he had come to care about the most...the first true friends he had in this world.

Clara leaned over, rested her head on his shoulder and said, "We might be able to help you, Gabriel. Emilia is a lawyer who has helped victims of human trafficking get out of that life. We don't just want to help...we're *able* to help, but we have to know what's going on first."

Emilia's heart burst with joy at the light of hope that appeared in Gabriel's eyes as he looked directly at her and said, "You're really a lawyer?"

She smiled, nodded vigorously, and said, "Yes. And all I do is work with victims of human trafficking. It's my jam, Gabe. If I can help those I've never even met, imagine what I can do for someone I know and have cared about all my life."

Gabriel smiled and actually laughed for the first time since she ran into him that day.

Clara sat up and said calmly, "Okay, everyone take a big, deep breath and let it out slowly."

They all followed her instructions and felt the tension melt away.

"Now," Clara continued, "tell us what's been going on in your life since we last saw you and what's going on in the strawberry fields."

Gabriel took several more deep breaths and then paused before beginning his story.

"When we were ten years old and your family had been in London for a few days during that Christmas break, my parents told me..."

His voice trembled with emotion at the memories that came flooding back. He began crying again and shook his head to indicate that he couldn't continue.

"Told you what?" Clara asked quietly.

Gabriel sobbed once more then took a deep breath and cleared his throat.

"They told me I was going to California the next day...without them."

"Why would a ten year old go all the way across the country without their parents?" Emilia was flabbergasted.

"I was being sold to work at the strawberry fields here," Gabriel lamented. "I told them I wouldn't go, but they told me if I didn't go that we would all be killed. So I had no choice."

Emilia and Clara looked at each other in shock at his story. Killed?

"Why would you all be killed?" Emilia asked pointedly.

Gabriel shrugged and said, "I don't know. That's what my parents told me."

"What about your grandparents? Would they kill them too?" Clara asked with sympathy.

She was surprised when Gabriel smirked and gave an ironic laugh.

"Yeah...that's when I found out my grandparents weren't actually my grandparents. Apparently, they were our owners, but everyone kept it a secret from me to keep me innocent until the time was right. Talk about feeling like an idiot," he grumbled.

Emilia smacked her palm on the table and snapped, "Gabriel, stop it! There's no way you could have known. You are *not* an idiot by any stretch of the imagination."

"Oh yeah?" he challenged. "Then why am I still in this situation over fifteen years later? Huh? Tell me *that*, Emilia!"

Why *was* Gabriel still in this situation? She always knew him to be quite intelligent, so surely, he could have figured a way out of this by now.

Unless there was a *reason*, he was still involved in this. A reason unbeknownst to the rest of them...until now.

All of a sudden, it dawned on Emilia that Gabriel *was* here for a reason, and that reason had something to do with the fact that she and Clara were *also* here at this place and time!

Emilia studied Gabriel's face, wondering how much she should tell him. She knew he had been through far too much trauma already but felt it was necessary in order for she and Clara to accomplish their goal of taking down the human trafficking ring under which Gabriel was held captive.

And there would be more trauma coming. That was a given. There was no avoiding it.

Emilia and Clara listened intently, their eyes filled with compassion and determination as Gabriel shared his harrowing story. They knew they had to help him, to fight for his freedom and bring the perpetrators of this human trafficking ring to justice. As Gabriel spoke of the terrible conditions he and his fellow laborers endured, the sisters 'resolve hardened. Individually, they couldn't take down the human trafficking ring, but together they were powerful allies.

When Gabriel's story was finished, he said, "I feel so relieved. Thank you for listening to me. I feel free. I'm not going back. I'm coming with you and starting over."

"That's awesome," Clara crowed with a big smile. "You can stay with me. I have an extra room."

"*Gracias, mi amor*," Gabriel crooned.

Clara squeezed his hand and looked up at him adoringly.

However, Emilia was instantly alarmed.

"No!" she exclaimed. "You have to go back, Gabriel. We need you to go back and act normal, to be our eyes on the inside and keep tabs on what the traffickers are planning so we'll know where to find them and what we need to prepare for when the time comes."

Clara looked at Emilia with extreme sadness.

"How can you ask him to go back, Emi? Were you not listening to his story?"

"I *was* listening, Clara...very closely, and *that's* why he needs to go back. Do you think it's a coincidence that the three of us were all brought back together in this time and place under these circumstances? Gabriel, a victim; me, a human trafficking victim lawyer; and you, the best nurse on the whole goddamned planet?"

Both Clara and Gabriel looked at Emilia thoughtfully yet fearfully. Tears slowly began forming in Clara's eyes and spilling over onto her porcelain cheeks.

"Why are you crying?" Gabriel asked softly.

Clara looked at Gabriel sorrowfully and then mumbled, "She's right. It's no coincidence. We need your help. You have to go back."

"Clara, no!" Gabriel cried, obviously hurt by what he saw as Clara's betrayal.

"I'm sorry," Clara sobbed. "We'll get you out as soon as we can. I promise."

"She's right, Gabe," Emilia began. "We need some time to gather information and get our resources together."

"How *much* time?" Gabriel demanded.

"That depends on you," she replied.

"How does it depend on *me*?" He looked stunned.

"We need to know how many people we're rescuing. What physical shape they're in. How many traffickers we're dealing with. What kind of weapons they have, when they're at the fields, which ones we might be able to use to our advantage...stuff like that."

"What do you mean?" he asked curiously.

Emilia paused while trying to think of a way to explain.

"Some of the traffickers might also be forced into their positions and are biding their time until they can get away. Are there any who seem nicer than the rest? Some that the workers are maybe less afraid of than others?"

Gabriel thought a moment, as his mind went through the bosses he had seen. He knew Leandro was definitely *not* being forced into his position. At least, if he was, he certainly hid it well.

Then there was Diego and Magnus. They both seemed pretty cool, but he wasn't positive about Magnus. He was a bit hard to read, and he occasionally overhead him mumbling something in a language he'd never heard before, repeating the word "on-dart-uh" a lot.

Alfonso and Pedro seemed almost as mean as Leandro, so he didn't see them as victims in any way.

"Maybe Diego and Magnus," he began. "At least they seem to be the least threatening to us."

"What do they look like?" Emilia asked.

Gabriel thought aloud, "Diego looks a lot like me, but Magnus is white."

"Hair and eye color?" Emilia inquired, taking notes on her phone.

"Brown hair and green eyes," Gabriel said.

"Height and weight?"

"Tall...over six feet and medium build."

"How many others are there?" Clara asked.

"There are three others I know of. Leandro's the head boss. Then there's Alfonso and Pedro. They're all really bad, but Leandro's the worst."

"Weapons?" Emilia asked.

"Leandro carries a Desert Eagle...and I've seen him use it," Gabriel replied.

"On whom?" Clara asked worriedly.

"People who ask for something that he doesn't want to give them." Gabriel shrugged.

"Like what?" Emilia asked.

"I heard he killed an old lady who asked for water once. Last week, I saw him kill a teenager who ate one of the strawberries because he was hungry. The kid asked if he could have one. Leandro told him no, but when he thought Leandro wasn't looking, he picked one and ate it. Before he finished chewing it, he was dead."

"Over a *strawberry*?" Clara was horrified.

Gabriel nodded.

Emilia took a deep breath and let it out before asking, "Any other weapons?"

"All the others carry guns, except for Magnus. He carries a sword," Gabriel explained.

Clara and Emilia immediately locked eyes. A *sword?*

"What kind of a sword?" Emilia asked, trying to keep the excitement out of her voice.

"I don't know...a big one. I've never seen anything like it before. It's got some kind of scratch marks going down the middle of the blade. I've never seen him use it, but he always has it with him."

Emilia and Clara locked eyes again and couldn't help but give a little smile of hope.

"Do you have a phone, Gabriel?" Emilia asked.

Gabriel laughed," What would I need a phone for?"

"Meet me here tomorrow at nine, and I'll have a phone for you. I'll set it up to always be silent so nobody will know you have it. We'll use it to keep in contact and update each other on the plans."

"I don't think that's a good idea," Gabriel said nervously.

"Why not?" Clara looked surprised.

"If I get caught with it, it could be the end of me," he explained.

"Then what are we supposed to do? How will we know when and where to do the raid?" Emilia said with frustration.

"Can we plan to meet here every night at nine until then?" Gabriel pleaded. "I would feel much safer doing that."

Emilia sighed.

"Fine."

"I can't guarantee that I'll be here every time because my schedule changes every week, but I'll be here for as many meetings as I can," Clara promised.

"Okay, until tomorrow then," Gabriel said.

"Until tomorrow," the ladies chimed in unison.

CHAPTER 32

FIRST RESCUE ATTEMPT

After weeks of rushed nighttime meetings at the taco shop on Rose Avenue, the three friends felt the time was ripe for a rescue attempt and made their plans for the following night. Under cover of darkness seemed to be the best time to make their move. Before they parted ways at the restaurant that night, Clara gave Gabriel her phone and showed him how to use it. The three friends came up with what seemed like a foolproof plan to keep Gabriel from getting into trouble with the traffickers. He was to go back to the farm, pretend to go to sleep, and wait until the bosses had left for the night. Except for the one sentry they kept near the sleeping quarters to keep an eye out for escapees, the rest of the farm would be empty of bosses. The girls 'father already had the fire department in place to create a fictitious emergency near the offices, which would surely distract the sentry – especially if he thought everyone was asleep.

ᛏᚾᚠᛒᛉᛉᚲᛉᚻᛗ

As he headed back to the farm, Emilia and Clara waited at the restaurant for another thirty minutes so as not to draw attention. When the time came, the sisters drove to a shopping center that was within walking distance from the farm and parked their car. Gathering the necessary first aid kit, water bottles, flashlights, and emergency blankets, they started out on foot to the farm property. When they arrived, Emilia and Clara crouched behind a dark van parked alongside the entrance to the farm, waiting for Gabriel to signal that the bosses had left the sleeping quarters area.

They waited for what seemed like an eternity.

"Should we call him?" Clara wondered.

"And let the phone vibration alert everyone to us being here?" Emilia whispered back.

Clara sighed and said," What's taking so long?"

Emilia shrugged. Both girls stood up in anticipation as they saw Gabriel come jogging toward them.

When he reached them, trying to catch his breath, he managed to get out, "They're gone."

"The bosses?" Emilia asked. "Let's get in there and get those people out!"

She started walking toward the dilapidated building where the workers slept, and then heard Gabriel say, "They're *all* gone. Nobody is in there. It's empty."

Crap! That was not what they were expecting to hear. All three of them looked morosely at each other, knowing the traffickers had gotten the better of them and foiled their rescue efforts.

"Where did they go?" Clara asked.

"I don't know," Gabriel shook his head slowly, "but I'll find out. I promise."

"You don't think they killed them, do you?" Clara asked fearfully.

Gabriel shrugged and said, "Not all of them. They need them to work."

"Oh!" Clara sighed as her eyes filled with tears.

"Not now, Clara!" Emilia said sternly. "Our purpose is to *rescue* the ones who are still alive. *That's* what we need to focus on."

Emilia immediately noticed the familiar look of defeat on Clara's face...something she hadn't seen since they were kids. She walked quickly over to her, put her hands firmly on both sides of Clara's face, and looked into her eyes.

"Remember, Eir, this is why we're here. We *will* succeed. It's like college though. We have to keep going and figure out the way that works. Remember?"

At hearing her sister say 'Eir'," Clara's steely resolve quickly replaced the defeat in her eyes.

"You're right, Andarta," she replied.

"Air? Ondartuh?" Gabriel was confused.

Then he remembered something and said, "Wait! *Ondartuh!* That's the word that Magnus keeps saying over and over again! What does that mean?"

Emilia's head snapped toward Gabriel so fast she felt that familiar sharp pain in her neck.

"Magnus said 'Andarta?'" she asked suspiciously.

"Yes!" Gabriel practically yelled. "He speaks some language I can't understand, but he says the word 'Ondartuh 'a *lot!"*

Emilia and Clara looked at each other knowingly, not quite sure what to make of this new revelation.

Clara looked at Gabriel and asked, "When Magnus says that, how is he saying it?"

"I don't *know* because I don't know the language he's speaking," he said with exasperation.

"No," she began calmly, "what tone is he using? Does he sound angry, happy, sad, or what?"

Gabriel closed his eyes as he tried to remember how Magnus sounded. "The best way I can say it is that he sounded like he was begging...or maybe...praying."

He looked at the sisters like he was unsure if he was explaining it properly because he knew how crazy it sounded.

Emilia couldn't hide her excitement.

"Have you ever seen him use his sword or threaten anyone with it?" she asked eagerly, already knowing the answer.

Gabriel quickly shook his head and said, "Never. The only time I've ever seen him even touch it was when he was talking with one of the other bosses and he would grab the hilt but then let it go."

Emilia looked at Clara and mumbled, "If Magnus is what I think he is, this is almost too good to be true."

Clara chuckled at the situation, knowing they had more than Gabriel on the inside now.

"So why did you call each other 'Air 'and 'Ondartuh 'before?" Gabriel asked.

Remembering that he knew nothing about their goddess possession, the girls tried to play it off as a game.

"Oh!" Clara laughed. "Those are nicknames we made up for each other."

"Yeah!" Emilia agreed with a convincing smile. "Don't you have any nicknames?"

"Some people call me Gabe instead of Gabriel," he said with a shrug, "but nothing completely different from my actual name. How did you come up with those names? They're very unusual."

Clara winked at Emilia and said, "Remember how we used to play Vikings when we were kids?"

Gabriel smiled and nodded. How could he forget since those were the last happy days of his life?

"Our grandpa, the one who used to tell us stories about our Viking ancestors, told us we were related to these two warrior women named Eir and Andarta," she explained. "We decided to use those nicknames for each other."

"That's actually kind of cool." Gabriel smiled. "I wish I had a nickname like that."

"You do!" Emilia exclaimed. "Gabriel is the name of one of God's most important angels. You don't need a nickname to sound cool. Gabriel itself is one of the coolest names there is."

"Really?" he said, his face lighting up with a huge smile.

"Really!" the ladies replied in unison.

Gabriel laughed and said, "Awesome!"

CHAPTER 33

PROGRESS

The next morning, Emilia's phone rang before her alarm went off. Answering it out of a sound sleep, she said groggily, "Hello?"

"Hi, it's me, Gabriel," he whispered.

"Gabriel?" She was wide awake now and quickly sat up. "Are you okay?"

"Yes," he assured her. "I went back to the farm and waited for them to come back for me. I'm in the back of a truck now being taken to the next farm."

"Where are they taking you?" she demanded.

"I don't know yet, but I'll let you know as soon as I do," he assured her.

"Okay," she took a deep breath. "Stay safe and keep in touch every day if you can."

"I will," he promised. "And please tell Clara I love her and not to worry. I'm going to do everything I can to help."

Emilia was momentarily stunned. She knew Gabriel and Clara really liked each other, but she didn't know it went this deep.

"Uh...okay...I'll tell her," she mumbled.

"Thank you, Emi." He breathed a sigh of relief. "I'll call you again as soon as I have any information."

"Okay," she said, still taken aback by Gabriel saying he loved her sister.

"Bye," Gabriel said.

"Bye," Emilia said before stopping. "Gabriel! *Wait!*"

Silence.

"*Gabriel!*" She yelled.

"Did you say something?" she heard him say.

"Yes," she confirmed. "Stay close to Magnus if you can."

"Magnus?" he sounded confused.

"Yes, he's an ally," she told him. "I can't explain how or why right now but trust me. He's on our side."

"Uh...okay," Gabriel replied, still sounding quite baffled.

"Okay, that's all," Emilia said, glad she had given him that important bit of information.

When they hung up, Gabriel looked at the phone for several seconds and thought, *Magnus...an ally?* He certainly never saw that coming!

Days passed with no contact from Gabriel. Neither Clara nor Emilia dared call or text him in case the sound or light from the phone should alert anyone to the fact that he had a phone. Time passed slowly with both women growing increasingly concerned about his safety. Why wasn't he calling?

They discussed the situation with their parents one night over dinner and expressed their deep-rooted concerns about their friend.

"Maybe there's no reception where he is," Amalia suggested.

"That never even crossed my mind!" Emilia grumbled with chagrin.

"It makes sense though," Clara agreed. "Gabriel would never let us sit here and worry for this long. He must be going crazy himself not being able to contact us."

Emilia suddenly remembered the message Gabriel told her to give Clara.

"Oh, yeah...the last time I talked to him, he said to tell you he loves you and not to worry, that he's going to do everything he can to help," she said nonchalantly.

Clara stopped her fork halfway to her mouth and stared at Emilia openmouthed.

"He said what?" she whispered.

"He said not to worry," Emilia explained, trying to avoid the obvious elephant in the room. "He knows how you get."

Clara smiled and blushed.

"He said he loves me?"

Emilia rolled her eyes and nodded. "Yeah."

"Is this the same Gabriel I told you that you might run into again someday?" Amalia asked knowingly.

Clara blushed an even deeper shade of red, giggled, and nodded.

Amalia smiled and said simply, "Interesting."

"Yeah, yeah," Emilia said irritably. "Now, how can we find out what's going on where Prince Charming is? This is serious, you guys."

"Don't you have the tracking app on each other's phones?" Cauley asked.

Emilia and Clara looked at each other perplexed.

"No? I don't think so," they replied in unison.

"I think you do," he replied, "because I'm the one who set it up."

Emilia jumped up from her seat and yelled, "You did?!"

"Yes, I thought it was a neat safety feature that might come in handy someday."

"How do I find it?" she demanded.

"Here, let me see your phone," Cauley said as he held out his hand.

Emilia handed over her phone and watched as her father went to the Find My Friends app, tapped on it, and saw her contact photos appear for her parents, which were right on top of each other and her blue dot.

"Where's Clara?" she pressed.

"Hang on, pumpkin," he said calmly as he zoomed out the screen to cover a larger geographical area.

Pretty soon, Clara's icon showed up north of their location, but closer than the strawberry fields where Gabriel had last been working.

"I see him!" Emilia shouted.

"Where?" Clara jumped out of her seat, knocking the chair sideways onto the floor.

"There!" Emilia pointed.

"Where is that?" Clara yelled.

"I don't know," Cauley replied. "Let's see."

The ladies watched as he zoomed in on Clara's icon, showing Gabriel's location more clearly and the surrounding area. It looked like farmland, which they expected, but there didn't seem to be anything else around it for miles – not like the last place where he worked.

"He definitely has reception," Cauley commented.

"How can you tell?" Emilia asked.

"If he didn't, we wouldn't be able to find him on here," he explained.

"So why isn't he calling?" Clara moaned.

"I don't know, little fawn," Amalia said.

She wanted to tell Clara that she was sure Gabriel was fine, but it certainly wasn't looking too promising. Suddenly, Emilia's phone rang, and Clara's image popped up on the screen. All the Bennings were momentarily stunned, but Emilia quickly reached over and pressed the speaker button and said, "Gabriel?"

"Hi," he whispered.

"Are you okay?" Clara asked, concerned.

"I'm okay, but a lot of the others are not. Things are really bad here. You need to come soon!"

"Where are you?" Emilia asked.

"We're at the Rosales-Guermo Strawberry Farm in San Paolo," he breathed.

"When is the best time to come?" Emilia asked, taking notes on her napkin.

"Between 10 p.m. and 4 a.m."

"Dad, how soon can the teams be ready?" she asked Cauley.

"I can have them mobilized in as little as two hours," he replied with confidence.

"We'll be there in three hours," Emilia told Gabriel.

"Okay, thank you," he said gratefully. "What do you need me to do?"

"I'll call you when we get close so you can guide us to your exact location," she instructed.

"Okay."

"Be sure to keep the phone on silent so it doesn't make any noise," she advised. "You never know if one of the bosses might still be hanging around."

"How will I know when you're calling?" he wondered aloud.

"The phone will vibrate, so keep it on you," she said.

"Okay," he said. "Oh...gotta go."

He hung up before they could say anything more.

In the silence that followed, the Benning family took in the moment they all felt would be a turning point in their lives. Then, along with their father, Emilia and Clara devised a plan to gather evidence, exposing the human trafficking ring, and rescue Gabriel and the other victims from captivity. With Emilia leading the legal battle and Clara providing much-needed medical support, they were determined to bring hope and healing to those who had suffered so much.

ᛏᚾᚠᛒᛦᛦᚲᛟᚻᛗ

The moon hung low in the night sky, casting a soft glow over the sprawling farm. When they arrived at the edge of what appeared to be the farm property based on the Find My Friends app, Emilia placed the call to Gabriel.

"Hello?" Gabriel whispered.

"We're here," Emilia announced, "but we don't know where to go."

"What's around you?" Gabriel asked.

"There's a gate with a chain locking it closed, a fence on both sides with some brush growing, and a dirt road that runs under the gate. There's a very small building on the right on the other side of the gate, but everything else looks like fields."

"Okay," Gabriel began, "it sounds like you're at the east entrance. The building we're in is at the south of the property in the middle of the hills."

"How far is that?" Emilia was getting frustrated, since it was dark and she couldn't see anything further than about twenty feet with her flashlight.

"About a quarter mile," Gabriel replied.

"Oh, good Lord," she mumbled. "And where are the bosses?"

"They're in a house that's along the dirt road you're standing on."

"Gah!" Emilia almost screamed. "Is there another way to get to you without going by the boss's house?"

"Yeah, walk along the fence to the left. When you get to the end of the fence, it will be attached to the hillside. Climb over the fence and walk along the bottom of the hill until you get to our building. It'll be the only decent-sized building. The other ones are outhouses, so they'll be really small. It should take you about twenty minutes. I'll wait outside for you and keep an eye out for any movement from the bosses."

"Okay." Emilia hung up and turned to Clara. "Let's go."

The sisters, shrouded in darkness, crouched behind the fence as they walked, their hearts pounding with anticipation as they surveyed the layout of the farm.

"Keep your eyes peeled," Emilia whispered. "We need to find the victims and get them out of here safely."

Clara nodded, her eyes scanning the darkness for any sign of movement. Suddenly, she pointed toward a figure darting through the shadows.

"Look at that cat! It's huge!" she exclaimed in a hushed tone.

Emilia's eyes widened in shock as she recognized her cat, Tyrell, running along a dirt walkway, chasing a mouse.

"Tyrell!" she whispered demandingly, making kissing noises at the cat.

Clara's eyes bulged at her sister while she asked, "You *know* that cat?"

Emilia nodded her head and whispered, "Yes, that's *my* cat, Ty!"

"How did he get here?" Clara wondered aloud.

Emilia shrugged and made more kissing noises at Ty. Tyrell paused for a moment, swishing his tail in acknowledgment before darting off into the darkness once more.

They reached the end of the fence and climbed over it, following the bottom of the hill as Gabriel had instructed. The terrain was more difficult in this area, which slowed their pace quite a bit, but the cloud cover parted allowing the moonlight to see where they were going...and their intended destination.

"I see it!" Clara whispered loudly.

They heard a whistle and looked up to see Gabriel waving at them not even ten feet away. They waved back and hurried their pace.

Suddenly, a voice broke through the silence. It was Ángela, a young woman with a gift for sensing things before they happen.

"Andarta is coming to save us!" Ángela exclaimed, her eyes wide with conviction.

The other victims exchanged uncertain glances, their brows furrowed in confusion.

"Andarta? Who's Andarta?" they whispered amongst themselves, thinking Ángela had finally succumbed to the madness of their captivity.

Before anyone could respond, they were shocked to see Gabriel enter the building with two women they had never seen before.

"Do they speak English?" Emilia asked Gabriel.

"Not enough to understand what you're saying," he replied.

"Tell them they need to get up and go with us right now," she ordered.

"These women are here to help us. We all need to go with them right now," Gabriel said to the half-awake farm workers in Spanish.

"Where will they take us?" Kahlo asked with concern.

Gabriel looked at Emilia for an answer.

"Somewhere safe," she replied with conviction.

Gabriel relayed her answer in Spanish.

"And then what?" an elderly woman asked as Gabriel translated.

"And then we will help you get your lives back," Clara promised.

"But there's no time to talk," Emilia interjected. "We need to leave *now*!"

Gabriel, Emilia, and Clara all helped gather the men, women, and children and hurry them out of the shack that had been their home for the last several months. They guided them along the foot of the hills toward the fence from which they had come, knowing Cauley's teams would be waiting on the other side to help the victims.

As they ran, Emilia called Cauley's phone and announced they were on their way and would be at the fence where it meets the hill in a matter of minutes.

"We're waiting for you, pumpkin," he said.

Gabriel was leading the charge and helping people over the fence and into the hands of the social workers or paramedics, depending on each victims 'needs.

As Clara, Emilia, and the last handful of escapees were nearing the fence line, they were spotted by one of the bosses, who let out a shout of alarm. In an instant, chaos erupted as the bosses jumped into their trucks, guns blazing as they opened fire on the fleeing victims.

Kahlo fell to the ground, his body limp and lifeless, as Coleta was struck by the speeding truck and left lying in the dirt, blood pooling around her.

But Clara and Emilia refused to give up hope. With steely resolve, they guided the remaining victims to temporary safety, their hearts heavy with grief for those they had lost.

As they returned to retrieve Coleta, they were met with a surprising sight. Leilani, a twelve-year-old girl with a spirit as fierce as her Hawaiian namesake, stood before them, her eyes blazing with defiance.

"The bosses are gone now," she declared, a triumphant smile gracing her lips.

Emilia wasted no time in calling her father for help, and within minutes the area was swarming with vehicles. With their combined efforts, they were able to transport the victims to safety and bring an end to the reign of terror that had plagued the strawberry fields for far too long. And as they drove away from the fields, the victims safe at last, Emilia and Clara knew their work was just beginning. They also knew that as long as they stood together, they could overcome any obstacle and fight for justice for those who had been silenced.

As the days passed in the aftermath, the sisters worked tirelessly to gather evidence and build their case against the crime ring. With each new piece of information they uncovered, their resolve only grew stronger, fueled by the knowledge that they were fighting for justice and the chance to give Gabriel and the other victims a second chance at life.

Aside from losing Kahlo and Coleta, Ángela had gone missing from the group of rescued victims and was nowhere to be found.

Did they miss one? Emilia wondered, concerned that Ángela had been held back by one of her captors.

CHAPTER 34

ANCIENT GUARDIANS

In the realm of Asgard, the great hall of Valhalla shimmered with ethereal light as the gods and goddesses gathered to observe the mortal realm below. From their celestial vantage point, they watched as Emilia and Clara, two mortal sisters, embarked on a daring mission to rescue victims of forced labor from the clutches of their captors.

Vahagn, the mighty god of thunder, gazed down at the mortal world with a furrowed brow.

"These mortal women show great courage and compassion," he remarked, his voice booming. "Perhaps it is time we intervene and grant them the power of the gods to aid them in their quest."

Hermes, the cunning trickster god, smirked mischievously as he lounged on his throne.

"Ah, but which of us shall bestow our blessings upon them?" he mused. "Surely, they would benefit from the power of the mighty Vahagn or the wisdom of Gungnir."

But it was Kara, the goddess of love and war, who spoke next, her voice calm and measured.

"No, my brethren," she said, her gaze piercing as she looked upon the mortal sisters below. "Emilia is not ready yet."

The other gods and goddesses exchanged puzzled glances, their curiosity piqued by Kara's cryptic words.

"But why, Kara?" asked Gungnir. "She shows great promise and has already done much to help those in need. Why deny her the power of the gods?"

He gazed down at the mortal world with a furrowed brow while the goddess paused a moment to gather her thoughts.

"I have lived with her for three years now. She is very stubborn, and her passion to help others consumes her to the point where she doesn't always look at the big picture before acting."

She looked up to see a few of the other gods and goddesses nodding in agreement.

"During her first rescue attempt, both the victims and the perpetrators had already fled before she arrived."

Kara noticed a few more of her fellows agree as they had all watched it happen from their realm.

"Her last attempt was partially successful, but the victims who were lost during the fray have haunted her ever since," she explained. "No matter how much power we give her from our world, it's not going to change the fact that her mortal heart is not yet equipped to withstand such great loss."

There was silence all around as the gods and goddesses pondered the situation and began thinking of ways to make it work without destroying the humanity in Emilia.

Kara continued, "Emilia already knows she is the chosen body for Andarta, and she has been preparing for this since she was ten years old."

"And what of Clara?" Gungnir inquired. "Does she know she is the chosen body for Eir?"

Kara nodded.

Hermes giggled and asked, "And does she know she needs to go to the Hall of Souls and give up her human form?"

Kara nodded slowly, then said, "They do. They both know. Clara was ready when she was younger, but she has had such a successful career as a nurse on Earth that it would be devastating to everyone who knows her. It is my belief that Clara is no longer ready for the Hall of Souls."

"Kara," Mihr said softly, "very few are ready for the Hall of Souls until they get there. Perhaps if we bring them back together immediately after Clara's human body dies, so they'll know they can still see each other..."

"Emilia is not ready for that," Kara stated firmly.

"What do you think would happen if Clara died soon?" Gungnir asked Kara.

"I think Emilia would lose her mind from heartbreak," she said matter-of-factly. "Those two mean everything to each other."

Gungnir sighed, "I think you've gotten too close to your charge and it's affecting your ability to see things how they should be. This problem with the humans is getting worse every day. Andarta and Eir are becoming more frenzied as each day goes by, and they are left with their hands tied."

"But the twins..." Kara fretted.

"Kara," Hermes began, "the twins will still be together, but not in the same way they are right now. Andarta and Eir *need* to intercede here. It's their purpose, and they've been held back for far too long. Emilia and Clara have known about this for fifteen years. If they're not prepared by now, they never will be. It has to happen so things can be set right in the human realm. We, as gods, cannot let our own feelings interfere with the greater good."

Magnus slapped his thigh and said, "I think that's the most brilliant thing I've ever heard you say, Hermes. Well done!"

Hermes continued, "Or we can do things Kara's way and watch the whole world go to Hel."

"And...there it is." Magnus smirked. "He's back."

The other gods rolled their eyes and chuckled.

Gungnir roused himself and said, "Andarta was revered as the protector of the innocent and the champion of justice. Her name is still whispered in reverence by mortals and immortals alike, yet her protection hasn't been invoked for over eleven centuries."

"Has it been that long?" Hermes asked with genuine surprise.

"It has." Gungnir nodded. "At one time, her domain was vast and varied, encompassing the wild forests, the raging rivers, and the windswept plains. She was the embodiment of strength and courage, her presence felt in every leaf that rustled in the breeze and every animal that roamed the Earth...including the humans. We are all her allies."

Everyone nodded in agreement.

Kara added, "I have long admired Andarta's strength and bravery, and we've become very close. We fought side by side in countless battles, our combined strength and wisdom ensuring victory for whatever cause we were fighting for at the time. She is more than a comrade at arms. She is a kindred spirit, a soulmate whose presence brings me comfort and solace."

"Where are they anyway?" Anahit asked. "Andarta and Eir, shouldn't they be here for this?"

Kara nodded and explained, "Yes, from our point of view, but as Gungnir explained, they are anxious to get going on this human trafficking problem. They both feel they need to stay close to Emilia and Clara so not a moment is wasted when their time comes to take over. I'm afraid that fate has intervened. I have felt my bond with Andarta be tested in ways I've never imagined."

"How so?" Gungnir asked with concern.

"Andarta had a vision of a mortal woman, a not-so-humble lawyer, who possessed the potential to become a true champion of justice," she began. "She knew Emilia was destined for greatness, but she also knew the path ahead would be fraught with danger and uncertainty. She turned to me for guidance and assistance, seeking my wisdom on the matter."

"And what did you tell her?" Mihr wondered aloud.

"I didn't tell her anything at first," Kara explained. "I listened to her, but my heart is very heavy with concern for the mortal Emilia. I didn't know what to tell her, so instead I asked her what she proposed we should do."

The other gods were leaning forward, taking in Kara's every word.

"She told me she believes Emilia is the key to bringing about change in the mortal realm, but she is not yet ready to wield the power of the gods."

Kara's brow furrowed in confusion as she continued, "I told her that surely Emilia's heart is pure and her intentions noble, so why deny her the power to make a difference in the world?"

Kara saw the other gods nodding in agreement, anxious to hear the rest of her story.

"She told me there are forces at play here that I do not understand. Emilia's heart is pure, but her soul is not yet ready to bear the burden of godhood. It is still young and untested, and she must face her trials and tribulations before she can truly embrace her destiny."

Kara sighed, her heart heavy.

"I told her I would trust her judgment but that I would also stand by Emilia's side, guiding and protecting her every step of the way."

Gungnir frowned in frustration, his grip tightening on his mighty Krighammer.

"But we cannot stand idly by and watch as mortals suffer," he declared, his voice resonating with thunderous authority. "God created them to be His companions, and He created us to watch over and protect them from themselves."

The goddess's gaze softened as she placed a hand on Gungnir's arm.

"Fear not, my brother," she said gently. "Emilia may not possess the power of the gods, but she is guided by something far greater...the strength of her own spirit and the love in her heart."

As the gods and goddesses continued to watch, Emilia and Clara emerged victorious, their compassion and bravery shining like beacons in the darkness. And though they did not possess the power of the gods, their actions spoke volumes, inspiring hope and courage in all who witnessed their deeds.

As Kara looked upon them with pride, she knew that one day, when the time was right, Emilia would indeed be ready to embrace her destiny as a true hero, with or without the power of the gods by her side.

CHAPTER 35

GAME CHANGER

Over the next several months, Clara oversaw medical care for the victims rescued from the strawberry fields and ensured they were in as close to perfect health as they could be before turning them over to social services for readjustment back into normal society.

Emilia continued to work on building the legal case against the human traffickers who had enslaved the rescued victims, but it was turning out to be a much more vastly interwoven network than she expected. It seemed that every piece of evidence she came across exposed ten more alleys she needed to explore.

Leandro Mammon's name was a common thread throughout all of them. Interestingly enough, he didn't have a criminal record, not even a parking ticket. He also didn't have a registered firearm, but Gabriel said he had a Desert Eagle – one of the most powerful handguns ever made – and he personally saw him use it to kill a teenage boy. Something in her gut told her that Leandro was the lynchpin in what was turning out to be a rather extensive human trafficking ring. Now she had to figure out a way to prove it. Her phone rang, distracting her from her project.

"Hello?" she asked irritably.

"I need to see you in my office," Judge Skarsgaard said and then hung up.

What could be going on? She wondered as she gathered her notepad and pen before heading down the hall to his office.

"Go on in." His secretary waved her in before she could even say hello.

This must be serious, she thought.

"Hey, kiddo, have a seat," the judge said as she entered the pristine office.

She took a seat in her usual spot and noticed he already had her Fireball on the rocks ready on the table in front of her. Emilia picked it up and took a large gulp to help calm her nerves.

The judge came over with his own drink in hand and sat on the chair opposite her and said, "I know you've been working hard on the strawberry field case, but there's something you and Clara need to take care of immediately. That case can wait, since those victims are now in safe hands."

Emilia's heart began pounding, but she said nothing.

"There are many people who are being held in a warehouse downtown and used for slave labor to make clothing," he explained.

"Slave labor?" Emilia questioned aloud.

"Yes, meaning they don't get paid. They're not allowed to leave. They're basically prisoners who are forced to work," he clarified.

Emilia gulped and whispered, "Prisoners..."

"Prisoners who have done nothing wrong except fall into the wrong hands," he explained. "We need you to get them out and into the right hands."

"When and where?" she asked, already starting to take notes.

"As soon as possible. It's a building downtown that is referred to by the locals as Jarrods Harrods, but it's not a store at all. It's legally considered an abandoned warehouse, but it's not abandoned. It's off the books, so to speak."

"Why do they call it Jarrods Harrods?"

"Because it's on Jarrods Street, and Jarrods rhymes with Harrods. Like I said, it's a local term. It has nothing to do with the Harrods store in London."

232

"Do they have security or any bosses around?" Emilia inquired.

"You can assume they do."

"How do we get around that?" she asked.

"I'll arrange backup to handle that part," he explained. "I need you and Clara to get the victims out."

"Okay, I'll get in touch with Clara and see when she can do this," Emilia said.

"Call her now," he ordered.

Emilia faltered, remembering she had left her phone in her office.

"Here." The judge handed her his phone.

She took it and dialed Clara's number, which immediately went to voicemail. Emilia began leaving a message when the judge took the phone away from her, hung up the call, and redialed the number. Again, it went to voicemail.

"Is she at work?" he asked.

Emilia shrugged and said, "Probably."

The judge smirked and dialed the phone again. They both heard it ring twice before a man's voice answered. Emilia immediately recognized Gabriel's voice.

She was stunned when she heard her own voice come out of the judge's mouth and say, "Hi, Gabe! Is Clara with you?"

"Hey, Emi! Yeah, she's right here. Hang on," he said cheerfully.

As the judge handed his phone back to her, Emilia's eyes felt like they were going to pop out of her head. How did he know Clara was with Gabriel, who now had his own phone? And how did he know Gabriel's phone number? And how did he make his voice sound like hers?

"Hi, Emi!" Clara trilled.

"Uh...hi," she said meekly.

"What's up? Are you okay?" Clara asked. "You sound weird."

The judge gave her a warning look that snapped her out of her reverie.

"I'm fine." She cleared her throat. "We have another rescue situation that is rather urgent. Can you come with me tonight?"

"Tonight?" Clara sounded disappointed. "Can it wait until tomorrow night? We're kind of celebrating something over here."

"What could you possibly be celebrating that is more important than what—"

"I'm pregnant," Clara said.

Emilia looked at the judge in astonishment. What the hell was she supposed to do now?

She held out her hands in defeat, pleading for guidance.

"Clara," the judge said, in his own voice now. "This is Judge Skarsgaard. Congratulations on your pregnancy! That's wonderful news. Emilia really does need your help with this though. There are a lot of injured people at this warehouse – many of them young children – and she won't be able to take care of them and rescue the healthy victims all by herself. Do you think you can help us out here? I'm going to have all the backup ready ahead of time."

"Oh!" Clara exclaimed. "Judge Skarsgaard! Sorry, I didn't know you were there. Did you say there are young children there?"

Emilia immediately felt remorse for not mentioning his presence to Clara, especially considering the very personal news she spilled.

"Yes, and I'm sorry. I happened to walk into Emilia's office, and she had you on speaker," he lied.

"Thank you," Emilia mouthed to him.

He nodded.

Clara continued, "It's not that I don't want to help, but Gabriel and I were going to Le Meadows to get married tonight. I really don't want to be pregnant and unmarried."

The judge said, "I'll make a deal with you. You and Gabriel come to my office. I'll marry you right here. Emilia can be your witness, and then you can both help her with the rescue tonight. Will that work for you? Then you can still go to Le Meadows for a honeymoon when it's all over."

"Oh my God, that would be amazing!" Clara squealed, and they could hear Gabriel laughing in agreement in the background.

"Great! Can you be here around five o'clock?" he asked congenially.

"Yes, we'll be there," Clara confirmed gleefully. "Thank you so much!"

"You're welcome, dear," he said with a smile and hung up.

"I can't believe she's pregnant," Emilia moaned.

"Why not?" he asked. "You knew they were in love. They're both adults. It was bound to happen sooner or later."

Emilia sighed. "I suppose. It never crossed my mind."

"Maybe it would if you ever got out yourself," he admonished. "How about if we make it truly special and include your parents in this little wedding and get a cake?"

She rolled her eyes, shook her head, and chuckled at the whole idea.

"You're too much, Judge." She smiled.

ᛏᚢᛒᚱᚱᚲᚱ�householdM

Emilia made the dreaded calls to both of her parents, who for some reason were thrilled at Clara's news and the impending wedding. They arrived at the law office at half-past four with a wedding cake, champagne, and gifts for the bride and groom.

When Clara and Gabriel arrived at five o'clock, *they* were the ones who were surprised at their own wedding. As thrilled as they were at becoming parents, they were dreading having the talk with Amalia and Cauley, so Emilia had actually done them a huge favor by telling them on their behalf. Everyone seemed very happy for them, which made the celebration even more heartwarming and perfect.

Gabriel almost wished his parents could have been there too but then quickly remembered how they had so easily given him up when he was a child and never reached out to him again...not even to see if he was okay. The Bennings were the only people since then who made him feel like he was part of a real family, and now he would be. It really was a dream come true. A dream he had never dared to dream before.

The ceremony itself was plain and simple, but emotions ran high and all the women were crying happy tears before it was finished. Gabriel let a few tears slip past his eyelashes too, but Cauley and Judge Skarsgaard kept theirs in check.

After a quick bite of cake and champagne toasts, which Clara abstained from, it was back to business.

"Okay, Emilia, Mr. and Mrs. Contreras, I need your attention over here," the judge announced as he unrolled a blueprint of the Jarrods Harrods building.

Once gathered around the table, they all looked at the large sheet of paper with squares and measurements drawn on it. The judge pointed to four squares next to each other.

"These are the rooms where we think the victims are kept," he explained. "They are locked from the outside so people on the inside cannot open them, but there are windows high up on each wall that exit to the alley here."

He pointed to the alley along the outside of the building wall.

"How high are the windows?" Emilia asked.

The judge sighed and looked at her shaking his head.

"We don't know. They can't be more than ten feet high, because the ceiling itself is ten feet high."

"If the doors are locked on the outside, can't we open them from the outside?" Clara asked.

"Possibly," he responded. "It depends on what kind of locks they're using."

"How can we find out?" Emilia asked, getting a blank stare from the judge.

"We have to go in, don't we?"

He nodded, his mouth in a grim line.

"Is there something we can use to quickly pick the locks in case we can't turn a deadbolt?"

Instead of answering, they watched the judge walk to a painting on the wall behind his desk and place his hand on the canvas. They saw the canvas vibrate slowly and make a chirping noise and then go back to its original appearance. He turned around and came back to the group and opened his hand. Inside was a small, amber marble.

"If you can't open a lock, put this on the floor in front of the door, and say 'opna,'" he instructed.

"Opna," Emilia and Clara repeated.

He nodded and then placed the marble in Emilia's hand.

"Time to go," the judge said.

ᛏᚾᚠᛒᛉᛉᚳᛉᚺᛗ

The moon hung high in the night sky, casting an eerie glow over the desolate warehouse where Emilia, Clara, and Gabriel crept cautiously through the shadows. Their mission was clear...to rescue the victims who were being held captive within its walls.

Emilia's heart pounded with a mixture of fear and determination as she led Gabriel and Clara through the maze of corridors, their footsteps muffled by the silence of the night. They knew they were walking into danger, but their resolve remained unwavering as they pressed on, driven by a fierce determination to help those in need.

Surprisingly, all the doors they came across were either wide open or unlocked. No form of security appeared either, which Emilia found a bit unnerving.

"We need to find them quickly," Clara whispered. "This seems way too easy, and the longer they're in there, the more danger they're in."

Emilia nodded in agreement, her eyes scanning the darkness for any sign of movement. Slowly, as her eyes adjusted to the lack of light, she saw one, then two, then several human shapes sitting and lying down on the floor of the open space before her.

"I see them!" she whispered excitedly to Clara.

"Hey!" she called to gain the attention of the people in the warehouse.

"They're here!" Ángela shouted gleefully to the others.

Before anyone could respond, their attention was drawn to a distant rumbling sound. It was the unmistakable sound of approaching footsteps, growing louder and louder with each passing moment.

Clara's eyes widened in alarm.

"We need to hide!" she whispered urgently, pulling Emilia and Gabriel into a nearby alcove.

But it was too late. Before they could react, the warehouse door burst open, flooding the room with blinding light as a group of armed men stormed inside, their faces contorted with rage.

The chaos that ensued was swift and brutal. Clara fought valiantly, her courage shining through as she defended herself and the other victims with every ounce of strength she possessed.

Amidst the chaos and despair, a miracle occurred. Tyrell emerged from the shadows, his eyes blazing with an otherworldly light as he stood beside her, his fur bristling with newfound power.

Emilia's breath caught in her throat, and she watched in awe as Tyrell transformed before her eyes. His gentle features contorted into something altogether more primal, his growl deepening into a menacing roar as he unleashed his newfound strength against their assailants. Tyrell was now at least eight feet tall and sprouted a thick, whip-like tail that he used to knock the men away who were attempting to grab the victims Emilia had come to rescue.

"Leandro!" a man yelled. "Look out!"

Emilia looked over at the man, Leandro, and watched as Tyrell's tail whipped toward him in a fury, but right before Ty's tail should have made contact, Leandro smiled menacingly at Emilia and vanished into thin air.

In that moment, Emilia knew there were other forces at work. Evil forces...something she had never encountered previously, and she was stunned. She had no idea how to combat such foes. No wonder there were so many human trafficking victims! They weren't taken by regular people...at least not this group.

Emilia suddenly realized why she and Clara needed the goddesses to guide their movements. They were up against something far beyond anything they could imagine, and it terrified her.

Who...or *what*...was the entity the man called Leandro?

"Emilia!" Clara cried out. "I need your help here!"

Snapped out of her momentary shock, Emilia yelled, "Coming!"

When she found Clara amidst the chaos, she was bent over a young girl lying on the ground. She noticed small pools of blood seeping through the girl's clothing, slowly growing larger as the girl bled to death from multiple gunshot wounds as Clara tried to stop them by applying pressure.

"What do you need me to do?" Emilia yelled desperately over the sound of screams and gunshots, as she saw the girl's flesh fade to a sickly white.

"Put her out of her misery!" Clara sobbed, tears pouring down her face and dripping off her chin onto the girl's motionless form.

Again, Emilia was stunned. Her beloved sister was asking her to murder someone. How could she do that? They were here to *rescue* these people!

"I can't do that, Clara," she stated firmly.

The girl suddenly cried out in pain, looked at Emilia, and begged, "Please help me!"

"I don't know what to do!" Emilia began crying, torn between wanting the girl to be better again,_and wanting her trauma to end.

"*Emilia!*" Clara snapped. "She will end up in the Hall of Souls by the end of the day. How long are we going to let her suffer?"

"I can't kill a good person." Emilia looked at her sister. "There must be some other way to get her through this."

"What's your name?" Clara asked the girl.

"Ángela," she gasped then coughed. "I knew you were coming, but they didn't believe me."

Clara and Emilia looked at each other in surprise. How did she know they were coming?

"What? How did you know?" Emilia asked Ángela.

"I have a gift...but I can't explain it now.. There's no time," she wheezed.

Emilia continued watching the girl talk and was amazed that she was able to communicate so well considering she was at death's door.

"You have to find Kahlo's paintings!" Ángela continued.

"Kahlo?" Clara was bewildered.

She assumed Ángela was in the process of dying and was saying random things as people sometimes did when they were moving from one plane to another.

"He painted pictures of the bosses when we were here before...and covered them up so they wouldn't be seen," Ángela coughed, her breathing getting weaker. "You have to find them and get them to the authorities….so they know who to look for."

"Are the paintings in here or in a different building?"

"Here, under the—" Ángela spoke her final words.

"Under *what*?" Emilia demanded of Ángela.

Clara sighed and murmured, "She's gone."

"Gone?" Emilia. "What do you mean?"

She couldn't comprehend what had happened.

Clara looked Emilia in the eyes and said, "She's gone to the Hall of Souls."

Emilia cried out in anguish as rage took over every fiber of her being.

"*Nooooo!*" she screamed. "Who did this to her?"

"I did." She heard a smug voice behind her.

Emilia whipped around and saw Leandro standing there with snakelike eyes.

"And now I'm going to do it to you too."

He smiled as he aimed his Desert Eagle at Emilia's forehead.

Before she could even think about how to deal with this new threat, Leandro disappeared.

Confusion reigned in Emilia's mind. She fully expected to have her head blown off, but now the threat was gone, at least for the moment. She looked over at Clara who was in shock herself.

"That man disappeared into thin air," Clara whispered in awe as she reached out to touch the area where he had been standing.

"I know," Emilia confirmed. "I saw him do that a few minutes ago too."

"I have a feeling we're not dealing with normal humans, Emilia," Clara stated.

Emilia nodded her head in agreement.

"No, there are other forces at play here."

"We need the goddesses," Clara said.

"We do," Emilia nodded.

Suddenly, they heard several people screaming across the cavernous space and more gunshots.

"Let's go!" Emilia demanded.

As they went running toward the heart-wrenching sounds of mortal destruction, Emilia felt a bullet whiz by her ear...so close she could feel its heat. She spun her head around to make sure that Clara was not hit, when she saw Gabriel stumbling after them, holding his stomach where the bullet had found its mark.

"*Gabriel!*" she screamed in horror and turned to go help him.

"*No!*" Clara yelled at Emilia. "I've got Gabriel — you go and help the others."

Shaken and numbed by the sight of her brother-in-law's condition, Emilia took off running toward the massacre that was surely happening on the other side of the building, based on the sounds she was hearing.

Noticing one of the men shooting at the victims, with his back to her, she quickly scanned the space around her for a weapon. Within seconds, she saw a long sword lying on the ground at her feet. She picked it up, not noticing the glowing colors that appeared on the sword as she ran it through the man's neck at the base, instantly severing his spinal cord.

As he crumpled to the ground, she quickly maneuvered herself between the victims and the other two shooters who had surrounded the victims, forcing them to back into a corner. The shooters laughed at her and took aim.

Emilia, grabbed the blade of the sword in her other hand and held it horizontally, bracing for the next bullets to come her way. She heard the simultaneous shots from the men's guns and waited for the force of the bullets.

But the bullets ricocheted off the blade and found their marks...into the heads of both shooters. Emilia and the remaining victims watched in stunned relief as the shooters were instantly killed from their own bullets and dropped on the floor, pools of blood pouring from their heads.

"Let's go!" she shouted to the people standing against the wall.

They didn't need to be told twice. Everyone followed Emilia out of the closest exit as she yelled over her shoulder, "Clara, I got them! I'm taking these people outside to wait for backup."

"Okay," Clara yelled back. "Gabriel's really hurt, so I'm going to stay here with him! Send the paramedics in here when they arrive!"

"You got it!" Emilia guided the rescued victims out into the quiet, clear night.

She grabbed her phone and called her father.

"Ready?" he asked anxiously.

"Yes," Emilia replied, "I have some of them outside with me, but Clara and Gabriel are still inside the warehouse. Gabriel got shot, but he's still alive. We need paramedics to check on him, and the police need to search the warehouse for any victims we missed."

"Hang tight," Cauley commanded. "Stay out of sight until you see our vehicles."

"Okay," Emilia replied shakily.

Now that it was all over, the events she had witnessed and participated in were whirling around in her mind.

ᛏᚾᚠᛒᛉᛉᚲᛉᛁᛗ

Shortly, the rescue vehicles arrived, and the grounds were soon swarming with the SWAT Team, police, paramedics and detectives. Several armored vans arrived that would be used to house the victims until they could safely be taken to hospitals for treatment.

She watched with relief as Gabriel was brought out of the warehouse on a gurney, surrounded by paramedics who had hooked him up to life-saving machines and tubing.

Emilia ran over to him and asked the attending EMT, "How is he? Is he going to be okay?"

The EMT removed a lollipop from his mouth and said, "He'll be fine. He needs to be patched up and monitored for a while, but it doesn't look like any major organs were hit."

She closed her eyes and breathed, "Thank God!"

"Emilia!" Cauley called from across the parking lot.

They ran toward each other and embraced, relief flowing through them both at seeing each other unscathed. At seeing her father, the one she had always turned to for advice and safety, Emilia broke down in tears.

"Dad, it was so awful!" Emilia cried. "I don't know how people can do this to other people. You should have seen how these people were living. It was horrible!"

"I know," Cauley agreed. "You did good, and I am beyond proud of you and Clara."

Emilia smiled at his praise.

"You should have seen her. She was so amazing, and talk about grace under pressure. I don't know how she did it."

They both laughed.

"Where is Clara?" Cauley asked. "I haven't seen her yet."

Emilia glanced over her shoulder.

"She's around. I'm surprised she didn't come out with Gabriel though."

Yeah, she thought, *why didn't she come out with Gabriel? Maybe there were other victims in need of her help still.*

"I'll go find her," Emilia offered.

"Okay, I'll be here," Cauley replied gratefully. "I have to stay here until the last person has left since I'm the one who sent out the invitations to this party."

Emilia went to each of the armored vans first to see if her sister was in one of them. No Clara.

She next went to the warehouse they had escaped from, back to where she had last seen her with Gabriel. All she found was an empty space with various spots and pools of blood and a dirty blanket. She picked up the blanket in a vain hope that Clara was underneath it.

No Clara, but she did see what looked like painted portraits that were part of the floor itself.

These must be the paintings Ángela told us about, she thought and took pictures of them with her cell phone. When she had finished taking pictures of all the paintings she could find, she continued her search for Clara. The warehouse was so quiet she could hear her heart beating in her chest.

"Clara!" she yelled.

Silence.

Beginning to panic, Emilia began running through every hallway and room in the warehouse, looking for her twin. Her other half was nowhere to be found.

"Clara!" Tears began forming in her eyes, blurring her vision as she ran.

She felt something against her leg and saw Tyrell. Giving him a gentle pat, she told him, "I can't find Clara. Do you know where she is?"

Tyrell settled down at her feet and gave a sad meow.

Certain that Tyrell would lead her to Clara, his lack of movement told her otherwise.

She ran back outside to her father and said, "I can't find her!"

"What do you mean?" Cauley's blood froze at Emilia's announcement.

"Clara!" he yelled and ran to the SWAT captain and explained that his other daughter was missing.

"We'll find her, Judge," he said tersely. "Wait here."

He handed Cauley a walkie-talkie so they could keep in touch. They spent the next two hours scouring every square inch of the warehouse, the farm property, and the surrounding neighborhood, but Clara was nowhere to be found.

"I'm not leaving until we find her," Emilia stated, crossing her arms for emphasis.

"She's not here, Emilia," her father sobbed. "Staying here won't do any good."

"How can you give up on her so quickly?" Emilia shouted.

"We need to let the authorities take it from here," he explained. "There's nothing we can do. The only thing we can do is take comfort in the fact that nobody has come across her body, which means she's still alive."

"THEN WHERE IS SHE?" Emilia yelled in anguish as she crumpled to the ground, wrapping her arms around her knees and rocking back and forth.

Cauley didn't respond but gently put his arm around Emilia's shoulders, helped her stand, and nudged her toward his vehicle.

"I don't know, but we will find her. I promise," her father said comfortingly, even though his own doubts were making it difficult to keep down the panic at Clara's disappearance.

Emilia was completely enveloped in grief and couldn't think of anything outside of how brutalized and defeated she felt.

ᛏᚾᚦᛒᚱᚱᚲᚱᚢᛗ

Once again, the gods and goddesses convened in the hallowed halls of Asgaard, their expressions grave as they gathered to discuss the fate of the mortal woman, Emilia, who had suffered a great loss. Kara stood at the center of the gathering, her eyes ablaze with determination as she addressed her fellow deities.

"My brethren," she began, her voice resonating with authority, "we have witnessed Emilia's deep grief and anger in the wake of Clara's disappearance."

Gungnir nodded solemnly, his one eye gleaming with wisdom.

"Indeed, Kara," he replied. "Emilia's heart is filled with righteous fury and her spirit burns with the desire for justice. Aye, Kara, Emilia's courage and determination in the face of such tragedy are a testament to her strength and resilience."

Hermes, the cunning one, spoke, "And yet, are we certain that Emilia is ready to bear the mantle of Andarta? She is but a mortal woman, and the burden of godhood is not one to be taken lightly."

Kara's brow furrowed in thought.

"I understand your concern, Hermes," she replied. "But Emilia's grief has awakened a power within her that cannot be ignored. She is ready to embrace her destiny as Andarta, the protector of the innocent and the champion of justice."

The other gods and goddesses exchanged uncertain glances, their expressions reflecting their own doubts and fears. But Kara remained steadfast in her conviction, her faith in Emilia unwavering.

"Trust in me, my brethren," Kara said. "Emilia's journey may be fraught with danger and uncertainty, but I believe she now has the strength and courage to overcome any obstacle that stands in her way. Together, we shall guide her on the path to her true destiny."

CHAPTER 36

PREPARATION FOR A GODDESS

Emilia's heart felt like a heavy stone in her chest as she stood before Clara's bed, eyes blurred with tears that refused to stop flowing. The sun hung low in the sky, casting a golden hue over the room as Emilia struggled to come to terms with the loss of her beloved twin sister.

Clara's disappearance had left a gaping hole in Emilia's heart, a wound that refused to heal no matter how hard she tried to ignore it. The pain was overwhelming, suffocating, consuming her every waking moment with its relentless grip. As the days passed, Emilia's grief turned to anger, a burning fire that raged within her every passing moment. She seethed with fury at the thought of Clara being stolen away by heartless human traffickers, their cruelty leaving behind a trail of devastation in its wake. What terrified her the most, and what she tried not to think of, was that Clara may have been taken by Leandro himself.

Amidst the anger and despair, Emilia's mind began to unravel, her thoughts enveloped by a darkness that threatened to consume her whole. Sleep became elusive, her dreams haunted by the specter of Clara, her waking hours plagued by nightmares that left her gasping for breath. It was during one such sleepless night that Emilia finally broke down, her sobs echoing through the empty halls of her parents' home as she sat in the kitchen clutching a framed photograph of Clara to her chest. The weight of her grief felt unbearable, crushing her beneath its suffocating embrace as she cried out for the sister she had lost.

The following morning, Emilia found herself still sitting at the kitchen table, staring blankly at a cup of untouched coffee as her parents hovered anxiously nearby. They had watched in helpless anguish as their daughter's mental state deteriorated in the aftermath of the last rescue plan, their own hearts breaking at the sight of her pain.

"Emilia, sweetheart," Amalia began, her voice gentle as she reached out to touch her daughter's trembling hand, "we're so worried about you. You haven't been yourself since Clara disappeared."

"She didn't *disappear*, Mom!" she spat. "Nobody has proven it yet, but I know she was taken from us by that evil *filth!*"

Amalia's eyes filled with tears, her heart breaking anew at the reminder of the senseless tragedy that had befallen their family.

"I know, Emilia," she whispered, her voice choked with emotion. "But we have to stay strong for each other...for Clara's sake."

Emilia shook her head, her anger boiling over as she pushed herself away from the table, her hands clenched into fists at her sides.

"No, Mom," she said, her voice trembling with rage. "I won't rest until those responsible are brought to justice. I'll make them pay. I swear it."

And with that solemn vow, Emilia stormed out of the kitchen, her heart heavy with grief and determination as she embarked on a quest for vengeance that would lead her down a dark and dangerous path. Emilia knew she would not rest until justice was served and her sister was found.

ᛏᚹᛒᚱᚱᚲᚱᛉᛗ

One portentous night, as Emilia was asleep in her bed, she was suddenly surrounded by a blinding light. It was so bright she had to shield her eyes from its brilliance. When she opened them again, she found herself standing in a vast, otherworldly realm, the air thick with the scent of ancient magic. Before her stood a figure cloaked in shimmering armor, eyes ablaze with power as they gazed upon her with a mixture of awe and reverence. She noticed Kara immediately.

"Kara?" she asked with confusion.

Kara, the goddess of love and war, stepped forward, her eyes ablaze with power as she addressed Emilia.

"Emilia, daughter of Midgard," Kara intoned, her voice echoing through the room, "you have been chosen to carry the mantle of Andarta, the guardian of the innocent and the harbinger of justice. With these powers, you shall defend the weak, protect the helpless, and bring hope to those who have none."

"When will I get my powers?" Emilia pleaded with desperation in her voice.

"When Andarta sees that you are ready," Kara explained.

"I'm ready *now*!" Emilia yelled and began crying. "I need to avenge my sister, and I can't do it without Andarta's help."

"We know," Kara said soothingly.

"We?" Emilia was confused. "Who's we?"

"The lesser gods and goddesses, like Andarta, Eir, me, and the others. We've been watching you for a long time and waiting for the right moment," she said.

"When will the right moment be, Kara?" Emilia sobbed. "I can't take this much longer. The despondency is making life unbearable. I can't do anything except grieve for Clara and her unborn baby."

Kara nodded.

"I understand. I do. But for you to handle the powers of Andarta, you need to move beyond your own feelings about Clara and the baby. Andarta is much bigger than that. She is here to save humanity itself, not one or two people."

Emilia let out a heartbreaking moan and cried, "But she's not just anyone, Kara! She's my twin. She's a part of *me*. Clara is literally my other half. You're telling me to not feel something for half of *myself*. How is that even possible?"

Emilia began sobbing uncontrollably.

"Clara is not gone, Emilia," Kara reminded her consolingly. "Clara will never be truly gone, not even when her human body dies. When that happens, she will become Eir. Yes, she may be the overseer of the Hall of Souls, and you may be here on Earth tending to humanity as Andarta, but you will still be able to see each other as often as you want."

Emilia looked at Kara's spirit for assurance and felt complete warmth and soul-reaching comfort.

"So what do I need to do?" she begged.

Kara smiled encouragingly.

"You need to let her go. When the time is right, you will find her again, but keep in mind that you and Clara will be together for all eternity…no matter what happens to your human hosts. Even Leandro can't take that away from you."

At the mention of Leandro's name, Emilia's focus snapped back to attention.

"Who is Leandro?" she asked sharply.

"He is one of the most evil entities that ever existed, intent on destruction everywhere he goes," she explained.

"Can he be defeated?"

"Yes." Kara nodded.

"How?"

"I cannot reveal such information," Kara said before vanishing.

CHAPTER 37

SKULDALIÐ

The next morning, Emilia went to her parent's house to visit Clara's room. This had become a daily ritual, and every day she spent more time there than the day before, hoping with every fiber of her being that she would wake up from this nightmare and be able to hold her sister once more.

Just once. That was all she needed to make her somewhat whole and functional again.

"Clara, please," Emilia sobbed as she sat on Clara's bed. "I can't do life without you. Please come back."

Emilia said these same words every day to the cold and empty room that summed up her sister's life. Her twin sister. Her other half. It really did feel like a huge part of her was gone since Clara went missing. She remembered a conversation they had when they were ten years old and visiting their grandparents in London. The year they first figured out they were human hosts for the goddesses Andarta and Eir.

"If I'm Andarta, then you're Eir. That means you have to go to the Hall of Souls. How will you get there?" Emilia recalled asking Clara *so many years ago.*

"The same way everyone goes to the Hall of Souls," Clara replied with a shrug.

"I hope it doesn't happen for a very long time," Emilia said.

Clara gave Emilia's hand a comforting squeeze but said nothing.

Why didn't Clara say anything when I told her that I hoped it didn't happen for a very long time? Emilia wondered. *Did she know something way back then that I didn't?*

Emilia got goosebumps at this realization. For the first time ever, it seemed like she was the one who was left out of this understanding. During their entire lives together, Clara was always the one following Emilia, but now Emilia wondered if it was really the other way around. Clara certainly seemed to have had some kind of foresight into the future and didn't let Emilia know. But why?

Emilia's world had shattered into a billion pieces when Clara disappeared. Each day felt like a battle against the suffocating weight of grief, the pain of loss threatening to consume her whole.

She suddenly felt a warm breeze move through Clara's room that lifted the tendrils of her hair slightly. There was a calmness in the breeze, one she hadn't felt since she was a child, and she couldn't help but smile a little. She glanced up at the curtains, expecting to see them moving in the breeze, but they were as still as a statue.

At first, confused by the breeze she felt and the lack of movement of the curtains, Emilia slowly felt a glimmer of light begin to emerge within her soul. She felt a strange energy coursing through her veins that wasn't from Andarta. This was a different kind of power unlike anything she had ever known before. It was as if Clara's spirit spoke to her, guiding her toward a destiny she could not yet comprehend.

ᛏᚾᛒᛟᚱᚲᛟᚺᛗ

The next night, as Emilia lie awake in her bed back in her apartment, wrestling with the demons of grief that haunted her every waking moment, she felt a strange sensation wash over her. It was as if the very air around her crackled with electricity, sending shivers down her spine.

Once again, Emilia was transported to a now familiar, otherworldly realm. Before her stood a figure cloaked in shimmering armor, it's eyes ablaze with power as it gazed upon her.

She heard an ethereal woman's voice say, "Emilia, daughter of Midgard, you have been chosen to carry my mantle. The mantle of Andarta, guardian of the innocent and the harbinger of justice."

Emilia's heart pounded in her chest as she realized what she was hearing. She was no longer a grieving sister but a chosen champion of the gods, tasked with a sacred duty to protect the innocent and fight against the forces of darkness.

She continued to watch the armor-clad woman, whom she now knew to be the goddess Andarta. The figure gently moved toward Emilia. As she moved closer, Emilia felt a warmth that filled her entire being. As Andarta was mere feet away from Emilia, she reached out.

"Take my hand, Emilia," Andarta said reassuringly.

Emilia felt compelled to take Andarta's hand, and she slowly reached out toward the figure in front of her.

With a flash of light, Emilia felt the power of Andarta coursing through her veins, filling her with a strength and courage that surpassed anything she felt previously. Emilia could feel her senses sharpening, her instincts honed to a razor's edge as she embraced her newfound destiny with a sense of purpose and determination.

"I need to say goodbye to Clara," Emilia told Andarta.

"Why goodbye...goodbye...goodbye?" Andarta questioned, her voice echoing around the brilliantly lit chamber.

Emilia looked at Andarta, not sure how to answer this question, since Andarta apparently did not understand what Emilia was feeling.

It must be a god thing, she thought.

"I have to let her go, Andarta," Emilia explained. "I haven't been able to return to normal life since she disappeared, and if I say goodbye to her, it might help."

Andarta nodded slowly once in understanding and faded away until she was no longer visible.

Emilia found herself once again sitting on Clara's bed. She had known for a long time that Clara would die before her, but she didn't know if Clara was alive or dead...and the not knowing was keeping Emilia's emotions in limbo. Clara was a good, kind, and gentle soul

who didn't deserve to disappear when her life was coming together so
beautifully.

She began singing the lullaby that Clara had written for her when
they were kids and found herself changing the lyrics to match her
anger.

Always happy,
Voice like a chime,
Our sweet, gentle, little fawn.
I turned my back
Just one last time.
Next thing I knew,
You were gone.

How can I do life without you?
Can't I just hold you once more?
My heart has been broken in two.
And what has it all been for?

This wasn't to be your story.
It's not how our tie should end.
I'll do my best to make it right.
Your departure, I'll defend.

How can I do life without you?
Can't I just hold you once more?
My heart has been broken in two.
And what has it all been for?

I've heard about these bad dealings,
But now it's really hit home.
I'll end all these evil beings,
Until their kind has flown.

How can I do life without you?
Can't I just hold you once more?
My heart has been broken in two.
And what has it all been for?

I hope you're in a decent place,
But I'm lost without your glow.
And now I've got a trail to blaze,
So I've got to let you go.

How can I do life without you?
Can't I just hold you once more?
My heart has been broken in two.
And now I'm ready for war.

And now I'm ready for war.

And now I'm ready for war.

AND NOW I'M READY FOR WAAAAAR!

She screamed the last line, letting out all the anguish she had been feeling since Clara's disappearance. By the time she was done singing, Emilia felt an undeniable sense of purpose and determination. Standing up, wiping the tears from her face, she took one long last look at Clara's photograph and said, "This isn't over, Clara. They may have started this, but I'll finish it."

ᛏᚾᚠᛒᛉᛉ᚜ᛉᚺᛗ

When she woke up, Emilia walked with purpose to Kara's room. She needed to learn about her newfound powers and how to utilize them. Kara should be able to show her.

She knocked on Kara's door but received no response. Impatiently, she quickly walked through the apartment looking for her roommate-turned-spirit guide, but she was nowhere to be found. Emilia texted Kara, feeling a sense of urgency to learn about her new self.

"Kara, I'm at the apartment and looking for you," she wrote. "I need to talk to you ASAP."

Within seconds, her text tone sounded. "Be right there."

Emilia breathed a sigh of relief. For a moment, she thought Kara was no longer in this realm after she was granted her powers, but she was still here, thank God. Before she could take another breath, Kara appeared before her in their living room, causing Emilia to shout in surprise.

"God, you scared me!" Emilia shouted, trying to catch her breath from the fright of Kara's instant appearance.

"You can do it too," Kara laughed.

Emilia looked at her doubtfully, "I can?"

"Try it," Kara instructed.

"How?"

"Focus all your attention on a place in this room. Block out all external distractions and focus on that one place," Kara said.

Emilia closed her eyes tightly and covered her ears, trying to focus on the back door.

Nothing happened.

She felt Kara's hands touch hers and pull them away from her ears. Emilia opened her eyes, confused about why Kara was doing this.

Kara calmly said, "You have to be able to do it without physically blocking out sights and sounds."

"That's impossible," Emilia argued.

"If you're in a rescue situation, you might literally have your hands full and not have them available to block out sounds, and you'll need your eyes to see what's going on around you," Kara explained.

"Hmm, good point."

"Let's try it again."

Emilia tried several more times to transport her body to a place near the back door, but nothing was working. Kara began to look a bit discouraged.

"What am I doing wrong?" Emilia cried in frustration.

"Maybe you need to get Andarta involved," Kara said.

Emilia looked at her quizzically.

"I thought Andarta was *already* inside me? Shouldn't that make it work?"

Kara laughed and said, "Andarta may be *inside* you, but you still have control over which one of you is running things. Andarta can take over when you are in certain situations beyond your control, but in the normal daily life of Emilia Benning, you are still in charge."

"Oh." Emilia mulled this over. "So how do I get Andarta involved right now?"

"Say, 'I am Andarta 'or, 'Andarta, help me. 'Something along those lines will call her to take over."

"OK," Emilia said and took a deep breath, ready for whatever physical changes she might feel, and then said, "I am Andarta."

A warm yet powerful tingling flowed throughout her body, as Andarta came forth. Emilia could still feel and think as usual but had no control over her movements.

"I'm here," a ghostly voice appeared inside her head.

"Andarta?" Emilia thought.

"Yes," Andarta replied.

"Can we transport to that spot over by the back door?"

Emilia felt an instantaneous *whoosh* as her body left the spot in which she was standing and reappeared next to the back door.

"You did it!" Kara exclaimed with glee.

Emilia smiled and shrugged.

"It wasn't me. It was Andarta. Apparently, we can talk to each other inside my head. She asked what I needed. I told her I wanted to transport my body to the back door, and she...did it."

"Awesome." Kara smiled.

Both women laughed at Emilia's triumph over this seemingly minor power.

"What else can I do?" Emilia asked.

Kara smiled and said, "Have a seat."

Emilia looked at her curiously but followed her as they both went to the couch.

"It's not what *you* can do, Emilia," Kara began. "Greater things can happen when beings work together. Your whole *skuldalið* is here to aid you in your quests."

"My whole...*what?*" Emilia was confused.

"*Skuldalið*," Kara repeated. "That's ancient Norse for 'family.'"

Emilia looked around, searching for her parents and Gabriel, the only family she had left, but the room remained empty except for Kara and her.

"Where are they?" she asked.

Kara smiled.

"They're here, waiting until you need them."

"I don't see anyone."

Kara raised her hands and slammed them together in one extremely loud clap that echoed throughout the apartment. Instantaneously, all the outsiders from the party they attended appeared, but they were dressed very differently. When Emilia thought they couldn't dress any more bizarrely, here they were literally looking like a group of adults going to a costume party...but a really fancy one. Some of their outfits looked seriously legit.

"Whoa!" Emilia yelled in shock. "These aren't my family. Where are my parents? Where are my grandparents?"

Magnus was the first to speak.

"Do you remember me?" he asked.

Since Emilia had only met these people one time, she was amazed to find that she not only remembered them but felt that old familiarity she had felt while sitting with them at the dining table at the party. Table seven. The one Kara commented on when she had said, "We'll be in seventh heaven!"

"I do!" Emilia exclaimed happily.

Magnus gave a gentle smile as delight lit up his eyes.

"I know this is all new to Emilia, but Andarta and I have known each other since the beginning of time. We are *skuldalið*, 'family 'as you call it. We are all here to aid Andarta in her quests, and since you are the chosen one to carry her mantle, you are also included in our family until the end of eternity."

"And what about Clara?" Emilia worried.

"She is also included in our family until the end of eternity," Brennhir said gruffly.

"Will I ever see her again?" Emilia asked worriedly.

Magnus nodded.

"When?" Emilia asked.

"Soon," he replied.

CHAPTER 38

REBIRTH OF ANDARTA

As Emilia began to explore her new skills, she felt confident in her ability to succeed, now that she had her *skuldalið* on her side. She also recalled that Tyrell, the stray cat who had befriended her during her college days, revealed himself to be more than a simple feline companion during the battle in which Clara went missing. He had transformed into something resembling part dragon, his fur bristling and gleaming in the moonlight as his tail became whiplike, which he used as a weapon to swipe away the human traffickers who were trying to hang onto the victims they were trying to rescue.

Well, all of them except one...Leandro.

With Tyrell by her side, Emilia embarked on a journey to bring justice to those responsible for Clara's disappearance. Together, they sought out victims of forced labor who had been wronged by the heartless human traffickers who plagued their world. Learning about an apartment complex where all the residents were victims of human trafficking, Emilia and Ty spent days observing the building from across the street.

Emilia learned how to transform herself to appear as other humans and used her power to change her appearance each day so as not to draw attention to herself while staking out the building. Knowing she would need her father's help to get law enforcement involved when she attempted to rescue the victims, she planned to meet with him that night to discuss her strategy.

Oh, how she wished Clara were still here to help.

Up until now, every rescue mission she had attempted had been with Clara by her side. At least Gabriel was still more than willing to help, since he had also lost his new wife and their unborn child.

Ding! Her cell phone gave a notification.

When Emilia looked at her phone, she was surprised to see a text from her boss, Judge Skarsgaard.

Meet me at your parent's house tonight at seven.

Taken aback but not wanting to cause any rifts in her professional life, she texted back, "Okay."

She immediately called her father.

"Hey, pumpkin!" her dad said in greeting.

"Hi, Dad," Emilia said quickly. "I need to meet with Judge Skarsgaard tonight at your house at seven. He sent me a text."

"Judge Skarsgaard?" her dad questioned.

"Yes, Kara's dad," Emilia explained. "And my boss."

"Oh! Um...okay," he began. "What is this all about?"

"I don't know," she admitted. "But I need to talk to you anyway, so can I come over a bit earlier?"

"Sure, of course!" Cauley said.

ᛏᚾᚠᛒᛦᛦᚲᛦᚺᛗ

Emilia arrived at her parents 'house half an hour early so she could explain her plans for the apartment complex to her father before her boss arrived, but before they could even get settled, the doorbell rang. Not wanting any distractions, Emilia ran to get the door to shoo away anyone who was thwarting her plans. Expecting to see a door-to-door salesman, she was shocked to see the judge arrive so early.

"Welcome, Judge," Emilia said half-heartedly, opening the door for Judge Skarsgaard.

"Thank you, Emilia."

He smiled as he looked around the entryway to her parent's house. She introduced her boss to her parents and was surprised to find that her father and boss already knew each other.

"How are you doing?" Cauley said as they shook hands.

The judge nodded and replied, "Not too bad, Cauley! Thank you for having me over."

"Anytime," Cauley replied as he led the judge into the family room.

"Can I get you something to drink?" Amalia offered.

"Do you have any chocolate milk?" he asked, and Emilia looked at him with a comical smile.

"Chocolate milk?" she giggled.

"Oh, it's my favorite! I never get any where I live, so it's a real treat when I can find it." He winked.

Amalia smiled. "I can make you some real quick!"

The judge beamed. "Thank you, Amalia."

"Honey, can I have a Belvedere martini with a twist of lime, please?" Cauley asked.

"Sure!" she confirmed. "Emilia, would you like anything?"

"I'll have a Fireball on the rocks," she requested.

"You got it."

As Amalia retreated to the kitchen to make the drinks, Emilia followed the men into the family room.

Once everyone was comfortably seated, Cauley turned toward the judge and asked, "So what are we all doing here?"

Judge Skarsgaard turned toward Emilia and said, "Yes, tell us...what are we all doing here tonight?"

Emilia looked at both of them, stumped for a response. After all, it was the judge who had texted *her*.

"I don't really know," she replied slowly. "I was planning on coming over to talk to my dad about something when you texted, saying you needed to talk to me tonight, and here, at my parent's house."

"What's the plan, Emilia," the judge demanded. "For the apartment complex?"

How did he know? she wondered.

Shaking her head out of confusion she asked, "How..."

The judge's human form quickly transformed into Brennhir, one of the outsiders. No...not outsiders, not anymore. Brennhir was *skuldalið*.

"*Brennhir!*" she shouted with laughter. "I *knew* there was something not human about you."

Cauley was alarmed at the transformation that had taken place in his own family room and the fact that Emilia not only seemed to know Brennhir but was happy about seeing him.

"What's going on here?" Cauley demanded as he stood up, bracing himself.

"Dad!" Emilia said excitedly. "This is Brennhir! He's one of the...uh..."

What exactly was he?

Emilia looked at Brennhir and asked, "How do I explain who you are?"

Brennhir gave a coarse, chuckle.

"That, lassie, is a bit of a story. Have a seat and I'll explain meself."

"*Meself?*" Cauley repeated as he took a seat. "Where are you from? Where did you come from just now? You have an accent, but I can't place it."

Brennhir leaned forward, cocked one eyebrow, and said, "That's because my language hasn't been spoken on Earth since the fifteenth century, brother."

"And what language might that be?" Cauley pressed.

"Most people these days call it Old Norse. It was the language spoken by the ancient Vikings," Brennhir explained.

Cauley slapped his hand on his thigh and began laughing.

"I should have *known* you Vikings would reappear at some point!"

Brennhir was taken aback at Cauley's reaction and simply nodded a bit.

"So, are we related?" Cauley's eyes were sparkling with excitement at this rare opportunity.

Brennhir dared a quick glance at Emilia before answering.

"Ye might say that."

Amalia entered the room with a tray of drinks. As she handed Brennhir his chocolate milk, she let out a little scream of surprise, since the last time she saw him, he looked like Judge Skarsgaard. This person looked like a Viking warrior from ancient times.

"What on Earth?!" she exclaimed, placing a hand to her heart.

"Mom, it's okay!" Emilia said excitedly. "This is one of our old Viking ancestors who Grandpa used to tell us about!"

"What happened to your boss?"

Brennhir cleared his throat. "I'm actually using Judge Skarsgaard as a disguise so I can work alongside Emilia and Andarta here on Earth."

"But you're such a good judge!" Cauley commented. "I mean, as Judge Skarsgaard. I grew up wanting to be like you."

Brennhir laughed and thanked him for the compliment.

"Wait...how *old* are you?" Cauley asked. "You were already a judge when I was a *kid!*"

"Let's see now..." Brennhir touched his chin and looked up, trying to calculate his age in modern terms. "By your calendar, I would be about 1,074 years old."

"Holy cow!" Emilia exclaimed.

Amalia gasped, and Cauley started clapping and laughing.

"That is *so cool!*" Cauley continued laughing until tears sprung from his eyes.

"How old is Andarta?" Emilia asked.

"That is a question for God, little one," Brennhir replied seriously. "Andarta has been around since the beginning."

"Since the beginning of what?" Amalia asked.

Brennhir shrugged. "Time, I guess."

"So, I'm older than *you*?" Emilia gasped.

"No, lassie," Brennhir corrected her. "*Andarta* is older than me. *You* have only been around since my wife gave birth to you and your sister."

All the Bennings looked quizzically at each other.

"Um," Amalia was offended. "Don't you mean since *I* gave birth to her and her sister?"

Brennhir shook his head.

"Emilia and Clara's souls were created when my wife conceived them in 965 AD. They were uniquely designed to be an earthly home to the goddesses, and they have worked in tandem with the goddesses ever since. *You* were specifically chosen to be the human mother to the goddesses in this lifetime because of your direct bloodline to the Armenian goddess Hovannah. The time has come for the Viking and Armenian bloodlines to merge for the sake of humanity."

"You're my *father*?" Emilia asked with suspicion.

"Aye," Brennhir nodded.

"Who is my mother?" she demanded.

"Her name was Kelda," Brennhir responded. "She was an amazing warrior, like you'll be once you get accustomed."

"What were our names when we were first born?" Emilia's mind was swirling with so many questions.

"The one you know as Clara was named Astra. She's always been the eldest until now. And *you* were named Embla," he said with a small smile and a faraway look in his eyes as he recalled his own family memories.

"Astra and Embla," Emilia repeated, savoring the sound of the ancient names.

"How did we get to be where we are now?" she asked.

Brennhir let out a little growl and said, "I don't like telling that story, lassie, but I will for you."

They watched as he downed the rest of the chocolate milk, burped quite loudly, nodded at Amalia in apology, and set the empty glass on the coffee table in front of him.

"My last battle was against a tribe of Senmarians. I thought we had the battle won when that bugger Kimbel Murphy came up behind me and cut off me head. You know his mother was a Viking, and here he kills one of his own, that bloody bastard! And then his Druid priest, Cathbad..."

Magnus suddenly appeared, giving everyone another fright.

He added to Brennhir's story with a chuckle, "That's me."

"Yes, this one..." Brennhir indicated Magnus without looking at him. "He comes over and curses me for all eternity to *serve* the very daughter to whom my wife gave birth. Isn't that like a Senmarian?"

Everyone noticed the glare Brennhir gave Magnus, and the tension in the room was palpable.

The Bennings had no response, still trying to wrap their minds around Brennhir's stories, which seemed to match pretty closely to what Grandpa Benning told them.

Brennhir cleared his throat and asked Amalia for more chocolate milk.

"Sure, but don't say any more until I get back," she said anxiously. "I don't want to miss anything!"

The rest of them chuckled at her excitement but waited patiently for her to return. When she returned, they had to wait another few moments for Brennhir to guzzle down the entire drink, burp again, nod at Amalia, and then clear his throat.

"He and his warriors killed everyone in our encampment after the battle, except for you two."

Brennhir was looking directly at Emilia, and it gave her the creeps...like he was blaming her for him getting his head cut off over a thousand years ago.

"He and his wife took you in and raised you as Senmarians, and the rest is history," he explained.

"Wait!" Cauley exclaimed. "You're Brennhir Torox, the notorious Viking?"

"Notorious, am I?" Brennhir laughed.

"That's how my father always referred to you," Cauley mumbled.

"Then yes," Brennhir said proudly. "I guess that's me."

"I thought you would be taller," Emilia commented thoughtfully.

Brennhir gave her a scathing look and said, "Height isn't might, lassie, and you're shorter than me...humph!"

"Sorry," Emilia apologized, thoroughly chastised.

Brennhir grunted in response.

"So, you're here to help me, but you don't want to," Emilia stated. "Am I understanding this right?"

"I have mixed feelings on the topic. I'm a Viking barbarian by nature. Destruction is in my blood, but since that bloody dolt Murphy cut off me head, I have no choice but to help you."

Then his expression softened and he said, "You are also me daughter, whom I love, so that makes me *want* to help you, even if I don't agree with you wanting to save the world."

Emilia could not understand that line of thinking. She had always wanted to help people, like Clara did. How could someone *love* causing destruction?

She couldn't even imagine the inner turmoil Brennhir must be experiencing now that he was assigned to be a helper to someone who believed in everything he did not.

"So, lassie, let's hear about your plan for this apartment complex."

"The apartment," Emilia mumbled, thinking. "Oh, right! There's an apartment complex I heard about where all the people living there are victims of human trafficking. The complex is locked and guarded twenty-four hours a day so nobody can enter or leave without one of the bosses letting them in or out."

"How are they victims?" Brennhir asked. "If they're living in apartments, it sounds like they've got it pretty good compared to some of the others we've seen."

"Apartments they can't get out of on their own," Cauley reminded him.

Brennhir's blank expression told them nothing.

Cauley explained further, "It's like the apartments are prison cells. Did you have prisons back in your day?"

Brennhir chuckled.

"Some places had cages, but we never bothered with that kind of nonsense," he explained. "Viking justice had its own way of dealing with scoundrels. Cages were never needed."

The rest of the group stayed silent as grim images of brutal slayings roamed around in their heads. After a few moments, Emilia brought the topic at hand back to the forefront.

"These people work in the clothing industry, and the apartments are owned by their bosses. They make them work exhaustingly long hours and don't pay them anything. They tell them that their apartment is their pay, but nobody can live like that without proper food, clothing, and whatnot."

Amalia, ever the concerned mother, asked, "How do they get food? People can't survive very long without food."

"They bring crackers and other cheap food for them...enough to keep them alive, but that's it. They have running water in the apartments, which will sustain them for a while."

"Oh!" Amalia cried. "That's awful!"

"Tell me about it," Emilia explained. "These are good people who want to live their lives in peace, but peace is the last thing they get."

Cauley shook his head mournfully at the thought.

"People are the *worst!*" Brennhir spat.

"Not everyone, Brennhir," Emilia replied. "But if we can take down the ones who are, then we'll be taking a step in the right direction."

Cauley nodded and said, "Agreed. What do you need from me?"

"Backup," Emilia replied tersely.

"When and where?" Cauley asked, removing a notepad from the coffee table and taking notes.

"1810 South Figueroa Street in Seraphim City," Emilia replied.

"And when?" Cauley prompted.

"I haven't figured that one out yet," Emilia replied quietly.

"Ye need to figure it out fast, lassie!" Brennhir growled.

"I'm doing the best I can!" she responded.

"Are you?!"

Emilia tore her eyes away from Brennhir. Was she really doing her best?

Brennhir continued, "These are the same people who took your sister, lassie. How much time are you going to give them?"

Emilia felt a surge of rage, glared at Brennhir for a moment, and then stood up while stating without conviction, "Time's up!"

They all watched as Emilia glowed a brilliant periwinkle, seemed to disintegrate into minute particles, and then slowly reassemble as the light around her slowly disappeared. When she reappeared, everyone was stunned to see her wearing Viking clothing. Her leggings and cape were a dark maroon, with gray and gold making up the top and skirts of her outfit. Large, amber, crystals lined the sleeves and outer skirt, with one at the throat that kept glowing softly.

Emilia blinked for a couple of moments to get her bearings and then looked sharply at Brennhir.

"Where is everyone?" Andarta demanded from Brennhir in an authoritative voice that echoed throughout the room.

"Remember, Andarta, all you have to think or say is '*skuldalið,*'" Brennhir whispered.

Skuldalið, she thought with extreme focus.

Suddenly, liquid drops of golden light fell from the ceiling and landed on the carpet in the shape of full-size human beings.

Before her human form was even completely solidified, Torreya whipped her head from side to side and demanded, "Where's the fight?"

"Bloody hell, woman!" Brennhir complained. "Could you at least greet our hosts first?"

Torreya looked around the room until she spotted Amalia and Cauley, gave her head a terse nod, then turned back to Brennhir and shouted, "Where's...the...damn...fight?!"

"You're so sexy when you're angry," Brandt said to Torreya right before she punched him out.

"Brandt!" Magnus chastised.

"Oh, Brandt," Brennhir moaned and shook his head, "when will you ever learn?"

CHAPTER 39

VIKING JUSTICE

Filled with stories of the riches available to immigrants in America, many had come in hopes of a better life for their families, leaving what they thought were poor living conditions. They made the long and treacherous journey to the land of opportunity, positive that their efforts were going to be met with impending wealth, health, and happiness. Upon arriving in the United States, they were met by their new employer who promised them a job and a place to live in sunny California. It really seemed like a dream come true, and it came so easily.

"See, *mi todo?*" Inocente told his wife Rosalita. "It's like I told you it would be."

She smiled warmly at him as the comfortable, air-conditioned bus they had all been loaded onto drove them to their new home. Rosalita had been looking forward to this day for years, having spent every ounce of her energy trying to put food on the table and keep her family in clean clothes. She breathed a sigh of relief and rested her head on Inocente's shoulder as she watched her little boys playing quietly across the aisle. Thankfully, at five years old, they were young enough that they would probably never remember the hard life they had endured in Honduras.

During the bus ride, their new employer's representative promised them all free health care and food. Their children were guaranteed the finest education, free of charge, and could grow up to become anything their hearts desired. It was like going to heaven, only nobody had to die first.

After a two-hour bus ride, the constant motion of the road finally came to a peaceful end in front of a large, plain-looking apartment complex in the bustling heart of Seraphim City. The name itself put a thrill in the hearts of the devout Catholics aboard the bus. Surely, this was a sign from the Divine Father.

As each family exited the bus, they were required to turn over their travel documents and were assigned an apartment number. After gathering their meager belongings, they were told to go to their apartments and wait for further instructions.

ᛏᚾᚠᛒᛟᛟᚲᛟᛉᛖ

When they entered their new homes, they were happy to find the apartments already furnished with tables, chairs, beds, linens, a sofa, and dishes. Most of them had never had a bed with a mattress before, so this was quite a luxury.

"Oh, this is amazing!" Lupita squealed to Roberto, her boyfriend, who she referred to as her husband to outsiders.

She had just given birth to their first child, a beautiful little girl named Carlita. Roberto chuckled at her excitement, proud that he was able to make this happen for his little family.

"I'm going to call my mother and tell her about this," Lupita jabbered on, walking quickly through the small apartment, searching for the telephone.

After a few minutes, she returned looking discouraged.

"Is everything alright?" Roberto asked with a frown.

"I don't see a telephone," she commented in consternation.

"Really?" he questioned. "There has to be one somewhere."

He walked around the apartment looking for the telephone but also didn't see one.

"I'll go ask them," he said. "Be right back."

He went to the front door but was unable to open it.

"I think the door's stuck."

He sounded confused and kept pulling on the door. No matter how hard he tried, he was unable to open it and eventually gave up.

"Maybe see if you can go out the window," Lupita suggested jokingly.

"There are bars on the window," Roberto pointed out sullenly.

They looked at each other in alarm, realizing the gravity of their situation.

In her panic, Lupita went over to the window, opened it, and shouted, "Hey! Is anyone out there? We can't get our door open!"

Quickly, a man in a security uniform came over and said, "Close the window and wait inside until someone comes to give you further instructions."

"But I need to call my mother, and we can't find the phone," she explained.

He repeated his message and waited until she closed the window before walking a few feet away and standing guard.

"I don't like this, Roberto," she said worriedly. "Something's not right."

"Let's wait and see what they say when they come with the instructions," he said calmly. "Maybe there's something wrong with the door, and they don't want people yelling out into the courtyard and upsetting the others."

Lupita looked at her boyfriend but said nothing while they waited.

ᛏᚾᛒᚱᚱᚲᚱᛏᛗ

Rosalita was busy making the beds when she heard the front door open and Inocente and another man speaking. She quickly hurried to finish her task so she could join them, curious about what was being said.

"Oh, thank you," Inocente said.

"No! Mama! Papa!" her children screamed.

Concerned, she rushed into the living room to see her children being ushered out of the apartment by two strangers.

"What's going on?" she exclaimed. "Where are you taking my children?"

"To school," one of the burly, security guards said.

"Oh no!" she cried. "They need a few days to get settled. Please!"

"In America, kids go to school every day," the man explained. "If they're not in school, you could be arrested for your children being truant. You don't want to start off your new life here by being in jail, do you?"

Rosalita and Inocente were speechless and looked on helplessly as their little boys were taken away from them.

"When do we start our jobs?" Inocente asked quietly.

"Tonight," the man responded. "Miguel will be by soon to train you."

"Where do we go for work?" Rosalita asked.

"You're already there, lady." He smirked as he closed the door behind him.

Rosalita cringed as she heard him turn the lock on their front door...from the outside. In a panic, she ran over to the door and tried to open it to no avail, and began pounding on it and yelling, "Open the door! Let us out!"

In the distance, they could hear other people pounding on their doors and yelling as well.

"What are we going to do?" she cried to Inocente, tears pouring down her cheeks as her heart broke in two.

He slowly shook his head and said quietly, "We need to get out of here as soon as we can."

"How?" she asked desperately. "We can't even get out our front door!"

Inocente crumpled into a heap on the couch and sobbed, "I don't know."

"I don't know either," she said despairingly.

"Seraphim City, my ass!" Inocente spat. "It's more like Diablo City!"

ᛏᚾᚦᛒᛉᛉᚲᛉᚼᛗ

As all of the immigrants soon found out, hidden beneath the facade of a seemingly ordinary apartment complex, a sinister operation was underway. The complex's owner, a ruthless businessman, was exploiting vulnerable individuals by forcing them to work long hours for zero pay.

The immigrants were trapped in this grim situation due to a combination of fear, coercion, and manipulation. Their identification documents had been confiscated, leaving them with no proof of their existence outside the complex walls. The complex itself was surrounded by high-security fences and patrolled by armed guards, making escape impossible. Some of them had their children taken from them, making the idea of leaving impossible until they could get their children back. It didn't take long to realize they had left their home countries to deliver themselves into the hands of slave owners. The land of opportunity turned out to be a land of imprisonment.

ᛏᚪᚠᛒᚱᚱᚳᚱᚻᛗ

For several months, the women were forced to work during daylight hours in the factory beneath the complex to make personal protective equipment for medical facilities.

The men worked during the evening making footwear, specifically basketball shoes which were highly popular everywhere.

"Hey, Ricardo," Inocente whispered, "how much do you think they sell *these* for?"

Inocente held up an ultra-fancy pair of light blue, high-tops he had just completed.

Ricardo shrugged and said, "I don't know, man, but I do know we'll never be able to afford them."

"There are a lot here," Inocente whispered. "I bet we can set some aside for us, and when we get out of here, we can sell them to make some money to get bus fare back home."

Ricardo looked furtively around as best he could with his head down while trying to look busy.

"How could we do that without getting caught?"

"Hide them in our clothes," Inocente mumbled quietly.

"OK, let's do it," Ricardo agreed. "You do the first pair, and then next week I'll do a pair, and so on. Before too long, we'll have a good stash."

"Exactly, man!" Inocente whispered excitedly. "And when we get..."

272

He stopped talking because one of the guards was coming their way. Both men continued working quietly as the guard paused for several minutes behind them, watching and listening, before moving on to another group.

When he left, both Ricardo and Inocente breathed a sigh of relief.

"That was close," Ricardo whispered.

"Too close," Inocente agreed.

"Let's wait until tomorrow night to try this," Ricardo whispered fearfully.

Inocente simply nodded. He had been shaken by the guard's appearance in the middle of their discussion.

When he arrived back at his apartment after work, Inocente woke Rosalita up for her shift, which was starting in thirty minutes. They had learned to savor the few precious moments together. He told her of his plans to stockpile the shoes so they would have something to sell when they were able to get away.

She looked terrified and said, "Papí, no! They'll kill you if you get caught!"

He gently put his arms around her and said, "Don't be afraid, Rosalita. We'll make it out of this mess. I promise."

"Like we were going to have a wonderful new life in America?" she asked bitterly.

She could feel his body stiffen before he let her go. Rosalita grabbed some crackers she found in the cupboard and drank some water from the faucet before heading down to the factory for her day shift.

Inocente headed off to bed.

ᛏᚾᚠᛒᛟᛉᚲᛟᚻᛗ

Emilia had been tracking the operation for weeks, gathering evidence and formulating a plan to free the workers. Now that she had the powers of Anðarta and her *skuldalið* and Gabriel working alongside her, she felt fearless in their ability to take down the oppressors of the enslaved victims imprisoned within the walls of the apartment complex.

The plan was for Emilia and Gabriel to enter the complex first, since the less visible bodies there were, the less likely they were to be spotted.

Under the cover of night, they approached the apartment complex, their presence undetected by the guards. Using her powers, Andarta created a dazzling illusion of a bright light in the sky, drawing the guards' attention away from their posts. With the guards distracted, Andarta took Gabriel's hand, and they instantly transported inside the complex, their movements as swift and silent as a shadow.

"Whoa, that was cool!" Gabriel whispered excitedly.

Andarta chuckled quietly.

"Meow."

Looking around, they saw Tyrell sitting on the edge of the roof of the complex across from where they were standing. His silver collar was shining brightly in the moonlight. Andarta was bolstered with confidence at seeing him and smiled at the sight.

Once inside, they quickly located the workers, who were toiling away in the dimly lit factory beneath the apartment buildings. The sight of their weary faces and the oppressive conditions fueled Andarta's determination. She approached the workers furthest from the guards and spoke in a calm voice, "I'm here to help. We're getting you out of here."

Gabriel translated her words into Spanish.

The workers hesitated, their fear palpable. They explained that the bosses had threatened their families and that any attempt to escape would result in dire consequences. Andarta and Gabriel listened intently, understanding the depth of their predicament.

She nodded. "We have a plan to protect your loved ones, and the authorities are waiting on the other side of the fence to help once you're free."

Suddenly, they heard shouting on the other side of the factory floor.

"No!" Inocente pleaded. "I wasn't trying to steal anything! I..."

BANG! BANG! BANG!

Inocente's body jolted with each powerful bullet that entered his body as he collapsed to the floor.

The room fell into immediate chaos as men began yelling, screaming, and running for cover.

274

"Skuldalið!" Andarta said loudly.

The building began to shake slightly as gold drops began raining down onto the factory floor, landing in the shape of human forms. Some were dressed as Viking warriors. One was dressed as a normal street person but was covered head to toe in tattoos. The last one to arrive appeared all in black with huge black wings.

Magnus didn't even bother to land completely. As soon as he arrived in the factory, he locked eyes with Leandro Mammon and scooped him up, taking him to another plane to battle it out. Doing it here would most likely end up killing everyone within a three-mile radius.

Torreya, who landed in front of the guard who had shot Inocente, promptly severed the man's torso with her Viking axe and watched as the top half of his body fell to the floor sideways while his legs twitched as if seizing for several moments before falling forward.

She then grabbed the shoes Inocente had been attempting to pilfer, dropped them on top of the man's legs, and said, "You're going to need these where you're going. I hear it's really hot there."

Andarta was deep in the fray, surrounded by several guards, swinging her sword with all her might, killing the men in her path quickly one after another until there were none left in her vicinity.

"Emilia!" She heard Gabriel yell in a muffled voice.

When she looked over, she saw Gabriel standing inside what appeared to be a large, glowing, transparent cube, suspended off the ground by several feet. His hands were pressed against the side, and he was pounding on it, trying to break it to no avail.

"What the..." She was momentarily stunned, having never seen anything like it. "Kara? What is that?"

"I don't know," Kara said in awe, "but it's obviously not of this world."

"How do we get him out of there?" she asked desperately.

Brennhir suddenly appeared in front of the goddesses.

"I'll handle this, lassies. You go help the rest."

"Thank you, Father," Andarta said gratefully.

Brennhir grunted and gave a nod before turning toward Gabriel with his claymore in hand. Andarta and Kara returned their focus to the remaining people in the room.

Brandt punched out one of the guards and said, "Who's the scum now, dickwad?"

Hearing a man scream, everyone's attention was directed to him.

They watched in horror as Leilani opened her mouth inhumanly wide, and a gigantic Leilani flower came out of it and enclosed the last guard's entire body before pulling it back into her mouth.

She swallowed the entire flower with the man inside, let out a huge burp, and said daintily, "Oops, excuse me!"

Everyone laughed, which helped relieve some of the tension.

Gabriel and Brennhir joined them, and Andarta was grateful to see Emilia's brother-in-law completely unscathed.

Brandt, thinking that Gabriel might be one of the gods, said, "Where's your costume?"

Gabriel blushed and said, "Oh, I'm not a god."

"Huh...could have fooled me!" Brandt chuckled.

Gabriel noticed that Brandt, although covered in tattoos except for his face and hands, was simply wearing a muscle t-shirt, joggers, and tennis shoes, so he asked, "And where's your costume?"

"This *is* my costume," Brandt replied.

"How is that a costume?" Gabriel spluttered with laughter.

"I'll show you," Brandt replied.

He transformed into his normal look, which looked exactly the same but with tattoos only on his arms.

"Why is the only difference the tattoos?" Gabriel wondered aloud.

Brandt shrugged and said, "You never know when I might need to get a job."

They both laughed heartily.

"Where's Magnus?" Andarta interrupted.

"He's dealing with Mammon," Brennhir said.

"Mammon is here?" Andarta was alarmed.

"He was," Brennhir confirmed, "but Magnus took him away so we can get these people to safety."

"We better act fast."

She turned to the victims who were waiting for directions from their rescuers.

"Gabriel, please translate quickly," she urged.

"Everyone, we know this has been a traumatic experience for all of you, but you need to do what we say and do it fast. Gather all the other victims still on the property and go to the south fence by the entrance gate."

Gabriel translated what the men were telling him. "It's locked.

"Don't worry about that," Andarta replied. "We can get it open."

With renewed hope, the workers followed her as she led them through the complex. She used her powers to disable security cameras and bypass locked doors, ensuring a swift and safe escape for those still trapped inside the apartments. As they neared the exit, a dark figure appeared, blocking their path. His metallic suit glinted menacingly under the lights.

"And what do we have here?" he sneered.

Andarta cocked her head to the side and said, "A cat."

The man was taken aback by her response. "Huh?"

In less than a second, Ty's whiplike tail sent the man flying into the electrified barbed wire at the top of the fence, impaling him in several places on the razors. The man screamed in agony, wriggling around in futile attempts to free himself from the electrical shocks and the slashes from the razors.

With the final guard defeated, they led the workers to safety, where law enforcement and social services awaited to provide assistance and protection.

ᛏᚾᚠᛒᛟᛟᚲᛟᛉᛏᛖ

Andarta stood watch over the crowd of rescued victims and officials who were there to help, satisfied that everyone had made it out alive...except for the man who was shot. It had been a good rescue overall, and she allowed herself a small smile.

Suddenly, she noticed a woman crying and going from person to person, seemingly in a panic.

"Gabriel," she said, "can you find out what's going on with that woman? She seems distressed."

"Sure," he said and walked over to Rosalita.

Approaching the distraught woman, he asked, "Are you okay? Do you need help?"

"I can't find my husband!" she cried.

"What is your husband's name?" he asked calmly.

"Inocente," she sobbed.

"I'll see if I can find him for you," he promised. "Stay right here so I can find you again."

"*Gracias, Señor*," she said gratefully.

Gabriel went to some of the men he recognized from the factory and inquired about Inocente. The first several men he spoke to didn't know him, but the last one he spoke to informed him that Inocente was the one who was shot to death. Dreading having to tell Rosalita that her husband was dead, Gabriel slowly made his way back to her.

"*Señora*, I'm sorry, but your husband did not make it," he said.

"*Que?*" Rosalita asked, not comprehending Gabriel's message.

"Your husband was killed by one of the security guards," he explained in Spanish.

"Nooooo!" She screamed, crumpled to the ground in a fetal position, and began rocking back and forth.

Gabriel bent down and put his hand on her shoulder in an attempt to provide some comfort, as other women began coming over to help Rosalita. He quietly explained to the women what had happened to Inocente and asked them to stay with her until she calmed down.

They agreed, grateful to still have their own families intact.

A man walked up to Andarta and asked, "What about our children? When will we see them again?"

She was bewildered by his question. There were several children here, so she didn't understand why he was asking.

"Your children?" she asked.

"*Si*," he said.

"What do you mean?"

"They took our children to school, but if we are going to go somewhere else or back home, we want our children with us," he explained.

"What school do they go to?"

The man looked at her blankly.

"They never told us."

"What time do they get home from school?" she inquired, knowing it was the middle of the night and the children should all be here.

"What time?" the man seemed confused.

"Yes." She was getting frustrated with this conversation. "What time do they get home from school?"

"They haven't been home from school since they took them when we got here in March," the man explained.

It was now October. Their children had been gone for seven *months*.

"How many children did they take to school?" she asked, trying to sound calm so she didn't set these already tortured people off into another round of panic.

"Oh," he shrugged, "I don't know, Señorita. They took all the children who were five years old and older. They took two of mine and four of my friends 'children, but I don't know how many others they took."

"Okay, we will find out and make sure you all get your children back," she assured him.

Now, how was she going to do that? This was definitely not something she was aware of when they were planning this rescue mission. She knew human traffickers simply used people for their own personal gain...but *children*? What benefit could a five-year-old possibly provide? The more she learned about these people, the more disgusted she felt...and the angrier she became.

CHAPTER 40

THE MISSING PROGENY

Once the victims were safely housed in a local hotel with guards provided for their protection, showered, fed, and given any necessary medical treatment, they were all gathered together in the attorney's conference room at the Law Offices of Skarsgaard and Skarsgaard for a debriefing.

"The first thing I want to say," Emilia began, "is that I am so deeply sorry that Inocente did not make it through our rescue effort."

Rosalita sniffled and dabbed at her nose with a tissue, hugging her little girl tightly.

"I told him not to take the shoes!" she sobbed.

"People don't get killed for taking shoes in this country, Rosalita," Emilia said firmly. "You were all imprisoned by some extremely bad people. Not everybody in America is like that. *Most* people in America are not like that."

"What did they do with our children?" a woman yelled out.

"I don't know," Emilia replied, "but I promise you we *will* find them."

"Inocente promised that he would get us out of that hell too and look what happened to *him!*" Rosalita spat.

This was getting out of control, Emilia realized. What would Clara do? She always had such a calming way with people. *God, I miss her!* Emilia had to take a few deep breaths to keep the tears at bay. Then it came to her. Clara would share something about herself that showed she empathized with whomever she was trying to calm down.

Gathering the strength she knew she would need to get through this, Emilia began her story.

"I'm going to share something with you that I've never told anyone beyond my family and closest friends."

She tried to swallow the huge lump that formed in her throat, to no avail. The tears quickly spilled out onto her cheeks, but she kept her voice steady.

"A few months ago, my twin sister, one of the most amazing nurses to ever come out of nursing school, reunited with the love of her life, Gabriel, a friend we had known most of our lives. They were so happy when she became pregnant and got married. And I finally had the brother I never knew I wanted."

She looked over the sea of faces and was satisfied that they were listening intently.

"The night they got married, I needed my sister's help to rescue some victims who were being held captive in a warehouse not too far from here. Having a nurse participate in a rescue situation is very handy at times, especially one as sensitive and caring as my sister, Clara.

"Since they had been married less than an hour earlier, Gabriel accompanied us on the rescue mission, not wanting to leave his bride's side. The more people we had on our team, the better off we would be...right?" She smiled wryly.

"When it seemed like we had gotten all of the surviving victims out of the building, a shot rang out."

She paused, needing to clear her head a moment.

"Oh!" Rosalita exclaimed with concern. "Did Clara get shot?"

Emilia looked at her and said, "I thought she did at first, but no. Gabriel was the one who got shot. I started to run toward him to help, but Clara told me she would take care of him and for me to finish getting the others out...which I did.

"I was standing outside with my father. He's a judge and had called in the medical and backup teams to aid in the rescue effort. We were standing there and watched as the paramedics wheeled Gabriel out of the building on a stretcher. I ran over to see how he was doing, and the EMT said he would be okay. My father and I were relieved but then quickly realized that Clara hadn't come out with him. She had left her new, injured husband alone with the EMTs...and we were sure all the other victims were already outside with us."

Emilia cleared her throat, needing a moment to collect her emotions before continuing.

She took a few deep breaths, then said," We spent the next two hours looking everywhere for Clara, but she was gone."

"Was she dead?" a young boy asked, his big brown eyes heavy with sorrow.

Emilia shook her head.

"We don't know. We never found her. To this day, we don't know where she is. We don't know if she is dead or alive."

She looked directly at Rosalita and said, "So you see, I do understand your pain, Rosalita. I literally lost my other half that day."

Although she tried to hold it in and maintain her composure, one last sob escaped her throat.

"So please believe me when I tell you that we *will* do everything in our power to find your children," she announced to the silently mournful faces looking in her direction. "We *know* your pain and will do what we can to stop it, but we need your help. We need pictures if you have them. If you don't have pictures, we need very detailed descriptions of what they looked like the last time you saw them, what they were wearing, their ages, things they like, things they don't like, anything at all you can think of that will help us identify your children."

"I have an old picture of my son," one woman offered, holding up a tiny photograph. "Will that help?"

Emilia smiled gratefully.

"Yes, thank you! Oh, I almost forgot! If there is something your children are particularly good at, please let us know. The traffickers might be exploiting those skills, which may make it easier to find them."

Tisha, Judge Skarsgaard's secretary, walked over to the woman to collect the photograph and write down the woman's name and any information she could provide about her son. The next few hours were spent with the law office employees gathering photos and information on the missing children. Each family was also given a cell phone and exchanged phone numbers with the law office. They were told to call Emilia at any time, day or night, should an emergency arise or any important information be remembered that might be helpful.

When information about every missing child had been collected, the families were escorted back to the hotel with their security detail in place. Lodging and security would be provided by the law office until their children were found and the families decided where they wanted to go next – back to their home countries or somewhere in the United States.

ᛏᚹᛖᛝᚱᚱᚲᛦᛘ

The next morning, Judge Skarsgaard arrived in his office to find Emilia asleep on the sofa, files askew on the coffee table. He gently shook her awake.

"Have you been here all night, lassie?" he asked with fatherly concern.

She nodded and yawned.

"Go home and get some decent sleep," he ordered. "We can address this when you're refreshed."

"I'm fine." She yawned again. "I need some coffee."

"And a toothbrush..." he muttered.

"Oh," she said as she covered her mouth in embarrassment.

"There are some extras in the executive restrooms for A-types such as yourselves," he offered.

"Thanks," she said then jumped up and quickly made her way to the restroom to freshen up.

Looking at herself in the mirror, she saw how awful she really looked. No wonder he told her to go home. She did her best to tidy up by running her fingers through her hair, brushing her teeth, and using the mouthwash on the counter. She straightened her clothes and tucked her blouse into her skirt, which helped with the wrinkles from sleeping in it. Emilia looked at herself and put on her best smile. Feeling like she could pass for "decent," Emilia turned on her heels and returned to the judge's office.

"Better?" she asked him with a smile.

He grunted and gave his head a slight nod.

"Great!" She clapped her hands together. "Let's get to work!"

Emilia went directly to the coffee table and began sorting the files, one for each missing child, into age groups. There were a total of one hundred and fifty-three missing children from seventy-eight families from that one apartment complex. Emilia's mind was swirling from the mere thought of how many others were out there that she didn't yet know about.

Thirty-two of the families in this pile were missing *all* of their children. She couldn't even imagine what they must be going through. Well, maybe a little. She was missing the only sibling she'd ever had, but somehow she didn't think it was quite the same as missing a child.

Overcome with rage at what happened to these poor people who had only come to this country for a better life, she burst into tears and threw her pen across room, screaming, "Goddamnit! What the hell is *wrong* with people?"

The judge still looked the same, but Brennhir's voice clearly came through when he said, "Calm down, lassie. Anger will only cloud your ability to see the solution to this problem."

"There *is* no solution, Brennhir. These people are *evil*. No matter what we do, they'll go somewhere else and find other people to traffic. It'll never end."

Brennhir's judge face suddenly lit up with a huge smile and said, "Do you see that, lassie?"

"See what?" she demanded angrily.

"Look in the mirror," he chuckled and nodded toward the full-length mirror on the wall behind her.

Looking bewildered, Emilia turned around and could see immediately what he was referring to. She was dressed in her full Andarta regalia from head to toe, and the beads on the trim were lit up and blinking rapidly in a golden-amber hue.

"What the heck?" she stammered, as she rushed over to the mirror to take a closer look. "When did *this* happen?"

"About a minute ago, when you were yelling about how this will never end," he chuckled. "I think if Andarta has anything to say about it…it just might."

"Do you really think so?" she asked hopefully.

"Perhaps," he said, peeking over the top of his glasses, "or she's reminding you who you really are."

"Why are these things blinking?" she wondered aloud.

"Those are your victims, calling for help," he explained matter-of-factly.

Emilia's eyes widened in alarm.

"Where are they?"

"There's only one way to find out," he said. "Pull one off, drop it, and follow it."

Emilia gently tugged at the closest one, but it wouldn't budge.

"It's not coming off," she whined.

Brennhir stood up and shook himself, shedding his judge's suit and appearing as the gruff-looking, ancient protector she had come to know and love.

"First of all, lassie, Andarta does not *whine*," he said with a stern look.

Emilia gave a sheepish look, knowing full well he was right.

"Second of all, I said, *pull* it."

He grabbed one of the beads, yanked it *hard,* and it came loose in his hand.

He placed it in her palm and said, "Now, give it a little toss and follow where it goes."

She tossed it gently onto the carpet and watched as it bounced once, blinked, and then began rolling toward the door. Quickly, they followed the blinking bead, not noticing that they passed through the closed door. They were so intent on following it that thoughts of keeping things looking normal for others didn't cross their minds. It rolled through the exterior window from the top floor of the building, and they followed along, their focus razor sharp. The bead, Andarta, and Brennhir all floated down gracefully to the ground, alarming people on the other floors as they passed by their windows, as well as people on the ground who saw them coming down. Neither of them noticed though due to their tunnel vision on the bead. It led them to an alley where they saw a teenage girl being yelled at by a young man in an alleyway.

"I know he gave you more than that!" the man yelled at her with his fist raised. "You'd better turn it over now if you know what's good for you...and I mean *all* of it, bitch!"

The man had his back to Andarta and Brennhir and was shouting loudly enough that he didn't hear them come up behind him. The girl noticed them but did her best not to be obvious about it, but their presence seemed to give her some courage.

She yelled back, "I did give you all of it, you asshole!"

The man's eyes began bulging in rage as he screamed, "What did you call me?"

He reached out and grabbed the girl by the hair, lifting his other arm and making a fist to strike her.

Brennhir noticed Andarta tense up, and knew she was about to yell at the man, but he grabbed her arm and whispered, "Shhh, keep your eye on the bead."

Emilia, who watched the action since Andarta was in control now, was stunned to see the bead go racing toward the girl. Right before the man's fist made contact with her face, the girl's body turned into liquid gold and got sucked into the bead, which immediately flew back to Andarta and reattached itself to her costume, blinked quickly a few times and then settled down to a gentle, steady glow.

"Whoa!" Emilia yelled. "What does that mean?"

"It means she's safe now. She's with you from now until you return her safely to where she belongs."

The man who was about to attack the girl heard them talking and spun around to confront them. He was stupefied to see the costume clad pair standing in his alley.

"What happened?" he howled.

"You lost one of your victims, brother," Brennhir said calmly.

"Victims?" He sounded confused. "She wasn't a victim! She was my *em-ploy-EE* and I ain't your brother!"

"It didn't sound like a very good employment arrangement to me," Andarta replied.

"Bitch, you better bring her back right now," the man demanded. "Taking away my employee is taking money out of my pocket, and I don't take too kindly to that."

"And I don't take too kindly to human traffickers," Andarta replied calmly as she ripped a steel stair railing off the staircase next to her and threw it at the man, viciously impaling him with it.

Enjoying the look of shock on his face as he suffered from the agony of his injuries, Andarta leaned over him and said, "Stick *that* in your pocket!"

As they walked away from the dying dirtbag, she sighed and said, "One down, one hundred and fifty-two to go."

Her adrenaline was rushing, and she was anxious to find the rest of the missing children. She grasped another bead and tossed it on the ground. It immediately rolled past her back into the alley at a much faster pace than the first bead had, so she and Brennhir picked up their pace, which eventually turned into an all-out sprint.

After running for approximately four miles through alleyways and streets lined with tents lived in by the homeless, they came to what appeared to be an abandoned building. The bead went straight through a wall in the side of the building, with Andarta and Brennhir following right behind. It led into a dimly lit, large, cavernous room filled with sewing machines and cutting tables. Men, women, and children were working at every possible workspace in the stifling heat with no ventilation. Everyone looked miserable, even those overseeing the operation.

Andarta's costume began twitching of its own accord, distracting her from their purpose.

"Brennhir, what's happening? Why is this thing moving around?" she said, beginning to panic.

"Hold on," he said as he picked up her cape and began pulling off the beads along the back that were flashing the fastest and tossing them on the floor.

Andarta watched as they sped to different parts of the room, turning some of the younger workers to liquid gold and then speeding back to her costume. The beads that had gone through the walls quickly returned and created liquid-gold circles on the walls before reattaching to her costume.

The other workers and bosses in the room began screaming at the disappearing children, not having seen Andarta and Brennhir, who were hidden in the shadows the entire time.

When all the beads had returned to Andarta, they quickly left the building through the wall they had entered it from.

Once outside, Brennhir slapped his thigh and let out a loud guffaw, "Oy, did you see the look on their faces? They must have thought the world was coming to an end!"

Andarta laughed along with him, realizing he was probably right.

"Okay, so how many was that?" she asked, having no idea since Brennhir was the one who pulled the beads off.

"Hmm, let's count how many are left," he said and pulled her over to a corner of the alley where they wouldn't be seen.

"Bloody hell, sixty-three!" he shouted with glee.

"*Sixty-three?*" Andarta shouted with a huge smile of triumph. "We rescued sixty-three more? How many are left?"

"No, no, no, lassie!" Brennhir corrected her. "There's only sixty-three left to rescue!"

"Wait! We rescued eighty-nine children in one place? There's no way there were eighty-nine children in that room."

She was stunned. That didn't seem possible. It happened so quickly.

"No, but some of the beads went to other places in the building, remember? Some of them went through the walls too."

"Wow."

She shook her head at the thought of so many people being trafficked in one place. One *very,* depressing place.

"I know we're on a mission to rescue the missing children, Brennhir, but when we're done, I want to deal with rescuing the rest of the people who are working in that factory...or whatever you call it. It's not only kids who are victims of human trafficking in that building," she lamented.

"I'm glad to see ye finally coming around, daughter."

He smiled with pride and Andarta blushed at his praise.

"Alright, let's get the rest of these kiddos back to their families."

She yanked off another bead, and they followed it to a local orange orchard, where they quickly rescued another sixty-two children.

Her entire costume was now full of solidly lit golden-amber beads, except for one.

She pulled it off and tossed it on the ground. It moved a little bit then faded to a light gray and stopped.

Her brow wrinkled in confusion.

"Why did it change color, and why isn't it moving?

"Oh, that's not good," Brennhir muttered.

"What does it mean?" she said in a panic.

He paused and looked at her, worried about how she might react.

"It means the child is in grave danger. We need to find them quickly," he explained.

"How can we find them if it's not moving?" she said anxiously and began wringing her hands.

"We need help." He looked at her knowingly.

"Skuldaliò," she said.

"What's up?" Brandt said right next to her, giving her a start.

"Where's the fight?" Torreya asked, already in her fighting stance.

Brennhir laughed, "Does there always have to be a fight, Torreya?"

She relaxed, growing contrite.

"Sorry, what's going on?"

"One of the beads turned gray and stopped moving," Andarta replied sadly.

"We need Magnus," Brandt said matter-of-factly.

"Here I am," Magnus said as he came floating down gracefully.

Andarta breathed a sigh of relief. "Can you help us find this last child?" She pointed to the immobile, dark bead.

"I can," he said, grabbing his chin thoughtfully, "but I can't guarantee he'll still be alive when we find him."

"He has to be," Andarta whispered, choking back the tears that threatened to burst forth. "I promised all the parents I would bring their children back to them."

"Did you promise you would bring them back alive?" Magnus asked.

Andarta's head dropped in defeat. She hadn't thought to mention that caveat, but then a righteous anger filled her entire being.

"No, but I *will* bring them all back alive, Magnus. I am Andarta! I don't let people down! Take me to that child, and I *will* bring him back alive."

"You can't bring the dead back to life, Andarta. None of us can," he replied gently.

"You're right, Magnus," she agreed angrily. "*We* can't, but *God* can! If we find him dead, I'll take him to God myself and trade places with that child so he can go back to his parents in perfect health! Now *take me to him!*"

"Yes, ma'am!" Magnus replied. "Grab the bead. We're going to need it."

After she picked up the lifeless bead, Magnus wrapped one arm around Andarta's waist, picked her up, and flew her across the city to an elegantly designed house in an upscale part of town.

"Here?" She looked at him quizzically.

"Here," he confirmed with a nod.

"How do we get in? Usually, we follow the beads through the wall right into the room where the victims are, but this bead isn't doing anything."

"Let's walk around the outside and survey the area for clues," he suggested.

The property was surrounded by ten-feet-high stucco walls and iron gates, so they walked through the walls to get inside the premises.

The grounds were immaculately kept and had a tropical theme. Lush palm trees surrounded the perimeter, and a well-manicured lawn covered the exterior. Beautiful rose bushes and bird of paradise bushes bloomed around the base of the house and outbuildings. They saw a man moving a pool vacuum along the bottom of the vast pool on one side of the house and quickly retreated to the other side so as not to be seen.

As they passed under an open window, they heard a woman say, "If you want something to eat, you have to say it in English. Until then, you get nothing."

They heard a small voice mumble something but couldn't understand what was being said.

Andarta felt a twitch inside her palm. When she opened it, she looked and saw the previously gray bead start to glow a faint yellow.

"Magnus, look!" she whispered excitedly.

He smiled at her knowingly.

"Now how do we get to him?"

He gave her a look that said they had to go in. She gave a light chuckle at imagining the face of the woman they heard chastising the boy when she saw them appear.

"Let's go!" she whispered with a wicked grin.

Magnus nodded and followed her through the wall.

"*Aaaagh!*" the woman screamed when they appeared. "*Help! Help!*"

Andarta simply walked over to the boy, who was sitting on the floor, limp and unmoving except for his eyes, which were following her movements.

"*Hola,*" she said with a smile and opened her hand to show him the bead, which was now glowing bright gold.

He slowly reached out and picked up the bead and put it in his mouth. Instantly, he melted into a pool of liquid gold, and his bead quickly attached itself to her costume and turned into a warm golden glow.

As Andarta stood up to leave, two armed guards entered the room and began shooting at her and Magnus. She felt excruciating pain with each bullet that hit her, but she was still able to move.

Magnus was completely unaffected by the bullets and walked over to the gunmen, grabbing their weapons from them and compressing them with his hands into scrap metal. The men screamed in fear and ran out of the house, while the woman continued to wail in panic.

"Ready to go?" Magnus asked Andarta.

"Yeah," she gasped. "I think I'm hurt though."

"You'll be fine," he said.

She looked at him like he was nuts, but he nodded in a way that told her to look at her wounds. When she looked down, she was shocked to see the bullet holes seal up on their own as the pain completely disappeared.

"How did you know?" she asked in stunned disbelief.

"Andarta has the power of self-healing." He shrugged. "Didn't anybody tell you that?"

"You know, it's been so long that I've forgotten most of what I'm capable of," she laughed with relief.

CHAPTER 41

REUNITED

Magnus took Andarta back to the law offices where the rest of their *skuldalið* were waiting anxiously to find out how the last rescue ended. When they arrived with triumphant smiles on their faces, an uproarious cheer could be heard throughout the top floor of the building.

"Congratulations!" Torreya yelled.

"Good job, guys," Brandt said, nodding his appreciation.

Brennhir walked over and gave Andarta a much needed hug and asked, "How was the little boy when you found him?"

She shook her head.

"Very weak, but I think he's better now. How do I get them out of the beads?"

"The 'beads, as you call them, are actually victim rescue pods, or VRPs for short," he explained. "To release them from the pods, you can do one of two things. Either pull each one off again or remove your costume and place it on the floor. If you only have a few, then pulling them off would be the easiest thing to do, but you've got many now, so you might want to go change so you can put your costume on the floor.

"Once you do that, say, 'You have been rescued by the goddess Andarta, one of God's helpers, and are no longer in danger. You are safe now and free to go wherever your heart takes you. 'Sometimes they come out right away, but some take a while. It depends on how much trauma they've been through.'"

She nodded and went to the bathroom to change her clothes.

When she returned, she gently laid her costume on the floor as her *skuldaliò* gathered around it.

She took a deep breath, released it slowly, and then said, "You have been rescued by the goddess Andarta, one of God's helpers, and are no longer in danger. You are safe now and free to go wherever your heart takes you."

She stood back, keeping her eyes on her costume, as they all watched with bated breath as the beads began to change from the tiny, solid warm golden glow they had seen since the victims had been rescued into something miraculous to behold.

At different times, each pod slowly changed to a twinkling shimmer that grew and moved outward in a brilliant white sparkling spiral.

As they grew in size, different flecks of sparkling colors could be seen swirling within the spirals as the children's bodies began to take shape. Slowly, the colors darkened into the colors of the children themselves, but the white sparkles continued to flicker around them for several minutes, even after they began walking around taking in the unfamiliar surroundings.

"Why are they still sparkling?" Andarta whispered to Brennhir.

"Those are God's healing hands at work. People can't see them, but we can. The longer they stay, the more healing is needed."

Andarta was speechless, not having a memory of seeing that before. She knew she had but couldn't remember it yet.

Kara joined them with awe in her eyes. "I'm amazed every time I see that."

"Yeah," Andarta breathed, savoring the moment.

She felt a tap on her shoulder and turned her head to see the teenage girl she first rescued in the alley.

"Hi!" She greeted her with a big smile.

The girl smiled sheepishly and looked down before saying, "I don't know how to thank you."

"You don't need to thank me," she replied. "The fact that you are alive and well is all the thanks I need."

"Are my parents alright?" the girl asked.

"Yes, and you'll get to see them very soon," she promised.

"Really?" The girls eyes filled with tears, and she hugged Andarta with all her might.

Andarta laughed, hugged her back, and said, "Really!"

"I think we've got a dud," Hermes giggled while pointing at one of the spirals that kept growing and then shrinking.

By this point, all the other children had fully appeared and been completely healed based on the absence of white sparkles around them. There were so many of them that it was hard to keep count.

Knowing they started out with so many missing children, Andarta called out, "Okay, we need to take a head count. Line up in groups of ten, please."

They all turned to look at her and then began sorting themselves into haphazard groups of ten.

She began counting the groups in her head.

Ten. Twenty. Thirty...

One-forty, one-fifty, one-fifty-one, one-fifty-two... That was it.

Where was one-fifty-three?

"We're missing one," she announced quietly.

"Told ya," Hermes smirked.

"Not now, Hermes," Kara said.

"Hey, I'm trying to help." He looked offended.

"You want to help?" She challenged. "Go back to Asgaard."

"Fine," he spat then vanished.

"What do we do?" Brandt asked worriedly.

"I've got this," Andarta replied determinedly.

She walked over to the struggling spiral and wrapped her hands loosely around it. Immediately, she felt the young boy's spirit struggling to revive. He wanted to come back. She could feel it in every fiber of her being, but something was holding him back.

"You are blessed by God, little one. Nothing can hurt you now. It is safe to come home. Follow my voice. Once you return, you will be made whole. Whatever happened to you at the hands of your oppressors is in the past. They are gone out of your life. They can't hurt you anymore."

Then she got an idea.

"Do you like to sing? I like to sing. I'm going to sing you a song I used to sing with my sister when we were very little. It goes to the tune of "Twinkle, Twinkle, Little Star," but we changed the lyrics when something bad happened to my sister to cheer her up. I hope you like it. Follow my voice and please come back home.

"Sometimes hard things come our way,
Clouds might hide the bright, warm day.
Good folks feel the hurt and pain,
But through storms we grow again.
Every trial helps us see,
How strong and brave we each can be."

Slowly, extra colors began shimmering within the white sparkling spiral. Encouraged by this beautiful sight, Andarta began singing louder as happy tears began falling down her cheeks.

"When we fall or feel alone,
Kindness helps us find our home.
Through the dark, we'll find the light,
Learning, growing, shining bright.
Sometimes hard things come our way,
But we'll grow more every day."

When she finished the song, the spiral had grown too large for her hands to contain, no matter how wide she spread her arms, and the cheering in the room grew to a roar as the young boy she and Magnus had rescued took shape. They watched in wonder as he began walking around and smiling at the others while a large cloud of white sparkles danced around his body.

He walked over to Tisha and asked, "Excuse me, ma'am, do you have anything to eat?"

Everyone laughed as she said, "Yes, I do!"

Brennhir announced, "Come on, kiddos! We've got a whole spread waiting for you in the conference room."

He led the way to the feast where Tisha had the kitchen staff prepare all the things they thought children would like. They had pizza, hamburgers, sandwiches, chips, soda, salads, tacos, brownies, chocolate milk, and bottled water.

"Wow!" the children exclaimed when they saw the options before them.

"Is this all for us?" A little girl squealed.

"Why, yes, it is, little lady!" Magnus replied with a laugh.

While the children were busy eating, Andarta faded into the background, leaving Emilia to her moment in the sun with the children.

She placed a call to Gabriel.

"Hi, Emi," he answered.

"Hi, Gabe. I think we're ready to bring the parents over now," she said.

"Okay, I'll get everyone together. We should be there within the hour."

"Great, thanks!" She said with a thrill in her heart.

Thankfully, the parents arrived while the children were eating dessert, so Emilia had time to greet them and prepare them for seeing their children again after their eight-month absence.

While they were talking in the office, one of the girls came out of the conference room, saw her mother, and yelled, "Mama!" She ran over to her mother, grabbing her in a hug and breaking down into tears.

At hearing her, the other children quickly came running out into the office to find their parents as well, some still with food in their hands or on their faces. Nobody minded though. They were so grateful to finally be reunited with their families again.

Emilia and the others who were watching it all unfold felt a warmth in their hearts they knew they would never forget…but it also reminded Emilia that a part of her was still missing.

Clara.

END MATTER

(...that really matters)

If you, or someone you know, are a victim of human trafficking or may be in danger of becoming a victim of human trafficking, call

1-567-Andarta

(1-567-263-2782)

This number will automatically forward to the Human Trafficking Hotline, where resources are available to help!

THE LIFE YOU SAVE MIGHT BE YOUR OWN!

**Keep going for important information about human trafficking - the catalyst behind this series.*

Human Trafficking – What Is It?

When most people hear the term "human trafficking," their thoughts almost always automatically go to one of two types: sex trafficking and child trafficking. Unfortunately, there are many different kinds out there.

What human trafficking is:

Human trafficking is a form of modern slavery involving the use of force, fraud, or coercion to exploit people for labor, sexual services, or other forms of exploitation.

It often involves traffickers targeting vulnerable individuals and manipulating or controlling them in ways that make it difficult for victims to escape.

Traffickers may use various tactics, including deception, threats, isolation, physical abuse, or withholding legal documents to maintain control over their victims.

There are as many as 25 specific types, all of which will be covered throughout the Ascending Veil Series.

Human trafficking is a significant and hidden crime that affects millions worldwide, and because it can happen in any community, it requires public awareness and intervention to help prevent it and support recovery for those who have experienced it.

If you enjoyed this first novel in

THE ASCENDING VEIL SERIES

please help the authors by posting a review on the website where you purchased this and also on Goodreads, your social media, and anywhere else you think would be a good place to post a review!

You can follow us on Facebook at:

PageTurnerBooksInc

and on Instagram at:

ptbooksinc

to be updated on the release of the audiobook and graphic novel

for

ANDARTA

THE ASCENDING VEIL, BOOK 1

And...be one of the *first* to know about our forthcoming novel,

EIR

THE ASCENDING VEIL, BOOK 2

www.ingramcontent.com/pod-product-compliance
Lightning Source LLC
Chambersburg PA
CBHW010736310726
48971CB00010B/2853